THE
CAUSE

THE
CAUSE
LOVE & WAR

ELLYN M. BAKER

TATE PUBLISHING
AND ENTERPRISES, LLC

Published by Tate Publishing & Enterprises, LLC
127 E. Trade Center Terrace | Mustang, Oklahoma 73064 USA
1.888.361.9473 | www.tatepublishing.com

Tate Publishing is committed to excellence in the publishing industry. The company reflects the philosophy established by the founders, based on Psalm 68:11,
"The Lord gave the word and great was the company of those who published it."

Book design copyright © 2013 by Tate Publishing, LLC. All rights reserved.
Cover design by Ronnel Luspoc
Interior design by Joana Quilantang

Published in the United States of America

ISBN: 978-1-62510-504-2
1. Fiction / Historical
2. Fiction / General
13.06.04

DEDICATION

To my family~ Thank you for teaching me about life. I could not have done this without you.

Gettysburg Circa 18

A. Mc Conaughyh Hall
B. Oakridge Seminary-Carri
   Home
C. Eagle Hotel
D. Mc Clellans Hotel
E. Globe Hotel
F. Court House
G. Public School
H. JL Schick- Dry Goods &
I. Fahnestock Brothers
J. Salome "Sallie" Myers R
Residence of Table Roc
David Blocher – Farmer
John Blocher – Blacksmi
Joseph Bayle Family-Far

ACKNOWLEDGEMENTS

To the citizens of Gettysburg, both past and present, thank you for showing me the meaning of courage and perseverance. Your strength under fire still shines through today. To the citizens of the past, your courage and compassion to help those in need gives us great tales of humanity and unconditional acceptance. For the present citizens who continue to struggle to preserve this history through preservation and endless dedication, you keep the fire burning for future generations. You are all heroes. Thank you for coloring these pages with your personalities. I am honored to tell your story. Please note: this is a fictional novel about non-fictional people. Any representation of non-fictional characters have been written with care and respect for those of the past. I could not tell this story without all of you who made Gettysburg history.

John Heiser, Ranger/ Historian Gettysburg National Military Park. Thank you for helping me "see" Gettysburg in the 1860s again. Your diligent work helped me keep the facts straight. You are an excellent teacher.

My darling husband, Shawn. You stopped the world and selflessly created a world for me to finish my first novel. You understood my dream and pushed me to make it happen. Thank you for allowing me to bounce ideas off you and giving me your honest opinion.

Kristine Berken. Thank you for your photographic talents. I appreciate the time you took to work with me regarding the right look for the author photo.

Tate Publishing team, for believing in the manuscript. It is a pleasure working with every one of you on this journey.

Mom and Dad—I did it! Thank you for all of your support through my early writing years.

PROLOGUE: WINDS OF CHANGE

It behooves every man who values liberty of conscience for himself, to resist invasions of it in the case of others: or their case may, by change of circumstances, become his own.

—Thomas Jefferson

AUGUST 1860
RICHMOND, VIRGINIA

The meeting room was stuffy and hot. The three large windowpanes let in more heat than relief from the sultry August afternoon. The clatter of wagons outside signaled this was just another day. No one in the room seemed to notice either the heat or noise. Heads bowed, each man was quietly lost in the details of the land-sale contract before them. Understanding every detail of legal jargon was tedious work for a man who worked the land.

"I don't see any provision for the workers I have left for you." Jacob Prescott's voice broke the muggy silence. His eyes showed serious concern. "You may not press them back into slavery when I leave, William. I won't have it."

"We've gone over this, Jacob. I will keep them on until the next planting season—pay them good wages. They will not be allowed to live on my land indefinitely." William had no idea what to do with the goods his brother was leaving behind. They were good commodity that could get him a good price. The man was strong and productive. He knew the plantation better than William did. William needed his knowledge. The female ran the house smoothly and controlled the house staff without much supervision. The boy was simply a commodity who would be sold for a good price later. This promise could be a sizable mistake.

"I can type up that addendum for you, sir. I will be happy to bring it out for you to sign," Attorney Abbot offered.

Jacob knew he would have to wait a little longer. "That's good." He said. "The harvest will finish next week, and we will be leaving after that. Once the addendum is added to the contract, I will be happy to sign it, William." Jacobs's younger brother shook his head.

"Why don't we sign the agreed-upon portions? I will give you the money up front, and when George gets the addendum to us, we will complete the transaction." William hated his brother's detail. Jacob was so fixed about everything—how things ran to how he hung his shirts. Meticulous, picky, details. He was sure his brother scheduled his bowels the same way. William shook his head in frustration.

"Fine, we will sign up to the final page. Add the addendum in two days." Jacob stood up and shook hands with his brother and the attorney.

The men got into the wagon to head home. William left Jacob to his thoughts. He understood the difficulties behind selling the plantation. William was only too happy to finally get a chance to make the land what it could be. It was a shame to see so much acreage go to waste, unplanted, not turning a profit.

"I know it doesn't mean much coming from me, but I think this is a good decision." William tried to be delicate. "The land can grow so much more. The profits will be there." William tried to hide the excitement in his voice. He planned to turn three times the profit within the first two years. He was giddy with the possibilities of so much money coming to him. He envied this opportunity since their parents bequeathed the property by the birthright to Jacob, their first born son. William despised being the younger child.

Jacob eyed his brother. "I have heard it all. I am weary from all the judgments cast upon me." He thought for a while, remembering the struggles that got him to this point. "We are close enough if you need our help. This move will be the best thing for my family. All I ask of you, William, it to remember what our ancestors went through to get here. Remember the stories of persecution and our family struggles. Don't let that happen here."

"It is not the same, Jacob. What you fight so hard to preserve is nothing like what the English did to our ancestral clan lands. This is a different breed altogether. They aren't like us." William was tired of his brother's logic; it simply did not make sense.

The beauty of the day was lost to them as they travelled home in silence, to a place that was dynamically different for each man. William Prescott now called this place *home*. As a former owner, Jacob was free to seek another home. The trouble started years ago when Jacob made the decision to release all the slaves and run the plantation with the help of fifteen men. Completely abandoning the traditions of the area, Jacob paid those who helped work his plantation. Crop sizes soon reduced as his employees could buy their freedom and move away. The owners of the nearby plantations feared the Prescotts' actions. Other owners feared blacks for hire would incite slave riots and encourage their slaves to run away. Peer pressure, gossip, and community shunning made life and belonging to this community unbearable. Jacob knew William would manage the plantation as he saw fit. The men never agreed on much. William adopted the current beliefs regarding slavery. Slaves were nothing more than property used to maintain the plantation. Jacob didn't see it this way, and this is why the family decided to move north, safely away from the accusing eyes and contempt of neighbors. He was free just like the men he signed papers for months before. A glimmer of happiness showed itself in him for the first time in years, and for that, Jacob was at peace.

A LONG WAY FROM HOME

There is no sanctuary of virtue like home.

—Edward Everett

SEPTEMBER 1860
PRESCOTT PLANTATION

Your life has many jump-off points. Taking the initial plunge into the unknown is always scarier than the danger before you. Leaving everything she had ever known put Emilie in that exact position, the point where there was nowhere to go but forward.

Dear diary,

Mother says it would be best to write to a friend to explain all my woes. Today we are leaving everything I have ever known to go into the unknown: a new place, new home, and new friends.

Today my life will change forever, leaving the only home I have known for seventeen years and leaving our farm life behind. I feel like a caterpillar wanting to come out of its cocoon. I am ready to break into a new life. I will miss all that is familiar here. My room and the comforts of home will sadly stay as we drive away. I am terribly torn up, that we have no room for our piano. I feel like I am saying good-bye to Mozart and Beethoven. Most of all, I will miss Seth and Martha and Big Jim. I hope they will be safe and stay free.

Pa says it will take two weeks to travel to our new home in the North. I hope Gettysburg will be a good place for us. Can a body feel happy and sad at the same time? All I can do now is pray for safe travel, and time will reveal the rest.

Your new friend, E. K. P.

"Emmie, the wagons are loaded. Time to go." Julia gently nudged her daughter. Emilie sat most of the morning on a crate, trying to remember every detail of the home where she was born. Emilie knew the home would never be hers again. The finality of this realization washed over her in a flood of emotion.

"Mother, will I ever stop feeling like my heart is breaking? What makes me want to stay in a place where no one wants us?" Emilie struggled to hold back the tears. These feelings were nothing like she ever felt before.

"It's called change, darling. You will be fine." Julia touched her shoulder, encouraging her to go. "Stop worrying. Come now, say good-bye."

Well wishes and good lucks were exchanged in the front yard. Aunt Jennie and Uncle William now owned the home—no more tobacco fields, no more blisters, no more hard labor. The family was free to begin their new life. Emilie looked at the garden in front of the house one last time. She remembered the tea parties she put on for her mother and Martha as she practiced the fine art of becoming a lady. Maybe her new life would allow her to serve tea with many new friends. The roses were past bloom. This thought tugged at her heart when she realized she would not see these roses bloom next year. She suddenly remembered she had one last thing to do.

"Where is Seth?" Emilie looked around to find her dear friend. "I need to say good-bye."

"You said good-bye last night." Jacob reminded her, not wanting another delay.

"They are in the drying barn," Uncle William interjected.

"Starlight is waiting for you!" Aaron handed the reins to his sister. Emilie smiled for the first time today. Starlight is Emilie's pride and joy. Helping his sister up, Aaron then took his turn saying good-bye. He shook hands with his uncle and hugged his aunt.

"I will be back after Christmas. Don't rent out my room while I am gone!" Aaron teased. Aaron and Henry drove the second wagon, while Jacob and Julia rode in the first wagon. The family headed north to a new life safely tucked behind the Mason-Dixon Line.

Waving until the family was out of sight, William hugged his wife. "I thought they would never leave in time. Horace Spree will be here with the shipment within the hour. Let's get some lunch before I have to break in the new darkies."

Jennie turned to her husband. "Martha's bubble and squeak should be about finished. She knows it is your favorite."

William smiled. "I am sure going to hate to let that one go. Her cooking is fantastic."

Jennie turned to her husband. "Are the new quarters ready?"

William nodded his head as they walked into their new house.

❧

Dear diary,

It feels like we have been traveling forever. Finally, we made it to Washington; this is a terribly busy place. Pa says it is good we made it through today. The weather has been seasonably warm. The nights are cold, but we are managing well. I miss our cook stove and Martha's good meals. I now know why Grandmother seemed so excited to get her new stove; I hate campfire cooking.

I have been thinking about how some of our so-called neighbors felt about us. Pa says they were angry because he freed Big Jim, Martha, and Seth. He says they don't understand why we would try to run the farm by ourselves when slave labor is available. It is confusing to me. Some say it is okay to have slaves, while others say it is not. I find those who condone slavery do not think of their slaves as people. How can they not? They live just the same as you and I, only at a different station in life. If there were a better way to manage a plantation, would there be no more slaves? I wish there was a better solution.

The farm is now in Uncle William's hands; he can run it as he chooses. Big Jim says he will stay on to help Uncle William during the first planting season. Big Jim knows the land just as well as Pa. Uncle William is smart to ask them to stay. Big Jim will have the place up and growing in no time.

Today we have a long way to go. I am going to ride with Aaron while Henry rides Starlight. The seat is more comfortable than the saddle right now. We are off and moving again.

Yours,
E. K. P.

The fall colors painted each tree—red, yellow, and gold. The sun's warmth broke through the chill of the morning. The road went on endlessly. It was hard to believe it would end at their home. Emilie tried to imagine what her new home would look like. Father described it several times. It was a story-and-a-half wood-and-stone structure. The parlor, he boasted, was the prettiest room of all. He could not stop talking about the beautiful stained glass windows in the parlor and stairwell. The property formerly owned and built by a gentleman farmer. The man had recently become a widower and since moved to the city to live with his son. Emilie could not wait to see if the house matched her vision of it.

"Aaron, how do you feel about us moving? Does it feel like you don't have a home, since you won't be living with us?" Emilie wondered if he felt out of place not having a room in the new home to call his own. Aaron would be returning to Richmond to finish law school in December.

"No. I am excited to get a home of my own. Maybe find a good woman to be my wife and open a law office." Aaron sensed his sister was anxious about the change the family was experiencing. Aaron knew she was worried about him. This would be the first time the family lived separately. He and his sister were remarkably close.

"This move is good for everyone. Who knows, I may come back to Gettysburg and open an office there. How would you like your brother living in the same town as you again?"

Emilie smiled at him. "No, you won't. You want to be a politician. You won't come anywhere near Gettysburg." She caught him again. He always tried to make her feel better about things. When she was four years old, her favorite hen went missing. Aaron told her, the chicken found a rooster to marry, and they ran away together. It was years later that Emilie found out they ate her for dinner. Aaron was always there for her.

Emilie turned to see Henry galloping past on Starlight. The horse bucked with protest. Angry, Starlight tried to throw her rider. Alarmed for Starlight's safety, Emilie stood up, horrified by the scene unfolding in front of her. Aaron pulled her down so she wouldn't be tossed off the wagon.

"Henry! What are you doing?" Emilie panicked.

"This horse has no discipline. She needs a good whip." He barely got the words out as the horse turned him round and round.

"Stop kicking her!" Emilie was more concerned for Starlight than her brother. "Starlight, stop!" Aaron slowed the wagon enough that Emilie jumped down and ran toward the horse and rider. "Henry, pull the reins back and tell her to stop!"

Henry regained control of the horse. Emilie rushed over to comfort Starlight and glare at her brother. "Don't ever ride her again!" Emilie was seething with anger.

"Fine, I won't! She is undisciplined, Emilie. That thing will kill you someday." Henry sat on the ground, trying to catch his breath. Hair tousled and eyes wide with excitement, Henry's face had a distinct smirk of mischief.

"What did you do to her?" Emilie shrieked. Starlight still acted skittish, backing up and dancing around, despite her owner holding the reins. Emilie turned to calm her horse, speaking softly like a mother to a child. The animal calmed enough for her to hop on and ride ahead.

Back in the wagon, Henry sat next to Aaron shaking his head. His older brother looked at him, eyebrow raised in suspicion. Henry sheepishly looked back at his brother. "I guess the horse doesn't like getting whacked with a willow branch."

❦

Ahead of the action, Julia turned in her seat as soon as she heard her daughter shriek. She saw her daughter galloping full speed toward their wagon. Emilie's hair flew wild and loose in the wind. As she approached, Julia noticed the furious look in her daughter's eyes. "Oh no, looks like we have trouble, Jacob." Julia described the scene to her husband. Jacob shook his head.

"That girl can scare the devil out of anyone, with that voice. No doubt Henry deserved it." Jacob knew his children well. Each child had his or her own personality, each as unique as the other. He and Julia raised strong-willed, determined children. His daughter was the strongest of all of them. She arrived in this world screaming, and she has taken control of it ever since. He loved them all but worried most about her. Emilie did not fit the mold of women of this time. Jacob knew there was no way to get her to fit. Emilie was a good girl, but she was undeniably her own person. His thoughts were interrupted by the sound of fierce galloping behind him. He turned to see his daughter, riding slowly next to the wagon. Face red with anger, she was ready to challenge anything that got in her way.

"Papa, we keep following this road for how long?" She was direct with her question. Emilie's voice quivered with anger. Her jaw set firm, eyebrows furrowed, making her look seriously in control of her emotions.

"Long enough for you to cool down and not take your brother's life," he said. "What happened?"

"He doesn't know how to ride." Her response was arrogant and sure. She rode off without another word.

"Why were we blessed with those two so close together?" Jacob asked his wife. "They fight constantly."

"God works in mysterious ways," Julia said, patting his hand. Julia always said that when she did not have the answers.

Somewhere between Frederick, Maryland, and Gettysburg, Pennsylvania

Dear diary,

I am excited to report that we will be in Gettysburg today. The journey has been long. We have been blessed with good weather and no problems with the horses or wagon. Pa says this is an easy trip as trips go.

I have decided to forgive Henry again. I know he antagonized Starlight. She is a good horse. He doesn't ride as well as I do, and he certainly doesn't know how to handle her.

I can't wait to see our new home, meet our neighbors, and begin our new life.

Details later as they are threatening to leave without me—again.

E. K. P.

It was a warm day for October. Emilie felt the nagging ache of being in the saddle too long, two weeks traveling with two wagons full of furniture and all the family belongings. How would the new neighbors welcome the newcomers? The questions flitted through her mind as she enjoyed the scenery, fresh and new. The leaves were still colorful—reds, golds, oranges, and browns— some leaves still hung on while most had left the trees to litter the ground with a kaleidoscope of color. The harvest was finished, yet life was just beginning for the family from Richmond.

"Say farewell to the South. We just passed the Mason-Dixon Line. We are officially living in the North. We have only seven miles to go, before we get to the borough of Gettysburg, then north to our new homestead. We will be home today."

Emilie was born just outside of Richmond, Virginia, on a third-generation family plantation. She grew up watching her family struggle to keep the tobacco farm profitable. The four hundred acres farm was a struggle for the family and a small group of workers to manage. Her earliest memories were the arguments she overheard from the neighbors, pressuring her father to either sell or own slaves to get the work done. Instead, Jacob employed fifteen black men and women and his own family to keep the farm running. This only infuriated the neighbors.

Emilie hated the hot, dusty fields. The humid weather and the long hours of monotony kept her from attending school. Emilie's mother chose to educate her daughter, when the work was finished. She knew the basics of reading, writing, arithmetic, but she lacked the finer skills young ladies acquire by socialization with others. While other girls were learning stitching, languages, and poetry, Emilie worked in the fields, miserable and resentful. Emilie loved to read and spent hours reading every book the family owned. Emilie's passion for learning was evident at a young age. She enjoyed teaching anyone who would take the time to listen to her. It was exciting to think this new home had colleges and schools. Emilie already discussed the possibility of attending school. Her parents simply told there was a lot of work left to set up the new farmstead, but the consideration of her education was not out of the question. At least there was a glimmer of hope.

"Emilie, pull your bonnet on. The sun is full on your face." Emilie wrinkled her nose; she enjoyed one more quick moment of warmth before dutifully pulling her bonnet upright. She resented the confines of the hat; it felt like blinkers on a horse. She would never put blinkers on Starlight. A girl should see what is front and behind her to better prepare her for what is coming.

Henry rode up beside his sister. "Look, Em! The town, it's right there."

She looked to where he was pointing. In the distance, she saw buildings appearing out of the fields, the road rutted with travel. The split rail fences became longer and more distinct. These farms fields now lay vacant and bare. The trees lined in uniform rows. Orchards! Emilie tried to imagine what fruits would grow on these trees. Emilie recognized apples, pear, and other fruit trees. She looked forward to making preserves with her mother.

Passing down the main street, Emilie took a mental inventory of residences and businesses as they passed. The streets were quiet, only a few people moving here and there. The town boasted tanners, cobblers, newspapers, hotels, and taverns. As the family proceeded through town, they came to the center. The street turned into a circle with roads pointing out in all directions.

Emilie turned in her saddle. "Where's the girls' school, Papa?" Now was a good time to remind her parents of the promise they made. Determined to finish her education, Emilie could hardly wait to enter the new school, meet her teachers, and make new friends.

"We have plenty to do over the next few weeks, child. Your schooling will be there for you when we are finished." Jacob's firm tone told his daughter he knew what she was asking, and now was not the time to bring it up. His eyes finished the sentence, saying, "I hear you, now hush."

"Just a few more miles to Table Rock Road and we will be home." Jacob could feel the pride bubble up in his chest. He was excited to show off the new home to his wife and family. His wife, Julia looked forward to changing from farm life to town life. The compromise was to own a small farm to support the family needs. The main source of income will be a town job for Jacob at the carriage factory. Julia will tend the home and socialize. The new start will be good for everyone.

Henry galloped up beside his father. "We are here!" The one-and-a-half-story wood-and-stone farmhouse stood nestled down a long drive lined with mature oak and aspen trees. The property was surrounded by fields on all sides, plowed under, and resting for the spring seed. The covered porch boasted two rocking chairs, inviting visitors to sit. Off to the right, the red barn stood majestic, clean, and fresh. The property was dotted with smaller outbuildings and outhouse. The well was situated on the right of the house. The property was beautiful.

The family dismounted from horse and wagon and stood in front of the large home. Jacob put his arm around his wife and pulled her close. "Welcome home!" he said, placing a kiss on her forehead. "I hope you like it!"

"Oh, Jacob, the home is beautiful. I can't wait to move in." Julia was more than pleased with her husband's choice. The home was simple yet elegant. It was large but small enough to manage. Julia realized for the first time that she would be in charge of the home without the help of her good, faithful housekeeper Martha. Julia missed her dearly. Martha was not only a good friend, but she was also an ardent organizer, who made the Prescott house a home.

"Well, family, you heard your mother? Let's move in." Jacob stopped, turned to his wife, and added, "After I carry you over the threshold." Jacob scooped up his wife as she giggled with delight. Aaron unlocked the door, and the family entered their new home.

NEW HOME, NEW NEIGHBORS

Home is a place not only of strong affection, but of entire unreserved: it is life's undress rehearsal, its backroom, its dressing room.

—Harriet Beecher Stowe

Moving day filled the hours with a flurry of activity. The men unloaded the large pieces of furniture. Julia directed where to place it. The parlor was as beautiful as Jacob described. It had birds' eye maple pocket doors, which closed out the noise of the rest of the home. It had a large fireplace with a beautiful screen. The gentleman who occupied the house left a few lovely pieces behind.

Emilie was eager to explore the rooms upstairs. The staircase went up, turned left, and finished on the floor above. The sweeping staircase was made of wood, dark and dusty. Her left hand brushed through the dust as she ascended the stairs. The hall was wide, leading to each of the four rooms on the left and right. The windows at each end of the hall let in plenty of sunshine up there. Emilie's room was bright with sunlight. She peered out the back windows. Fields and rows of fences and trees separated the large expanse of land. The land was extensive with gentle rolling swales. The rugged hills surrounding the area gave the region a protected, secure feel. Turning her attention back to her room, Emilie mapped out where she wanted the men to put her bed. Once decided, she went downstairs to tell her brothers.

Emilie took Starlight to the barn to unsaddle and feed. She helped her father walk the team into the barn. Brush in hand, she stroked Starlight's coat, singing softly to her friend.

"Starlight, star bright, first star I see tonight. Wish I may, wish I might have this horse as mine tonight." The song was a ritual

Emilie started on Starlight's birthday five years ago. She sang it like a lullaby every time she brushed her. Mesmerized by the methodical stroking of the brush, Emilie didn't hear the footsteps behind her.

"Nice piece of horseflesh that one is." The boy's voice came from behind her. "I'd say fifteen hands high and possibly a good runner but no good for racing. How fast can he run?"

"*She*"—Emilie emphasized the correction of the horse's gender—"happens to be a great racer." The boy popped around the front of Starlight. This was Billy Bayle, eleven years old. "Billy. Is it?" He shook his head in acknowledgment. "How do you know so much about horses?" Emilie studied this tall boy with tousled dark hair and an impish smile. She identified him by the stories her father told them when he talked about the Bayle family. Billy was the eldest of the six Bayle children. She noticed his eyes; they spoke of energy and mischief.

"My Pa taught me everything I know. He takes me to auction with him." There was arrogance about this boy. Was he arrogant, or did he clearly know about horses? "My Pa is coming. Do you want him to tell you?"

"No one needs to tell me about my horse, thank you." Emilie was eager to finish her chores.

"Your horse?" He sounded incredulous.

"That is too much horse for a lady. You need a gentle mare that doesn't have much spirit."

Seeing Emilie's reaction, Billy immediately asked, "What's her name?"

"I am sure you have no idea what you are talking about, Mr. Bayle." Emilie was trying to contain her irritation. "Her name is Starlight." Setting the brush aside, she busied herself with the rest of her chores.

"Why aren't your brothers doing that?" Billy had only seen his mother in the barn when his father was ill or out of town. This girl was very comfortable here. Did her brothers do the dishes? He smiled at his peculiar thought.

"Aaron and Henry are moving furniture into the house. I am taking this chore tonight." Emilie fed hay to the draft horses and secured their stalls. Finishing the work, Emilie prepared to leave. "Are you coming? I am sure there are things at the house to do." The boy seemed to be delaying the work that awaited everyone.

The yard was bustling with men unloading wagons, women directing, and small children trying to stay out of the way. It went as smooth as a well-rehearsed symphony. Once the wagons were unloaded and the beds made, the families sat together to share the chicken stew and biscuits Mrs. Bayle had brought for a welcome dinner.

"Mr. Troxel cannot wait until you start working. He says the company is getting very busy, and he needs the extra hands, Jacob." Joe Bayle was very familiar with the businessmen in town. He introduced Jacob to Mr. Troxel last fall.

Jacob smiled at his youngest son.

"Well, if they need more hands, maybe you would like to be an apprentice as a wheelwright, Henry. I am sure your math skills will come in handy."

Henry's eyes widened with excited anticipation. "I would like that very much, Pa. Do you think we can work together?"

"Lets finish settling in here, and we will go see about your future." Jacob had wanted to share his love for woodworking with his sons. There was never any time while they were in Virginia. He had hoped Henry would love this skill as much as he did.

Billy listened patiently for a break in the conversation to speak. "Pa, did you see Miss Emilie's horse? He is a great, big thing. She says he's a good racer." The boy's eyes sparkled with excitement. Emilie glared at him from across the table, whispering "she," hoping Billy would correct his error.

Joe Bayle turned his attention to Emilie.

"Do you ride, young lady?"

"Yes, sir. I have raised her from a colt." Emilie smiled as she always did when she speaks of Starlight. Like a parent speaking of their child, Emilie beamed with pride.

"Just five years you say? How does she handle?" Joe looked interested.

Jacob piped up, "Emilie handles her very well. They are practically inseparable. Be careful when you first meet her," Jacob advised. "Starlight is skittish around men with hats."

"The horse is possessed," Henry commented.

"Undisciplined and—"

Jacob cleared his throat and glared at his son. He observed his daughter turning red. Her nose wrinkled, eyes glared at her brother. Henry knowingly eyed his sister, liking her reaction as each comment made her turn crimson with anger. Henry enjoyed this power; he smiled with delight at his sister's expense. Jacob kicked his son's shin under the table. Henry jumped with surprise then immediately went back to his half-eaten biscuit. Jacob did not want his children arguing in front of the new neighbors. Joe smiled at the unspoken discipline happening at the table. It reminded him of his family.

"I will keep that in mind. Until then, I can't wait to meet her." Joe smiled back at Emilie.

"Aaron, what do you think about the upcoming election?" Joe was making his rounds to getting to know each family member.

"Well, Mr. Bayle, as I see it, Washington is starting to push the limits of states' rights versus what is outlined in the Constitution. It seems the slave issue should be a states' question not a federal one, since there is no mention of the rights to own or not to own slaves in the Constitution. Slaves are considered property, so is the federal government then infringing on our rights to own property? I am thankful Mr. Lincoln will not bring this issue to Washington if he is elected." Aaron had a lawyer look about him when he talked politics. Emilie noticed he was prepared and ready to defend the issue if warranted.

Joe Bayle smiled. "I hope the rest of the country can come to terms with the slavery issue, or we may have problems."

Jacob said, "We managed our farm without slave labor. On the contrary, I know some of the plantations will not survive without it. It is sad that our country is favoring the industrial North, when the agriculture is equally important."

"I agree with you. Our government is hard on the farmers. I can't imagine running a large plantation," Joe agreed. "How many acres did you say?"

Jacob swallowed, shaking his head. "The whole plantation is four hundred acres. We had to grow considerably less acreage to manage it with the limited hands."

Caught up in the conversation, Emilie added, "Why won't the North invent ways to help the farmers in the South? They boast of their industry, so why don't they do something to reduce the need for slave labor? We could eventually free all of the slaves." Emilie continued the conversation now more to herself, "Wouldn't that be a solution for both sides? Although I can't see Mr. Spree letting go of any of his darkies, and Mrs. Spree would be lost without her house servants—all eight or ten of them. No, I can't imagine there is help, let me think…"

The men stopped their conversation. Emilie instantly flushed, realizing she did it again. Speaking her mind within the family home was permitted, but she often forgot to keep her opinions to herself in the company of others. "Excuse me, I'll be quiet now." She looked around the table, all eyes on her, large with awkward disbelief. She wanted to slip under the table and disappear. She saw the look of disapproval from both of her parents. Aaron shook his head, willing her to stop, and Henry smiled, knowing she was getting in trouble again.

Julia broke in. "Does anyone have room for dessert?" The two families continued the conversation about the people of the town and shared need-to-know information to help them feel better acquainted with their surroundings. The evening was late, and the Bayles took their leave with sleepy children in tow.

Boxes, trunks, and crates scattered around Emilie's room. She finished putting the bedclothes on the bed and knelt to say her prayers as she did every night. Tomorrow will be the first day of the many new changes in her life.

GETTING TO KNOW YOU

The better part of one's life consists of his friendships.

—Abraham Lincoln

Crates, trunks, and packing materials littered the kitchen. It was a busy morning arranging new cupboards and pantry. The men were in the barn discussing repairs. Pa had already inspected the small fruit orchard, and Mother was excited to grow vegetables in the garden. It was still too early to grow, but the prospect of a new beginning was exciting for everyone.

"Emilie, finish up those snickerdoodles. I would like you to deliver those to the Bayles before night," Julia said as she finished emptying another crate.

Emilie brushed the flour off her hands and opened the oven. "The oven seems to be heating evenly, Mother. The cookies look perfect."

❦

The Bayle homestead was beautifully situated up Table Rock Road. The two-story, white home had a porch that wrapped around the front and side. It was neat and well cared for, reflecting the pride of its owners. As she reached the front door, Emilie heard a voice behind her.

"Mrs. Bayle is not home, Miss."

Emilie turned, expecting to see Mr. Bayle, only to see a man much younger. Stephen Byrne was a part-time farmhand for Joseph Bayle. He worked with Mr. Bayle to learn some of the finer points of farming. Stephen was a hard worker, and Mr. Bayle benefitted from both his labors and his friendship.

"When do you expect Mrs. Bayle to return?" Emilie's voice slipped into its sweet Southern drawl. She was delighted to meet someone new. "I have a thank-you gift for them."

Stephen was surprised by her Southern accent. "Don't know for sure. They went into town. I should still be here when she returns. Who should I tell her called?"

Studying him, she raised an eyebrow. "I don't know as I trust these fresh-baked cookies with the likes of you, hungry-looking stranger."

Stephen reached his hand to take hers. "Name's Stephen." He gently kissed the back of her hand with a slight bow. His eyes were a soft hazel. He looked at her with an intense gentleness.

Emilie smiled. "Stephen, it is a pleasure to meet you. Emilie Prescott. We just moved in up the road. I think I'll wait awhile for the missus to return." Emilie sat down on the rocking chair on the front porch, happy to delay the work at home for a bit longer.

Stephen sat across from her. They chatted about the move from Richmond. Emilie found out Stephen was born and raised in Gettysburg. His family owned a farm and orchard.

"I will inherit our family home eventually, once my parents approve of a girl for me to marry," Stephen answered Emilie's question regarding his plans.

"Your parents' approval?" Emilie repeated. "I thought the girl had to approve you, not the other way around?"

"Not in this case," Stephen explained. "Seems there are many who would like to marry their daughters to me. My parents have my life planned out." He let out a sigh of resignation.

Emilie smiled. It was odd to hear his parents were planning this man's life. He seemed to accept this fact without question.

"What are your plans, once you settle in here?" He interrupted her thoughts.

"I will get my teaching certificate," Emilie stated. "I have plans to have a large classroom of children and maybe run my own school for freed slave children and families."

Stephen dropped the stick he was holding. It startled Emilie as it hit the wooden porch. His eyes got wide, mouth agape. "What did you say?" Stephen was shocked. He never imagined such goals coming from a genteel southern girl.

She looked at him. "I didn't think my goals were that shocking."

"No, I just wasn't prepared to hear that from a lady." Stephen had to be careful. "I didn't expect that, I guess."

Emilie raised her eyebrow inquisitively. "Are you shocked because I have goals, or are you shocked because I didn't mention a husband and children?"

Stephen simply stated, "Both." Stephen saw her resign with knowing. It looked as if she had heard this all before. She smiled to reassure him. She wasn't surprised or angry at his shock.

"Let's just say, I believe a husband and a family have their place, and I will get to it when I am good and ready." Emilie tried to state that as gently as possible.

Stephen looked puzzled.

"And your parents don't mind that you are taking this path?"

"I am sure they would like me to marry and have many children to teach, but I feel there is more I need to do first." Emilie felt the pull of something more than just a dream when she thought or talked about teaching.

Stephen suddenly remembered he had to finish his chores. Getting up to excuse himself, he said, "It was a pleasure meeting you, Miss Emilie, but I must finish the chores before Mr. Bayle returns, if you'll excuse me." Stephen did not want to leave this charming girl's presence. She was smart and articulate. She laughed easily, and he truly enjoyed her company.

"You're right. I should go. It is getting late, and my mother will worry. Where shall I leave these?" Emilie looked around for a table where the Bayles would notice her gift.

"My stomach would love to hold those for a while." Stephen smiled.

"That's what I thought." Emilie scolded playfully. "You cannot be trusted." They laughed together. Just as they were ready to part company, they noticed the wagon coming up the drive. The Bayle family arrived home.

The wagon pulled up to the house. Emilie and Stephen walked over to greet them. Emilie noticed all the little heads of the Bayle children at the back of the wagon. Young Billy and little Joe jumped out of the wagon, followed by Sam, who felt he was old enough to get down himself. Stephen gave a hand to eight-year-old Jane and held little VanWyke's hand as he attempted a sizable jump for his little three-year-old body. Stephen caught the boy and turned him into a circle before setting him safely on the ground. Emilie greeted Harriett, who handed down baby Robert, just under a year old. His tiny body was wrapped in blankets, sleeping peacefully.

Emilie watched the little bundle in awe. His eyes closed, fists tightly clenched together. His body was warm and delightful to hold. Emilie felt a twinge inside of her she did not understand. "Why, aren't you the most precious thing I've seen in a long while," she whispered to the sleeping bundle.

"Emilie, dear, you look so natural holding that baby." Harriett smiled at the young girl, recognizing the look of wonderment in her eyes as she peered at the sleeping child.

"Oh, Mrs. Bayle," Emilie began, "I have a gift for you and your family. We really appreciate your welcome dinner last night." Emilie liked Mrs. Bayle; she had warm eyes and a gentle demeanor. She always seemed to be smiling despite the flock of children and immense chores demanded from her daily.

"Thank you. Won't you come in and sit awhile?" Emilie looked around for someone to take the baby. Mr. Bayle and Stephen were lugging parcels inside, while Billy was chasing after VanWyke so he wouldn't get his tiny self in trouble. Everyone's hands were full of parcels and packages.

Mrs. Bayle rounded up the scattering boys with one command. "Boys, come inside!"

The kitchen was a bustle of activity. Mr. Bayle, Stephen, and Billy brought in the goods and disappeared to the barn for the evening chores. Emilie set down the plate of baked goods and found a chair to sit with the baby still in her arms. Mrs. Bayle was busy with the other children and unpacking. The kitchen warmed up quickly as Jane stirred the fire; Joseph and VanWyke went to fetch wood. The house ran smoothly; everyone had chores. Emilie wondered if her home would run like that someday. She rarely thought about her future family. She focused on teaching and supporting herself. She knew a husband was inevitable; she was in no hurry. Emilie left the Bayles' thinking about her future.

Dear diary,

It was an amazing move-in day for us. My room is organized, and I now have a lot of ironing to do. I went to visit the Bayles to deliver cookies. Met a very nice boy, Stephen. He seems to have his life planned out for him. I think it is funny, his parents are choosing his wife for him. Something is strange about that. I like the Bayle family. They are so busy and always moving. Mrs. Bayle seems to have control over the whole thing. She is an amazing woman. I can't wait to get to know her more. I don't know how they do it. I wonder if I would be a good mother of so many children. It seems so overwhelming. First, I need to teach; then I will worry about children and family.

It is late, dear friend, will write more as it compels me later.

Yours,
E. K. P.

BRANCHING OUT

The love of learning, the sequestered nooks, and all the sweet serenity of books.

—Henry Wadsworth Longfellow

NOVEMBER 1860

Opening the last crate, Emilie let out a sigh of relief. Tossing the packing materials aside, she carefully lifted the book out of the crate. Longfellow. She loved his poetry. She tried to picture how she would teach someone to love this as much as she does.

Reaching in for another book, she pulled out her spelling primer, arithmetic, and another book on Shakespeare. Her mother had taught her from these books, and Emilie learned to appreciate their value. Handling them carefully, she opened the Longfellow book, its pages were fairly worn and yellow with age, to sit back and read. An hour later, she closed the book, determined to rehash the subject; she went downstairs to have a conversation with her parents.

The kitchen table had become the debate center of the Prescott house. Today, Aaron, Jacob, and Henry were deep into a debate about the latest news. Newspapers spread over the large farm table. The men were listening to Aaron make his point.

"As I see it, our new president has hard work ahead of him. The South is hot under the collar. If he cannot answer the slavery question, we may have a fight on our hands. He has to make right on this issue."

Henry broke in. "What is right, Aaron? What is the answer to this question?"

Jacob smiled. "I think the answer is who has the right to decide an important issue that affects so many people."

"The Constitution clearly does not address the issue of slavery. The issue of the right to own slaves defaults to the state's decision. That is clear. This should not be an issue. The South knows that. Why can't the North get it through their thick skull?" Aaron was getting ready to recite the Constitution when Emilie saw her chance to interrupt.

"What do you mean 'fight on their hands'? Will our states actually fight one another?" Emilie thought the question was not out of the question; she understood how the Southern culture lives for honor, determination, and respect. From what she overheard, she could see both sides of the argument. Her upbringing told her that the state for which she lived was her country. Her homeland. All of the states as a whole live under the under the large umbrella of the United States. Emilie decided not to discuss this further. It was a subject she did not have an opinion.

"Mother, Father, I think it is time I get ready to take the teachers' examination." Emilie had practiced this speech repeatedly. "I want to be self-sufficient."

Henry shook his head attempting to appeal to his sister. "Em, just get married. Educate your babies as Ma educated us. Why do you want to teach?" Henry could never understand his sister's desire to teach. He thought it was not ladylike to be a common woman who worked outside the home.

"Henry, how narrow-minded of you! As you can see, I have no prospects for marriage, and I am getting to the point that I do not want to live without helping support our family. I have always wanted to teach, and I will." Emilie stared down her brother.

"If you weren't so stubborn, maybe men would not be so afraid of you!" Henry knew how to irritate his sister. His words stung her pride like salt in an open cut.

Aaron added his opinion, "What Henry is trying to say, dear sister, is that men are intimidated by smart women. A woman should know her place in a relationship."

Emilie's face turned red with fury. Her temper bubbled up within her, causing her to sputter. "I…I can't believe you just said that, Aaron. I expect this barbaric speech from him." She pointed at Henry with accusation. "You mean to tell me, you will marry a simpleton who is at your beck and call, mouthing, 'Yes, Aaron. Whatever you say, Aaron.' This is disgusting, and I don't believe for one minute you would be happy. An intelligent woman is not a curse, and if it is, then may God curse me with smarts and the gift to teach it!" She finished her speech, slamming her hand on the hard oak table and glaring at her brothers, angry and willing to fight this point to the death.

Aaron smiled at his sister. "Good one, Em. You would make a great lawyer. Excellent closing argument, my dear." Aaron appreciated his sister's fire. He only hoped there was a man out there somewhere who could handle her determination and spirit.

Jacob looked up from his paper. "Boys, you have ignited your sister enough. The chores await you in the barn." Henry got up from the table, disgusted he was unable to finish tormenting her. Putting his cup in the sink, he left. Aaron got up from the table, winked at his sister, and left the room.

Julia wiped the flour from her hands and sat at the kitchen table. Both parents were acutely aware of her desire to teach. When she was ten years old, they remembered searching for her for hours. They found her teaching a young black boy, Seth, to read. Despite them scolding her, Emilie persisted defiantly, stating, "Everyone should know how to read." She was too young to understand the laws of the land, and it was illegal to teach blacks how to read. Emilie befriended Seth, and both Jacob and Julia knew the young ones had many reading lessons despite her repeated scolding.

"I agree it is time." Jacob was not going to argue with his daughter; she was still recovering from the scrap with her brothers. "Tell me this, Emilie. How long will it take you to take your exam? How long will you use it?"

"Father, I will teach forever. If not other people's children, it will be my own. Mother has instilled the importance of education." Emilie straightened up as she looked like a university professor giving a momentous speech. The room was now under her control. "I love to learn, and I want others to love it too. Since I have no prospects for marriage, I don't need to worry. As far as how long will it take me to pass my exam, I will have to be tested. I just need to find someone who will work with me."

"We agree you need to move forward and socialize. Just don't forget proper traditions of marriage and home." Julia did not want her daughter to forego becoming a wife and mother for a dream that would leave her empty. She knew Emilie's determination and independence were not good traits for the vows of honor and obedience. Julia could never understand why her daughter did not fit into the mold of most young women.

Emilie beamed with excitement. There is so much to learn, so much to study. Emilie couldn't wait to get started. "Do you think Mrs. Bayle will be able to help me locate the right person?"

"I agree that would be a good place to start. Mrs. Bayle said there are two ladies' schools in town that may be able to help: the ladies' school at Oakridge and the Female Institute. I believe Miss Sheads and Mrs Eyster may give you some direction."

Jacob enjoyed seeing his daughter's joy. She glowed with excitement. "Emilie, do you understand what an opportunity this is? This will give you a chance to create your own reputation. Gettysburg is a small town. Everyone knows everyone's business."

"Father, you have taught me the importance of reputation. I will make you proud." Emilie knew she had hard work ahead of her.

Over the next few days, Emilie travelled to town to find someone to help her achieve her diploma and prepare her for the teachers' exam. Emilie's first stop was at the Oakridge Seminary for Young Ladies to inquire with Miss Carrie Sheads. Over tea, Emilie made her case.

"I want to become a teacher," she explained to the school's principal.

"What qualifies you to teach?" Carrie studied the young girl sitting across from her.

"That is where I was hoping you could help." Just like Aaron in the courtroom, Emilie was forward and distinct with her case. "I have been taught by my mother, and I don't know if I am prepared to take the teachers' exam."

"At this point, I am sure you are not prepared, but I may be able to help you." Carrie easily saw this girl wanted to teach but wondered if she was a natural teacher.

Carrie listened to Emilie explain her school experience and what she studied, her love for books, and her desire to teach. Carrie noticed Emilie's voice had a gentle accent which brought more questions to the principal's mind regarding this girl's history.

"Where did you say you were from?" Carrie asked when the girl took a breath. She listened to Emilie describe her experiences and her hopes for the future.

"Near Richmond, Virginia. My family recently moved here," Emilie said matter-of-factly. "I am excited to meet new friends here in Gettysburg."

"I am sure you will have no problems making new acquaintances. You are outgoing and very pleasant." Carrie liked this girl, and she decided she would be willing to help her. "I will test you, and then we will see what you need to study. After that, you will need to study algebra, geometry, and Latin." Carrie pulled out primers and study guides. "You will need these subjects in order to teach the older children. Once you get to learning Latin, I will need to send you to Mrs. Eyster at the Female Institute on High Street. She is more proficient at this subject than I." Carrie looked up from the books to see Emilie, wide-eyed and bubbling over with excitement.

"How can I thank you?" Emilie felt dizzy. She was happy to make this woman's acquaintance. "What can I do to repay you for your kindness?"

"Do you have a job?" Carrie studied the girl.

"No, madam." Emilie's bubble burst; she felt dejected and suddenly sad. Her face clouded over; her expression darkened with disappointment. "I was hoping to work for you."

Emilie watched Carrie for a sign of approval. She pressed on. "I could help teach the younger children, while you work with the older ones. I would love to help you grade papers. By the time I finish my studies, I will have teaching experience. I would be willing to trade your help for mine."

Carrie smiled. "You have some good ideas, Miss Prescott. Let me think about how best I could use your talents, and we will discuss that when we finish winter break. Now let's discuss your study schedule."

The teacher and apprentice sat down to work out Emilie's study schedule. Just as, they were concluding their meeting, they heard a piano downstairs. As Carrie escorted Emilie out, she stopped by the parlor.

"Let me introduce you to my cousin, Salome Meyer. She is your age. She may be able to introduce you around town." Carrie turned to her cousin. "Sallie, I would like you to meet my new friend, Emilie Prescott."

"Pleasure to meet you." Sallie smiled and gave a brief nod. "Cousin, I came to visit a bit if you have time."

"You play beautifully," Emilie complimented.

"Do you play? I teach other girls in the area," Carrie chimed in. "Sallie, when are we going to resume your lessons?"

Emilie stayed longer than she anticipated. Emilie learned more about her new friends and listened to stories about the people of Gettysburg. Before the visit ended, Sallie invited Emilie to call on her Saturday. Emilie excitedly accepted the invitation. The girls made plans to sew and have tea that afternoon.

As she rode home that evening, she sent thanks to God. Her mother had always said, "Thank God for your blessings. He wants to know you appreciate him." Emilie smiled to herself. Everything seemed to be working in her favor. She looked toward the sunset. "Thank you for all your blessings. Come on, Starlight, let's get home. I need to study."

The sun painted the sky orange and red. Emilie pushed Starlight to run faster to get home before dark. Her parents worried if she was out past dark. The evening was beautiful but cold. She started thinking about the warmth of the kitchen and all of its comforts. It was a long day and Emilie was ready to go home.

About a quarter mile away from home, Emilie was still feeling the excitement of the day. She felt giddy with new books to study and a chance to teach. She didn't care if she only taught the alphabet; she had a chance to teach children how to read.

Starlight was moving along nonchalantly, when Emilie leaned in close. "Starlight, what do you say we run the rest of the way home?" The horse perked her ears, listening. Emilie spurred the horse to a run and raced to the driveway of the Prescott home. As they flew by the Blocher residence, Emilie did not notice Mr. Blocher watching from his driveway. The man shook his head in disgust, when he noticed the rider had long, loose hair and billowing skirts.

BLESSED CHRISTMAS

Christmas is the season for kindling the fire for hospitality
in the hall, the genial flame of charity in the heart.

—Washington Irving

❦

DECEMBER 1860

The Prescott family celebrated their first Christmas in Gettysburg
with a Christmas tree. Emilie scurried around to gather pieces
of old materials and scrap paper to make the decorations. The
excitement of preparation and festivities surrounding the season
gave Emilie a much-needed break from her studies.

It was a busy Saturday afternoon at Sallie Myers house. The
girls worked to finish their sewing projects. Emilie diligently
embroidered a collar for her mother while Sallie focused on a
cloak for her sister Jennie. Emilie noticed something was bothering Sallie.

"What's wrong, my friend? You seem distracted today." Emilie
gently broke the silence.

Sallie looked up from her sewing. "Oh, my mind is so heavy
with thoughts."

"Worry? Are your students giving you trouble?" Emilie was
always eager to hear about Sallie's teaching experiences. She
marveled at how Sallie seemed to have control of her classroom
and how she enjoyed teaching. Emilie hoped to learn much from
her friend's experiences. Sallie was a teacher at the public school
in town.

"No, class is finished now until January 14.

I heard that Mrs. Warren's son, Eddie, is ill with typhoid fever.
He is such a beautiful boy. I hope he recovers soon." Sallie's brow
wrinkled with concern.

"What are you planning for your vacation? I am excited to be in class with your cousin Carrie." Emilie found it difficult to contain her excitement. Sallie only shrugged her shoulders with indifference. Emilie quickly changed the subject. "How is your geometry?"

Tying off the thread, Sallie shook her head. "It is a good subject for me. Are you having trouble with it?"

"I guess not. The terms are confusing." Emilie tied off the end of her thread. "I am worried I won't remember all of the terms for the test." Emilie put aside her work and dug into her bag to show Sallie her plans for tree decorations. "I have some ideas to show you for tree decorations I found."

"You have a tree this year?" Sallie seemed to perk up. "I wish we had one. Are you going to have visitors?"

"That is why I came to you. Will you help me make them?" They discussed Emilie's ideas while they strung popcorn and cranberries. The afternoon passed quickly with tales of funny family stories and jokes. Hands sticky from cranberries and bellies full of popcorn, the clock in the parlor chimed, telling Emilie it was time to go.

"Thank you for all of your help. My tree project may get finished after all. There is one last ornament project I want to try." Emilie finished wiping the table. "Here, this string is for you."

"Emilie, I won't have a tree this year." Sallie was surprised with the gift. "You take this. Make sure you have enough."

"Sallie, it is a tabletop tree, very small." Emilie demonstrated the size with her hands. "Besides, I have plenty here. Put it on a tree outside. The birds will love it." Emilie smiled at her friend. "Smile my friend. Do not take so much on your shoulders at once." Emilie studied her friends face for a glimmer of hope. Sallie smiled in spite of herself. Emilie added, "Thank you for everything." Emilie surmised her friend was very responsible. Too many expectations seemed to have made Sallie a natural worrier, despite how hard she tried, her worries always got the best of her.

At the door, Sallie bid her friend good-bye. "See you soon, good luck studying."

"Thank you for everything, and Merry Christmas to you and your family," Emilie called back as she turned Starlight toward home.

❦

The next few weeks bustled with activity. Emilie finished the tree in time to show it off to the families on Table Rock Road. Neighbors called on the Prescott home between Christmas and New Year's. There were always more gingerbread cookies to make and cider to warm. The weather was either unusually cold or very snowy this season. The family celebrated a quiet Christmas with a small gift exchange. Emilie received writing paper from Aaron and a new pen and ink from Henry. Her most cherished present was from her parents. Emilie held the tiny gold heart-shaped locket in her hand. She examined the beautiful etchings on its face. The locket had a tiny key and two purple beads hanging from it. The piece was simply beautiful. Emilie watched how the light glistened off the heart, mesmerized by its beauty. It was sturdy for it had a strong chain and a tight clasp. At that moment, she recognized something on the back of the locket. Turning it over, the inscription read "Courage." Looking up at her parents, they smiled at her knowing she understood its meaning.

"I will treasure it always." Emilie felt overwhelmed with gratitude. "Thank you." Now it was her turn to give gifts. Emilie proudly gave gifts of knit scarves and mittens to the boys. She was delighted to present the embroidered collar to her mother. Emilie felt the sense of Christmas that day, knowing this holiday was one she would never forget.

New Years Eve the family went to visit the Bayles for a New Year's celebration. The family left for the Bayles' around 11:00 a.m. Emilie could not wait to meet more neighbors and celebrate with them.

Arms full of pies and gingerbread cookies, Aaron helped Emilie out of the wagon. The cold air nipped at her face and hands. The Prescott family was not the first to arrive. Several wagons circled around the Bayle yard. "I didn't think there were so many people coming today. How does Mrs. Bayle have time to manage the children and throw a beautiful party?"

"You will have to ask her yourself. I don't know how you women do half the things you do." Aaron handed back her things once her feet were set firmly on the ground.

The house was warm, brightly lit with sunlight through the windows. The snow glistened in the yard, making the sun brighter than usual. The smell of baked ham and fresh deserts wafted through the air, inviting anyone in who came close enough to smell its goodness. Emilie set the pies on the table as baby Robert started to wail from his crib. She slipped out of her coat and gave it to Jane, who was waiting to hang it up.

"Oh, Robert, you just ate. What seems to be the trouble now?" Mrs. Bayle had her hands in dishwater, searching for a towel.

Handing her a towel, Emilie rushed to the crib. "May I see if I can soothe him?" Emilie was surprised at her fascination with babies. Picking him up out of the crib, she smiled at his pinched, pink face, mouth open with a high-pitched squawk.

"Be my guest, Miss Emilie. He may need to burp, the rocking chair works well for that." Mrs. Bayle went back to her work. Julia stopped as she entered the kitchen. Seeing Emilie soothing the baby, Julia couldn't help but smile. It was a dream come true, maybe there was hope for her daughter after all.

Joe came into the kitchen. "Welcome, Julia, Jacob, and family." His smile was inviting, especially since Joseph Bayle was a serious man on most occasions. He ushered the family into the family parlor to introduce them to the rest of the guests.

"May I get you a beverage? We have apple cider, eggnog, and wine. Before I get your beverages, let me introduce you to some of our neighbors."

Joe finished the introductions of the Blochers, Mr. and Mrs. Jack Byrne and son Stephen, and finally, "Mr. and Mrs. James Marsh and their sons, Thaddeus and—where's young Ian?" Joe looked around the room.

"I believe he and Billy ran off to amuse themselves," Thaddeus said.

"Thaddeus, I am sure you would be interested in getting to know Aaron and Henry. They are new in town." Joe left the young men to become acquainted as he slipped back to the kitchen to retrieve the beverages ordered.

Back in the kitchen, Emilie had baby Robert over her knees, rocking the small bundle peacefully. She patted his back, speaking soothing words of comfort to him. Just as the baby quieted hypnotized by the rhythmic rocking motion, the heavy door crashed open. Little VanWyke, pink cheeked and cold, stood shivering in the open doorway. Behind him was Sam, also cold, missing his mittens and scarf.

"Frozden, frozden," Van repeated proudly. Jane rushed to the boys, shoving them inside the kitchen and slamming the door behind them. She removed their coats, hats, and scarves. Both boys' hands were red with cold. Despite the slamming door, the baby slept blissfully on Emilie's lap.

"Where are your mittens, Van?" Jane scolded him like a mother.

The tousled-haired, red-checked toddler pointed at the door. "Wet, frozden."

"Were you playing near the pigs again?" Jane insisted.

"Piggy bite, piggy eat!" VanWyke insisted, still looking at the door.

Jane turned to Sam. "Sam, were you playing near those pigs again?" Sam only shook his head. Jane groaned with frustration. "You boys are going to get in big trouble with those pigs. They will eat you, you know." Jane closed her hands like a big mouth in front of the boys' faces. The clap of her hands made the boys jump with surprise.

Seeing their eyes widen in fear she was satisfied by their reaction. Jane hung up their coats and then rubbed their hand in hers to warm them.

"Ma, I can't warm their hands. They are so cold and red." Jane was concerned.

"Give them some warm milk to hold in a mug. Set them at the table and with something to eat. They'll warm up soon enough." Mrs. Bayle was nonchalant and unnerved by the whole scene.

Jane picked up the squirming toddler and sat him at the table as she pointed to the four-year-old to sit down. She placed the mug and cookie in front of them and went back to her chore. Emilie noticed how she was becoming a mother so fast. Would she ever get the chance to pursue her own dreams?

"Miss Emilie, may I pour you something to drink?" Joe gathered what he needed and looked down at the young girl. "There is a nice gentleman in the parlor waiting to meet you." Joe pointed to the parlor and raised his eyebrows, teasing her.

Emilie blushed. "Don't fuss over me, Mr. Bayle. I will get something to drink after I convince the baby to fall asleep."

Joe walked over, peered down at his son, and said, "I think you work miracles, young lady. He looks like he's sleeping to me."

"I'll finish helping Mrs. Bayle. I will be in soon." Emilie picked up the sleeping baby and patted him on the back. The infant let go of the bubble he was holding with a small burp. Satisfied with her work, she settled him into his crib. The baby lay peacefully, sucking his thumb in a blissful sleep.

"Mrs. Bayle, how can I help you?"

"I am finished here," she said. "Would you like some cider or eggnog before we go to the parlor?"

The parlor was a buzz of conversation. As the door opened, Emilie heard David Blocher question Jacob.

"So since you are from Virginia, are you supporting those rabble-rousers down there? Do they really think seceding from the Union will get them their way? It sounds like trouble to me." Mr. Blocher was a cantankerous sort, who had the reputation of stirring up trouble. He was a thin man, shoulders hunched over from long hours in the fields. Mr. Blocher looked grumpy, with deep creases worn by sun and worry etched deep in his face.

"We still have family in Virginia. Whatever they choose to do is up to them," Jacob calmly responded. "We live in the North now."

Jack Byrne interjected, "What made you move up here? Why Pennsylvania?"

"The land is beautiful, soil is fertile, and there are many opportunities for the family."

David spoke up. "You can remove a leopard's spots, but he is still a leopard."

Maura Byrne turned to Julia. "How do you like Gettysburg so far, Julia?" Maura wanted to learn more about her new neighbor.

Julia smiled. "I like it very well. I am looking forward to meeting more good people."

Stephen noticed Emilie enter the room, standing up and going over to her. "Emilie."

"Stephen, how are you?" Emilie smiled at her new friend.

"I can't complain. Let me introduce you to my friend, Thaddeus." Emilie allowed Stephen to escort her to the middle of the room, when Joe Bayle popped up from his chair.

"Everyone, this is the last of the Prescott family to introduce." Emilie smiled at everybody, speaking little, polite, gracious words to everyone she met. At last, she turned to see him: Thaddeus Marsh—tall, strong, and with the bluest eyes she had ever seen. He smiled at her, his voice deep and resonant, speaking something she couldn't understand because she was lost in staring into his eyes. Mesmerized by him, she felt his eyes look straight to her soul. Emilie's heart pounded. He gently took her hand in his and placed a gentle, soft kiss.

"It is a pleasure to meet you, Miss Prescott."

"Nice to make your acquaintance, Mr. Marsh." Emilie heard her voice crack. Blushing with embarrassment, Emilie sat down on the nearest chair she could find. She suddenly felt lightheaded. He was exceedingly handsome. It felt like her corset suddenly tightened, leaving her breathless. Taking a sip of eggnog, Emilie was hoping to recover quickly. She felt everyone watching her fall in love at that very moment.

David Blocher suddenly broke the silence. "Are you the girl who races that horse past my farm?" His eyes narrowed with determination, willing her to answer him.

She turned her attention to the older man. She replied, "Racing, no. Starlight likes to run. I am just obliging her. She isn't so sassy if she runs regularly."

"What? That is preposterous. Obliging her, it's a darn animal. It is meant to work, not have tea." His face wrinkled with disgust at the thought.

Emilie smiled at the thought of Starlight having tea. "I am sure she would only want the sugar cubes, Mr. Blocher." Emilie giggled at the thought.

Together, Jacob and Julia gave her the look. Everyone laughed to ease the tension.

"Besides, she is a best friend to me."

"Yeah, she runs fast too. You should race her, Miss Emilie." Billy's excited voice came out from the open room off the parlor. Billy and Ian were eavesdropping on the whole conversation.

"Boys, there are plenty of chairs. You're welcome to join our conversation." Mrs. Bayle directed the boys to chairs.

Billy sat in the chair next to Emilie, leaning close to keep her attention. "You should race, we could build a good wager on her, and you could get rich. Ian here has an excellent horse I bet you can't beat."

Perturbed by his comment, Emilie moved in close to him. "No one races my horse but me. I am not racing for any money. That is called gambling and gambling is a sin, Billy." Emilie turned her back to the boys. Facing Stephen and Thaddeus, she smiled. "How have your holidays been, gentlemen?"

The evening was celebrated with talking and dinner. Emilie and Thaddeus had a great conversation. He made her laugh. Emilie enjoyed getting to know both Stephen and Thaddeus. She found they were boyhood friends. The young adults enjoyed the evening getting to know one another. After a wonderful meal of ham, sweet potatoes, cranberries, and sweet desserts, everyone returned to the parlor for wassail and music. Jacob tuned up his fiddle. As soon as the he was ready, Stephen offered Emilie his hand. "May I have this dance?" Emilie blushed and nodded her head towards her dance partner.

"I would be delighted to dance with you Stephen." The dance was a quick two-step. Stephen held her firmly and whisked her around the floor. Emilie laughed with delight. Before she finished the customary curtsy to her partner, Thaddeus took her hand and requested to dance a waltz with her.

Emilie's heart quickened. "I would be delighted," she said as he turned her around and settled into the waltz position. Emilie noticed he had a firm hand on her back and a gentle grip on her other hand. The contrast between the two gave her a secure, confident feeling until she missed a step onto his right foot.

"I'm sorry, for that." Emilie blushed red with embarrassment.

He chuckled. "It's alright; you may walk on my feet anytime." She looked up at him, surprised by his words. Her mouth formed the silent question *What?* He grinned wider, seeing her confusion.

"So what do you do when you are not dancing?" Emilie asked him. She hoped this waltz would be a long one so she could get to know him better.

"I work with your father at the carriage company in town as well as manage the farm at home with my father and brother."

Thaddeus told Emilie. They felt an awkward silence, neither knowing what to say because they were so newly acquainted. Just as he was about to ask her something, the waltz ended.

"Thank you for the dance." Emilie smiled as she did the customary curtsy to his bow. Thaddeus gave her a smile and a wink that made her tingle with excitement.

"It was my pleasure." Emilie took his arm as he escorted her off the dance floor. Seeing the crowd in front of her, she noticed her mother smiling from ear to ear. Emilie didn't think too much about her mother's happiness because she was still smiling about him.

Everyone sang carols and danced throughout the evening. Emilie always had a dance partner with Stephen and Thaddeus. Billy and Ian tried to dance with her too. They seemed to dance with two left feet, tripping on Emilie's feet and their own. Emilie graciously thanked each of her dance partners for a lovely evening. The celebration lasted well past midnight; when the Prescott family arrived home in the early that morning hours, it was already 1861.

> Dear diary,
>
> It is late and already 1861. I am too tired to welcome the New Year with any great enthusiasm. We had a lovely evening meeting new neighbors and making friends. Stephen introduced me to Thaddeus Marsh. He is very charming. We laugh together very easily. He likes my jokes and patiently listens to my stories. I smile when I think of him. Have to turn out the light, just got yelled at. More tomorrow.
>
> Happy New Year!
>
> E. K. P.

NEW YEAR, NEW LOVE

Let our New Year's resolution be this: we will be there for
one another as fellow members of humanity, in the finest
sense of the word.

—Goran Persson

JANUARY 1861

Once the holidays were finished, Emilie resolved to get back to
her studies. She worked through her spelling words, pacing her
room spelling and respelling aloud. The weather was blustery and
rainy, a perfectly miserable day to stay inside, trying to cram difficult words into her brain. These spelling words were long and
hard to memorize. Closing her eyes in concentration, the bang on
her bedroom door startled her.

"What! Henry, don't scare me like that!" Emilie jumped over
her bed and swung the door open to find her mother waiting
impatiently on the other side.

"I called you several times. Why didn't you answer?" Julia said,
perturbed by her daughter's disobedience.

"Mother! I'm sorry. I didn't hear you. I'm focused on these
spelling words. What do you need?" By the surprise on her
daughter's face, Julia could see she was telling the truth.

"Mrs. Bayle is ill. Will you please go up and see if you can
help her? Be a good neighbor. I have some extra biscuits for you
to bring them. Maybe it will help ease the dinner preparation."

Suddenly worried for Mrs. Bayle, Emilie hurried to get her
things to leave for the Bayle's. Gathering her basket, she went
to the barn to saddle Starlight. The barn was warm, smelling
of sweet hay. Emilie loved the barn; it was warm and inviting.
Gathering blanket, bridle, and saddle, she called out to Starlight.

"Emilie. What are you doing?"

Jacob was hooking up the team to the wagon.

"Mother said Mrs. Bayle needs help. I'm heading up there."

"I was just getting ready to go into town. Ride with me. It's too rainy to leave Starlight out all day."

"Thank you, Father." Emilie put the riding equipment away and climbed onto the wagon.

"Where are you going?"

"I have a few things to do before work today." Emilie could see her father was thinking about something. "Thaddeus is a nice boy."

"Yes, yes, he is." She realized her father was hinting. She smiled. Her father was as easy to read as *The Sentinel*. "I enjoyed his company at the Bayles' on New Year's Eve."

"If he asks, you should get to know him better." Jacob needed to push his daughter toward marriage because she obviously wasn't going there on her own accord.

"I may consider it if he asks. Stephen is also a very nice boy. We have chatted at the Bayles' awhile back." She felt his eyes on her. "We will have to see if either comes calling. Until then, I am continuing my studies. I have a classroom to teach."

Jacob shook his head. "All I am saying is that I give my permission if he wants to see you."

"Thank you, Father." Emilie dropped the subject like a hot, red poker. She did not want to complicate her life when she had a great opportunity to teach within her grasp.

The wagon rolled up to the Bayles' farm. Emilie kissed her father on the cheek and hopped down from the wagon. Joe Bayle came out of the house.

"What have we here, Miss Emilie?" Emilie handed him the basket of biscuits.

"Hello, Joe, I am lending you my daughter to help. Sorry to hear Harriett is under the weather." The men shook hands.

"Sure glad you could lend a hand. The children are rambunctious today. Poor Jane is at her wit's end trying to run the house."

"She's only eight, Mr. Bayle." Emilie was surprised to hear about so much responsibility for one young girl. Mr. Bayle did not seem concerned by his daughter's age or responsibilities.

"I better get going." Emilie took the biscuits from Mr. Bayle and hurried to the house.

The house was quiet as she entered. Emilie saw a pot on the stove, dishes on the table, and something spilled on the floor. No one was around. Walking toward the parlor, she heard a noise from the room to her left. Peering inside, she saw Mrs. Bayle changing the baby's diaper.

"Mrs. Bayle?"

Harriet turned to see Emilie in the doorway. "Emilie? What are you doing here?" Her face was pale, eyes darkened by deep, black circles, sweat beaded on her face. The woman looked as if she were about to fall over.

Emilie gasped. "Mrs. Bayle, you need to go back to bed. You look awful."

She sent Mrs. Bayle back to bed, tucked Robert in for a nap, and found Jane reading to Sam and Van in the boys' room before sending them to nap. The house was lacking its normal hustle and bustle. Emilie went back to the kitchen to get started cleaning up and begin dinner preparations.

"You must be the Prescott girl my brother has told me so much about." Emilie did not recognize the man at the kitchen table.

Emilie looked at him. "And you are?" He looked like a younger version of Joe Bayle, but she wanted to make sure.

He smiled at her. "I am John Bayle, Joe's younger brother. I live here too."

The house already seemed stuffed to the brim. Where would they possibly fit another person? Emilie said, "Why haven't I met you before?"

"I just returned from visiting relatives in New York. It's good to be home. What's for lunch?" John looked like a cookie cutter cutout of his older brother, in looks and mannerisms. They had the same eyes, build, and speech. John seemed to have a lighter sense to his personality than his brother, Joe. He was quick with a joke and exceptionally thoughtful of speech. Emilie would have guessed he went to a university like Aaron but did not ask.

"So, Miss Prescott, where are you from?" John was stirring his soup, watching her clean up the dishes.

"We live up the road on the way to town," Emilie replied as she put the last of the dishes in the cupboard. Moving to the pantry, Emilie gathered some potatoes, carrots, and onion. Taking out a cutting board and knife, she returned to the table.

"Not with an accent like that. I'd say Virginia. When did you move in?" John had a keen ear for accents. He wanted to become a politician but did not have the education to do so. His family farmed, and he was stuck. As circumstances happen, John did not have a place of his own, so he was living with his brother's family until his luck changed.

"Yes, sir. Virginia. I was born there." Emilie chatted while she cut up vegetables for stew.

"So what side of this war are you going to be on?" His question was direct and abrupt.

Emilie looked up. "War? Has war been declared?" Emilie knew South Carolina and Louisiana had seceded from the Union, but no one said anything about war.

"There is nothing yet, but if the South keeps up their temper tantrums, there is going to be a brawl." John watched her as she cut the vegetables. She chopped with precision, each cut even and uniform. It was easy to see she had done this many times before.

Emilie looked up from her work. "I think President Lincoln will manage to fix this problem. He needs to satisfy both side of this situation. There won't be a war." Why did this idea disturb her so?

"You know better than we do. The South will never talk about it. They need the slaves," John said matter-of-factly. "They cannot survive without the labor."

"Not everyone needs or wants them. It is the right to own them that we dispute, not the slave itself. I wish we could get rid of slavery. It isn't right to own another human being. Maybe if the North would find some way to remedy the problem, we could all get along." Emilie held fast the idea that industry will eventually take the place of human labor. There were many strides made so far; it would only take time.

"We did come up with a solution. We are limiting slavery in the new states that join the Union." John was surprised. "How do you know so much?"

"With all due respect, sir, that is not a solution. It only adds fuel to the fire. Our government does not have the power to decide a matter that should be left up to the state? No sir, the solution is not to take away the very thing that makes the farmer productive. It is to create something to replace it. The North seems to think they know everything with all of their industry. Why won't they come up with something to replace the need for humans in the fields?" Emilie was desperately trying to control her temper. Emilie put her cut vegetables in a pot and tended the fire.

"Miss Prescott, I am impressed." John found this girl to be fascinating. She did have her own opinions, and she was well educated. "Just curious, what side would you pick?"

She quickly tried to calculate the correct answer. It should be the North—the home she was creating, the neighbors she made. She thought of the comfort she was feeling in her new environment, but her heart still screamed the South. How could she turn her back on her upbringing and all she knew?

Looking at John with passion in her heart, she whispered, "I don't have to choose right now. There is no reason to choose because there is no war." Emilie picked up the water bucket and left the room.

The quiet of the early afternoon was shattered when the boys woke up and needed food, entertainment, and diaper changes. Mrs. Bayle stayed in bed all day, awake enough only to nurse the baby. Emilie managed to make dinner and start bread for the next day. As she was finishing the last of the dishes, Stephen came into the house with the milk from the barn.

"Joe said you may need this." Stephen handed her the pail of milk.

Emilie quickly dried her hands. "Oh yes, Jane, where do you store the milk?"

"Here is the pitcher, Miss Emilie." Jane handed the pitcher to Stephen.

He poured the milk into the pitcher as he addressed Emilie. "Looks like you have made quite an impression on John. He says you are one of the most opinionated women he has met in a long time."

"He asked my opinion, and I gave it to him. What's wrong with that?" Emilie shot back, irritated at his probing.

"Everything." Stephen became frustrated with her. It baffled him. "Women are not supposed to discuss political affairs."

"Stephen, isn't it correct, if you are asked a question, it is only proper to answer it?"

He nodded.

"I was asked, and I answered. If my opinion is interjected, all the better to make my point." Emilie turned back to the stove to finish stirring the rice pudding. She could feel Stephen's eyes still on her. She knew he wanted to say more, but he never did. She finished pouring the pudding when Joe came into the house.

"Miss Emilie, your ride is here."

"Thank you, Mr. Bayle." She turned to Jane. "Remember the biscuits in the oven and don't let the boys eat the pudding until it is cold."

"Thank you, Miss Emilie." Jane smiled.

"You're welcome." Emilie put on her cloak and finished her good-byes to the boys.

The day was already gone; the sun was setting over the mountain. The clouds of the day moved away. Tonight the sunset showed orange and red. She stopped to admire the colors setting over the mountain. Emilie did not realize how late it was. Approaching the wagon, Emilie grinned to see who was waiting for her.

"Thaddeus! What a surprise."

"Hello, Miss Emilie. Your father asked me to pick you up on my way out to your place. I hope you don't mind." He smiled at her and offered to help her onto the wagon.

"Thank you." She was excited to see him again. "Are you staying for dinner?"

"Yes, I have been invited to dinner." Thaddeus smiled at her. His dark hair, naturally wavy gave him a carefree, handsome look. His blue eyes, still crystal clear, excited Emilie as he looked at her.

Emilie smiled. She felt so carefree whenever this boy was around. She wished the ride home lasted longer. Thaddeus and Emilie talked about everything and anything. She was surprised how easy it was to talk to him. He laughed at her jokes, questioned her thoughts and opinions, and challenged her to think beyond her ideas. They enjoyed each other's company.

"So, Miss Emilie, I must say, I do enjoy your company," he said, testing the conversation.

"As do I. You are delightful to talk to." Emilie felt awkward; it wasn't a feeling she was used to having.

"May I call on you more regularly, with your father's permission, of course?" Thaddeus smiled at her to cover up his own discomfort.

"I am sure Father will be delighted. You may ask him." Emilie's cheeks hurt; the smile would not leave her face. As she watched him, he winked at her.

They arrived home to a warm house full of family. Tonight they will have a farewell dinner for Aaron. The holidays were over, and it was time for Aaron to travel back to Richmond to finish his degree.

The table conversation was full of laughter. Thaddeus seemed to fit right in, with witty comebacks to Henry's stories and thought-provoking questions to Aaron's philosophies. The night ended with Thaddeus and Jacob on the front porch. Emilie watched from the hallway window upstairs. The two figures below talked in low tones, head shaking and finally handshaking. Thaddeus left with a good night. As he drove away, he waved to the upstairs window. Emilie felt giddy with happiness.

The next morning was filled with activity. Aaron packed his saddlebags while Julia prepared food for his trip back to Richmond. As happy as Emilie was last night, this morning she was equally saddened with the loss of her brother's presence.

"You take care of yourself and make me proud to see you ace that certificate." Aaron hugged his sister, who had large tears in her eyes. She shook her head in response.

"When will you come back for a visit?" Emilie felt a little of her security leaving with him. She always had her father and brothers to protect her.

"I will be back early summer, just after I graduate. Take care, little sister." Aaron hugged her one last time before saying good-bye to the rest of the family. This was the first time the Prescott family separated from one another. Everything was beginning to change.

Emilie suddenly remembered. "Aaron! Say hello to Seth. Tell him I miss him."

"I will," he replied before he rode away.

> Dear diary,
>   I don't know how I can feel two emotions at once. Thaddeus is coming over to visit tomorrow. I am happy to see him. We always laugh together. He is interesting to lis-

ten to, and more importantly, he listens to me. Aaron left to go back to Richmond today. He will be living with Uncle William and Aunt Jennie. I hope he has safe travels. I am feeling empty now he is gone. I expect this is how a sister feels when her older brother moves away. I sure wish it were Henry going back; he aggravates me in the worst way today. I still love him, but that doesn't change him. Will he ever change? I guess I can hope and pray he will. Need to say my prayers before bed.

Good night, diary.
E. K. P.

Emilie finalized her testing and graduated from the Oakridge Seminary for Young Ladies with her certificate at the end of February. She continued her studies to train for the teachers' examination in May. Emilie started teaching with Miss Carrie in February. She began teaching the younger children to read. Between her work and studies, she enjoyed visits with Thaddeus. They spent pleasant evenings with the courting candle and her father just outside the parlor door.

Tonight, they sat together watching the fire, holding hands. In the peaceful stillness, Thaddeus asked, "How long do you plan on teaching after you find someone to marry?"

Emilie smiled; he always had a way of asking a question as if he wasn't involved in it. Still watching the fire, she replied, "I will teach as long as life lets me. I know the man I marry will understand my love to teach. He will realize I too can provide for the family to make things easier for us. If he is smart, he will allow me to pursue my happiness until the children start arriving."

"You know, there aren't many men who would understand, much less put up with that point of view." He was testing her. Thaddeus's voice was calm and soothing. He stroked her hair, encouraging her to open up to him. He understood she knew what she wanted, and he appreciated her focus. Her spirit was unfailing and strong. He didn't think there was anything that would stand in her way, not even him. He either had to accept all of her or none of her.

She turned to him. "I know there is someone out there who will understand. It is a perfect compromise."

"Some would think the man is less of a provider to allow his wife to work." He pressed on.

"It's not work, Thaddeus. It's a gift I give. Why should we care what they think? We are doing what is best for us. Isn't that what matters?" Emilie realized her use of *we* and *us*. She instantly closed her mouth, hoping she hadn't been too forward.

His eyes reflected in the firelight; a soft smile crossed his face. Thaddeus looked at her, shook his head, and leaned in to kiss her. She tenderly accepted his kiss as if to say he understood her, and it would all work out.

Putting her head on his shoulder, she spoke to him. "So what do you say about me opening a school for freed blacks? I would like to principal a school like that."

"Let's not push it." He pulled her close, kissing the top of her head. "Why must you always push an issue to the edge of all reason?"

"I don't want to miss out. I have it all planned." She suddenly became agitated. The look of concern on her face made him want to protect her. He knew he could never tell her that was his intention, she was too independent, but he would do it nonetheless.

He held her close as they sat quietly; he felt her relax. Just as they were about to speak, the courting candle snuffed out. It was time to go. Thaddeus stood up and offered her his hand. The young couple embraced one last time before Emilie walked him to the door.

"Have a good day tomorrow. Enjoy your students."

"Thank you, you too." she replied. Emilie felt her parents and brother watching from the kitchen window. Thaddeus saw the look in her eye and immediately took his leave. Giving her one last bow, he untied his horse and left.

Emilie watched him ride down the drive. She suddenly realized that she hated to see him go. She didn't want it to stop; she wasn't worried about her goals. She was sure he would give her his blessing.

RACE HORSE ALLEY

A horse never runs so fast as when he has other horses to catch up and outpace.

—Ovid

MARCH 1861

"Billy, how are you going to get that horse away from her? She keeps it closer to her than a tick on a hound dog." James was immensely interested in seeing how this venture was going to work.

"It goes like this," Billy explained. "I will go to her and ask if I can borrow the horse, we take it up to Race Horse Alley, and race. When the horse wins, you give me the winnings, and we're done. I take the horse back, and she doesn't have a clue."

Billy's plan was finally coming together. Ever since he met Starlight, he had to see how that horse ran. Beautifully sculpted, muscles defined, sleek and shiny chestnut coat—that horse would be envied by any good horse trainers. The horse had a perfect, white star on her nose. She was as beautiful as her owner was. Billy knew Starlight was well run, he often saw Emilie run her up and down Table Rock Road. Billy wanted to feel the strength of Starlight under him, he wanted to see how he could handle her. These envious thoughts haunted him ever since he met her. He and Ian Marsh hatched the plan complete with bets and winnings. The bets came as a result of Billy and Ian's pride and inability not to brag about their plan. Their friends were more than willing to bet just to not listen to any more of Billy and his stories.

"What is so great about this horse anyway?" Sam asked.

"A horse is a horse."

"You city boys don't have a clue. That is the most beautiful animal I have seen in a long time, and I have to see if she can run." Billy's palms sweat with anticipation. "Besides, Emilie brags about her horse all the time, and now I am putting it to the test. Who wants to wager a bet? I am putting in my bone-handled pocketknife to say that the horse can run." Billy slapped down his pocketknife and stared down his friends, daring them to raise the price.

Gates Fahenstock, suddenly appearing around the corner, interrupted the betting. "She…she…" He was struggling to catch his breath. "She is in the store, and…and…the horse is out front."

❧

"Good morning." Emilie was in a pleasant mood today. She was picking up some goods for the house, and this was her chance to look at some new fabric for a dress she was hoping to start. Stopping at the dry goods store first, she arrived at the store just inside the diamond in town.

"How may I help you today?" Mrs. Sarah Schick smiled back.

Emilie suddenly remembered what her mother told her. Good impressions are essential. Emilie pulled her list out of the pocket of her dress.

"I would like to see your fabrics and trimmings for a new dress, please." Eyeing the shelf behind the clerk, Emilie was impressed by the goods available.

"Are you new in town?" the clerk who interrupted asked.

"Yes, I am Emilie. My parents are Jacob and Julia Prescott. We recently moved here from Virginia. Do you have any new patterns in?"

"We just got this silk. What color are you looking for, miss?" The clerk finished pulling her order form the self behind her. "Will you be buying the fabric today?"

Shaking her head, she answered, "I am just getting some ideas today. I need cotton or homespun, please." The clerk led her over to the fabric wall. Colors of all kinds decorated the wall. The splash of color was exciting to see.

Emilie took her time looking at the fabric colors, imagining the possibilities of what was going to be her new dress. Her favorite color was red. The print was bold and refreshing. The blues were subdued and boring. Emilie then spotted a green-red print but dismissed it as too seasonal. Thoroughly enjoying her shopping, she noticed a flash in her peripheral vision. Looking out the front window, she saw Billy bouncing up and down, trying to get her attention. Emilie excused herself and left the store.

"Miss Emilie, I have to borrow Starlight. My friend needs her." Billy was excited. He had several friends around him, shaking their heads and agreeing with him.

"Billy, I need to get home. Can't someone else help?" Emilie was suspicious of the boy. He seemed too interested in Starlight, and her instincts told her this was a lie.

Boldly, Billy jumped up on Starlight and attempted to ride away. Angered by his audacity, Emilie grabbed Billy's leg and pulled.

"Stop, Billy! Get down this instant!" Emilie suddenly felt something was terribly wrong. Emilie restrained Starlight and glared at Billy.

"We have to go! Be right back." Billy tired to yank the reins from Emilie's hand.

"I'm going too." In one swift motion, Emilie was up on Starlight's back. "Let's go."

"She can't come. It'll ruin the race." Young Gates threw down his hat in disgust. "I want my money back!" The other boys poked him to shut him up.

Billy shook his head at Gates. The boys shuffled and whispered. The word *race* echoed in Emilie's mind. She realized what was happening.

Emilie looked at Billy. "What are they talking about?

"Oh, nothing, it's just I was hoping to borrow Starlight for a race. Sam here doesn't believe that I can win. So I was hoping Starlight could fill in." Billy's ears turned red with embarrassment.

"Billy Bayle, you lied to me," Emilie scolded him. "Why didn't you just ask me?"

"Because I was afraid you'd say no," Billy sheepishly replied.

"Well, I am sayin' no. This is a horrible idea." Emilie turned to go, pushing Billy to get off the horse. He hopped down and turned to appeal to his crowd of friends.

"Starlight isn't a good runner anyway. Sorry, boys, we ain't gonna see this horse run. Ever! This sure saves our disappointment." Billy was making every effort to impress his friends and push Emilie. He knew Emilie was competitive. He knew with a few properly placed phrases she may be willing to let him race.

Emilie turned in the saddle and glared down at Billy. "How much money did you boys think my horse was worth?"

"Aw, not much. Just a few dollars." Billy knew he was getting under her skin. "This sure saves us all the trouble."

Just as the confrontation was getting heated, Ian Marsh galloped up on his horse, Diablo. "When's the race? Can I still enter?"

"No, we're going home." Billy announced. "Emilie won't race. The horse won't win anyway."

Emilie noticed Ian immediately. He looked like his brother. His eyes were bright blue, a stark contrast to his dark, wavy hair. Ian had a strong build. Remembering he was only about fifteen years old, Emilie dismissed him as a boy, not yet a man. She knew he would certainly be a ladies' man when the time was right.

"The horse will win, but no one's riding her but me." Emilie would not risk anyone else riding Starlight.

"No! Not the girl," Gates whined. "Girls can't race. I want my money back." His frustration grew the longer the race was delayed. He knew Ian was a fast rider, and it would be hard enough to beat him, but a girl on her horse? That was simply impossible in his mind.

"Fine with me. This will be the easiest race since I raced you, Billy." Ian laughed. "What's the wager?" Ian made sure it looked like Billy's idea; he didn't want to steal the boy's thunder.

"If there is, the winner gets it all," Emilie stated clearly. "You want to bet on my horse—I get the winnings."

"Only *if* you win. Let's go to Race Horse Alley." He noted the girl had determination. Nothing held her back. Most girls he knew would never be caught gambling, much less racing. This girl was different.

Race Horse Alley was named for its tendency to attract horse races. The long alley was perfect for a race among friends. The group travelled together to the top of the alley. Emilie and Ian set up next to each other. Gates drew the line in the dirt. Billy and his gang waited at the end of the alley. They waited to call the race at its finish. Gates pulled out his handkerchief, raised it in the air, and shouted, "Go!"

Emilie spurred Starlight into action. Starlight took off running. She had a hard time getting into the rhythm at first, but just as she hit her stride, she saw Ian race up beside her. He ran his horse hard and fast. Emilie pushed Starlight harder. She had to win this, it was simply pride, but it would feel good to win. Just as the finish line was in sight, Emilie noticed the boys scatter in different directions. There was a man standing in the middle of the road just beyond the finish line.

Ian yelled, "Stop! Sheriff!"

Emilie reined in Starlight. The horse snorted with protest. As Emilie came to a stop, noticing the sheriff as a portly older man, looking very disappointed next to the sheriff, stood an equally upset Thaddeus. He glared at his brother. His eyes met Emilie's; he was very surprised to see her. She dismounted. Her hair had fallen out of its pinning. Curls blew into her face; Emilie knew she must have looked disheveled and messy. She could not get over how he made her feel—giddy, happy, and carefree. Emilie wanted to feel like this always.

"Gentlemen." Emilie inclined her head in greeting.

"Where did the others go?" She suddenly felt abandoned. The street was surprisingly vacant of the gang of boys that stood there moments earlier.

The sheriff sternly answered, "What was the wager?"

"I have no idea. Billy Bayle was the ringleader." She was catching her breath. "He wagered this race, but he was not going to ride my—ow!" Ian stepped on her foot. She glared at him.

Addressing Ian, the sheriff turned to him. "Mr. Marsh, this is the third time that I am aware you have been racing down the alley. Will you please recite the law for this alley?"

Ian respectfully answered, "Yes, sir, I believe the law says that one may travel no faster than a boy can walk."

"Well, Mr. Marsh, I don't believe anyone can walk as fast as you two were running those horses. Are you aware that there is a fine for racing in this alley?" The sheriff seemed to be satisfied with his catch. He turned to Emilie. "What is your role in this situation?"

Calculating her answer, she approached the subject with her usual charm. "I raced out of pride, and even though I won"—Emilie emphasized these words as she glared at Ian—"I realize how foolish my actions have been." Her big, green eyes stared them down. "I assure you, this was not my idea. I was caught up in the excitement of the boys who have since disappeared." Dismissing the men, Emilie gathered the reins and walked away.

The sheriff stopped her. "Miss, we are not finished here. You and Mr. Marsh have some business with the Borough of Gettysburg. You owe us a fine."

She turned back. "With all due respect, Sherriff, I explained my situation here. This is not my problem."

"Would you rather explain it to the judge, Miss? Court is held on Tuesday." The sheriff left Ian and Emilie standing in the alley holding their fines. Emilie seethed with anger; she did not know where to turn. She was angry with Billy for goading her into this and angry with herself for falling for it.

"What were you thinking?" Thaddeus broke his silence of disbelief. "Do you realize how embarrassing this is for us?"

"Us who?" Emilie questioned. "I am hoping this will disappear. I just wish I could string up Billy Bayle. How did he think of this?"

Ian looked at her sheepishly. "I helped him."

"Oh, good." Emilie handed him her ticket. "You can pay for this then."

"Oh no, I won't." He dropped the fine to the ground, defiantly looking at her. Shocked at his behavior, Emilie swept down and picked up the fine.

"You conjured this up. Now you get to take care of it." Emilie was frustrated. Realizing her stupidity, she felt angry and embarrassed. "If you don't want to do this on your own, you'd better call on Billy." Ian shook his head, refusing to take the fine back in his hand. Knowing she would not get anywhere with him, she crumpled the fine in her hand. Not wanting to hear what Thaddeus had to say, Emilie walked away.

"I am finished here." She mounted her horse and turned to Thaddeus. "Will I still be seeing you tonight?"

Thaddeus quietly responded, "How about six?"

"I will see you then." Emilie turned Starlight and headed home.

The longer she rode, the hotter her temper simmered to a boiling point. Stopping at the end of the Bayles' drive, Emilie debated about giving Billy a good piece of her mind. She was angry for giving in to verbal challenges by someone years younger than herself.

She could not leave this alone; Emilie started up the drive, telling herself she was going to be the adult in this situation— simply discuss her disappointment and then tell him under no circumstances was he to ever look at her horse again. Stomping up the drive, head down with determination, Emilie almost ran into Sam Bayle.

Dancing around Emilie, Sam jubilantly said, "Did you win? Did you win? Billy said you were winning."

"Sam! This is not something I want to discuss."

The young boy stopped. "Billy said." His eyes were wide with excitement as he bounced up and down like a rabbit. Sam was always full of energy. His excitement was contagious, hair messy and shirttails sticking out of his trousers. Emilie smiled despite her foul mood.

Billy met Emilie outside the house. "Did you win?"

Emilie glared at him. "You disappeared. You coward." She grabbed his hand and put the fine in his palm. "You pay it— this is your doing. I am sure Ian will be delivering his fine to you. We got caught by the sheriff."

"He knew the risk." Billy was annoyingly nonchalant about the subject.

"He did. I did not. You will stay away from my horse. Your antics embarrassed me, and the sad part is that I am angry with myself for allowing you to get to me."

Disgusted, Emilie left Billy on the porch.

Billy called after her, "I knew she was a good runner."

She did not look back as she ran Starlight home. She took care of Starlight in the barn. Her anger still seething within her, she entered the house and slammed the door behind her. Her family, who filled the kitchen, looked up at her, surprised to see her—hair disheveled, face red with fury. Emilie stomped by the family and up to her room to clean up.

"What did you do this time?" Jacob looked accusingly at his son.

"It wasn't me." Henry was surprised at the accusation but somewhat astonished someone or something could set her off like he could.

As she slammed her bedroom door, her father asked Henry, "Do you know how to repair hinges?"

His son shook his head.

"If this keeps up, you'll learn fast." Jacob shook his head. "I think I should see what is going on."

"I would wait. She needs to settle down. She needs time to cry it out, slam things. She should be herself by dinner." Julia knew her daughter.

Jacob was shocked. "Slam things? I won't have any door left by the time she is done!"

"Patience, Jacob. She'll come around. If you go up there now, you will only be stirring a hornet's nest." Julia calmly assured her husband the doors would stay intact.

The evening meal was silent; Emilie spoke only when spoken to. She was calming down, hoping to be in a better mood when Thaddeus arrived.

Emilie broke the silence. "Pa, do you remember Thaddeus is coming to call this evening?"

He eyed his daughter deliberately. "I remember. Are you going to tell us what happened today?"

Emilie shook her head. "I took care of it." Emilie said nothing further. She quietly prepared for Thaddeus's visit.

The wood in the parlor fireplace popped and sputtered as its warmth filled the room. Emilie curled up in her father's large chair with her new book. Her legs curled underneath her, skirts draped over the chair. Emilie was happy to leave her hoops upstairs; she only wished she could shed the restricting stays that threatened to stab her ribs with one wrong move. Reading always relaxed her. She pulled *The Missing Bride* by E. D. E. N. Southworth off the bookshelf. This will be the best way to escape for now. She worried about Thaddeus's reaction to today's events. Through the weeks they had been seeing each other, Emilie valued his opinion. She couldn't imagine disappointing him.

Engrossed in her story, she did not hear the doors open to the parlor. Thaddeus slipped into the room. He knew she was concentrating because she did not look up. He leaned over the back of the chair and whispered, "How's my jockey this evening." Her hair smelled of lavender and sweet hay. Emilie smiled, her cheek less than inches from his lips. She pressed her advantage and turned her head to feel his lips against her cheek. He kissed her gently.

Looking up at him, she quietly whispered, "I am sorry. I am impetuous that way."

"I can tell. You almost won! I was rooting for you." His smile was genuine, his dimples deeply engraved in his cheeks, and his eyes sparkled when he looked at her. He moved away from her chair as she adjusted and sat up. Thaddeus sat across from Emilie as all good courting gentlemen do. They knew it would only be moments before her father entered with the courting candle.

Just as, expected, Jacob entered the room with the courting candle. "I expect you both know the rules, and I can trust you alone this evening? When the candle goes out, Mr. Marsh will be on his way." The couple nodded in agreement. Jacob left the room, sliding the doors partially closed.

"Are you upset with me? How many people in town are going to know?" Emilie was concerned with her reputation.

"I don't suspect the sheriff will care to gossip about this news. Ian has been a thorn in his side for some time. The gossip would only make the sheriff look bad. I suspect you will be safe, provided you won't pull that stunt again." Thaddeus had thought about the potential damage control. He already planned how they would handle the fall out, if needed.

Thaddeus told her about the latest project he was working on at home. "I just can't seem to get the piece to fit. The table is almost complete, but there is just something missing."

She could see the frustration on his face. "Maybe you could ask my Pa. He may be able to tell you what's missing." Thaddeus looked doubtful. Emilie stood up, put her book back on the bookshelf, walked over to Thaddeus, and offered her hand.

"Come on, let's go see Papa." Still holding his hand, Emilie led him out to the barn where she knew her father would be working on a project. As they turned the corner, Emilie heard Henry ask, "What are we going to do about it, Pa?" Henry's voice was urgent and uneasy. Henry sounded surprisingly older than she had ever noticed before.

"We need to keep this between us. I don't want your mother or sister to worry. I am concerned about what Virginia will do now that eleven states have seceded. The South is occupying forts. It may be coming faster than we think."

Emilie could smell the cigar smoke. She knew her father did not smoke unless he was worried about something. Emilie walked to the barn shudder and banged it to announce they were in the barn.

"Papa!" she called. "Where are you?" She took Thaddeus's hand and led him to the area where her father worked on his projects. They passed Henry. Emilie smelled cigar smoke on him.

"Henry?" she said. "Are you smoking?"

Henry said nothing except to glare at her and shake his head as he walked out of the barn.

Thaddeus and Jacob discussed woodworking while Emilie tended Starlight. She checked her for swelling in her legs. The run didn't seem to affect her, and for that, Emilie was relieved. Emilie decided to take care of the fine as soon as possible and leave the whole episode behind her. She had so much to look forward to.

At the end of the evening, Thaddeus and Emilie said goodbye in the yard. He took her hand and then pulled her close to hug her. His embrace gave her strength; his closeness made her feel strong and confident. She fit perfectly in the spot below his shoulder. She tried to memorize how it felt to be in his arms. Emilie took a mental inventory of him. She noted the fresh scent of him, the soft cotton shirt on her cheek, how his eyes sparkled when he laughed with her. The more she was with him, the harder it was to let him leave. Emilie started to imagine what it would be like to be his wife and mate for life.

Back in her room, Emilie turned down the bed and crawled in. The covers felt invitingly cool and soft. The quilts were made by her mother and grandmother. The heavily stitched blankets gave her a protected, comfortable feeling. Settling into the blankets, she opened her diary. She carefully set her ink on the table beside the bed. Emilie was careful with the ink; her mother would never understand ink stains on the sheets.

> Dear diary,
>
> I am falling in love. I am worried about my future. Confused by what is happening to me, I can't seem to make sense of it. I am losing the strong desire to live by myself. I thought the only way to teach was to live alone. I don't want to be alone. What is to become of me and my teaching? Will he allow me to teach and be his wife? He hadn't asked, of course, but what will I do? It has always been teaching first, husband second. Will it survive? Will I be happy with this? I am confused. I hope my dreams will tell me what to do. I will ask God to guide me and talk to me in my dreams so my heart can be content again.
>
> Worried about my future and excited at the same time.
>
> E. K. P.

Putting her diary aside, Emilie blew out the lamp and settled into the warm bed. She remembered his words, they were the last memories she had before she fell asleep. "Good night, my love." His whisper echoed in her ear. She thought little of what she heard in the barn that evening. She only thoughts focused exclusively about their love.

RUMOR MILL

A rumor is one thing that gets thicker instead of thinner
as it is spread.

—Author unknown

❧

APRIL 1861

Arriving early to the courthouse, Emilie slipped in, hoping no
one would notice her. She gave the clerk her ticket and money for
the fine. The clerk was a tall, thin gentleman with glasses perched
on his beaky nose. He read over the fine and looked up at her.

"Paying this for your brother, are you?" He looked at her accusingly. "That alley is going to get someone killed."

Pleasantly, Emilie corrected him, "No, sir, this belongs to me."
She handed him the money.

"Oh, so you are the lass that got the sheriff's tongue wagging.
You sure did impress him."

Emilie looked at him in surprise. She felt the color drain from
her face, and her stomach began to feel queasy. Then she saw him
looking at her.

He looked at her approvingly. He wasn't approving her riding
ability, but he was approving her looks. He gave her that *I can see
everything under that petticoat* leer. Feeling uncomfortable, Emilie
glared at him.

"I would like my receipt if you please." Even though she
wanted to scratch him like a cornered cat, she instead smiled
as sweetly as she could. She wondered why when she was about
to do something improper, she could hear her mother's quotes
and lessons. This one was, *First impressions are lasting impressions.
Always make them good impressions.*

"I see here, Mr. Marsh did not pay his fine." He looked at her over his glasses.

"I am sure he will be in promptly," she said, looking out the window. The street was now bustling with people. Emilie could not imagine how the streets got so busy in the few minutes since she arrived. She tapped her foot impatiently as she waited for the clerk to write her receipt. Watching him out of the corner of her eye and watching the street with the other, Emilie prayed no one would recognize her.

Finally, he finished his careful writing. Handing her the receipt, he reminded her about second and third offenses if they were to occur. The lecture droned on for what seemed like a week. Losing her patience, she took the paper from his hand and mumbled something like, "It won't ever happen again." And she walked out.

Closing the door behind her, Emilie scanned the street. It looked like no one saw her. Just then, Sallie waved from across the street. Emilie reluctantly waved back. Emilie pointed down the road to indicate she was in a hurry. Sallie mimed for her to wait a minute and crossed the street. Dodging wagon and horse, Sallie called to her friend. "Emilie, wait for me."

Seeing her good friend again was always a pleasure, but today was not the day Emilie wanted to meet Sallie on the street. "What are you doing today?" Emilie asked sincerely, hoping Sallie would have to turn around and go the other way.

"I was just heading off to school. Class begins in forty minutes, and I want to be ready." Sallie looked at Emilie, waiting for her friend to tell her why she was leaving the courthouse. Sallie didn't pry; it was something she considered un-Christian-like. Sallie was a devout Methodist, who prided herself in following her religion and its teachings to make herself a better person.

Emilie replied, "I was headed to school myself." The girls walked in that direction, talking about their holidays. Sallie reported her holiday was dampened by Eddie Warren's funeral.

Sallie expressed how thankful she felt for finishing a dedication piece for Eddie. Mrs. Warren was proud to see it published in the paper. Emilie empathized with Sallie regarding her loss. Sallie simply smiled. It was Emilie's turn. She expressed her joy of the Christmas holiday and told Sallie some details about the gathering at the Bayle residence. "We had a wonderful time bringing in the New Year." Emilie chattered on. "I danced all night. I had a dance partner for almost every dance." Emilie could not help but smile as she told her friend about the party. It brought back good memories. Emilie suddenly noticed a change in Sallie's mood. Sallie seemed very quiet. Emilie suddenly felt remorseful for bragging. "I am sorry Sallie; it was horrible of me to sound boastful. Please forgive me. Maybe you could come out to my home. We can dance in the parlor. My father plays a great fiddle." Sallie intervened at this suggestion.

"We don't dance," Sallie said abruptly.

"I'm sorry?" Emilie was confused. "I don't know what you mean?"

Sallie reiterated, "We don't dance. It is not what our church believes, nor do we consume alcohol." Sallie was uncomfortable.

Emilie felt relieved Sallie wasn't upset with her. "That's fine, I wouldn't want you to be uncomfortable. When you visit, I'll have Pa give us a concert instead." Sallie shook her head.

"What were you doing in the courthouse, if I may ask?" Sallie blurted out.

Emilie explained that she was paying a fine for racing down Race Horse Alley. Sallie shook her head as she was trying to imagine her friend facing the sheriff. Sallie knew him because her father is a judge in town. Emilie explained her embarrassment.

"I am just glad this is all over." Emilie smiled. "I am very happy I didn't have to face your father."

"You have no idea." Sallie laughed.

The girls parted company as they came to the crossroad where they had to part ways. Each school was in the opposite side of town. Emilie continued on to the Oakridge School to start her day. The day went by smoothly; Emilie taught spelling and reading to a small group of girls. Emilie was having difficulty getting young Annie Sullivan to memorize her alphabet. She then realized the girls were distracted by the day's good weather. The sun was out, and the birds were singing. They were preoccupied with thoughts of anything but their studies. Today's lessons were not sinking in, and Emilie soon realized she would not keep her students' attention much longer.

At the end of the afternoon, Emilie instructed the group that there would be a test tomorrow on letter recognition. "If any of you fail this test, you will have to stay inside at recess to practice with me. Now, who wants to stay inside tomorrow?" She eyed the girls, who watched her with large, concerned eyes. Emilie waited a moment and then interjected, "I don't either, but if you need help, we will get the work done. Do you understand?"

Annie began crying. Emilie took the young girl aside and explained the lesson one more time. Firmly, Emilie reassured the child she would understand it very soon; she just needed to pay attention. The little, curly-haired, blue-eyed girl shook her head. At the end of their conversation, Annie was smiling as she left the room. Emilie finished up for the day and said good-bye to Carrie.

"You are doing a good job with those girls," Carrie said. "They are earning high marks on their tests. You have their respect."

"Thank you, Carrie." Emilie was encouraged. "Will there be anything else today?"

Carrie shook her head. "I will see you tomorrow."

On her way home, Emilie thought about her day. Reviewing the day, deep in thought, Emilie did not see Stephen walking toward her. When he grabbed her arm, she winced as the pain shot up her arm. His body was stiff with tension. Stephen's eyes narrowed, he was angry.

"So are you up for another race?"

Stephen immediately got her attention.

Emilie looked up to see Stephen glaring at her. "I don't race." She immediately felt defensive. Trying to calculate how he would have found out or who would have told him, he accused.

"You are not a lady either, so what is it going to be? Who are you?" Stephen was back on his high horse again, attempting to control Emilie as others controlled his life. The longer she delayed answering him, the angrier he became. Emilie was trying to understand why he was attacking her. Stephen had a disagreeable habit of charging into her life to announce how upset he was with her behavior. Why did he care?

His attitude set her off.

"What concern of yours is my reputation?"

He retorted, "Someone has to care. It obviously is not you. Do you know what people are saying about you? Do you know where they think your brother ran off to? Do you have any idea what a negative situation this horse race is to your reputation?"

His face was red with anger. The more he said, the closer he stepped toward her. She quickly became defensive. Emilie matched his glare and hissed. "There are only four people who know about the alley. If there are more, then I can only believe that you are the one spreading the rumors. Why would you do that?" She put up her arm to protect herself from him coming any closer.

"What you need, young lady is a severe whipping to put you in your place. You have too much independence. I only wish I could be the one to save you from a marriage of beatings." The words hissed from his mouth; his eyes narrowed. Stephen suddenly grabbed her arm.

"Let go of me, Stephen." Emilie tried to control the terror in her voice. "No one will ever control me. I'd rather live without a man than have one control me like you are trying to do." His fingers dug deep into her arm. Her word stung him harshly; she did not understand her place. She did not understand him.

"You may just get your wish."

His voice suddenly became controlled.

"Why, Stephen? Why would you do this to me?" Her voice was soft, pulling the words from his heart. He let go of her with resignation.

Taking two steps back, he simply said, "Because I care but can't love you." He choked on the words as they spewed uncontrollably from his mouth.

She saw how he struggled to express himself. He could not look her in the eyes. Emilie saw the pain in his eyes, but she did not feel sorry for him. The words sat on the surface of her anger. She heard *can't* and *love* in the same sentence. Studying him, she finally said, "You will never fully love someone you control. If you love me, truly love me, you will find a way to accept me the way I am. No changes. No control. Until then, you can choose to be my friend or just my acquaintance." Saying all she could, Emilie walked away, leaving him alone with her words echoing in his head.

Emilie felt sad. She liked Stephen as a friend. She worried about how Thaddeus would take this news. She was unsure if she would even tell him. Stephen was the first to greet her here in Gettysburg. She never realized how much he really cared about her. Emilie felt sad that he felt he could change her somehow, making her better fit into his ideal. It was all up to him; if he wanted to continue a friendship with her, he would have to change. Emilie was not going to change for him.

Emilie was happy to arrive home. The thoughts of the day weighed heavy on her mind. She looked forward to a good dinner and conversation with her family. No matter how Henry tormented her tonight, she was going to be thankful. After checking in on Starlight, Emilie opened the door to the house. Inside she knew something was desperately wrong. Her mother was in tears. Her father did not smile at her when she came in. Henry held the newspaper in front of him, looking at the page, shaking his head. The room had an eerie stillness.

"What happened?" Emilie's words echoed in the room.

"Em, the country is falling apart." Henry's voice was not teasing her. He wasn't the melodramatic type.

Emilie looked down at the paper. The *Republican Compiler*, page 2, clearly stated the following: "Bombardment of Sumter—Progress of a Battle." Looking for answers from her father, mother, and brother, she finally asked, "What does this mean? Are we in trouble?" Emilie felt the security drain from her. Suddenly she was afraid of the unknown. Where did the family stand on this?

"Papa, what are we going to do? Are they really fighting?" Questions started flowing through her brain. She could not ask them fast enough. She watched her mother burst into tears. Her father comforted her and gave her a handkerchief to dry her eyes. Henry sat stunned.

"Papa, what are we going to do?" Emilie did not like the desperation in her voice. Her head was still reeling, trying to absorb the news and its possible implications. Do we have to choose a side? "Oh my God. Aaron, Thaddeus." Emilie felt faint. The room started to spin around her. She suddenly felt short of breath. As she tried to catch her breath, the room went black.

CALLING IN THE TROOPS

Every citizen should be a soldier. This was the case with the
Greeks and Romans, and must be that of every free state.

—Thomas Jefferson

APRIL–MAY 1861

The Prescott family spent the evening discussing how they felt
about the possibility of war. Emilie was numb. She did not know
how she should feel. Her upbringing taught her all of the culture
of the South. She had no animosity toward the North or anyone
in Gettysburg. She felt free to be in the company of people who
did not believe in slavery. She heard rumors of the Underground
Railroad through the area. Emilie knew slavery was not the only
reason for this war. The Southern states were angry, and they
were, in the tradition of Southern culture, expressing their anger
with the issues.

Jacob was clear with his family. "If there are any questions
about our loyalty, we must side with the North."

Angered by his words, Henry stated, "Pa, why? Didn't you hear
anything Aaron taught us? Lincoln is wrong. States' rights come
first. No one should dictate to us what we can and cannot own.
First it will be the darkies, then it will be the right to own guns,
and then what else?" Henry understood the lessons his brother
taught him. His beliefs were very strong.

"Henry, I believe in the Constitution of the United States, but
we cannot be seen as Southern sympathizers. If things get ugly,
you or I could die for it."

"Now what? Do we sit this out or fight for our rights?" Henry
shouted at his father; his anger grew more intense. He didn't
understand his father's logic. Henry always looked up to him. He

saw a strong man who was an excellent instructor of life. Why was he turning his back on Virginia? You never turn your back on your homeland.

"I want us all to get through this together, son." Jacob could not say any more. It felt like he was contradicting himself. He knew the family would only be safe if they stuck with the Northern decision. It was simply dangerous to think otherwise.

Emilie curled up into her father's chair to protect herself from the harsh words in the room. She became quiet and withdrawn, not knowing what to think. "No one will make me choose sides," Emilie whispered from her father's comfortable chair. Worry overwhelmed her; she thought about Aaron, Seth, Big Jim, and Martha. It felt as if the South put up a large wall of separation, and she would never be able to go back to her birthplace again.

> Dear diary,
>   The government did it. My friends are fighting my family. How am I supposed to feel? I feel numb, unable to move past the unknown. Will write more later.
>
>   Sadly,
>   E. K. P.

War fever hit Gettysburg hard. The streets bustled with men signed up to fight. Parades and patriotic impromptu speeches broke out on any available street corner. The borough seemed to be alive with the idea of war and the romance of adventure. The day after news of the attack on Fort Sumter arrived in the papers of Gettysburg, a Union support meeting was held to rally the young men of the town to answer President Lincoln's call for seventy-five thousand troops.

Henry and Emilie went to town to purchase some dry goods from Scott Grocery, when they came upon a group of men rallied up and excited about volunteering. The pack shouted loudly, whooping and hollering, slapping each other on the back. The group made it impossible for the pair to pass. Emilie chose to skirt around them on the left and Henry on the right. As Henry passed, two of the men grabbed Henry by the arm.

"Hey, they still need more volunteers. Did you sign up yet?" The stranger was about a foot taller than Henry, his eyes peering down at him in anticipation.

Caught off guard, Henry shook his head no. He looked for Emilie, who disappeared in the crowd ahead. He tried to release the man's grip on his arm. The man tightened his grip and shouted to the group with him.

"This one's still waiting out the war. Let's help him get in." The jubilation started again as the boys pulled Henry along down the street toward the volunteer office. Henry heard bits of advice and congratulations as they whisked through the crowd. Well wishes and cheers greeted him from people around him.

Pushing her way through the crowd toward the store, Emilie turned around when she realized Henry was not pushing her from behind. Throngs of people filled the streets. Bands were playing in the distance; general jubilation surrounded her. Emilie carefully scanned to street to find her brother. Her height prevented her from seeing over most of the men in the crowd. Pushing toward the street, Emilie saw his yellow shirt. A group of boys, moving him away from her, surrounded Henry.

Exhausted by continually excusing herself as she pushed through the crowd, she found her way to the clearing in the street. Henry was still yards ahead of her, moving quickly down the street. Picking up her skirts, only high enough not to trip, Emilie took off to catch up to her brother.

Passing by the others in the street, she heard gasps of shock and "good days" by the ladies and gentlemen. The more she hurried, the less she could breathe. Her stays constricting her breathing and shoes slipping on the road, Emilie felt faint by the time she reached them.

"Henry!" She meant to shout at him, but she could not. Struggling to catch her breath, Emilie stopped, leaning against the building to regain control of her body. Hoping Henry could talk himself out of this one, Emilie urged herself to keep moving. The boys, who had taken Henry in their excitement, had long since disappeared.

Briskly walking the last half block, Emilie finally reached the recruitment office. Trying to think of an excuse for her brother, Emilie reached for the door handle. Suddenly, the door opened; Emilie stepped aside as three more boys came out, slapping one another on the back. Whooping and hollering at their exploits, the boys never saw her standing there. The excitement was contagious.

Inside, Emilie saw scores of boys and men all waiting to reach a table at the head of a very long line. The cigar smoke hung in the room like it had another ceiling. One ceiling made of smoke, the other of plaster. No one could talk without shouting, because the noise and excitement escalated by the excitement of the men there. Men in uniform lined up the recruits for instructions, shouting at them and demanding a response. Pushing herself through the crowd, she heard her name. Turning around to locate the source, Emilie saw Thaddeus dragging Ian behind him.

"Emilie, what are you doing here!' His face was red with anger, and his brother looked like a scolded puppy. They were arguing, and from the look on Ian's face Thaddeus was winning the argument. Thaddeus waited for her to respond.

"I lost Henry." She looked around for him, now feeling panic overtake her. Emilie hated crowded rooms. The smoke and congestion overwhelmed her. The confusion in the room suddenly engulfed her. Fighting against the fear of claustrophobia and worry about her brother's safety, Emilie began to search for a quick way out of the room.

Thaddeus saw the panic on her face. "What happened to him?" he sternly spoke to her to keep her attention. Emilie looked as if she was about to faint. Her cheek flushed red, and she was unable to focus on his face. Emilie blinked several times to try to keep Thaddeus in focus. His image was blurry; the visions nauseated her. Emilie felt the curtain of darkness surround her. She heard him call her name before she gave into the blackness and fell forward into his chest.

The darkness lightened as she came out of her spell. Feeling a breeze on her face, she noticed her head was laying on something soft. She felt someone tenderly stroke her temple. Unable to break into consciousness, she fought harder to open her eyes.

"Will she be all right?" Ian's voice spoke quietly above her.

"She's coming around. I wish we had some salts. That would bring her out of it quick enough." Thaddeus's voice was calm. He continued stroking her head.

"She has been doing that a lot lately. Out cold. I don't get it." Henry was frustrated and felt helpless at the moment.

"Maybe if you kiss her, she will wake up," Ian teased his brother. Thaddeus smacked him. "Ow."

"Why did she say she lost you, Henry?" Thaddeus was getting to the story now.

"We came into town. Ma didn't think she should come alone. We were off to Scott's, when these boys gathered me up and dragged me to the recruitment office." Henry cleared his throat; his voice was still shaky from the ordeal.

"Lucky!" Ian interjected. "I was gonna sign up when Mr. Gloom came down to tattle my age." Ian sounded dejected. "I will never get in now. It'll be over by the time I get to sign up."

Thaddeus shook his head. "Be careful what you wish for. If you are going to be patriotic, at least tell Ma and Pa first. You will worry them sick disappearing like you had planned." Thaddeus refrained from any more scolding.

"I am not ready to commit to this," Henry said. "I have heard horror stories about war. It doesn't appeal to me."

"You're safe," Emilie whispered from Thaddeus's lap. Her eyes opened to see three concerned faces peering down at her. She struggled to sit up, when she felt Thaddeus push her down.

"Slow down, Em. I don't want a repeat episode." He was concerned for her. She saw it in his eyes as they tenderly looked at her. He didn't have to speak. She knew what he was saying: *Don't scare me like that again, and I love you more than I can say in front of these two.* Emilie raised a knowing eyebrow at him smiling.

"I feel better. Let's go home." Emilie sat up, instantly regretting she moved from his lap. It was comfortable there, and she could watch him from that vantage point without him seeing her study him.

"We will take you home." Thaddeus ordered his brother and Henry to get the wagon. The boys left them alone. He turned his attention to her.

"You scared me, Miss Prescott."

His stern voice, spoiled by his smile.

"I can say the same for you. Were you signing up today? Are you leaving without telling me?" Emilie was surprised at how those words tore at her heart. She didn't have to search his face too long before she saw the answer.

"I would never leave you without telling you first." He looked hurt that she would suggest he would be so dishonorable. "I love you, Emilie Prescott, and I would ask your father's permission right now if we were ready to marry." Thaddeus kissed her tenderly. She was so delicate to him. He understood her stubborn exterior was a shield to a tender, beautiful heart. He loved her more than he could ever hope to express. He knew this was going to be a discussion for later.

The clatter of wagon wheels interrupted the lovers' kiss. Emilie knew she had to stop; any sort of scandal her brother saw, would certainly come back to haunt her later. She squeezed his hand reassuringly as he helped her up. Directing the boys to the back of the wagon, Emilie sat next to Thaddeus as they rode home. She like being on his arm; it was exactly where she belonged. As the wagon moved toward the Prescott home, Henry expressed his concern. "I don't want to go back into town for awhile. I am not ready to enlist."

Thaddeus reassured him he would not be bothered again. "No worries Henry. The Captain and I have an understanding." Thaddeus told Henry and Ian about his discussion with the Captain. He told the captain that Henry and Ian were underage and under no circumstances was he to enlist. The captain wrote down both Henry's and Ian's names after Thaddeus expressed the boys would return another day. He pointed out how terrible it would look to the community if he took underage boys from their mothers. It seemed the captain agreed.

"So, Henry, if you are going to fight in this skirmish, you will have to enlist elsewhere because you and my reckless brother are blacklisted." Thaddeus smiled as he felt Emilie squeeze his hand in appreciation.

"What about you?" Henry questioned. "When are you going in?" Henry admired Thaddeus. He certainly made Emilie more bearable to live with, and he genuinely liked him as a neighbor and friend.

"I haven't decided yet. There is a lot of business to attend to at home. If the president calls again, I may have to answer his call." Thaddeus's answer seemed to satisfy everyone.

Henry's adventure was the topic of conversation at the dinner table that evening. Jacob listened patiently to his son embellish his story. He read from his daughter's head shake and eye rolls his son's story was getting bigger by the minute.

Emilie had her chance to retell the story, which only differed slightly. The part about her saving her brother from certain enlistment made her parents smile. Emilie relayed how she was surprised to see so many men gathered in one place.

"The jubilation in town is certainly exciting. I overheard some say this would not last but a few months. What do you think, Pa?" Emilie was getting more animated as she relayed the events.

"I think this will last as long as God wishes. I pray it is short, but I also know my fellow Southerners. All we can do is pray for the safety of our country." Jacob was stern. His wisdom told him this was not going to be an easy fight.

"Speaking of God," Julia broke into the conversation. "Emilie, we have a meeting on Tuesday, and I volunteered you to help."

"Help where?" Surprised by her mother's announcement, Emilie listened intently.

"With the men leaving home. Mrs. Harper is forming the Ladies' Relief Society. I have volunteered us to help." Julia was happy to participate. She was making great strides in the social circles in town. She enjoyed her new friends.

"Before Tuesday, make sure to go through your scrap material and pull out extra fabric. We will need it." Julia saw the dejected look on her daughter's face. "What's wrong?"

Feeling guilty for not being generous, Emilie tried to pass over the question. Her mother insisted. "I had plans for that fabric," she finally said. "I wanted to make Thaddeus a quilt for Christmas next year. It was supposed to be a surprise."

"Sounds like you are keeping that one around, huh?" Jacob saw the love in his daughter's eyes. He was glad to see her so happy. He was worried about the timing of their love.

"We will go over what you need for the quilt and give the extra to the cause. I know you have plenty." Julia knew her daughter scurried away fabric like a squirrel and its winter nuts. Emilie was fascinated with fabric and wouldn't waste a scrap if she could help it.

Dear diary,

The town is full of celebration. Do they know whom they will be fighting? I don't understand how men are always ready to shoot each other at a moment's notice. It does not make sense. I have searched through my fabric. Mother says we will be making things to send with the troops when they leave. Is the discussion table closed for them that all they can do now is fight?

Thaddeus told me he loves me today. My heart leaps for joy. I am happier than anyone could ever be. I hope when he asks, Father will approve with an outstanding *yes*. I am starting to imagine my life as both a teacher and a wife. I feel my blessings are many, and God is smiling upon me.

Good night, dear diary.
E. K. P.

PATRIOTIC CELEBRATION

True patriotism hates injustice in its own land more than anywhere else.

—Clarence Darrow

The weekend before the first troops left, the town celebrated. Emilie franticly searched through her trunks to find the ball gown she had not yet unpacked. She felt excited to attend the ball with Thaddeus. This would be their first social event together. Feeling around near the bottom of the last trunk, her fingers felt the slippery coolness of the silk dress.

Emilie gently tugged at it to free it from its hiding place. She pulled it in one big tug, and it fell out in a big *swoosh*. The plaid gown boasted beautiful colors of blues, yellows, and greens. The lace delicately accented the neck and arm sleeves. Emilie loved this dress. It was made for her two years ago for a ball held for celebration in Richmond. She held it up in the mirror. She hoped it would fit. Remembering it had accoutrements; she set the dress on her bed and went back to digging in the trunk. Where were her lace gloves and shawl?

The knock on her door interrupted her search. Looking up to see her mother at the door, Emilie stopped. "I found it, Mother. I hope it fits."

Julia came in, picked up the dress, and held it out to her daughter. "I don't know, Em. I think you have grown since. Let me help you try it on."

The dress was a bitter disappointment. It was at least six inches too short, and it did not fit in the shoulders anymore. Emilie was mortified. Tears sprung to her eyes. "Please tell me we have more fabric to alter this. I only have two weeks. I can't make something new in two weeks."

Julia turned her daughter away from the mirror. Holding her by the shoulders, she tried to be gentle. "Emilie, you are a woman now. This is a little girl's dress. Let's find you a new one."

"Two weeks, Mother!" Emilie was desperate. She pictured herself going to the ball in petticoats or, worse yet, not at all or, worse than that, in a day dress.

"I have something for you." Under protest, Emilie was led to her mother's room. The bed was cluttered with dresses and fabric. Her mother was obviously searching for dresses too. Setting her to the front of the mirror, Julia turned back to the bed. Emilie stood there looking at herself waiting. Fidgeting in her petticoats, her chemise, and corset, Emilie waited.

She could hear her mother shuffling fabric around on the bed. Emilie could identify its make by the sound it made. Hearing the skirts rustling behind her, Emilie was tempted to turn around. Just as she was about to give in, Julia popped into the mirror with a beautiful, rose-colored, checked silk gown held in front of her. The trim accented the skirt in a diagonal sweep. Accented with black lace, it made the gown rich with contrast, yet it popped with color. The dress made Emilie's cheek a beautiful, rosy pink. Her dark, curly hair complemented the black lace. Her green eyes sparkled in contrast to the dress.

"It is beautiful." Emilie stood mesmerized as she studied her refection in the mirror.

🌿

The night of the ball, Emilie took great care with her appearance. She fussed endlessly with her hair and cheeks. Hairpins in place and tight, cheeks not too rosy. She reviewed her checklist one last time before she heard her father's announcement from the parlor. "Time's up," her father called from the kitchen. The buggy was leaving, and he threatened to leave her behind.

Carefully descending the stairs, Emilie greeted her father and brother in the entryway. Amazed at how grown up Henry looked in his frock coat, cravat, and crisp, white shirt. She noticed her father looking equally handsome. She noted his dark hair was now accented with gray that she hadn't seen before. She saw her mother's skirt whisk past the parlor entrance.

Turning to enter the parlor, Emilie saw him. Thaddeus looked taller in his black frock coat than she had remembered seeing him. Emilie already thought she enjoyed him dressed up. So handsome in a cravat, she had never seen him so dashing. He held a gloved hand out to take hers. She gave him her hand. She dipped into a curtsy as he placed a gentle kiss on the back of her hand without either of them breaking the eye contact.

"You are breathtaking, my dear." Thaddeus could not stop looking at her.

"I might say the same for you—very handsome, all dressed for the evening." She smiled and winked at him. The couple had three conversations at once: one with their words, the other two with their body language and thoughts. Both had a keen sense what the other was thinking, it was easily expressed through action and spoken word. The world disappeared when they looked at each other. They only saw each other as they were now. When they looked into each other's eyes, they saw their hopes for their future. Emilie was taking in all she could—the way he looked, how he smiled at her in appreciation. Thaddeus loved watching her float into the room—head held high and a smile that could melt any man's heart. He was very glad she chose his heart and no one else. He did not let go of her hand the whole trip into town.

McConaughy Hall, located between North and York Streets and a tall brick building, held many balls in the past. Tonight, charity groups raising money for the war effort combined to hold the ball. The event's attendees were a mixed group: some who supported the cause and others who enjoyed an evening out.

The ballroom was decorated with patriotic flags, streamers, and decorations. Refreshment tables were placed at one end while table and chairs lined the sides of the room. The floor was large and spacious, roomy enough for many couples to enjoy the evening. It was a perfect starlit night, the air cool enough to invite a shawl, but little else was needed. The military band was superb. The dance floor swirled with waltzes, schottische, polkas, and Virginia reels.

Thaddeus and Emilie finished their first waltz. Leaving the dance floor, he escorted her to the refreshment table. Emilie noticed Stephen standing alone at the table. The couple went forward to greet him.

"Stephen, good to see you here this evening." Thaddeus shook his friend's hand.

"You too, my friend. How are things?" Stephen nodded toward Emilie in acknowledgment. Emilie inclined her head in response. They talked about the pleasantries of the day and a little bit about family, when Stephen began his plea to his best friend. "So, Thaddeus, what do you say—you and I sign up for this thing?" Stephen patted Thaddeus on his back, leaning in close to conspire. "We could get this war over with, right quick." His casual reference to the war made Emilie gasp. Ignoring her, he went on. "You are a great squirrel hunter. We could take out a few Rebs. Come home heroes." He finished his drink in one gulp.

Thaddeus stared at his friend. Stephen was out of character tonight. "Have you been drinking, man?" Stephen picked up another drink and shook his head.

"Yup, as I see it, we can get in and get out before anyone gets hurt. These boys leavin' tomorrow will soften them up for us. Come on, what do you say?" His gestures got bigger as he excitedly told of his plan. Stephen grew unsteady as they watched him.

"Stephen, let's step out for some fresh air." Thaddeus turned to Emilie. "Let me take you back to our table. I will be back in a moment."

"No, I will go." Emilie started to go when he stopped her.

"No, I will escort you." He motioned for Stephen to stay there, and he took Emilie back to the table where her family sat. It was improper to allow a woman to cross the dance floor unescorted. Thaddeus was not going to disgrace her like that. He pulled her chair out for her and set his refreshment on the table.

"Please excuse me. I will return in a moment." Thaddeus was off quickly. Julia turned to her daughter, interested in "why on earth" he would leave Emilie so quickly. They were becoming inseparable.

"He and Stephen are talking," Emilie answered her mother's question for her.

"Is the boy all right?" Jacob asked his daughter.

"I think so. Stephen is out of sorts this evening. I think the men are going out to walk it off." Emilie scanned the crowd to locate Thaddeus. She saw him escorting his friend outside.

Handling him with some force, Thaddeus sat Stephen on a bench outside of the hall. "What are you thinking?" He was angry at his friend's insensitive remarks. Stephen looked up at his boyhood friend, trying his best to focus on him.

Stephen blinked his unfocused eyes and said, "I am signing up. Come with me. We could get out of here." Stephen had so many emotions. He was tired of his parents running his life. He couldn't erase Emilie from his thoughts. He was obsessed with the independent, driven woman. She would not leave his dreams at night or his thoughts in the daytime. Now she looked like a dream dressed in a ball gown, dancing so happily with his best friend; drinking helped him watch without the pain.

"I am not talking about the war, Stephen. I am talking about your insensitive conversation about Emilie's family. How much have you been drinking?" Thaddeus knew he had plenty. Stephen smelled like a whiskey.

"Oh, her." Stephen slurred his words. "She is a tough gal. You know she has opinions about everything. She is smart, and she'll tell you too. She's not upset about a little war talk. She'd probably shoot a reb faster than you."

Thaddeus cuffed Stephen upside the head. "She is a reb you idiot."

Thaddeus shook his head, trying to rearrange the words his friend was spewing forth. Stephen was not right. He knew he should get his friend home. Thaddeus knew they didn't spend a lot of time together ever since he and Emilie started seeing each other. For that, he regretted not keeping in contact as often. Stephen had changed; he was unsure what was causing it.

"Do you love her?" Stephen asked.

"Yes, I do," Thaddeus answered with definite finality.

Stephen shook his head; this was not the answer he wanted to hear. Changing the subject, he asked his friend again, "What do you say? What are you going to do about this war?"

"Stephen, I'm busy trying to keep Ian from signing up. I have my parents' farm to look after as well as my job. Let's let the first group take care of it. If the president needs me later, I will follow, but now, I am waiting this one out." Thaddeus's responsibilities overwhelmed him sometimes. He could not take on more at this time. Indications predicted the war would only last three months. If that was true, then he felt his contribution would not be necessary.

"I think it will be a great adventure. I am going as soon as I can. It will give me a chance to do what I want for once." Stephen truly believed, even in his drunken state, his life would change by following his patriotic duty. Maybe when he came home, he would be able to get Emilie out of his heart.

"I wish you the best of luck, my friend. If you do sign up, do it when you are sober." Thaddeus smiled. He heard another waltz beginning in the ballroom. Thaddeus had promised her he would dance the next one with her. "I need to get back. Do you want someone to escort you home?"

"No. the walk will do me good." Stephen stood up. "Please let me know if you reconsider. We would be great together in the same company." Thaddeus shook his friend's hand. Thaddeus watched his friend walk away. It was hard to believe the only thing they once cared about was not coming home late for dinner. Times had certainly changed. There was so much more responsibility for those farm boys.

The waltz had just finished when Thaddeus appeared back in the ballroom. He was pleased to see Emilie and Henry finishing the dance. This was the first time he saw both of them smiling at each other. If he did go off to war, he wanted to remember her as she was now—beautiful, happy, and all his.

He stepped onto the dance floor as Henry escorted Emilie off. "May I take her from you, Henry?" He held out his hand to receive hers. She was happy to see him return.

"Be my guest. If you want to marry her, you have my permission for that too." Henry had a great sense of humor. He loved teasing them; he could see how much they were in love.

"Thank you, Henry." Emilie felt better now that Thaddeus was back. He moved her effortlessly into the waltz. She felt as if she was floating. He guided her around the floor with a firm but gentle hand.

"What is your relationship with Stephen?" Thaddeus could not shake the nagging feeling that Emilie and Stephen may be in love. He felt jealous by that thought. He looked down at her, waiting for her to answer.

"Excuse me?"

Emilie never expected that question from him. Shocked by his questioning, she felt the color rush from her face.

"Do you like him?" Thaddeus rephrased the question. He observed her reaction, keenly aware she was not comfortable with this question.

"I think of him only as a friend. There is no more than a friendship between us." Emilie felt panic at the thought of him thinking there was someone other than him in her life. "What's wrong?"

"He wants to sign up and leave as soon as possible."

Thaddeus thought it over. They danced in silence for a few moments. Emilie left Thaddeus to his thoughts. She wondered what transpired in their conversation. Did Stephen tell him of their last confrontation?

Emilie finally offered more information. "Stephen does not like my opinions. He's always there to lecture me when he thinks I have offered too much."

"Why would that bother him?" Thaddeus was thankful for that information.

"I guess it is not what he considers ladylike. Why does he care?" Emilie was getting angry thinking about their last confrontation. She stiffened and stepped on Thaddeus's foot. He held her from falling, placing her back on her feet.

"Careful, dear, I need that foot. Relax. You are getting upset. I am worried about my friend." He saw the crease of frustration in her forehead. He gently reminded her to allow him to lead. She easily fell back into step with him.

Emilie focused on the waltz, saying no more about Stephen. If he wanted to go to war, that was fine with her. She didn't like his constant reminders to follow the role of a submissive woman. She would never show that kind of weakness.

Emilie danced most of the night between Thaddeus and her father; she was very tired on the ride home. Resting her head on Thaddeus's shoulder, she listened to him breathe. His arm securely around her, she drifted off to sleep as the men discussed work and plans for the upcoming planting. Emilie was warm and safe in his arms; she didn't want to be anywhere else at the moment.

> Dear diary,
>
> What an exhausting night. I danced as many dances as I could. The ball was lovely. The ladies' dresses were beautiful. The decorations had a patriotic feeling. The whole family seemed to enjoy the festivities. Henry even danced a good waltz with me. I hope this gives hope to the troops

leaving next week. I hope all of the troops get a send off as we had for our boys. Stephen was out of sorts tonight.

I think he is going off to fight. I wish him the best, as he is only a dear friend. I am sad others control his life. Maybe he will find happiness, doing something he feels compelled to do. I hope he finds happiness. I must end here. I am falling asleep writing tonight.

Good night.
E. K. P.

RETURNING FAMILY

But friendship is the breathing rose, with sweets in every fold.

—Oliver Wendell Holmes

MAY 1861

Only a few weeks left of the school term, and with her teachers' exam looming, Emilie once again focused on her dreams. She began to see her goals transform; with Thaddeus in her life, she found herself beginning to see the possibilities of him permanently with her. In a few weeks, she would have time to relax, without books. No rest for the weary, Emilie thought as she saw the sewing projects lined up on the chest in her room. The Ladies' Relief Society moved full speed ahead, supporting the troops making shirts, socks, and other supplies they would need. There was plenty to do without books. For now, the teachers' examination was her next goal; her test was in three days.

The Gettysburg Independent Blues commanded by Captain Charles Buhler slipped out of town on the train in the early morning of April 21. The town, still excited by the national news, had quieted in comparison to the first few weeks. Troops still recruited. The ones waiting for federal service served as border security. Pennsylvania worried about its precarious spot, sitting between states that had already seceded. Maryland was still a slave state, but not officially seceding. It made people suspicious. The town felt safe with the borders patrolled, and the war was not specifically bothersome at this time.

School let out early today. Emilie felt exhausted by the children's inattention to their studies. Spring fever had come, and they didn't give a hoot about their spelling or math subjects. Finishing a test of her own, Emilie handed in her paper to Miss Carrie.

"Finished?" Carrie looked up from the mounds of papers she was grading.

"I did the best I could. Dare I say, this one was easy?" Emilie attempted a smile.

"Yes, you should dare."

Carrie loved her bouts of worry and self-doubt. Emilie commanded the classroom and her world. It was good to see this girl doubt her abilities somewhere. It endeared her to people. This made her human and not arrogant.

"I will grade it tonight. We will go over the result tomorrow." Carrie smiled at her student. "You are ready, you know."

"Why don't I feel ready?" Emilie responded.

"Because you worry too much." Carrie admired Emilie. She was a hard worker who demanded more from herself than her students. "Go rest, and I will see you in the morning. We have testing to do now for the next week. I will need your help."

"Thank you, Carrie." Emilie knew there was no arguing with her mentor. "I will see you tomorrow."

Riding home that afternoon, Emilie noticed Starlight limping. She refused to run and balked when Emilie tried to force her.

"What is wrong with you today?" Emilie dismounted, grabbed her head, and pulled her in. The horse pulled her head away from her upset owner. "Did you throw a shoe?" Emilie tied her to a tree and went around inspecting her shoes. She tapped the horse's leg and commanded, "Foot please!" Starlight allowed her to lift her lower leg to inspect her shoe. Finding the offending shoe, Emilie walked the horse back toward home.

The Blocher blacksmith shop was on the way home. Emilie stopped in to see if Mr. John Blocher could fix the shoe. Mr. John was father to Mr. David Blocher, whom she met at the Bayles' New Year's Eve party. Her father had used Mr. John's services previously, so Emilie had made his acquaintance.

Making her way to the blacksmith shop, Emilie saw there were several men in the shop. She tied up Starlight and walked over to inquire about the wait. The men seemed to be heatedly discussing some political issues but stopped as soon as Emilie appeared.

"Excuse me, Mr. Blocher, do you have time to look at Starlight? Her shoe is not right." Emilie smiled sweetly, acting as they expected her to act. She learned early that in order to get attention in these surroundings, it works best to turn on the charm and act as expected. This grated on her nerves, because for her, it was an act. Emilie was usually more direct.

"Miss Prescott. I would be happy to look at it for you."

Mr. Blocher got up from his seat. "Where is he?"

"I tied her up out here." Emilie noticed Mr. Blocher's hat. Remembering Starlight's aversion, she stopped him.

"Excuse me, sir. May I ask you to leave your hat inside?"

"What? Why?" John was confused by the strange request.

"You won't be able to look at her with that on." She pointed to the man's hat. "Starlight doesn't like men with hats." Emilie was embarrassed to try to explain.

"Aw, that horse won't remember," he said confidently. "I'll show her who's boss."

Emilie tried to stop him. "She'll not let you near her."

John stopped. "Then I suggest you control her." He brushed past her.

Despite Emilie's protests, the old man walked out of the barn straight toward the horse. Emilie hoped he was right, but she knew what would happen. Emilie took her reins and held her tight, trying to distract her from the man.

Just as John approached, Starlight turned her head hard, pulling Emilie off her feet. The horse nervously started dancing to avoid the man approaching her. Emilie scolded Starlight, trying to calm her. The closer Mr. Blocher came to the horse, the more Starlight fought against Emilie. Too small in height and weight, Emilie was no match for the terrified horse. Emilie tried to warn him. Mr. Blocher looked up in time for the horse to turn and knock him on his backside.

Mortified, Emilie released the horse to go over to help him up. "I am so sorry. Are you all right?" Emilie was concerned for his safety.

Pushing away her efforts to help him, he got up and dusted off his pants. "What is wrong with that thing?" He pointed accusingly at Starlight.

"I tried to explain," Emilie broke in. "She doesn't—"

He cut her off. "I can't help you if she won't let me close to her." He threw the hat on the ground in disgust and stood there staring at the horse. He had never seen this before.

Emilie whispered behind him, "Leave your hat on the ground and try again. Let me grab her and distract her. Then slowly approach her again."

Having no other solution, the man followed her directions. Emilie talked Starlight into calm, and he approached. Taking her leg, Emilie commanded, "Starlight, foot please." The horse lifted her foot as if the incident moments before never happened.

The shoe repair went effortlessly. Emilie requested a bill from Mr. Blocher and promised she would return with the payment. John agreed, and Emilie thanked him one more time before departing.

Emilie and Starlight started up the drive when she noticed Thaddeus waving to her. Taking Starlight to the barn, he followed her. "What took you so long?" He seemed suspicious in asking.

She turned to him. "Did we have a date? Am I late?" She couldn't read him. Emilie raised her eyebrow in suspicion. She brushed past him as she undressed the horse for the evening. Thaddeus went to get some hay for her.

"Starlight threw a shoe on the way home. Mr. Blocher fixed the shoe for me. I have to give him the money next week."

She looked frazzled to him. "Did everything go all right?"

"Yes. Starlight almost ran over Mr. Blocher, but it turned out all right in the end." She stopped brushing and looked at him, asking, "Why don't people believe me when I ask them to remove their hat around my horse?" Emilie was irritated at not being taken seriously.

"Because you are too beautiful." He smiled at her, his dimples showed mischief. "They don't believe you could possibly be smart and beautiful at the same time." She loved the way he looked at her. She felt important and loved.

"That has nothing to do with it." She countered, trying to stay angry. "I know this horse like a mother knows her child. Why do they doubt me?"

Thaddeus could see she was working herself into a fit. He wanted nothing to do with her rants today. He took her hand to stop her. "Let's go for a walk to calm down. I want to tell you about my day." His voice calmed her; she forgot her anger and allowed him to take the conversation.

She nodded. He took her hand, and they walked in the yard behind the house. The apple trees were in bloom. The fragrant white flowers smelled sweet. The cherry trees blossomed pink flowers, less fragrant but no less beautiful. With his hand in hers, the stress washed from her. Relaxed, she smiled for the first time since they met today.

"What is your news of the day?" Emilie leaned her head on his shoulder as they sat on the bench in the middle of the orchard. Blissfully relaxed in his arms, she enjoyed listening to his voice as it resonated in his chest. Her head was nestled perfectly below his collarbone. She fit there as if it were made only for her.

"I talked to Stephen today. He is going to wait to enlist for a while yet. He wants us to enlist together." Hearing Stephen's name instantly made Emilie grumpy. She was still angry with his comments at the ball.

Alarmed, Emilie looked at him. "Is he pressuring you to join?"

"I am not going until everything is settled here." He tried to reassure her, but he did feel pressured to make a decision. Thaddeus knew she would not take the news easily.

"Exactly what needs to get settled here?" Emilie was preparing for the day he would finally tell her. Neither one wanted to hear it, but they knew Thaddeus had no reason to stay home. He supported the North, and he was brought up to defend his country. It was only a matter of time before she would have to say good-bye. Emilie felt strangely jealous. She was angry that events caused by others would take him from her. How would she say good-bye?

Their conversation was interrupted. Emilie heard a wagon arrive. The reins and harness noise was telltale that someone had arrived. Getting up to investigate, they rounded the side of the house. Emilie recognized them immediately. Aaron had come back, and Seth was with him. Seth was tall like Big Jim. Built strong and sculpted by hard work, he was no longer the boy she had once known. Excited, she didn't know whom to hug first. She ran to Aaron.

"You're back!" Emilie jumped into Aaron's embrace so fast, he almost dropped her. Thaddeus and Aaron shook hands. Thaddeus and Seth exchanged greetings. Emilie could not believe Seth was here. "You're here. I have missed you."

"Someone had to help drag this thing from Richmond." Emilie hadn't noticed the large parcel they had tied on the back of the wagon. She looked at her brother, confused. The door opened to reveal an excited Julia, followed by Henry and Jacob. They happily spilled into the yard to greet them.

The excitement carried on until Henry said, "Aaron, you actually got that piano across the lines?"

Emilie stood silently shocked. "My piano?" Once the reality hit, she hugged both Seth and Aaron, thanking them endlessly for their hard work. Circling the wagon, she untied the ropes holding the instrument. They packed it snug in the wagon, tying the lines down, which were still taunt. Safely cushioned with tarp and padding, she could not wait to run her fingers over the keys. She missed her piano.

"My—" she began to inquire.

"Right here, little sister. I packed all of your piano books and music." Aaron signaled to Seth, who gave her the heavy box of music. Julia and Emilie made a path for the piano as the men struggled to get it into the house. She smiled at the reality of it sitting exactly where she imagined it. Emilie carefully dusted it and set the music on it. She stood back, admiring it in its new place. Thaddeus took his leave. The family sat down to a hearty dinner of fried chicken and potatoes. It was Aaron's favorite meal. This was Seth's first meal with the family. It was strange to see him at the family table, but it felt right nonetheless.

"How was graduation?" Julia inquired from her son.

"It was a hot and uncomfortable day. Richmond is going to have another hot summer," Aaron said as he took another mouthful of potatoes. He loved his mother's cooking as much as he loved Martha's cooking. Both women knew their way around a kitchen, and he appreciated that talent.

"That will be good for the crops," Jacob broke in. "Seth, how did you manage to get away from the farm this time of year?"

Seth looked surprised. "Oh, Mr. Will has plenty of help. I offered to help Mr. Aaron move Miss Emilie's piano. 'Sides, I sure missed all ya." Seth smiled his big, toothy grin.

Thinking that was peculiar, Jacob said, "So you must have gotten an early start on the planting." He shook his head, convincing himself that must be the reason. Jacob looked at his eldest son, who had an eye on Seth, willing him not to say anything else. Seeing that look from Aaron before, Jacob added, "That is the answer, isn't it?"

"Things have changed around the plantation, Pa," Aaron simply said. The family listened intently as Aaron talked about the changes. After the family left, William had bought 250 slaves and borrowed a wicked overseer from Mr. Spree's plantation.

He managed to use double the land that Jacob was using when he sold the farm. With the plantation under new management, William Prescott ran the Prescott Plantation with an iron fist. He threatened to tear up the freedom papers signed by Jacob for Big Jim and Martha if any one of them disagreed with him. The family was kept under control with William holding the papers until he feels he could let them go. Aaron managed to convince William that Seth was needed to go with him.

Deeply disturbed by the news of the plantation, Emilie retired to her room early. She could not imagine what was to become of Seth and his family if Uncle William decided to enslave them again.

In the parlor, Jacob, Aaron, and Julia talked about what they could do about the trouble at the plantation. No one could think of a good answer. They sat quietly pondering the situation. Jacob meditatively smoked his cigar. Julia sewed busily at her work, and Aaron watched the fires, thinking to himself.

"Julia, are you sure we do not have another copy of those papers?"

Julia sat thinking a moment. Her husband always had a backup plan. Yet it was so long ago since they had made the arrangements. "I believe you do have another set. It would be in your desk file. Would you like me to look?"

Comfortable in his chair, he could see his wife settled in the other with her sewing laid on her lap. He did not want to disturb her. "No, I will look in the morning. I think I have a second set, but how would we get the papers to them?"

"Pa, I think you should give Seth his set of papers. Free him and I will bring the second set back with me." Aaron was thinking through the plan. "If William won't free Big Jim and Martha, then I can bring them up here with the papers. He won't have a choice." Aaron was disappointed in his uncle going against his father's wishes. He was willing to help right the wrong that may be done to a family he knew his whole life, even if it meant going against his uncle's wishes.

"Are you moved out of the plantation yet?" Julia asked her son.

"Yes, I found a place in Richmond, close to the law office I am working for." Aaron was happy to be living on his own. Richmond suited him just fine. He enjoyed social events with his new friends, meeting new people and his new job.

"How's the war news in Richmond?" Julia asked, looking up from her work.

"Oh, they are ready to fight. Most think they can win and make it quick," Aaron surmised. "The war needs to end quickly before we lose some good men." He told of the military school increasing drills. They wanted to develop the students and officers for war. The military school divided students and faculty, picking sides, either leaving or staying. The city of Richmond was busy preparing for war just like every other town in the North and South. Aaron shook his head. "I have been thinking about what I should do with this mess." He hesitated, not wanting to go on.

Jacob set down his cigar and looked at his son.

"What are you deciding, son?"

Aaron looked at his parents. "I am going to fight for the South. I have thought about it long and hard. I can't shake it. I believe the South is right to hold on to the states' rights. This isn't strictly a slave issue; it's about the federal government making decisions that do not belong to them." He looked to the fire sparking in the fireplace, knowing his resolution sounded right. Aaron spent hours working this matter out in his head. The decision felt right, but the blessings from his parents would secure that feeling for him. Julia dropped her sewing. Cursing under her breath, she reached for her handkerchief to catch the blood oozing from her finger.

Jacob looked at his son. Where had the time gone? Aaron was a man, sitting there. He had grown up, and Jacob and Julia could not be prouder of his accomplishments. "Do you need our blessing, son?"

"Only if it freely comes from you. I am going whether I have it or not." It still felt awkward talking to his father like that. Aaron looked at his father, man to man. Solemnly he looked at both of his parents. They looked older than he remembered. The tell-tale signs of grey hair and more defined wrinkles showed more prominently now.

Jacob cleared his throat and said, "It is your decision, son. You will always have our blessing to live your life in your best interest. This country has forced us to pick sides, and that doesn't come easy for those of us who have family on both sides."

Aaron nodded. "I will stay until you decide what you would like to do with Seth. I brought him to you because I wanted to save at least one of them. I wanted to bring them all Pa, but I know that could not have happened."

"Do you think the others are in danger?" Julia asked.

"I don't know, Mother, but I am concerned." Aaron used his powers of induction. He knew his uncle contradicted his father at every turn. This was no exception. He expected William to sell the others simply because he could.

The threesome continued talking about what to prepare for Aarons leaving. The men believed Aaron would most likely enter as an officer. Julia prepared a mental list of what to send with her son. She had extra items from the Ladies' Relief Society. The men talked quietly about what to do with Seth. What was best for his safety? The family went to bed that night with worried minds and heavy hearts.

CELEBRATION AND TEARS

Chaos is rejecting all you have learned, Chaos is being yourself.

—Emile M. Cioran

JUNE 1861

Emilie stood in front of the Board of Education to receive her long-awaited teacher's certificate. The thick diploma paper heavy in her hands, the certificate proudly proclaimed that Emilie Kathryn Prescott passed all of the required tasks to become a teacher in the public schools. Beaming with pride, she thanked the school board and walked out of the room filled with applause and congratulations.

Outside the stuffy room, Carrie waited to greet her former student and newly eligible teacher. She was proud of Emilie. Emilie expected as much from herself as she expected from her students. It showed in her work and the love her students gave her through their hard work and dedication. Carrie thought long and hard about hiring Emilie as her assistant teacher. She did not want to lose Emilie's skills to public school. Her school was growing fast, and Carrie felt grateful for all of the help Emilie gave her. Emilie deserved a teacher's pay for her work.

"Congratulations, teacher," Carrie greeted her with a handshake and hug.

Wide eyed, Emilie looked at her mentor and said, "That's me, isn't it?" Emilie showed Carrie her diploma. "I couldn't have done this without you. Thank you!"

"It was my pleasure. You are an excellent student and a very good teacher. I suppose you will be leaving me for a job in the public school?" Carrie said with a hint of teasing in her voice.

"I don't want to leave the students." Emilie sobered up at the thought. "I would love to teach for you, Carrie, if you have room for me."

"How about you enjoy a few weeks without having to study and pay me a visit in three weeks? I think we can work something out for the next term." Carrie was still waiting on the incoming tuitions for the next term. She would know better in a few weeks if she could keep Emilie as a teacher.

"I will see you in three weeks then." Emilie was excited to get home to show her family her accomplishment. It was written and officially on parchment. On the way home, Emilie enjoyed the warm summer sun. She enjoyed the walk. All of the stress from studying and tests eased its way out from her muscles as she took the long walk home. It was a bright, cloudless day. The fields were showing signs of growth. Little, green sprouts peeking out of the black dirt promised good, hearty crops. Emilie looked forward to the celebration tonight. Her mother tried to keep the celebration quiet but failed to remind Aaron it was a secret. She enjoyed having Aaron and Seth home.

When she saw the blacksmith shop, she remembered the payment she owed Mr. Blocher. Emilie entered the shop to find Mr. Blocher working on a large chain. Behind him, the links fastened to one another with a ball on the end. It reminded Emilie of the slaves' chains at Mr. Spree's plantation. She waited patiently as he finished hammering the hot piece of metal. When he finished, she interrupted him.

"Mr. Blocher, I have the payment for you," she said, adding, "What are you making?"

Wiping his sooty hands, he ignored her question. "How's that shoe holding?"

"Fine. She hasn't a problem with the shoe since you fixed it." Emilie saw the man smile. She was pleased. She could charm the most cantankerous man with just a compliment and a smile.

"I have to say, that horse has some spirit. Keep her close when the troops come knocking." He took the money from her, counted it to himself, and stuffed it in his dirty pants pocket. "They'll take her for sure."

"Take her where?" Surprised by his comment, Emilie did not like the way it made her feel. "Who will take her?" She did not like the panic in her voice. Emilie always felt safe here; she never worried about herself or Starlight. It was not an issue of concern ever.

"Any persons in need of a horse." He saw the panic in the young girl's eyes. "Cavalry most likely. They get their horses shot out from under them all the time." Mr. Blocher wasn't usually in the habit of terrifying young girls, but he certainly hit the mark here. Emilie was mortified. She could not speak.

Before she left the shop, he asked whom the black man was at their home. He assumed her father hired the man to help around the farm while he worked in town. Emilie assured him. "Seth is a free man. He will work for no one but himself now." Emilie believed Aaron brought Seth home to stay. She did not fully understand the dire situation her friend faced with her Uncle. "Seth is a good friend of the family." Emilie recovered from her initial shock. "He's like a brother to me." If she thought before she spoke, the comment would have never been spoken aloud.

The old man shook his head at her. John knew this girl was different, but now he seriously doubted her common sense. No one would think of describing anyone like that as a brother. "Well, all I'm saying is he best watch himself. It's dangerous being so close to the lines."

"They can't. He has free papers." Emilie was getting defiant.

"Ain't no matter, child," John said. "They take anyone they please. Our own population is scared to death when those rebs come knocking."

She thanked Mr. Blocher for his work and left the shop shaking uncontrollably. He watched her leave. He thought she needed to hear the truth; men were looking for good horses all the time. Her horse was prime target for confiscation. It was all in the name of war.

Tears sprang to her eyes. Emilie could not imagine Starlight getting shot. With the added thought that Seth may be in danger, she longed for the simple life on the plantation. Anger replaced fear. Vowing to protect her family and her horse at all cost, she didn't care which side wanted them; she was not giving up her family, possession, or loved ones. She felt a desperate desire to gather all that she loved and cherished and pack everything away like fine china dishes. Emilie wanted to protect her world to keep it untouched by the changes happening around her.

She was walking hard and fast, anger and fear driving her. When she entered the kitchen, she slammed the door behind her in frustration. He father looked up from the table. Her mother panicked and carefully checked the cake in the oven. Aaron and Seth came out of the parlor to see the source of the noise. Their smiles faded as they saw her face streaked with tears and her hair a mess about her face. Emilie looked like she had been through a windstorm.

"Welcome home," Jacob calmly said. "Tell me, daughter, what did the door do now to deserve such a greeting?"

Moving in close, she looked into his eyes. Driven by fear and anger, the words bubbled out of her, intense and angry. "Tell me the truth, Pa. Will there be men stealing Starlight? If so, do I have a right to shoot them or hang them for thieving?" Emilie's mouth formed a serious pout. She looked at him with passionate intensity.

Jacob put his paper down and took her shaking hands in his. Her fingers were small and delicate compared to his work-worn, calloused hands.

Smiling at her, he said, "You will first have to learn how to load a musket fast enough to shoot them. I don't think hanging a grown man will be easy for you either."

Her eyes flashed angrily for him teasing her. "*No*, Pa. Tell me the truth." She was in no mood for his teasing.

He spoke gently to her. "If troops come this way, we will take precautions to guard Starlight. If they take her, we cannot shoot them or hang them. We must give her over or be killed ourselves."

"They can take what they want and call it an act of war," Aaron added his two cents.

These words started her tears all over again. Julia came over to hand her daughter a handkerchief. Everyone was baffled. When Emilie left the house, she was excited to receive her certificate. No one expected to see a tearful mess arrive home.

"What is this?" Julia tried to calm her daughter. Seth and Aaron joined them at the table. Emilie explained what transpired between her and Mr. Blocher. Although her concerns were real, the family dispelled most of them. Emilie's family assured her Seth would be safe and Starlight would have to stay close to home to keep her safe.

"I don't understand why he would scare you so. What has gotten into that man, Jacob?"

"I don't know, Julia." Jacob could not think why John would discuss such a subject with his daughter. "I think he is trying to show Emilie some realities she doesn't need to know now."

Seth added, "No worries, Miss Emilie. I sleep Starlight. Mista Jacob, wills ya teachn me to shoot? I's a fast learner." Seth was so sincere; Emilie smiled for the first time since she arrived home.

"Sleep with Starlight?" Emilie corrected her friend. She noticed Seth's speech had deteriorated since she left Richmond. Emilie eyed Seth knowingly; he looked away embarrassed.

Julia got up from the table to check on the cake. As she pulled it out of the oven, the aromas of spicy cinnamon, nutmeg, and ginger wafted through the kitchen. Everyone smiled breathing in the wonderful smells while anticipating its taste. Julia looked at her daughter.

"No one is getting a snitch of this cake until I find out if we have a teacher in our midst?" Placing the cake on the cooling rack, she looked to her daughter for the answer. Everyone in the room turned to her, awaiting the verdict of the day.

Forgetting her immediate crisis, Emilie smiled, nodding. "Yes, yes, I did it!" She held up the certificate proudly. The room burst into applause. Aaron scooped her up and gave her a big hug.

"I knew you could do it, Em. Congratulations!"

"You make a good teacher. You taught me to read." Seth smiled proudly at her.

Emilie laughed. "You by far, Seth, are still my best student."

❦

Aaron gave Emilie her night of celebration before he announced he was leaving to enlist in Richmond. The family gathered in the parlor for Aaron's announcement. He was brief and honest about why he felt it was his duty to enlist.

His announcement did not surprise Emilie; she expected Aaron to do the right thing. He was dedicated, and this was another one of his convictions. Emilie insisted he write to her. She felt it would help everyone to receive letters from him. Aaron agreed; it would be best to try to get letters home.

Henry thoughtfully sat on the settee, watching the exchanges between his brother and sister. When Aaron announced what day he would leave, Henry got up from the settee and announced, "Pa, I will need a horse, and, Ma, please pack two of everything. I am going too." He looked at his family as they gaped at him in surprise."

Julia looked faint as the color drained from her face. She shook her head no. "Please, Henry, I can't let two of you go."

"Why? I believe everything Aaron just said. I believe in what the South stands for. I would best serve my country by fighting for my birthplace." Henry had been thinking about joining the war for some time. He felt uncomfortable with thoughts of joining the Union. Aaron reminded him of his beliefs, and in this, he decided to join his brother.

Aaron shook his brother's hand. Congratulating him for making his own decision, Aaron wanted to approach his brother earlier about enlisting with him, but felt a immense sense of pride knowing Henry made this decision on his own.

"We will enlist together so we won't get split up." Aaron saw the concern on his mother's face. Aaron knew his mother saw them as her little boys. She would never stop worrying.

"Don't worry, Ma, we will be there for each other." Henry added to the comforts his brother bestowed on his mother. "I have to do this. I am not your baby anymore. Ma, let me go." His eyes pleaded with his mother.

Julia looked at her sons. They looked at her with resolve; neither had a doubt on his face or in his heart. She worried for their safety, but moreover, she knew each son made his decision through what she and Jacob instilled in them. If they were this convicted, then she brought them up right. For that, she had a reason to beam with pride. Julia smiled at them with tears streaming down her face.

"Someone has to lose this war," Emilie piped up. "Who do we support, Pa?"

Jacob looked at his family, wondering how many others faced this dilemma. He knew there were other families facing this decision, torn apart by loyalties. Support was important to the soldiers. It gave them courage, hope, and strength to fight. Support from family, country, and loved ones made the horrors of war bearable. He paced the floor, mulling over what he heard. Walking over to his wife, he gathered her in his arms, whispering a private conversation. Julia nodded in acknowledgment. Together they faced their children. Aaron and Henry stood side by side, both proud and firm in their resolve. Emilie looked worried and thoughtful, waiting for what was next.

He began as if he were telling another one of his stories. "We are in a different situation here. Most families are concerned about one side of the war. I cannot tell you which side to support. We have good reasons to support both sides. Henry and Aaron have made their choice. Your mother and I are staying neutral, as we were raised in the South but our choice to live here in the North was thought out with deep consideration. We will support our children because we do not believe they are wrong. Some families are torn apart by this. Thankfully, ours is not, but we Prescotts walk a fine line. We'll be true to our beliefs and support our neighbors to support our country. To do this well, you must be a strong person. Emilie, you will choose the side that feels right when the time comes. Boys, your mother and I support you. You have our blessing and prayers to go forward." Jacob gave his blessings with the support of his loving wife. Emilie watched the whole scene unfolding, questions still unanswered.

After the house settled into a sleepy darkness, Emilie slept restlessly. Her mind busily working over the questions in her head, Emilie slipped into a restless dream. She saw herself sitting on a fence, watching the pasture ahead of her. The wheat blew a pattern of waves in the field. In the distance, she saw the glint of steel in the sun. The field filled with sparkling, shiny glints of steel. Out of the field on the other side, she saw it again. The waves of wheat were interrupted by glitter of steel, the wave silently moving toward her. On one side emerged blue-coated men, the other side, gray coats. Both troops were closing the distance of the field as they came together. Behind her came Henry—happy, carefree, and laughing as he tried to push her off the fence. On the other side, Thaddeus saved her from the fall. Henry passed on, wearing a gray coat; he walked to join the others. Thaddeus kissed her soundly, passionately. Looking into her eyes, his smile melted her heart. The thrill of his kiss tingled her to her soul. "Good-bye, love." His voice was husky in her ear. He held her as long as he could before joining the men opposite Henry. Before she could ask, he walked to the other side of the field. Men raised their guns toward one another. Emilie saw Thaddeus aiming for Henry and Aaron aiming for Thaddeus. Emilie tried to get off the fence. Desperate to stop them, she could not move. She opened her mouth to scream, which was drowned by cannon fire.

Emilie woke sweating, her face covered in tears. Emilie lit the lamp with shaking hands. Terrified, she got out of bed. Her legs shaking, she fell to her knees and prayed. Once her body calmed down, she picked up her diary to write.

> Dear diary,
> I woke up tonight with the most terrible dream. I feel helpless. I am afraid for my family, both for my present and future. My brothers are leaving to fight in Richmond. There are many brothers from North and South who were already gone; I now know how it feels to be one of those sisters. There are sisters like me who worry about their loved ones' safety, concerned for their health and strength. I don't even know if we will get letters from them. How would a Southern letter get up here? I prayed tonight for God to be with them in their every step, protecting them so they can come home to us. I beg him bring them back to us unscathed. My dream tells me something bad will happen. How can you root for both sides of a fight? I honestly don't know how to feel except I will miss them dearly. Even Henry, as much as he torments me, we are still blood. Morning will be here soon. I must try to sleep again.
>
> Good night.
> E. K. P.

Aaron, Henry, and Seth left to return to Richmond two weeks later. Emilie and Julia prepared an extra set of clothes for the boys and sent as many provisions as they could carry. After much debate, Jacob decided Seth would return to the Prescott Plantation. Seth missed his parents and he wanted to keep his family together. Seth kept with him an extra copy of the manumission papers for each of his family members. If William decided to press anyone back into slavery, Seth would have some form of freedom with him. There was a small chance the document would be recognized, but a small chance was better than none.

Stomachs full of a hearty breakfast, Emilie and Julia tried to hold back their tears for after the boys left. Emilie made sure to pack enough paper and pencils hoping to receive a letter or two from each of them. She told Seth to write to her if there was trouble. She carefully wrote their address on paper and sewed it into his jacket. His writing was still crude, but she made him promise to keep practicing. Emilie looked at her friend. "Seth, practice your speech, you sound more distinguished when you speak proper. Do you understand?"

Seth shook his head. "Yes, um…" He broke into a big smile when Emilie raised her eyebrow, ready to correct him. "Yes, Miss Emilie." They laughed together. Seth still liked to tease her. He knew how to make her laugh. They had been playmates as long as either one could remember.

Saddlebags packed, there was nothing left to do but say good-bye. The men exchanged hearty handshakes and hugs. Jacob smiled for his boys, so proud of them that he felt his heart would burst. Julia held on for a long time to each of her sons, saying a prayer and telling them to care for each other. If letters got through, she would respond as soon as she could. With tears in her eyes, she let them go. Emilie hugged Seth first; he was the easiest to say good-bye to. She did love him like a brother, but saying good-bye to the others was so much harder. Her dream followed her in her thoughts for days. Aaron scooped her up in his arms. His good-byes always made her happy. She always felt he would be right back. Tears formed in her eyes as she let go. "Hurry home." Looking at her little brother, she felt emotionally fragile. He was no longer the boy she grew up knowing. He looked older and more prepared than she imagined.

She hugged Henry tighter than she ever did. Suddenly feeling like water, her body overwhelmed with emotion, she burst into tears. "Please be careful and hurry home." Henry kissed her cheek.

"Take care of Ma and Pa. They need you now." His brown eyes sparkled as he teased. "Now look who gets to do my chores."

Emilie tried to laugh, but the tears would not stop flowing. She smiled and nodded her head. Why did he always make her cry? Tucked safely between her parents, Emilie waved good-bye to her brothers and Seth. When the boys were out of sight, Emilie and Julia went in the house for a good cry. Jacob went to the barn to work. Each family member was trying to best deal with the leaving of the boys. All they could do now is wait for the letters.

🌿

Feeling the security of her life chip away after her brothers left, Emilie needed some relaxation. Thankfully, she still had Thaddeus. Today they spent the afternoon riding in the hills around some outcroppings called Devil's Den. The area filled with rocks and crags. The stream that meandered through was a popular place for picnics and gatherings. Today Emilie felt like climbing the steep hill called Little Round Top. The climb was strenuous. It was work for Starlight too; the horse went slowly, testing the footing with each step. Gently encouraging her to continue, they made it to the top. The trees blew in a gentle wind, giving just the right amount of shade for a picnic. Adjusting the blanket, Emilie spread before them the meal she prepared. The sun was warm but not hot. It felt good to see the green trees and listen to the singing birds. Emilie felt happy and content. It certainly felt better than the stresses of the previous weeks. Thaddeus finished tying up the horses and came to join her. His shirt billowed in the breezes on the hill. His hair fussed wildly around his face, making him look very attractive indeed. Emilie took off her hat to catch some sun on her face. They enjoyed a hearty meal of ham sandwiches and lemonade; they sat together enjoying the view.

"This is exactly what I needed," Emilie said as she watched a bird hopping over the rocks. "Now that the boys are gone, it is so quiet around the house."

"No work and all play, are you?" He kisses the top of her head. "I hear that makes trouble for someone like you." The wind blew the red ribbon from Emilie's hair. Thaddeus caught it with one quick motion. He handed it to her. "Red is a perfect color for you. It is bold. I don't know of any other woman who fits this color like you, Emilie."

"You wouldn't be satisfied with any less of a woman, Thaddeus. The bolder the better. I keep you thinking." Emilie raised an eyebrow at him.

"So right you are, my dear." He pulled her close. She snuggled closer to him. They sat looking at the landscape, peaceful and fresh, each lost in their own thoughts. Suddenly Thaddeus got up. Emilie looked at him curiously. He reached for her hand and pulled her up. Together they hiked up over the large rocks, finding new vantage point to look over the landscape.

Finally, sitting on large rock to catch their breath, Thaddeus turned her to him. "I can't picture my life without you. I love everything about you." His eyes were serious, searching her eyes for an answer. "I would like to ask for your hand, Emilie. Would you do me the honor of becoming my wife?" She knew he was serious. She saw this look before. He was asking her to marry him.

"Didn't you want to wait?" Emilie felt the excitement burst within her. She imagined many times how he would ask her. She thought of so many scenarios. She loved him. Emilie never thought love would be like this.

"I want you to be my wife before I leave." His voice was steady and solid; his words alarmed her. She knew it was coming—just not this soon. She barely recovered from Henry and Aaron's departure. How would she deal with him going too?

He saw her thinking it. He knew she wanted to say something, but what? Encouraging her to say the words, he said, "You give me hope, Emilie. I know I can get through this with you by my side."

"When? There will be no time for a wedding." Emilie was surprised by his admission. She knew he loved her, but he seemed to be in a hurry now. She pressed him. "Do you know when you are leaving?"

He held her in his arms to protect her from his words. "We are leaving at the end of the month. We leave here June 25." He felt her gasp. There was no way to prepare her. Leaving would be hard for both of them.

"I want to take you as my husband. Is it fair for us to rush this?" Emilie tried to keep her emotions in control. "I want us to celebrate our wedding with family and friends. It takes time to prepare." She looked up at him, eyes glassy with tears. "I can't live without you, Thaddeus."

"You know I have to go. It is my duty." He held her tighter.

"You will be fighting my brothers." The reality struck her, vivid as her dream. "What will you do if you meet them on the battlefield?" She began to shake. He sat her down and held her, rocking her and hoping to comfort her.

"Each one of us has a duty," he began. "I pray that we never meet. I could not raise my gun against your brothers." He knew there was nothing he could do if faced with this situation. All he could do is hope it would never happen.

"Ask him, my father must give you permission," Emilie whispered urgently. "I can't live without you." He saw the love in her eyes. He saw her more beautiful than he ever had before. Her hair loose from its pins framing her face, he saw her eyes bright with tears, her pink lips pouting. She stirred a longing inside of him; he knew he had to wait. Boldly, he took her mouth and kissed her deeply. She responded with a boldness he never felt from her before. She let go, giving herself to him. Pressing her body as close as she could without shedding her clothing, Emilie needed him. Kissing him deeply, she obeyed the stirring inside of her.

Laying her down, he pressed his body against her, wanting to claim her and keep her to him. Her body surrendered to his hands, wanting him as well. She melted against his touch, following his every movement with her body. She needed him. He wanted her. Each kiss followed by another, he explored her body, desiring to touch her intimately; he pushed himself as far as he could. She followed each kiss with an exploration of her own. Memorizing his body with her hands, she arched against him, not wanting his hands to leave her body. She wanted more, knowing they were dangerously close to a full commitment of body and soul.

A sigh escaped her lips; she pulled him close, breathlessly close. She wanted more, knowing she was crossing the line. She stopped. "Please make me your wife. I need your touch, your love. I need you, Thaddeus." Her eyes were full of excitement of the moment. She wanted his commitment. "How am I going to watch you go?"

Sobered by her words, he pulled her close. "Together we will get through it. And I will come home as your husband, and we will grow old together in love." He sealed his words with a kiss that told her he was hers.

The afternoon passed quickly, they lost themselves in deep, thoughtful conversations about their future together. The sun was setting when he dropped her off at home. Emilie felt a renewed excitement. She knew she had to wait for Thaddeus to ask her father. Memories of the afternoon excited her. She was hopeful for their future.

> Dear diary,
>
> Today it is obvious I am ready to commit myself as a wife. Thaddeus has made his intentions clear, and I accepted his proposal. He must talk to Father first, but I am confident we will have his blessing. I am excited to start my new life with him. I am sad we will be separated for a

while. Thaddeus is going to enlist for as short a period as he can. Driven to do his duty for country, we will serve our country—him in the field, me at home. When this is all over, we will be one. I am so happy my life is falling into place, and I am going to be Mrs. Thaddeus Marsh.

Excited for her future,
E. K. P.

PROPOSAL OF LOVE

Being deeply loved by someone gives you strength, while loving someone deeply gives you courage.

—Lao Tzu

Thaddeus watched Jacob chisel an intricate ivy pattern into the cabinet board. He concentrated on his work, slowly inching the chisel through the cherry wood. Thaddeus admired Jacob. He was a good man, he quietly commanded respect, and it was granted by anyone who met him. He could see himself as the man's son-in-law.

"Did you have something to say?" Jacob looked up from his work, blowing away the wood shavings. He took up the sandpaper to smooth out the grove.

Nervously, Thaddeus twisted some straw in his hands. "Yes, sir. I want to ask you for permission to marry your daughter." The words spilled out of his mouth, simple and to the point. Thaddeus was happy the words came out so easily.

Jacob looked at the young man. He had prayed for this moment for a long time. A father wishes to marry his daughter to a good man, who will provide for her, love her, and make her happy. It was only months before he was wishing for someone to come into Emilie's life. Now that the time came, he never thought he would feel like this. He put down his work and sat across from Thaddeus.

"Emilie tells me you have enlisted. Why do you want to marry her so fast? Is there a problem I need to know about?" Jacob was concerned. He had many questions for this boy. *Why so fast?* was the first.

Shocked by the intention of the question, Thaddeus's face turned red with embarrassment. "No, sir. There is no emergency. I respect your daughter and you. I feel the upcoming days will be easier if I know she is waiting to start a life with me when I get home. I love your daughter, Mr. Prescott."

"I can see your love for her. I don't doubt your feelings. I am concerned about the time separating both of you. Why not wait until you return? We can have the wedding I am sure she has been planning." Jacob could see the young man was hopeful.

"I don't want her to feel alone. She has had a hard time since her brothers left. It would give her hope to see the ring on her finger. It would give me something to fight for. I love her, Mr. Prescott."

"Your love for each other will give you courage to do what you must on the battlefield. I am worried about what if you don't come home. You will widow my daughter before the honeymoon ends." Jacob's words surprised him. Thaddeus shook his head.

"How much do you like my daughter, Thaddeus?" Jacob was not going to have any question unanswered. He was going to find out his intentions before he would give permission. "She is quite a trying young woman. Can you handle her?"

Thaddeus smiled at this. "I have liked your daughter since the first day I met her. I admired her challenge to Mr. Blocher at the New Year's Eve party. I love how she challenges me every day. She is smart and passionate. I don't want to live without that." He stopped to think a moment before adding, "I love her spirit, Mr. Prescott. She makes me feel alive."

Jacob shook his head. His daughter certainly had spirit. From her first day on earth, she kicked and screamed heartily when she was born. Her stubbornness would never be taken from her no matter what he tried. Luckily, Emilie was a good girl who learned honor and respect; he never had to discipline her too harshly. Remembering his daughter's antics, Jacob smiled.

"You will have to keep plenty of door hinges on hand. That girl has a temper." He looked at Thaddeus, who smiled at his joke. Emilie certainly knew how to get her point across, slammed doors and all.

"I will keep stock of door hinges and extra lumber." The men both appreciated Emilie for who she was. "Mr. Prescott, I will do my best to keep her happy, secure, and provided for. My job will still be here when I return. If something happens to it, I still have the farm. I will provide for her." Thaddeus tried to think of everything he would be asked during this interview. He fought for her as if his own life depended on it.

Jacob shook his head, considering what the young man was saying. He had no doubt they were in love. He saw his daughter's happiness. He saw how tender Thaddeus was with her. Holding hands and hugging each other when they thought no one was watching. Their love had grown steady since they met last January. This man was asking for her hand in marriage. Every father's moments came to this.

"Thaddeus, I am going to be straight with you. I appreciate your desire to go to war and fight for your beliefs. I gave my blessing to my sons not three weeks ago. You must see how worried I am about your return. I will allow you to be engaged to my daughter, only to marry her when you come home at the end of this war." He saw Thaddeus's face fall with disappointment. He could not tell this man his fears, the fear he felt for his sons and anyone else who engaged in war. It was the simple fact he may not come home. He could not bear to see his daughter a widow so soon.

"I think we can all live with that, sir." Thaddeus was reasonable. He knew the hard part was over. He had permission to marry Emilie, just not this moment. "When can I tell her?"

Jacob shook his head. "You know if you wait, she will hunt you down or not let me get any rest. We had better go in to tell her." They stood up and walked into the house.

Emilie stood at the kitchen window, watching for Thaddeus and her father to walk out of the barn. Pacing back and forth from table to window, she finally sat down at the table. Emilie tried to keep herself focused on her sewing but could not concentrate. Julia watched her daughter fidget nervously. She wanted to say something but did not want to risk making a joke out of a serious situation. Her daughter was on edge, and jokes would not make things better. She was content to watch her for now, knitting socks and waiting for the door to open.

Emilie suddenly stood up. "Here they come." She didn't know what to do. Looking around, she asked, "Do I look all right?"

Julia raised her eyebrow, nodding yes. "You are very anxious tonight. What are you worried about?'

"Anything could happen," she said. "Was Pa in a good mood?" Emilie honestly could not remember her father's mood at dinner. He seemed pensive. What did that mean? Emilie nervously watched her mother. "What will he say, Mother?"

Julia set down her knitting and looked at her daughter. "I guess we will find out."

The door opened. Thaddeus walked in, followed by Jacob. Emilie got up and looked at both men. They seemed happy. Thaddeus smiled and winked at her. She looked at her father, waiting for him to speak.

"Julia, it has come to my attention that Thaddeus wishes to marry our daughter. After some consideration and dire warnings to this young man, he has not changed his mind." Jacob worked hard to control his face. He wanted to keep his daughter in suspense.

Emilie broke in, "Papa, what?" She did not find any humor in his joke to dissuade Thaddeus. "Did you say yes?" Emilie stood beside Thaddeus; he put his arm around her for comfort.

He raised his hand to quiet his daughter. "I think due to the circumstances, you will marry him after he comes back from serving. At that time, if your love is still strong, you have my permission to become engaged now and marry when he returns."

Emilie jumped into her father's arms. "Thank you, Father. Thaddeus, that's good, isn't it?"

He shook his head. "Having you in my life is very good." She rushed over to him and hugged him. He stopped her. Bent down on one knee, taking her hand in his, he placed a kiss on it before he looked up at her. "Emilie Kathryn Prescott, will you do me the honor of becoming my wife?" The proposal was interrupted with Jacob clearing his throat. "When I return, as soon as I return," he added. Holding her hand in his, he reached for his pocket with the other. He pulled out a simple ring with a single diamond in the center. He slipped it on her finger.

Looking down at him, she smiled. "I would be honored to be your wife, so hurry home to me."

He stood to receive her in his arms. He kissed her deeply and whispered, "I love you."

She winked at him. "I love you too. I can't wait for you to come home." They stayed locked in each other's arms until Julia interrupted the moment with a suggestion.

"I just finished a strawberry rhubarb pie." She wiped the tears from her eyes. She saw the joy in the young couple's eyes. They were hopeful and excited about their future. She was thankful for such a great pairing. They matched, complemented each other; she could not have chosen a better husband for her daughter, and for that, Julia and Jacob were thankful.

🌿🍃

Two weeks after their engagement, Thaddeus and Stephen packed to take the train to Harrisburg to begin training for the war. Emilie finished his quilt just in time to send it with him. Emilie fussed for weeks, trying to think of everything she could send with him to keep him comfortable. Finally finishing all the necessities, Emilie put together one last present for him. Taking the locket from her neck, she laced the red ribbon through its loop. Inside the locket, she cut a picture of herself and clipped a lock of her hair. He had her with him. She tied this around a packet of paper and bound pencils to it—a care package from home. She knew she would desperately need to hear from him as soon as possible. Her emotions were up and down, laughing one minute, crying the next. She told herself that if she could be strong, it would help him come home faster. As time drew near, she was losing that battle with herself.

A small gathering of five men readied near the train platform to leave with Captain McPherson. Jacob and Emilie arrived at the station to say good-bye. No bands played today. Small groups of family members were there to say good-bye to the men. Emilie felt heavyhearted. The scene was solemn, dusted with a glimmer of hope. Each family member secretly prayed this would not be the last time they would see their loved ones alive.

Emilie found Thaddeus and Stephen shaking hands with friends and hugging family. She stood watching him, waiting for him to turn around. Suddenly she saw him tense. He was aware she was behind him. Turning to see her, he smiled, his eyes telling how he really felt. Clouded with sadness, he smiled to try to cover it up. She saw through him, both looking at each other, blocking out everything else around them.

"There you are." Thaddeus took Emilie's hand. He looked down to admire the ring he put on her finger just weeks before. He kissed her hand. "You are a beautiful sight. I will remember this until I see you again."

Emilie smiled bravely. She was so close to tears. She fought them every moment they were together. "You look happy today." She knew he wasn't. "Are you ready for this adventure?"

He nodded. "I am ready to go so I can come home to you." As he spoke to her, she pressed the locket in his hand. "What's this?"

"It is the only way I can come with you." She looked into his eyes, trying to shut out the rest of the world. She wanted to be with him out of the eyes of the public. "I love you."

"Please, you two lovebirds are attracting attention," Stephen broke in. "Will you write to me dear, Emilie?"

"Only if you write back," Emilie teased. "I have to keep on your nerves somehow."

"Just what I needed," he chided back. "I want to apologize for my bad behavior at the ball." He was serious now. "I am sorry."

Emilie shook her head. "I forgive you. Now both of you take care of each other and come home soon." Emilie bravely smiled at them. She liked Stephen's sense of humor. He was fun when he was not complaining about her opinions.

"Hey, where's your brother Henry. Isn't he coming too?" Stephen looked around the crowd.

"Henry already enlisted," Thaddeus broke in. "He left awhile ago."

"Excited to get going, I see." Stephen seemed satisfied with Henry's commitment. "I didn't think he was going to do it, being from…" He stopped, not wanting to hurt Emilie's feelings.

Emilie reached in her basket. Pulling out a packet of paper, she gave it to Stephen. "Here is some paper to write home. Don't leave us worrying about you." He took the paper from her. Bowing his head in appreciation, the train whistle sounded. It was time to go.

"Thank you, Emilie. I will leave you two to say good-bye." Emilie stopped him from leaving. She took his hand in hers.

"Take care of yourself, Stephen. Take care of each other." She smiled at him and let go of his hand.

Wordless, he acknowledged her with a wink and walked toward the train. She turned to Thaddeus, who had not left her side since she arrived. He held her close. She felt the rough wool coat on her check. She held on to him with both hands, not wanting to let go. Holding on to this moment as long as she could, she took a mental inventory of him. The feel of his coat on her cheek rough and new; she fit perfectly into his body. How his arms tight around her told her he would never leave her. She could smell him. His scent, fresh to her, it belonged only to him. She prayed she would never forget how he smelled. She listened to his heartbeat, strong and steady; it was exciting to hear how close he was to her. How could she let go now? She felt him kiss the top of her head. She fit perfectly in his arms. Her head cradled into the soft spot under his collarbone, she held tighter.

"Be strong, little one. Know every day I am closer to coming home. Be strong for us." His voice was soothing to her sadness.

"I love you, Thaddeus. Stay strong. I want to become your wife." His chest shook as he laughed.

"I consider you my wife already. I have to go." He lifted her chin to kiss her. Soft and delicate, she felt him for the last time in she didn't know how long. She wanted more, more kisses, more tender words. He gently let her go. "Be brave, my love."

Shaking her head, she bit her lips to stop the tears. She watched him step onto the train. Waving to him, she watched the train leave the station. Frozen in place, she could not move. If she moved, she knew the tears would come. Her body shook fighting the tears that were at the surface. The crowd dissipated around her. Finally, her father was at her arm. He gently touched her elbow.

"Em, time to go." He gently steered his daughter away from the train station. During the ride home, she didn't speak. Emilie closed her eyes. Trying to remember how he felt, how he smelled, she didn't want to forget a thing about him. If she could remember, he would always be with her.

Emilie walked from the barn to the house, hoping to get to her room without breaking down. Entering the house, she saw her mother. Julia's eyes filled with sympathy. One look at her daughter, she rushed over to hold her. Once their eyes met, Emilie broke down into tears. She cried for him. She missed him and her brothers. She cried out of anger for the country that took them away. She felt stripped of the security they brought to her life. Emilie retreated to her room for the rest of the day.

Dear diary,

Today I feel naked. I have no one except my parents to look after me. I feel vulnerable to the world, no one to protect me if I need it. I am uncomfortable and upset. How am I supposed to carry on without this security? Is it within me to carry on without them? I pray God shows me what to do. I will start writing letters every day to be close to him. Thaddeus said I am his wife already. I can't imagine me belonging to anyone else. I am exhausted by the day. Praying I get a good-night's sleep.

E. K. P.

Stephen tried to distract Thaddeus from thinking about Emilie. He told stories about what he thought about the adventure to come. The train arrived at Winchester by mid-afternoon. It was a short ride to Camp Wayne. The five new recruits were joining the Company K, First Pennsylvania Reserves, Thirtieth Regiment. The first of the troops left Gettysburg a few weeks previously. The regiment still needed men; this is how Stephen and Thaddeus were able to join their neighbors.

The rigors of setting up their quarters and settling in added to the exhaustion of the day. There were many people to meet. Thaddeus and Stephen knew this was going to be very different from the life they came from. Men from all walks of life were wandering through camp. Thaddeus and Stephen learned quickly the expectations of Company K. The troops were already well groomed in marching and taking orders. The expectation that the five new recruits would step up and learn just as fast was blatantly clear through the rigors of marching and barking of orders. It was all around them all the time. Stephen learned the drills quickly. Thaddeus learned he could not let home distract him. Once he focused, Thaddeus fell into army life feeling alone for the first time in his life.

There was no time to think about home. Thaddeus felt guilty that he did not write Emilie those first few days. He busily tried to learn the drills, chores of camp. Building friendships with his comrades was important to learn how to get what you needed. On the third day of camp, everyone received care packages from home. The packages contained housewives and goodies for the making the camp more comfortable. Thaddeus heard someone complain that his housewife was missing the sister or lover to use the sewing kit.

"They call this darn thing a housewife. All I see is the needle and thread. Where is the wife to complete the mending?" He got chuckles and slaps on the back for his witty comments.

Back in his tent, Thaddeus sorted through his belongings. He pulled out Emilie's locket. He opened it for the first time. Inside he found her picture and lock of hair. His heart began to ache missing her. He missed her laugh, her teasing him, and the witty way she turned his comments into jokes. He wondered how she was doing.

Pulling out a piece of paper and pencil, he began his first letter. Just as he began, Stephen blew into the tent. "Hey, I have searched these grounds and asked about. No one knows Henry." Stephen wanted to see his friend again.

"He may not be here. I don't know what company he was assigned." Thaddeus could not tell Stephen about the family secret. He didn't want them under any suspicion of being Southern sympathizers. Stephen had a great way of saying too much; he could not risk telling his friend where Henry and Aaron went.

Stephen sat right in front of Thaddeus, staring him down. "Why wouldn't she tell you which company he was enlisted?" Thaddeus could feel his eyes demanding answers. Stephen laughed off his friend's bad attempt to weasel an answer out of him.

"Simple. She didn't know." Thaddeus was keeping things simple. It was true. Emilie had no idea where Aaron or Henry enlisted or what branch they even enlisted. They could have decided on the navy for all she knew. As of the latest news, the boys hadn't gotten back to Richmond.

Stephen thought for a few minutes. Just as Thaddeus was ready to begin writing, Stephen interrupted him by his revelation. "Did he go back to Richmond?" Stephen jumped up with excitement. He could not believe how scandalous it would be for the family to be living in the North and having their son fighting for the enemy.

Thaddeus hushed his friend. "Stephen, do not draw attention to us. We don't know how these people will react knowing I have family from the South."

"What are you talking about? Did you marry her?" Stephen could not believe Thaddeus did not share this news with him. He was hurt. He watched his friend put away his writing. Thaddeus sat next to his friend.

"Emilie and I are engaged. Her father wouldn't allow marriage until I come back." Thaddeus watched his friend's face for clues to his perceived relationship with Emilie. Thaddeus suspected Stephen was enamored with Emilie. He did not want to share his excitement about her, especially if it meant that Stephen would have hard feelings for both of them.

"I didn't know," Stephen added. "How did it happen?"

"Two weeks ago. I asked her father's permission." Thaddeus smiled. He was glad that was over. It was nerve-wracking imagining what Jacob would say. Now that it was over, he enjoyed his new status of being Emilie's betrothed.

"Congratulations, she's a great girl." Stephen smiled. The bugle call suggested the men were ready for the evening meal. Putting away his papers, Thaddeus vowed he would write before the sun went down tonight. He was excited to start receiving letters from her. He wanted to surprise her by being the first to send a letter.

MILES APART

If I had a single flower for every time I think about you, I could walk forever in my garden.

—Claudia Ghandi

The days since Thaddeus left seemed to drag on. Emilie did her level best to keep busy to keep her mind from thinking about him. Sitting under the apple trees in the family's small orchard, Emilie tried to immerse herself into Shakespeare. The green leaves of trees provided lush, cool shade from the late June heat.

Sonnet 47
Betwixt mine eye and heart a league is took,
And each doth good turns now unto the other;
When that mine eye is famish'd for a look,
Or heart in love with sighs himself doth smother,
With my love's picture then my eye doth feast,
And to the painted banquet bids my heart;

As she read these words, Emilie found her heart aching. She missed him, and Shakespeare was not helping her to forget him. Throwing the book onto the dirt, she shouted, "You are not helping me, Mr. Shakespeare." Her mood changed from melancholy to grumpy. Thinking hard, she got up, picked up the book, and stomped into the house.

She said nothing as she walked past her mother into the parlor to put the book back on the shelf. After inspecting it for damage, Emilie brushed off the book and placed it carefully in its spot. Emilie turned to see the piano. Music always lifted her mood. Turning to the Beethoven music, she began playing. The music was healing. It felt good to let her soul sing its way out of her depression. Her fingers gliding over the keys made her smile. She loved this. She knew she had to move on. She refused to wait for him while feeling sad and insecure. She hated how moody she had become; normally upbeat and happy, she now felt depressed and mournful. Just as she finished the piece, she heard the parlor open.

Julia swept into the parlor carrying a tea tray. She sat down on the settee, waiting for her daughter to acknowledge her. When the music stopped, she said, "You still play that one beautifully."

Emilie smiled. "Thank you. I remember thinking I could never play this piece."

"It did challenge you, but look how far you've come." Julia was very proud of her daughter's accomplishments. "Will you have tea with me?"

"Yes," Emilie said as she slid off the piano bench. She saw the cookies arranged on the tray. The teapot and cups were also arranged perfectly on the tray. Emilie remembered the days when her mother taught her the etiquette of serving a proper ladies' tea. Emilie had been excited to be the server at her first tea. Some of her mother's friends had come over for a visit. Emilie watched Martha prepare the tea, while she, herself helped arrange the desserts on the tray. Emilie felt like a grown-up for the first time. It was a pleasant memory that made her smile every time she thinks about it.

"We have a new project starting with the ladies' society," Julia said. "We will be making shirts and knitting scarves. I will need your help if you aren't busy teaching this quarter."

Emilie smiled. She was hoping Carrie has room for her this quarter. Emilie wanted her life to feel normal again. "I have to meet with Carrie before I can say. I'm planning a trip into town later this week. I think I need to socialize again." Emilie offered her mother her teacup. Julia poured her tea and handed Emilie the creamer. "When did you make these?" Emilie bit into the butter cookie. It was light and crisp. The cookie melted on her tongue as soon as she bit into it.

"I made those when you were sulking in your room the other day. You need to move on. Get busy. Did you write to Thaddeus yet?" Julia sipped her tea, looking at her daughter's face change mood when she mentioned him.

"I honestly don't know what to say. I want to write an upbeat, happy letter, letting him know I am fine, but I don't feel fine." Emilie set her cup down. "He will read it in my words. He will know."

Julia set down her cup and placed her hand on Emilie's. "Just write him. The words will flow, and you will feel connected again." She had a feeling this was what was bothering her daughter the most. The loss of connection with him made her feel isolated and alone.

Emilie smiled.

"I will work on that letter. I know it is all he has from home."

Gunfire and smoke filled the air. The heat was oppressive, and the sulfur smell of smoke from the firing rifles added to the suffocation. Drilling became intense; as the rumors grew hotter, the troops were being prepared to move in a few days. Lieutenant Bailey barked orders to a group down the line as the rest of the group sat by and watched them drill again. Bailey was a stickler for movement and precision. At the end of that drill, everyone reassembled to march in formation again before given orders to break rank for water and food.

Thaddeus felt the effects of continuous effort in his feet. His brogans were still new. He watered them and wore them, praying they would break in. It wasn't fast enough. Taking off his boots, he saw the blisters forming at his toes and heels. He was lucky the boots fit in length; he just needed to break in the width.

"This heat is horrible. All this drilling, my drawers are beginning to sag." Stephen sat next to his friend. "Sure glad they gave us a few more days. I think I am getting the hang of this drill. I wonder what they'll do when we finally get it. It would be nice to stop moving for a while." Stephen took another drink of water from his canteen. Finding it almost empty, he shook his head in disgust. He had no energy to find water just now.

"How are your feet holding up?" Thaddeus questioned.

"Fine, once my brogans gave way, calluses replaced blisters. My feet are as tough as cow's hide." Taking another drink from his canteen, he continued, "I expect we will be moving soon. Tyler says there's rumor to be fighting all over this area."

Stirring the fire, Thaddeus hoped they would not move for a few more days. A letter from Emilie would sure lift his spirits. He needed that now. He was tired both physically and mentally. Thoughts of her gave him a moment to relax and not think about drills or maneuvers. He worried about her well-being. There was little time to think about anything but what the army wanted now. The troops were being pushed to fight hard and train harder so everyone could go home.

Later that day, the excitement grew. The company received their uniforms: white duck pants, flannel shirts, and gray jackets—all contributions from the home front. Caps and overcoats with arms and accoutrements were also distributed. The feeling of camaraderie grew. The men, driven to drill harder, put all their effort forward. The troops focused on perfecting their drill, finally feeling like a formidable army. It struck Stephen as peculiar. He thought, *All dressed up and nowhere to go.* The troops looked like a fighting force, but where was the action? He shared this sentiment with some others in his regiment.

"We seem all drilled and dressed for the fight, but where's the action?" Stephen sat pondering this question as he chewed on a toothpick.

"I hears them saying we still don't have enough men. I guess no one else wants to whip the enemy like we do." Amos was a farm boy from Heidlersburg. He had the fighting spirit in him. Eyes wild with anticipation, he was itching for action. "I can't wait to kill my first reb!"

Seeing his fervor, Stephen shook his head. "Be careful what you wish for. I am sure we will be shooting in no time. We are so close to the South. They can't cross the Mason Dixon without running into one of us."

Thaddeus was rather tired of listening to the bragging and boasting. He wanted some quiet time with Emilie. He pulled out his paper and began writing.

> My darling girl,
>
> It feels like eternity since I last held you in my arms. President Lincoln has set to either make us into strong fighting men or kill us trying. We have been drilling constantly, waiting for word to move to the front lines. There is so much to learn, I often wish I had your scholarly brain to remember all of it. We have been getting many gifts from the home front. Last week we received housewives and other goodies. I still have the one you made me, only wish you were here to help with the sewing when I need it. Your closeness would be a welcomed relief.
>
> Today we received our uniforms. They are very clean and new. I can't imagine what they will look like in a few months. Our companies are still waiting more men to finish their numbers, as we are still too few to be a complete regiment. I expect we will be here at Camp Wayne for a while yet.
>
> Next week is the Fourth of July. I want you to celebrate and have a good time. Know that all of the men here are doing our duty to finish this and come home. Whatever the outcome, it is in God's hands to see it done.
>
> I look forward to your letters. I miss you and hope all is well with you. Do not miss me sadly. Miss me with hope that I will be home soon. Put a bright smile on your face, and know I love you, my girl!
>
> Write when you can. I can't wait to hear from you!
>
> Always in my heart,
> Thaddeus

It felt good to finish the letter to her. For more than a moment, he was with her. Sealing up the envelope, he placed it in his knapsack to send tomorrow. He hoped the next mail call would have a letter for him.

Thaddeus went to sleep that night wondering how Aaron and Henry were doing. Would he ever have to face them, and what would that do to Emilie? The thoughts weighed heavily on his mind. All he could do is pray they would never meet. Thaddeus finally gave in to sleep, his body nagging him for rest, his mind still mulling over the dreadful thoughts of facing, not an enemy, but brothers.

Aaron began looking for a place to stop for the night. He had enough riding for the day. They were making good time on the way back to Richmond. Seth was a good rider; he helped pass the long hours by telling stories and asking questions about the boys upcoming adventures.

Henry and Seth bantered back and forth, talking about women, courting and who would marry first. They bragged about their first kiss, trying to make the non-event sound real. Aaron breathed a sigh of relief when he saw the tavern. They had just crossed into Virginia. It felt good to be in their home territory. Aaron thought a drink would soothe their dry throats and refresh their minds.

The other two took the news quite well. Henry was excited. This would be his first ale without parental permission. He grinned from ear to ear when Aaron announced, "I figure you will be fighting like a man. You may as well partake in a man's drink." Henry's eyes lit up with anticipation. "Only one ale for you, brother," Aaron warned Henry. "I don't want to hear complaints about riding with a headache tomorrow." Aaron saw the anticipation in his brother's eyes.

"What about Seth? Will you buy him one too?" Henry was eager to share this event with him. He looked at Seth, eager to hear if Seth would join him.

"Oh no, Mama says spirits are the work of the devil. I don't need that, Aaron." Seth was astonished Aaron offered. "I don't want that devil's drink."

Aaron appreciated Seth's views. He knew Seth's culture was superstitious about some aspects of the white man's culture. This was one of them. "Well, I don't think anyone will allow you in the tavern, Seth. Let's find some shade, and you can tend the horses while we step inside. I will bring you back something to eat."

"Thank you, Mr. Aaron."

Seth was happy he didn't have to explain anything else.

Finding a cool, shady spot across from the tavern, the boys tied up the horses. Seth sat on a horse blanket while Henry and Aaron went across the street. Inside the tavern was cool and dark. Cigar smoke filled the air. Men dressed in military uniform crowded most of the tables in the taproom. Civilian men gathered around another table, giving the man information.

The uniformed sergeant asked, "Do you have a reliable horse, and can you ride?"

The man shook his head. "Yes, sir. I can ride one handed at a gallop and shoot while riding too." His sandy, mussed-up hair shook as he regaled his exaggerated story.

The sergeant eyed him suspiciously. "We'll see how good you are. Sign here and report back in two days. We will be leaving then."

The man scribbled his name on the paper and happily walked over to the bar to order a drink. The men around him slapped him on the back with good cheer and congratulations. The atmosphere seemed to be very jolly in this place.

Aaron found a table. Henry sat down while he went to inquire about a meal and some good ale. Aaron wished for some good whiskey, but he was still watching the money they had. It needed to last until they could enlist.

The barmaid eyed him up. "Welcome, stranger. What can I get for you?" He first noticed her face, inviting and bright. Her other assets threatened to spill over her chemise, her pretty, blond curls falling out of her snood. It looked as if she had been busy working all day.

Aaron could not help but flirt with her. "I'd like a look at your menu, and two ales and one sarsaparilla, please." She nodded, handing him the paper menu, all tattered and well read. He looked it over as she poured the drinks. Aaron excused himself to bring Henry the selections and his ale.

On his way to the table, a man called out to him, "Excuse me? Do you boys have a unit yet?" Aaron turned to see an officer addressing him. The man was tall, dressed in full cavalry uniform complete with knee-high boots and saber. He looked very distinguished.

Aaron nodded toward the table where Henry sat. The officer followed him to his table. Seeing the man approach, Henry's eyes widened with surprise. Aaron leaned over to Henry and said, "Go give this to Seth and ask him what he wants to eat." Henry jumped up. Aaron grabbed his sleeve. "Be sure to pour this in his mug. I don't want to cause any trouble with the patrons."

Henry nodded and took the drink and menu out to Seth. Turning back to the officer, Aaron said, "No, sir. We are looking for a unit. We have someone to deliver back to my uncle's plantation first."

The man nodded his head. "Caught that one back, eh?" He continued to scrutinize Aaron's looks. He surmised Aaron was a fit young man, decent in build. His speech was educated.

"We are a newly formed cavalry unit. Do you ride?" He took a swallow of his ale.

"Yes, we both ride and rather well. My brother and I were hoping to join a good cavalry instead of infantry unit." Aaron was experienced since he was a boy. He enjoyed learning tricks and handling his horse with one hand.

"The boy looks rather young. I don't know if we can take him in the horse unit. I may think he'd be best on foot." The officer was skeptical.

"I can assure you, sir. He is a talented rider. Taught him everything I know." Aaron was thinking about the promise he made to his mother. "We boys have to stay together."

"I see, you promised your mother, did you?" The officer had heard that story many times today. He understood the young man's desire to keep a promise to his mother.

"We'll see what we can do. Do you have good horses?" That was the man's last question. They were finished talking by the time Henry returned from outside. Cup in hand, Henry came to sit down with Aaron and the officer. Just as he sat, the officer got up and shook Aaron and Henry's hand.

"Go sign up with the sergeant, and we will meet you in Ashland in a few weeks. We will begin our training." The officer took his leave. Henry sat looking at his brother, waiting. Aaron looked at Henry.

"What do you think about the cavalry? Do you think you can do it?" Henry and Aaron discussed the options for weeks. Henry felt the infantry would be very taxing; the physical labor and all the marching did not suit him.

He surmised the artillery was too specialized, and since he was not a great swimmer, the navy was out. Cavalry would have been their first choice.

"That is my first choice. What do we do now?" Henry was excited to start this new venture. "Will we be together?"

"Looks like it. We have to go register with the sergeant over at that table." The boys left their drinks to find out what was in store for them.

The sergeant reviewed their credentials, gave them papers to sign, and swore them into the unit. He explained once they arrived at Ashland for training that they would need to pass a physical exam. The horses would be reviewed for health. They listened to a laundry list of things they would need to bring with them and what would be expected. Finally, each was given a military pass stating they were assigned to the Third Virginia Cavalry Company K.

Returning to the table, Aaron congratulated Henry, and they toasted their success to serve in the Confederate Army. Henry drank half of his ale and began feeling the effects of it quickly. Their food came just in time. The smell of fresh chicken pie and biscuits set his stomach to a ravaging hunger. Aaron, having the same, watched steam rise from his plate. When Seth's meal was set in front of them, Aaron remembered Seth was still waiting outside with the horses.

Getting up to deliver him his meal, there was shouting and commotion outside. Aaron hurried to the door. Pushing his way through the crowd, he saw men surrounding Seth. One man held Henry's horse while the others accused him of trying to steal it. Seth was doing his best to explain.

Hurrying through the crowd, Aaron approached the mob. Seth was terrified. The mob was looking to hang him without any questions asked. Aaron broke into the conversation.

"What is going on here?" His voice was gruff with anger.

"This darkie was stealing this horse. I saw him attempting to ride away." He pulled Seth in front to show Aaron the accused.

"He belongs to me."

Looking at Seth, he asked, "What's happening?"

Meekly, Seth's voice was low and scared. "Mr. Aaron, I was just exercising him. They were too close and biting each other, causing a ruckus. I's only moving him."

"You actually believe him?" the accuser scoffed at Aaron. "He was planning to steal and ride his way North."

Aaron tried to control his growing anger. Stepping forward, he took Seth's arm and pulled him closer to him. Seth cringed but realized Aaron did not handle him roughly. "He belongs to me, and you all can go about your business." Aaron's six-foot stature was formidable when he got angry and his deep voice brought attention to him when he spoke.

The crowd quickly dispersed. The men gave their comments regarding Seth's freedom, and derogatory remarks toward Aaron being soft on slaves were thrown about as they reluctantly went back to their boring lives. Aaron sat down next to Seth. Seeing him frightened did not sit well with him. It bothered him to see his friend in distress. "Are you all right?"

Seth shook his head. He was still shaking from the incident. Aaron sat him down, gave him his dinner, and tethered Henry's horse away from the others. Coming back to Seth, he encouraged him to eat. "We will finish up inside and be out in a bit. We'll move out to find a place to rest tonight." Seth watched Aaron; he didn't say anything even though Aaron knew he wanted to. Aaron thought it better not to press the issue. There would be plenty of time to discuss the situation later.

Returning to the tavern, Henry finished his meal. Satisfied, he held the mug of ale in his hands. He looked delightfully relaxed and on the verge of sleep as the ale's effects were overpowering his senses. Suddenly noticing his brother sitting at the table, Henry asked, "Where ya been?" His words slurred a bit.

Aaron focused on eating his meal, which was now cold. He grabbed his mug for a swallow and found it empty. His brother had a smug look on his face. Aaron shook his head. "No more for you. You drank mine, didn't you?" Aaron went back to eating.

Henry shook his head, grinning ridiculously. Aaron took his mug from his brother's hands. "We have to go. Finish up." He got up from the table to pay the barmaid. Henry sat stupidly numb in his chair. Aaron came back to the table, scooped up his brother by his arm, and escorted him out of the tavern.

Seth jumped up as he saw the boys coming across the street. He noticed Aaron escorting Henry across the street. Henry weaved and tripped. Seth watched the scene, wide-eyed. Shaking his head in disbelief, Seth surmised it must be the "devil's drink" that made Henry weak. Seeing this solidified his faith in his mother's teachings.

Aaron helped Henry up into the saddle. They rode away in silence to find a place to bed down for the night.

LIFE'S NEW NORMAL

There are many ways of going forward, but only one way of standing still.

—Franklin D. Roosevelt

Emilie hurried to finish her first letter to Thaddeus. She needed to get into town so she wouldn't miss the letters out at the post office. Lighting the sealing wax, she willed it to hurry to melt onto the envelope. She impatiently counted the drips. Grabbing the brass stamp, she carefully sealed the envelope. The stamp set her initials in a perfect red seal. Putting away all her supplies in the writing desk, Emilie hurried downstairs.

"Mother, do you have the list I need?" She whisked past her mother in the kitchen, stopping short as her skirt caught on the bench at the table. Annoyed, she yanked at the fabric.

"Slow down, you are anxious today," her mother observed. "I am glad you got his letter done. Here's the list. Starlight should be ready, I asked your father to saddle her."

Emilie grabbed a slice of bread, smoothed some butter on it, and attempted to eat it as she ran out the door. Behind her, she heard her mother scold. "Emilie Kathryn, your manners." Emilie nodded in acknowledgment but continued on her course to the barn.

Inside the barn, she greeted Starlight, "Hey, girl, are you ready to run into town?" The horse greeted her with a snort and head-shake. Emilie searched the barn quickly for her father. She found him in the woodshop, shaving down a piece of wood for his most recent project.

"Papa, thank you for saddling Starlight. Aren't you going into work today?"

Her father shook his head. "Not today. The shop slowed production since the war started. It gives me time to work on a few projects for your mother." He attempted a smile, but she saw worry etched in his face. The deep creases in his forehead and lack of bright-eyed smile told her he was concerned about something. She regarded him knowingly. "Papa, are you worried about the boys?"

He sighed heavily. "I always worry about them. They should be back at the plantation by now, greeting your aunt and uncle. It will only take time until they find a unit."

By her father's quiet, broody mood, Emilie knew this was no time to get into a long conversation with him. She knew he wanted to be alone when he came to his workshop. She gave him a one last smile and said good-bye.

It was late June, and the sun was already promising a hot day. Emilie and Starlight headed toward town. Three things were on her list: Emilie would first stop at the post office and then it was off to see if Sallie was home. She wanted to have Sallie show her how to turn the heel of the sock she was working on. Her mother tried to show her, but Emilie just could not get the hang of it. She hoped Sallie would give her new perspective. After Sallie, there was the stop at the general store to fill her mother's list and then off to check in with Miss Carrie. Emilie looked forward to working with Carrie this semester. Emilie knew it would take her mind off missing Thaddeus. She worried about Thaddeus and her brothers constantly. The unknown was always a source of worry for her.

The town bustled as usual for a weekday morning. Emilie arrived at the post office in time to get her letter included in the outgoing mail. Popping into the post office, Emilie saw Mrs. Buehler behind the counter.

"Good day, Mrs. Buehler. Do you have any letters for me?" Emilie waited for her answer, hoping there was one for her.

The clerk shook her head. "I have a few things for you." She handed Emilie the small stack of letters. She smiled at the young girl as she thumbed through them. Suddenly her face looked dejected with disappointment.

"I still have to sort the incoming train. Come back after 1:00 p.m.. It may be there for you when you come back." Mrs. Buehler knew how she felt. She waited every day for a letter from her husband today too. "I have been receiving more soldier letters every day. The boys are very busy, my dear."

Emilie took the letters and thanked Mrs. Buehler.

"I will be back this afternoon."

Emilie attempted a smile despite her disappointment. Leaving the post office, Emilie felt as if she would burst into tears. The anticipation took her by surprise. She wasn't planning on a letter today, but it would have delightfully surprised her if it came.

Emilie stopped by Sallie's to see if she was home. Knocking on the door, she waited. Sallie called from the backyard. "We are back here." Sallie was dressed in her work clothes, hair tied back in a kerchief.

Emilie found her friend tending a large pot of wash water. "Almost done washing. I just have a few more pieces." Sallie focused on her work.

"No worries." Emilie found a chair to sit while she talked to her friend. "I just wanted to stop by to say hello. We haven't visited in a long time."

Sallie smiled at her friend. "Things have been extra busy around here since Jefferson left. Mother and I are having difficulty getting along," Sallie whispered, not wanting anyone else to hear.

Emilie sat closer to the edge of her seat to listen intently.

Emilie knew Sallie was very fond of a family friend named Thomas Snyder. Yet Emilie was still unaware of any romance between the two. Emilie hoped Sallie would disclose some information so she could disclose about her news about her and Thaddeus.

"I am sorry to hear that," Emilie said.

Sallie rolled her eyes. "Father is talking about enlisting, and Mother is none too happy about it. Either way, I am doing extra chores and learning some extras in case Father decides to enlist."

Emilie saw the exhaustion in her friend's eyes.

"How will you manage all of this and school when it starts?" Emilie was concerned.

"We will manage well enough. I am not giving up my teaching." Sallie was determined. "We are getting into a routine now, so I imagine it will all settle down by the time the next semester starts. We have no choice."

Sallie put everything into perspective for Emilie. Emilie realized she needed to stop wallowing in pity and go on with life. Emilie chastised herself for being so selfish. Her best friend was surviving with the prospect of no men in the house and had still had an attitude of adapting. Sallie's strength to persevere made Emilie realize she was not the only person suffering from loved ones going to war. None of the men went to war under duress. They chose to go with honor and dignity, each focused on completing their duty to come home as soon as possible. Emilie wanted all of them to come home. She knew the possibilities ranged from all to none completing this war. For the first time since Thaddeus left, Emilie realized she needed to refocus her energies to help the cause. The men needed hope to make it through their time in the war. Everyone had a stake in this war whether they wanted it or not.

Emilie could see she was intruding on Sallie's work and stood up to take her leave. "I can see you are very busy, so I won't keep you. I would love to get together when we have time to sit in the parlor and sew."

Sallie looked up from the steaming pot. "That would be lovely. It sounds like a luxury right now. What are you sewing now?" Sallie always took the teacher role. It came so natural to her.

"Mother and I are working on socks for the Ladies' Relief Society. I'm having difficulty turning the heel. It looks awful, and Mother is frustrated with me." Emilie shook her head.

"I don't understand." Sallie looked perplexed. "What is keeping you from getting it?"

"She is left handed, and I am right. It is backward for me."

Sallie shook her head knowingly. "I will be happy to show you."

"I will call on you another time, or better yet, please feel free to call on me. The porch is a beautiful place to sew and have lemonade. The ride out is beautiful." Emilie wished her friend would come out for a visit. Looking at her pocket watch, Emilie announced, "I have to get back to the post office. I look forward to seeing you soon."

Sallie waved to her friend as she left through the gate. Still thinking about all of the changes in Sallie's new life, Emilie wondered who else's life had changed so dramatically. Emilie finished gathering supplies at the store and then returned to the post office. It was bustling with patrons. Emilie squeezed through the crowd. She didn't realize the mail was so popular. Mrs. Buehler was too busy for conversation now. She just handed Emilie two letters and smiled, before attending to the next customer.

Pushing her way back out of the crowed post office, Emilie broke free from the crowd. Securely packing the letters in her saddlebag, she decided to leave the crowd behind. On her way out to see Carrie, Emilie thought about her students. She sincerely hoped each one would come back. They had made great strides before leaving on break. She wanted the opportunity to push them harder this semester.

The Sheads' home, a beautiful two-story wooden structure, stood majestically on Chambersburg Road. Riding up the drive, Emilie noticed someone in the garden. Carrie came out of the house to greet Emilie as she tied Starlight to the fence.

"Hello, Emilie." Carrie walked toward her. "I have water for Starlight over here." Carrie brought the bucket to Emilie and showed her where she could retrieve the water.

"Hello, Miss Carrie. I have come to inquire about the upcoming semester and how you've been, of course."

"Of course," Carrie echoed. "We are faring well since my brothers, father, and uncles have left for the war. The women have taken over the house. It will be a much-needed relief to get back to school."

The ladies walked over to the table and chair set under the big oak tree. Sitting down, Carrie popped up and asked, "Would you like some tea?"

"Yes, please."

Emilie's throat felt parched after her hectic morning. Carrie left Emilie sitting to enjoy the coolness of the shade while she went in for tea. Emilie surveyed the land. It was a beautiful farm with orchards, a well, and outbuildings. She tried imaging what life would be like when she and Thaddeus owned a beautiful place like this one.

"You look so dreamy. What are you thinking about?" Carrie broke into her thoughts. Emilie saw her set out the tablecloth, a plate of cookies, and tea. She set the table in minutes and sat down to inquire about her thoughts.

"Well?" Carrie waited for an answer.

"Oh, just about what life will be like when Thaddeus comes home and we begin our life together." Emilie blushed with the confession. It sounded still new and exciting to her.

"I knew it wouldn't be long until I lost another teacher," Carrie teased. "I thought it would be to public schools, not marriage."

Taken aback by her words, Emilie watch her a moment before she realized Carrie was teasing her. She shook her head in denial. "Oh no, I will be teaching well into my marriage. It has been discussed."

Carrie hesitated, not sure she heard Emilie correctly. "What? Your new husband will allow you to work after marriage?" Carrie continued to pour the tea.

The shock factor always made Emilie laugh. She could never understand why women gave up who they are as soon as a ring was put on their finger. This was a concept she never grasped and didn't want to either.

"I will be teaching with you until either you kick me out of the classroom or our first baby is born." Emilie was proud she and Thaddeus had discussed their future. She felt confident their life would be wonderful together.

"Well, I am not going to kick you out, but this semester is going to be difficult." Carrie became very serious. The tone of their conversation changed. Carrie continued, "I am not getting as many students this semester, Emilie. I can't hire you. I am sorry."

"I was hoping to come back." Emilie felt as if her world shifted again. It was uncomfortable and upsetting. "I don't want to leave the classroom."

"I will certainly miss your help." Carrie saw Emilie deflate. She felt bad for her. "With the men gone, families have to change to adjust."

"Everything is changing so fast." Emilie struggled to find an answer. "How about if I volunteer my time? I can't imagine myself not teaching."

Carrie shook her head. "It wouldn't be right to have all of your hard work, and you have nothing to show for it." Carrie admired the girl's tenacity.

"How about we barter?" Emilie's idea sprung forth.

"Barter?" Carrie couldn't wait to hear this.

"I will volunteer my services to help in the classroom for trade for music lessons—only if that works for you." Emilie was proud of her offer. She wanted a reason to practice music, and lessons would be just the thing to get her back to the piano.

Considering the offer, Carrie took a meditative sip of tea. They sat at the table pensively, each wrapped in her own thoughts. Just as Carrie began to speak, a brisk wind blew through the orchard. The tablecloth blew fluttered briskly and the cookie plate moved with the breeze. The trees rustled in the wind. Emilie noticed the clouds had moved in quickly. It looked as if a storm was threatening. Her observation was verified as Starlight whinnied by the fence. Emilie saw her horse stomping the ground. Emilie returned to Carrie, who snatched a napkin that threatened to blow off the table.

"I like your idea, Emilie," Carrie said. "I would be happy to hear you play, and I could certainly use your help in the classroom."

Emilie agreed. Both women hastily finished their tea, concerned about the sudden change in the weather. Looking to the sky, Emilie offered to help clean up the tea before leaving.

"No, it looks like this storm could come up fast." Carrie noticed the sky fill with thick, gray clouds. "Would you like to wait this one out inside?"

"No, I need to get home."

Emilie heard Starlight call for her. "Thank you, Miss Carrie, I look forward to working with you again."

"Be careful going home. I will see you in class in two weeks." Carrie gathered all of the supplies in her arms. "Here, give this to Starlight." Carrie gave Emilie a sugar cookie for the horse.

"Thank you, she will love it. See you in two weeks." Emilie rushed to gather Starlight and ride home before the clouds dumped rain on them.

Just as they reached Table Rock Road, thunder clapped in the distance. The lightning followed close behind. This was going to be a great summer storm. Emilie pushed Starlight harder; she didn't cherish arriving home soaked to the skin.

Starlight picked up the pace as lightning lit up the sky and thunder announced the storm had arrived. The wind fiercely blew by the time they reached the driveway. The wind was warm; the rain fell in large drops. Emilie was thankful the barn was in sight. Dismounting in the yard, Emilie led Starlight into the barn. As she put away Starlight's riding equipment, Emilie finally looked at the letters Mrs. Buehler gave her that afternoon: one from Aunt Jeanie and the second, perfectly scripted, had Emilie's name on it. She recognized Thaddeus's handwriting. Stuffing the letters into her pocket, she ran to the barn door. As she looked out, she saw another flash of lightning, followed by a clap of thunder, and the hail came pouring down. Surprised to see the tiny hailstones rain from the sky, Emilie decided to run to the house. In her hand, she held a piece of him. She could not wait one moment longer to be close to him. The hail pelted her bare skin, stinging everywhere it hit. She couldn't move fast enough. Throwing the door open, she held tight to the screen door as the wind threatened to pull it out of her hands. Slamming the inside door, she finally shut out the angry storm.

"Emilie!" Julia scolded her daughter. Dress soaked and dripping on the floor, Emilie was a sight to see.

"It is brutal out there. I have letters and your supplies." She set everything on the table and waved the letter at her mother. "He wrote." She beamed with excitement.

"Go change before you catch the death of cold." Julia picked up the other letters, reading each one.

Emilie pulled off her wet shoes. She brought them to the stove and set them under it to dry.

"You missed one." Julia turned with another letter in her hand.

"He wrote me two?" Emilie was surprised.

"I don't know who it's from. It's hard to read." Julia looked at her daughter.

Too excited about the letter in her hand, Emilie took the letter from her mother as she opened Thaddeus's letter to read as she walked slowly up to her room. Her heart raced with excitement. The opening line filled her with love: "My darling girl." Emilie narrowly avoided the candle sconce on the wall. She carefully put the letter on her bed. It lay there with its fragile pages open for her to read. Emilie went to the bureau to retrieve a dry dress. Trying to read his words as she wiggled out of the wet gown, this was a challenge she soon abandoned. Finally donning a dry gown and underpinnings, Emilie settled in to read his words and to be as close to him as she could. His words made her smile and her heart longed for his voice and his touch. The opposing emotions tortured her with sadness and joy.

Dear diary,

I realized today that I am not the only one missing loved ones who went to war. I am reluctant to say I am more fortunate than most, only because I don't know how to measure the emptiness I feel inside. I miss my brothers. I miss my future husband. Today I realized there are more people missing fathers, brothers, and uncles. Women in Gettysburg are running their lives and homes without their men. I admire their bravery, but most important I learned today that I must change my ways because I have my father here. Mother and I are not alone like the Meyers or the Sheads.

Today I vow to be supportive. The only way I can ensure the comfort of my loved ones is to send letters and gifts from home. These acts will bring them home safe and sound.

Thaddeus's letter made me smile as always. I will have to write him tomorrow.

Bursting with excitement,
E.K.P.

HOME TO RICHMOND

All change is not growth, as all movement is not forward

—Ellen Glagow

❧

LATE JUNE–EARLY JULY 1861

The heat in late June was oppressive in Virginia. The three men were excited to see the main house of the Prescott Plantation come into view. The boys made plans to meet up with the Virginia cavalry unit back in Richmond in two weeks. The last leg of their ride was hard. Henry welcomed the shade of the trees that lined the driveway of the home. He remembered the trees were always taller than he, but now he was glad of it. It provided cool and shade from the sun. He looked over at Aaron and back at Seth. Both seemed pleased as he was to see home.

A tall black man at the front of the house greeted them. Henry asked his name. The man spoke in a small voice, replying he would water and stable the men's horses.

The boys dismounted and walked up the steps. Henry turned around, missing Seth for the first time since they left Gettysburg. He remembered Seth was now home, which also meant that once they were on this property, he was no longer Henry's or Aaron's equal. Seth disappeared to the stable with his horse in tow. Henry felt saddened by this realization.

Aunt Jeannie swept into the foyer to greet her nephews. She was a small woman, tiny in frame but big in personality. Her light-brown hair and dark-brown eyes spoke of a good and gentle woman. Once she spoke, it was easy to see she liked to laugh, and she enjoyed life.

"Welcome back! Henry, what are you doing here?" Jeannie was surprised to see her nephew. She set down the small embroidery hoop on the table and hugged her nephews.

"Are you hungry? I can send for Maggie to fetch you something." Jeannie reached for the bell.

"Maggie? Where's Martha?" Aaron was surprised at the change in house staff. He had never met the stableman outside or Maggie. Things had changed. He was suspicious.

Jeannie, surprised by the question, attempted to cover her reaction. She cleared her throat and said, "She has been ill. Dr. Hudson is tending to her. We are told she has a touch of rheumatism but will recover soon." She did not make eye contact with either Henry or Aaron. "Come, let me get you some cool, sweet tea." She escorted the boys into the parlor. "We still have your room upstairs. Why don't you stay the evening."

That evening, the dining room table was formally set. Servants at their disposal, Aaron and Henry felt uncomfortable with this formality. The atmosphere of the house changed from what they knew when they lived here. Their Aunt and Uncle enjoyed the spoils of slave labor and wealth their parents willingly gave up. William sat with his nephews to discuss the latest news. Everyone enjoyed a hearty meal of fried chicken, biscuits, and greens. William spoke in generalities about the plantation.

"So, Uncle, how is the new crop?"

Aaron tried to get more details.

"Growing well, it is green and fragrant. Provided we have continued good weather, it should be profitable indeed." William took another puff of his cigar. "You know, boys, this is not your father's plantation anymore. I run it as I please." His eyes bore into the young men.

Henry shifted uncomfortably, sensing the stress that hung in the room. Aaron nodded his head. "We appreciate your hospitality, Uncle. Henry and I have to be going to Richmond tomorrow.

We will be connecting with the Third Virginia Cavalry once we get there." Aaron took a sip of brandy.

"What made you come back? Your family is clearly living in the North." William was curious about the boys' return.

"We were born and raised in the South, Uncle. We believe in the rights of the states and we believe this government is violating the Constitution as it was written; for that, we cannot tolerate such behaviors. We will fight with our countrymen to preserve these rights," Henry spoke clearly.

"How many slaves are here, Uncle?" Aaron asked.

"Between the house and the plantations, we have 240 bodies in the fields and grounds. That leaves 10 house hands. We have doubled the land we are farming. The profits will be the best in the plantation's history. Next year we are going to plow the last twenty acres to plant a different crop out there."

"Sounds like you are running a fine place, Uncle." Henry tried to sound positive. He knew his father would be sorely disappointed. There was nothing he could do.

"Will you need to add another set of slaves with the extra acreage?" Aaron had a good business mind. It was plain he was calculating figures in his head, trying to imagine how his uncle was managing everything.

"We have time to wait. The auctions are still regularly held every month." The tension was easing in the room. The men were getting comfortable with one another. No one felt threatened. Both Henry and Aaron realized this was no longer their father's place, and they had to accept the changes.

"I hope it is profitable for you. Thank you for allowing us to stay this evening. We are leaving tomorrow to meet up the Calvary. We have to get onto Ashland as soon as possible." Aaron assured his uncle. William poured another round of brandy, and the men drank to health and protection.

Seth walked out to the cabin he shared with his parents. The dirt floor, small and dirty windows, and primitive furniture were a drastic change from the Prescott stable room he had in Pennsylvania. Inside the home, his mother, Martha, was cooking at the hearth. He crept into the home, set down his things, and stood behind her.

"You ought to be greetin' your momma instead of creeping around like a rat boy." Martha did not look at her son. She continued stirring the stew. Seth put his arms around her waist, hugging her close. She was familiar and comforting.

"I will never be too old to hug you, Momma. It is good to be home." Seth buried his face in her back. His mother always made him feel safe. Turning to hug her son, Martha looked at him through her good eye. He saw her left eye was black and blue and mouth still swollen and cut. Seth stepped back, shocked at the sight. The joy of this reunion washed away from him instantly.

"What happened?" He could not say any more.

Whatever it was, Seth suddenly lost the comfortable feelings of being home again.

"You shoulda stayed with Mr. Jacob and Missus Julia. Things changed round here, son." The creases in her forehead worn deep into her face verified her statement.

Seth retrieved his bag. "I got it, Momma. We leave tomorrow. There is a community of free blacks up in Pennsylvania. We can go there. We will be near Mr. Jacob. He will help us." Shuffling through his bag, he took out the writing paper, pencil, and finally a copy of the manumission papers given to him by Jacob.

"See, we have papers." Seth pushed them toward her. His proof would certainly spare them.

Martha dropped the papers like a hot cinder. "Put that away, boy. Don't show them to anyone. They say theys a fake, and we'll be whipped." Martha shoved the papers back into the knapsack. "Go bury em hind the house. Don't tell anyone!"

"What are you talking about?" Seth could not understand how things could change so fast in just four weeks. He carefully smoothed out the creases in the papers and tucked them safely into the knapsack. Seth sat down at the table to listen to what had changed while he was gone.

Martha poured coffee for her and her son. She began to explain the changes occurring at the Prescott Plantation. Production in the fields kept Big Jim working from sunup to sundown. He works under a harsh overseer who believes Big Jim is soft and does not drive the workers hard enough. It seems William sides more with the new overseer than he does with Big Jim. In an argument, William threatened to tear up the freedom papers and sell the family in the next auction.

Mrs. Prescott assigned Martha to teach Maggie the cooking role in the home. Maggie was a feisty girl who wanted favor with Mrs. Prescott. She refused to listen to Martha and told Mrs. Prescott Martha was stealing. When Mrs. Prescott confronted Martha, Maggie elaborated the lie. When words were exchanged, Mrs. Prescott slapped Martha. At the time of the altercation, the overseer intervened and took Martha outside. Without a word, he punished her with a black eye and cut lip for talking back. "I think theys tryin to get rid of us, Seth. The new owners wants new staff, and they ain't gonna honor those papers." Martha felt deeply saddened by the prospect of leaving the plantation. The family had been here since Martha was seventeen years old. She married Big Jim here. Seth was born on this land. The Prescott Plantation was home for this family.

"We have to go." Seth was determined not to let this happen to his family. "We will move. I have the papers."

"Member your place, boy! You been livin wit dem whites too long," Martha scolded her son. She worried his ideas would get him killed. It would be best for everyone to know their place.

"Momma, Gettysburg gots a big community of free blacks. They has farms and jobs. No one owns them there," Seth pleaded with his mother. "Let's go please."

Martha shook her head. Seth had never seen his mother look so defeated. She had always been a proud woman; today she looked broken and frail. Seth became angry. He got up from the table and went into his room.

That night, the family ate without Big Jim. He was made to work as long as there was still light in the sky. The late summer's light finally faded, and only then were the men released from the fields. Big Jim was tired and sore; his body ached from the demands of his job. Happy to see his wife after a long, grueling day, Big Jim was glad to open the cabin door. Her smile breathed life into him; her touch gave him comfort. He treasured their love, and he still dreamed of the day that they would farm their own land.

Tonight, he was surprised to see his son and wife waiting for him. Big Jim felt the extra joy of seeing his son, Seth writing at the kitchen table. Seth hunched over the table, the lamp pulled close, lighting a piece of paper on the table. Seth focused carefully, putting pencil to paper.

Seeing her husband, Martha went over to the hearth and retrieved a bowl of stew. She set the table with a small meal in minutes. Pouring water into a basin, Jim washed off the dirt from his face and hands. Martha fetched him a clean shirt and towel. The family existed in silence. Once Jim sat at the table, he spoke to his son.

"You get that piano safe to Miss Emilie?"

His voice was deep but gentle.

Seth looked up from his page. "Yes, Pa. She hugged me like I delivered it myself."

Jim smiled; he loved Emilie's enthusiasm. She was a good girl who had the spirit of a bird, always free to soar. He remembered the day she was born. Jacob was as proud as a papa could be. He missed the family dearly.

"Practicing writing? Miss Emilie be teaching you again?"

Jim tried to read his son's writing. He knew it was futile; he can't read. Jim was thankful for Emilie taking time teaching his son to write and read.

"No, I'm writing to tell her I's home again. I don't want her worryin." Seth went back to his writing.

"He will tell her our troubles. That boy is going to get us killed." Martha never looked up from her knitting.

Jim noticed the tension in the room. "Seth, what are you writing?"

Seth put down his pencil in frustration. "I am writing her we's home. She made me promise." Seth was persistent.

"Things changed here, son. You be ready at sunup. Work won't wait. You come to the fields with me tomorrow. Glad yous home here. I will not have a repeat of what happened to your mother." Jim looked at his son. He could see Seth had changed. "These Prescotts are not our friends. Do as yous told and we be fine."

"We don't have to do this. I have the paper to set us free." Seth showed Jim the papers. He read the script and waited for his father to answer.

"This aint the place you left. I beg you, son, do as you be told." Jim needed time to speak to Martha. "Go to bed, son."

Seth signed the letter, closed it in the envelope, and went to bed. "I got to saddle the horses in the morning. I got to say good-bye." Seth watched his father.

Jim only nodded. "Get to them fields and don't delay."

"Thank you!" Seth kissed his mother and hugged his father good night. He went to bed with mixed feelings.

Early morning came quickly. Seth put the finishing touches on his letter to Emilie. He would give it to Henry to mail, and the family would be off this plantation in a month. Seth was sure Mr. Jacob would help them. They were good friends.

Horses saddled, Seth waited for the boys to emerge from the house. The boys came out of the house with William and Jennie close behind. They exchanged good-byes as Seth took the boys' saddlebags and secured them to the horses. Seth handed Henry Emilie's letter.

"I wrote to Miss Emilie, saying we're home. Will you mail it for me, please?" Seth handed the letter to Henry. Before the letter passed to Henry, William intercepted it.

"I will be happy to mail it for you, Seth." William glared at Seth. "I didn't know you could write."

Seth said nothing except to step back with a nod. Henry intercepted. "Uncle, I will be happy to mail the letter. It will travel faster mailed from Richmond."

William tucked the letter into his pocket. "No need, son, I will take care of it."

Aaron nudged Henry. "Time to go, we have a small window to catch the Third before they leave the area."

Good-byes were exchanged, and the boys rode down the drive. Seth turned to leave for the fields. William called after him. "Boy!" His voice was harsh and hard.

Seth turned to look as William tore the letter up and dropped its pieces to blow away in the wind. "Know your place, or it will be written in your hide. Get to the field."

"Yes, sir." Seth watched the papers and his hope blown away in the wind. He now understood how his parents felt. For the first time in a long time, he was reminded he was a black slave on a big plantation.

THE WAITING GAME

Such is the state of life, that none are happy but by the anticipation of change: the change itself is nothing; when we have made it, the next wish is to change again.

—Samuel Johnson

JULY 1861

Drill, drill, drill. Thaddeus and Stephen fought the heat and continuous days of drilling. In the coolness of the night air, the men busied themselves writing letters and talking by the fire, too exhausted by the work of the day. Camp life was becoming all too familiar for the farm boys of Adams County. Music from the military band played in the background. The band practiced by serenading them almost every night with a concert to keep moral high.

Stephen and Thaddeus sat around the fire. Thaddeus poking at the fire with a long stick, watching the embers glow as sparks released into the air. "Do you think we will ever leave this camp?" Stephen looked for a stick to whittle with his knife.

"I am sure they won't keep us here forever." Thaddeus was tired and missing Emilie. He wrote to her days ago, and still there was no return letter. He was sure she didn't forget him. Maybe she didn't have time to write with the new term starting soon. He found himself looking at her picture often. He didn't want to forget her eyes and that smile that lit his heart into happiness.

"Oh no, not again," Stephen's voice broke his daydream. Thaddeus looked at his friend. "I knew it. You gotta keep your mind on the battle. Don't let her distract you."

Thaddeus broke his stick, throwing half into the fire. "What are you talking about?"

Stephen continued to concentrate on his stick. "You are thinking about her. I can see it on your face. What is that going to do for you in battle?"

"I am not in battle right now. I do miss her, and I'll think about her." Thaddeus was annoyed. He knew Stephen was trying to distract him, but he was annoying him. The only thing that could get him out of his mood was to read a letter from her.

Stephen went back to his stick. The silence dragged on. Just as Stephen was about to break into another conversation, Lieutenant Bailey walked up and called to them.

"Marsh, Byrne. The captain wants you to report to his tent." The lieutenant gave the order and passed by, looking for others in the camp.

Surprised to see the lieutenant, Thaddeus and Stephen stood up quickly, saluting the officer. It was unusual to see such a rank wandering about camp. Thaddeus added another small log to the fire; Stephen pushed his stick into the ground and put away his knife. Both men got up and walked toward the captain's tent. The men knew there was little time to linger. The captain was most likely watching to see how fast the men reported to him. They wasted no time in responding to the order.

On the way, they passed other campfires with men quietly cleaning their muskets or washing out their laundry. The night was full on, so everyone was back from bathing in the river for the evening. Card games and games of chance being played here and there, the men did not have free access to alcohol; most were quietly enjoying the time away from drilling.

"The captain is waiting for us." Stephen noticed him outside his tent, scanning the camp for his subordinates.

Thaddeus saluted the captain.

"Marsh and Byrne reporting, sir."

Slowly smoking his cigar, pondering other thoughts, Captain McPherson asked them to wait by the fire. It seems they were expecting more men to show up. The small group of twenty men gathered quietly. Captain McPherson spoke quietly to the group.

"We have a deserter from the other company here at camp." His tone was serious, his eyes troubled. "I have watched each of your performances, and I am impressed how you men drill. I am trusting that you will find this man and bring him back. I hope none of you have any qualms about shooting him if he resists. Can I count on you?"

"Yes, Captain." The unison response was clear. The captain dismissed them to go gather their weapons and accoutrements to set out for the search.

The search party spread out through the woods. Each man secretly hoped to be the one to find the deserter. Stephen and Thaddeus waited, listening in the woods. The others spread throughout the area. Some cavalry on horseback circled through the area.

The night wore on as the group searched. They moved, stopped, and listened. Standing in a copse of pines, listening for any sign of movement, Stephen felt a twig on his left shoulder. He told himself it was only squirrel, willing himself not to react too soon; he gently nudged Thaddeus. The dark of night surrounded them, but they could make out each other's outline. Stephen saw Thaddeus shake his head.

Thaddeus shifted his musket quietly to the other hand and carefully reached to his shoulder to lift a twig to show Stephen he felt it too. Returning the musket to his shooting hand, the men turned to look up into the tree. The form was black in the dark night. The light of the moon showed it was a man and not an animal.

"Soldier, is that you?" Thaddeus spoke in a forced whisper.

"Hell yeah, it's me. Go away, I'm not going back." The man's voice showed his fear. It shook and cracked as he spoke. "My feet are sore, my back aches, I can't stand another moment in Mr. Lincoln's army."

"What's your name, man?" Thaddeus was keeping focus on him. He didn't know if he had a musket pointed at him or not. The shadows of the trees were too dark. It blocked out everything except the man's form and branches of the trees.

Stephen broke in, impatient with this man. "You signed up for this, man. You have to go back or get shot."

"You might as well shoot me then. I ain't goin'." The man shifted on his tree branch, cursing as the branch threatened to give way. Thaddeus and Stephen shifted their weight, muskets pointed at the man.

"You can't stay up there all night. Did you see the surgeon?" Thaddeus was good at reasoning with people. "If the surgeon thinks you can't do it, you may be able to go home. Do it with dignity, man. Don't make us shoot you."

"I could go home if the surgeon says?" This seemed like a new concept to the man. "I can hardly move. My joints ache. I feel so old."

Their talking attracted others to the site. Stephen hushed them as Thaddeus continued talking. The soldier was beginning to see reason. He asked more questions. He shifted uncomfortably on the narrow branch.

"That is no place for you. If you fall and break your back, you'll go home an invalid. Come down, we are attracting attention." Thaddeus's tone was more urgent now.

"All right!" Impatient, he moved to leave his branch when the flash of musket fire rang out into the darkness. The lifeless body fell at Stephen's and Thaddeus's feet. Thaddeus looked up to see a cavalry officer glaring at them.

"Get that body back to camp. We have to get to bed." Callously, he turned his horse and rode away, gathering his troops to move back to camp.

Anger seethed through Thaddeus. He couldn't understand the senseless act. "What the hell was that?' He was pointing at the body. "He was getting out of the tree. We had him ready to go back to camp. Now he goes home in a box."

Sergeant Stewart appeared out of the darkness. "He was not following orders. We don't ask questions. We take care of business. Can't run an army with morons like that."

"With all due respect, sir, he was hurting. He needed medical attention." Thaddeus pleaded his case for the dead man.

"He should have reported to the surgeon instead of hiding in a tree." The answer was simple and unarguable. Thaddeus watched as they removed the body. He had nothing else to say; it was done.

They walk back to camp was shrouded in silence. Thaddeus felt Stephen beside him, walking in step with him. He knew his friend silently supported him. The whole incident left Thaddeus feeling empty. He longed to hold Emilie, hear her laugh and joke with him. She always made a bad situation better. He longed for his home, his brother, and his parents with the security.

"You had him convinced," Stephen spoke gently. "He would have gone back with you."

"He's going back all right." Thaddeus felt dejected knowing he had to shake these feelings. He knew this was not the first dead man he would see before this was all over.

The next day was business as usual: roll call, breakfast, and drilling. The afternoon brought relief. The heat finally broke by a downpour of rain and lightning. All of the men reported to their tents.

As the sun came out, the last cold wind blew through the camp. The troops assembled, and it was a welcome sight to see the mailbag waiting for them. Everyone stood waiting for word from home. Thaddeus knew there was a letter for him. He dreamed about her last night. He saw himself reading her letters.

Finally, Thaddeus heard his name. He received two letters. One he recognized was from his mother. On the second letter, he saw her delicate handwriting. Smiling from ear to ear, he knew she must have timed this letter perfectly to arrive when he needed it the most. As he was getting ready to leave, he heard his name again. There was a small box waiting for him.

Thaddeus opened the letters. His mother wrote about how the farm was running. She spoke of gossip about the neighbors. Father and Ian were both well. His mother sent the box full of extra socks and sweets, lemon drops and oatmeal cookies. Knowing these treasures were more valuable than gold, he stowed the package under his arm and went to find a quiet place to be with Emilie.

Her letter had a faint scent of lavender. He remembered how the smell permeated delicately through her hair. He loved being that close to her. Emilie wrote the following:

> My darling,
>
> It is so quiet here without you. I miss everything about you. Our rides and our long talks on the porch, these are some of my favorite memories. The weather has been so agreeable. I can imagine us spending long nights out there planning our future. I think of you when I am not thinking of anything else.
>
> I have been keeping busy with the Ladies' Relief Society, making socks and knitting scarves. I finally understand how to turn the heel on the socks. I have knitted about twelve pairs. I hope you get one I made. I sew so much love into every pair. I imagine each one is for you. I hope you get a chance to come home for Christmas. On our first Christmas together, we didn't even know each other. It would be a blessing to spend some time with you.
>
> I haven't heard if I will be teaching this term. I'm going to pay Miss Carrie a visit after I drop off your letter. From your first letter, it sounds like you and Stephen are getting on very well in camp. Is Stephen receiving letters from home? If not, may I write him a few? I want your blessing to do so. I can't imagine not getting a letter from home. I love reading your letters. I need to know you are healthy and safe. Do you know when you will be leaving camp?

Work hard and stay safe. Know you are in my dreams nightly, and most of all, I *love* you with all of my heart.

Yours,
Emilie

Thaddeus reread the letter before he tucked it into his haversack. He wanted to keep her most current letter with him. The bugle call announced it was dinnertime. Thaddeus searched the camp area for Stephen, before going to the get his evening meal. He would write her letter later that evening. He found Stephen bargaining with a fellow soldier. He traded molasses cookies for horehound candies. Mail day was also known as bargaining day as men enjoyed goodies and news from home.

❧

Making good time, Henry and Aaron found themselves in Richmond as the sun was setting. The boys found the company was not at the meeting place as specified. They arrived a day early. Aaron and Henry found a quiet place to camp outside town. They had dinner that evening in the small tavern before setting up a camp for the night.

Freeing his horse of her saddle and bags, Henry tethered the horse to a tree. Gathering his bedroll and haversack, he went to sit beside Aaron. "It feels good to be on our own for a while. This is the calm before the storm." He reached into his sack for his knife. Feeling around trying to locate the knife, he pulled out a piece of paper. "Oh good, I didn't lose my orders."

Aaron scowled. "That is not the orders. It looks like a letter. When did you write that?"

"I didn't." Henry investigated the writing. "It's for Emilie." He turned the letter over to see if it was sealed. The paper was carefully tucked into itself, but no seal. Henry looked at Aaron.

Aaron took the letter from his brother. He looked it over. "It's from Seth. He slipped the letter into your haversack." He smiled as he figured out the whole scene at the plantation that day. "He is one smart boy."

"What letter did Uncle William take from him?" Henry was thinking it through. "Who did he write that one to?"

"He knew William wouldn't allow communication to our family. He was not too happy about all the changes Father would never allow." Aaron broke down his thought. "I wouldn't be surprised if Seth had two letters, one to slip in and the second if he got caught. I wonder what is says."

"It is addressed to Emilie. She would kill us if we read her letters." Henry knew how temperamental she was about her privacy. He leaned forward in anticipation to see if Aaron would open the letter.

"No, I am not opening it." Aaron gave the letter back to Henry. "We can't do anything about whatever he tells her. Tomorrow we will be in the Confederate cavalry. We better get a good-night's sleep."

At sunup, they packed up the camp and rode back into town to mail the letter. On their way back to the meeting place, they met up with a wagon, and a band of cavalry arrived to recruit more men.

Crowds of new recruits swarmed the small community building. Aaron and Henry finally got to the front of the line. Showing the officer their enlistment papers from the tavern, the boys moved to the next station. By the end of the day, they signed up and were sworn into the Confederate cavalry. The next day, they started the ride to Camp Ashland to begin training.

The next few weeks filled with drilling, marching, and tactical maneuvers on horseback. Aaron and Henry stayed together. Henry took to their new adventure with great enthusiasm. Aaron was impressed with how his younger brother showed discipline and determination. He was proud at how quickly he learned to load and shoot while keeping Penelope calm and focused. Aaron remembered how he handled Starlight, rough and careless. It took two weeks for him to handle Penelope expertly. Henry developed into a strong soldier.

Aaron's natural leadership skill transferred well. He adapted quickly to a soldier's life. He caught the eye of his superior officers. Aaron worked his way into learning tactical maneuvers by making acquaintances with other enlisted officers. By the end of eight weeks, Aaron accepted the first of many promotions to come.

One night after the camp settled into a quiet calm, Aaron sat by the fire watching it glow. Henry sat beside him. "I miss home," Henry said it so quietly, Aaron hardly heard him.

"We should write. It will give Mother some peace of mind." Aaron spoke without looking at him.

Henry shook his head. "Yes, Mother is probably worried, and she doesn't even know where we are." Without another thought, Henry went to retrieve the paper and pencils. Thinking about how much has changed in the last few weeks Henry had plenty to write. He penned his first letter to Mother and Father, and then he wrote a letter to Emilie. He smiled as he wrote to her. He playfully wrote telling her about his world, teasing her about all the chores she had to do now he was gone. Henry sealed the letters, feeling closer to his family. He was now ready to handle whatever tomorrow would bring.

LETTERS HOME

Letter writing is the only device for combining solitude with good company.

—Lord Byron

❦

JULY–AUGUST 1861

On laundry day, Emilie woke up early; she wanted to finish the majority of the chore before the morning sun became too hot. Lugging the heavy basket toward the clothesline, Emilie clipped the clothespins to her apron. As she struggled to flip the sheets over the line, a wind picked up and blew it back over her head. Emilie grumbled with frustration. Fighting to get out from under the sheet, she felt the wet sheet lift from her head.

"Do you need a ride into town today?" her father asked as he helped secure the sheet over the line. "I am going into work today."

"How long will you be in town?" Emilie asked as she quickly pinned the blowing sheet to the line. "I have school this morning and a post office stop after that."

"I will be finished by three," he said as he pulled another sheet from the basket.

"I have to finish the last batch of laundry. When are you leaving?" Emilie thought she would love a ride into town. She looked over to see Starlight happily munching on hay left for her in the pasture. Emilie didn't feel like getting her ready today.

"Your mother said she'll finish. I am sure she will save the ironing for you. Can you be ready in fifteen minutes?" He pulled a clothespin from her apron to secure the last sheet to the line.

"I just need to change. Meet you in the yard? Thanks for helping." Emilie smiled. She could tell she missed Henry. They once enjoyed hours in the workshop together. She didn't know exactly what they did out there, but she figured it was talking and wood-working, something they both enjoyed.

Emilie prepared to go into work.

Shuffling through her dresses, she decided on a white calico print. She hurried; her father hated to be late.

Downstairs, she met her mother at the door. List in hand, Emilie took the list, grabbed her basket, and hurried to the carriage waiting in the yard. Climbing into the seat, Emilie fussed about securing her basket and finally looked at her father. Watching her, he couldn't help but chuckle.

"What? Did I miss something?"

Confused, she looked at him.

"You're a whirlwind," he said. "A flurry of activity."

"I don't want to be late," she said. "You hate being late."

"We're fine." He signaled the horses, and the carriage was off to town.

Emilie could not stop thinking about the letters waiting for her at the post office. She looked forward to letters from Thaddeus. She didn't yet get one from Stephen, but she didn't really mind. She wrote to him because she wanted to make sure he received messages from home. Today, she sincerely hoped to hear from her brothers. They hadn't written since they left over a month ago.

The class was small today. Emilie spent some time tutoring Annie. Carrie was concerned as the child always wrote her letters backward. Emilie showed her how to draw loops and where to start and stop the letters. The afternoon finished before they wrote half of the alphabet. Annie presented Emilie with her work, tears in her eyes. She was clearly disappointed in her work. Emilie assured her that she would not scold her if she tried.

The class had a spelling bee contest during the last hour before school finished for the day. As the words became more difficult to spell, the younger children became antsy, wiggling in their seats. Mary Adams won the spelling bee by spelling *adequate*. Carrie rewarded the class with early release.

"I think Annie understands the letters we reviewed today," Emilie said to Carrie as she finished wiping off the chalkboard.

"She doesn't take her time. I don't know where the fire is. All that girl needs to do is to slow down." Carrie shook her head, obviously frustrated.

"I don't think she remembers where to start the letters." Emilie thought about her student. "She doesn't seem to remember. I don't know if she is afraid to make mistakes or if she can't remember. Did you hear her read?"

"Not lately."

Carrie was interested in what Emilie discovered.

"Annie is not reading the words. She's adding and deleting words." Emilie put down the eraser cloth. "I wonder if it's more than just being in a hurry."

"I don't know. I appreciate you working with her." Carrie closed up her books.

"I'll keep on her until she gets it right." Emilie was determined to see Annie succeed. "I am off to the post office. Are you going into town?"

"I have to go too. May I walk with you?" Carrie and Emilie left to walk to the post office. The trees that lined the street provided good shade as they walked. Summer was half over. They walked along, discussing how they missed the men that left for the war. Emilie told Carrie about how she enjoyed making scarves and shirts for the troops.

Carrie stopped to buy a newspaper. Carrie paged through the paper. Stopping on the second page, she read intently. She frowned. Emilie watched her carefully, wondering what she was reading.

"Good news or bad?" Emilie finally asked.

"Not good. Looks like our boys have lost a battle." Carrie continued reading. "There were many injured and killed. The Union retreated to Washington."

Carrie showed her the newspaper print. It read "Battle of Bull Run." The scrolling words filled the page, detailing military movements, list of dead and wounded. Emilie scanned the page for any word that would connect the troops to Thaddeus and Stephen. The last she heard, the boys were still at Camp Wayne. Giving the paper back to Carrie, Emilie suddenly remembered Aaron and Henry.

"Wait." Emilie reached for the paper again. Carrie gave it back to her.

"Did you see something?" Carrie was surprised at her reaction.

"No." Emilie changed her mind. "Oh, I'll buy one. I don't want to trouble you." Emilie reached into her pocket and pulled out the money for her own paper.

"We better get to the post office before Mrs. Buehler goes home for the evening." Emilie folded the paper and put it under her arm; they travelled on to the post office.

Mrs. Buehler pleasantly greeted the ladies. "I have some letters for you, Miss Emilie. I hope it is good news." Emilie took the letters from her.

"Thank you." Emilie counted the letters: two for her parents and two addressed to her. Emilie recognized his handwriting. Thaddeus sent her a letter. She didn't recognize the handwriting of the second letter addressed to her. The writing was elementary and simple. It lacked the style of an adult's hand. Confused, Emilie opened the letter.

"Miss Emilie, will you please read your letters outside," Mrs. Buehler said. "I have many customers."

Suddenly remembering she was standing in line, Emilie excused herself, thanked the postmistress again, and went outside to read her letters on the bench.

She carefully tucked Thaddeus's letter under her skirt and pulled out the letter she had just opened.

Dear Emlee,

I am home. You brothrs leave tomorrow for the horse army. Big change here. Pa works all day and nit. Ther bad overseer, he hit Ma, she look awfl. I am very worrit. We cant leave and more blacks here than ever befour.

I heard some ar going to auctin next month. We all in line four it. Pa says we can't show the papers Mr. Jacob gave me no one will believe it. I hope we is not going.

Thank you for havin me at you home. Happy seeing you again. I hope to see you soon.

Seth

Emilie reread the letter, trying to understand exactly what Seth was telling her. *Could Uncle William sell them at auction if he wanted to?* The emotions washed over her mixed with anger and betrayal. The disrespect was so blatant; Emilie seethed with anger. She carefully put the letter in her bag and then looked at Thaddeus's letter. She was excited to read what he was doing next.

My darling Emilie,

It feels good to be with you again. I miss you and our rides up to the Round Top. I miss your smile and the thrill of your kisses. I want to talk with you and laugh with you again. I am doing well. Stephen and I are now accustomed to camp life. If we are not drilling, we are sleeping. No one knows when we will leave Camp Wayne. Our troop numbers are full, so now all we do is wait for the call from President Lincoln.

Please tell me how you are doing. I long to hear from you. Your last letter was wonderful to read. I had a hard day the day I received it. Your words felt like a breath of fresh air. I smiled for the first time that day. Tell me how good old Gettysburg is faring. Are the crops growing well? From what I see around here, it will be a good summer for growing. Did you get back to the classroom this term? I would love to hear about your students. Tell me everything you can. I miss home, and I miss you more.

I received some goodies from my mother a few weeks ago: new socks, candies, and cookies. They were very popular here. I had to hide them not only from my friends but also from the animals that frequent our tent when we are in the field. If you have time to bake, I could sure use some of your molasses cookies. I love the way you make them. I am doing well with the rest of my supplies. My boots are holding up well, and I have as much as I can carry of everything else.

Time is short. The bugle just sounded for assembly. I will write as soon as I know where and when we are leaving good ole Camp Wayne. I hope it is soon. Until then, take care of yourself. Whenever you need a hug from me, close your eyes and think about me. If my spirit could travel while I am still living, I would be right there to give you what you need. Know I am thinking of you often and I love you!

Always with you,
Thaddeus

Emilie held on to the letter, thinking about being with him. Her daydream was interrupted by her father's voice.

"Good news?" She heard him say.

Emilie looked up and nodded.

"Very good news from Thaddeus."

She frowned thinking about Seth's letter.

"How come it doesn't look like good news?" he questioned; the frown on her face told him she was not happy about something,

Changing the subject, she asked, "What was the agreement between you and Uncle William?"

"It was a standard property transaction. Why do you ask?" The question caught him off guard.

Emilie reached into her bag and retrieved Seth's letter. "I will let you read for yourself." She handed him the letter. "From what I understand, things don't look good for Seth and his family."

Jacob saw the serious look on his daughter's face. She had no glint of happiness, the sparkle in her eyes gone, her forehead wrinkled, eyebrows furrowed. "Let me read it when we get home." It was the only answer he could give her now.

Satisfied, Emilie broke into what her day had entailed. She brought up the newspaper article. "They called it Bull Run, and the North had to retreat. What do you think Henry and Aaron are doing?" Emilie finally paused for a breath. She had been chatting nonstop since they started for home.

"I hope they found a good company to serve under, and they are staying out of harm's way." Jacob slowed the horses to turn into the drive. "It is my prayer every morning and every night."

Emilie helped him feed the horses before they went into the house. Inside, she could smell the results of her mother's labors. Fresh chicken and rhubarb pie—their smells decorated the house to make it a home. All of the windows open, the breezes blew in, attempting to cool the overworked kitchen. Emilie hung up her bag on the hook behind the door. Pulling the letters out of her bag, she put them on the table. She searched the house for her mother. Peering out the kitchen window, she saw her sipping tea in the arbor. She looked peaceful enjoying the late-afternoon breezes. Emilie saw her father greet her mother, kiss her gently, and sit beside her while they talked. She admired how they revered each other. Emilie noticed how her mother still glows with happiness whenever she looks at him. She noticed how her father softened whenever he talked to her. They spoke in quiet tones. The words were unclear, but their tones were filled with love and respect for each other. Emilie waited a few moments before going out to join them.

"Dinner smells wonderful," Emilie said as she greeted her mother.

"How was school today? Do you have any letters from the post office?" Julia asked.

"Oh yes. Here they are." Emilie handed her mother the letters. "I have one from Thaddeus and Seth. Here are your letters." Emilie handed Julia the small stack.

"Seth wrote to you?" Julia looked up from the letters in her hand. "We have one from the Henry and Aaron." She opened the letter with a smile. Silence fell over the group as Julia lost herself reading the news.

Emilie looked at her father. They exchanged looks of surprise and suspense. Jacob made a face at Emilie. Her giggle broke the silence. Julia looked up from her reading, both husband and daughter waiting for her to tell them what she read.

"What is the news?" Jacob asked his wife.

Julia read the letter to her family. They talked about the good fortune the boys had to enlist in what seemed to be a good company. Emilie was dumbfounded that Henry agreed to the cavalry.

"He can't ride," she insisted. "Have you seen him on Starlight?"

Jacob laughed. "He rides her like that to make you mad." His confession did not surprise Emilie; it only made her laugh. Jacob reasoned they probably wanted to stay outside the line of fire. They could do that as cavalry better than they would as infantry. Jacob explained the roles of both armies.

"What did Seth and Thaddeus have to say?" Julia remembered there were more letters. It was Emilie's turn. She gave a brief synopsis of the letters. Her concern concentrated on Seth.

"I think they need help." Her concern welled up in her voice.

"I feel like we let them down."

"They made their decision to stay. It was worked out in the sale of the land," Jacob stated.

"Did you sell them with the property?" This was the first Emilie heard about this. "Why did you sell them? I thought they were free?"

Jacob was angered at his daughter's accusations. "Wait one minute, young lady." He did not appreciate his daughter accusing him. "When we left, they were going to work at the plantation and then move. A contract is only valid when followed by all parties. I don't know what happened."

Taken aback by her father's harsh words, Emilie quietly stated, "Seth said Martha was bruised and cut. We promised them a good life."

Julia gasped. "Martha? Jacob!" Julia looked to her husband.

"Seth said there's a bad overseer. His writing is not good. I wish I had worked with him more while he was here." Emilie was frustrated she didn't have all the answers. Both women turned to Jacob, silently pleading for him to do something.

"What do you want me to do? I gave Seth the papers. They are free." Jacob felt angry for trusting William. Their views on humans in bondage were very different. Jacob did not believe in binding any human to another, no matter what color his skin. William went along with popular opinion. People of color are not equal to whites.

Timid now by her father's outburst, Emilie whispered, "They worry the papers won't be honored."

Jacob sighed. "I don't know what my brother is up to, and I am not supposed to care, but he is hurting people we care about."

"Can we sit by and do nothing?" Julia's question hung in the air as everyone contemplated all the ramifications of their actions. When most of society doesn't care about someone, it takes a stronger person to take action. The Prescott family was not like others in this society. They celebrated their lives alongside Big Jim and Martha. Jacob and Julia celebrated Jim and Martha's courtship and Seth's birth. They didn't see their color, they saw each other as people who shared the same milestones in life. Julia and Jacob watched Emilie and Seth become not only good friends but close companions. In any other culture, they were as close as brother and sister. There was no denying the families' commitment to each other. This family felt like family; no color or social constraints could keep them apart.

At the same moment, they looked at one another. Jacob knew in his heart he could not and would not wait. "I will leave for Richmond as soon as I can."

"I am going with you, Father." Emilie did not request; she stated it boldly her chin set, eyes determined. "I will tell Carrie I won't be available for a few weeks. I have to pack and write Thaddeus before I go." Emilie listed off the other things she needed to accomplish as she got up and started for the house.

Once she was out of sight, Julia looked at Jacob. "You are not letting her go with you, are you?"

"I don't think I have a choice in the matter." Jacob shook his head. "I could use her company. Do you want me to have Joe look after you while I am gone?"

"No, I am fine here. It will be quiet and very peaceful." Julia smiled at him. "I can take care of things."

"I know you can. I just want you to be safe." Jacob held her close. "I want all of us to be safe." Jacob's words echoed in his brain. He wasn't worried about Julia, but he was very concerned about what his brother was doing at the Prescott Plantation.

ALL ROADS LEAD HOME AGAIN

I had rather be on my farm than be emperor of the world.

—George Washington

❦

SEPTEMBER 1861

Warm days and frosty nights set in as Emilie and her father traveled toward Richmond. They spent time talking about his childhood, and how values and lifestyle changed from then until now. Emilie listened intently. She thought about how she would raise her and Thaddeus's children. She liked the way her parents raised her. Her mother was strict with manners and appearances. Emilie knew how to prepare a proper tea and the details about the social skills needed. Emilie's father raised her to think for herself. She developed these skills well, but she also understood that society still viewed women as second-class citizens. She didn't like it, but she understood the importance of controlling her actions in public.

"I think you and Mother raised me very well," she added.

"I am free to think as I please and learn about how others think. I don't have to sit by and keep all of these thoughts in my head like the other girls do."

"I can't imagine you keeping anything to yourself, my dear." Jacob laughed. "You're growing into a fine young woman. You recognize where your opinions matter and where they don't."

"I think women should be able to voice their opinions. We have good ones, you know," Emilie chided her father. "This could be a whole different world if people listened to women's opinions, you know."

"I am afraid to think about it," he teased back. "I don't know if women could think to make such important decisions."

"Oh, Father, that's only because we have been told to keep quiet so long. Just because we don't express our thoughts doesn't mean we don't have them." Emilie's smile faded as she became serious.

"You are the fairer sex, my dear." Jacob could see her mood begin to change. "You are meant to be taken care of, and your role is to create families and be a dutiful wife."

"You are right about that. I can't wait to become a mother and wife." She loved thinking about it.

"What about teaching?" He was surprised to hear how easily she had changed her mind. If he asked her about this issue a year ago, she would not have given the same answer. He was happy to see the change.

Her brow furrowed, and she began to wrinkle her nose. Jacob knew this meant she was thinking about something that she was hesitant or afraid to ask. He waited.

"Do you think, if needed, of course, that women could run the country?" Emilie had thought of this question many times. She was still on the fence about the answer. It felt strange to imagine women in such a position of power.

"Never underestimate a woman. People are remarkable." Jacob had seen this before. "Think of our forefathers who settled this land. They had many obstacles to overcome. If it is one thing I learned being married to your mother is that when pushed, women are just as strong as men."

"Not physically."

"No, but physical strength has no comparison to determination and resilience."

Emilie thought about their conversation in silence as they continued to travel. The trees were beginning to show color, and the cool winds spoke of the pending fall weather. Emilie enjoyed the quiet time during travel. She thought about Thaddeus and her students at school. The rocking movement of the carriage lulled her into a peaceful sleep.

Sometime later, she woke to harness jingling and men shouting. Emilie sat upright in the seat. Looking around, she saw men on horseback passing the carriage. Turning to look behind her, Emilie saw files of men, all in line marching. She struggled to see the end of their line. It went on for a long distance.

"Who is this?" Emilie asked her father.

"Looks like Union troops marching past." Jacob kept the horses in line. The horses were getting skittish with so many people suddenly upon them. "I think we will wait over here until they pass."

Emilie walked around the carriage while they waited for the army to move past them. She saw units of men pass by. Some waved, while others didn't look past what was in front of them. Growing tired of watching the parade, Emilie went to the basket to pull out some bread, cheese, and ale. They ate their lunch while they waited.

"Good lunch," Jacob said as they finished.

"Where are they going?"

Emilie referred to the army that passed.

"They are off to Washington, I would think. If we get going, we will be through the city before dark." Jacob stood up, offering a hand to his daughter to help her off the blanket.

"Thank you." Emilie stood up and gathered the remnants of their lunch, tucking it into the basket. "Why does this trip feel so long?" Emilie couldn't remember the last trip from Richmond feeling like it took years. "Why didn't we take the train?"

"I get to learn more about you this way," Jacob teased his daughter. "Besides, if we need to bring anyone back, they wouldn't get to travel in our part of the train. It wouldn't be safe for them."

"Always thinking ahead, aren't you?" Emilie smiled at her father. He truly did think of all the angles when it came to planning. He wouldn't want his family sitting in a boxcar anymore than he would want to see Seth and his family there.

Washington was busy! It was not like it was when they traveled through a year before. The city was teeming with people, soldiers and recruits. Emilie noticed a horrific smell as they rode through the downtown streets. Reaching for her handkerchief, she covered her nose. "It smells like the outhouse. How do people live here?" Emilie covered her nose and mouth to keep from breathing the stench.

"This is city life," Jacob said calmly. "I am going to stop to get a paper. I want to see if we need to change course. We don't need to run into a battle." Spotting a general store, Jacob parked the carriage, tied up the horses, and helped Emilie down.

"This won't take long, I hope." Emilie looked around. She was surrounded by so many people. Everyone was moving at their own pace, faces stern with no expression. Turning, she noticed the shop window, the beautiful display of cameos and green glassware caught her eye. "Oh my!" She stood in front of the window mesmerized.

Shaken from her wonderment by a shove from her left side, the bump was a reminder she was not the only one on the walkway. "Keep walking." The cantankerous woman glared at her through tiny spectacles. Dressed in black, the large woman looked like a black cloud. The layers of black draped over her body.

"Excuse me." Emilie struggled to walk against the crowd to slip into the door of the store. Her body pushed and shuffled through the crowd. Reaching for the doorway, she grabbed on to the door handle to anchor her body to the door. Pushing herself through the door, she entered the store.

Inside, she gravitated to the glass display. The lights on the display made the glass sparkle. Emilie could not resist; she reached in to touch a goblet. The glass was etched with deep groves forming diamond-shaped pattern. It was beautifully made; it must cost a fortune.

"Careful, miss, that glass is part of the whole set. If it is broken, you will own the whole set minus one." The storekeeper's voice was stern but kind. "May I help you find something?"

Not taking her eyes off the glass, still hypnotized by it beauty, Emilie replied, "I lost my father in here." Gingerly, she replaced the glass back to its original spot. Turning, she saw the tall, handsome shopkeeper still looking at her.

"We don't sell lost fathers." He smiled at her. His eyes were the same blue as Thaddeus's. His dark hair was wavy but kept in place with oil. His hair was shiny and slick. The resemblances to Thaddeus were close, but not close enough. Emilie caught herself looking into the man's eyes. She quickly looked away.

"He came in for a paper. Do you sell those here?" She looked past him to see if her father was there. The shelves were packed with goods of all kinds. Emilie could get lost looking in this store for hours. She loved wandering through places like this. These stores were filled with an assortment of curiosities.

"Tall gentleman, with a Southern accent? Dressed in dark-green shirt and black trousers?" He caught Emilie's attention. She confirmed his description with a headshake.

"He just left," he said pointing out the window. Emilie looked outside to see her father waiting impatiently by the carriage.

"Thank you. You found him." She carefully brushed past him to the door. The bell on the door jingled, announcing her departure.

Outside, Emilie saw her father reading the paper. She climbed into the carriage and plunked down beside him. The springs were giving in to her weight, and she bounced on the seat. It was Emilie's way of announcing she had arrived.

"I thought I lost you." Jacob continued to read the paper, fully aware of his daughter's arrival.

"Did you see the glassware in the window? It is amazing! I think Mother would love it as a birthday present." Emilie was excited by her announcement. Maybe he would buy it for Julia, and Emilie would inherit the find down the road. She thought it would make a great family heirloom to pass through many generations.

"Too frivolous at a time like this, my dear." He never looked at her. His attention focused on the news.

"But, Papa," she began. "Mother would love you forever. I know as a woman—"

"Yes, Em, you have the 'as the woman' charm down. We have weeks to travel. This is no time to have to worry about glassware." He gave her the "I am finished with this conversation" look. "We have another hour to travel. How would you like to stay at an inn tonight?"

"An inn?" The announcement was far better than any green glassware. Emilie was growing tired of sleeping outdoors. The nights were getting very cold. Mother would be angry if they both came home with pneumonia. "That is the best idea I have heard all day. I finally have a place to write Thaddeus."

The travelers continued on their journey out of Washington. The countryside was a welcome relief to the bustle of the city. Feeling more comfortable, Emilie continued to think about her family. It helped to pass the time as they rode closer to Richmond.

❦

Traveling as a regiment seemed to be the slowest kind of movement anyone could possibly imagine. Thaddeus and Stephen had been marching for weeks. All they knew is that they were assigned to march toward Washington. As they walked, the men told jokes, teased one another about their lovers back home, and generally tried to make the time pass until they could stop for the night. This was not a forced march, but it sure felt like a demand on all of them.

Today Thaddeus was at the brunt of these jokes. "Hey, Marsh. I hear you has a lassie back home. Is she pretty?" McCabe was a boisterous, small man, whose obnoxious banter made up for his size.

Thaddeus shook his head. He was drawn into this conversation and had no choice but to participate. "Yes, she is beautiful, inside and out." Thaddeus smiled as he always did when he spoke of her.

"Ohhh, did she write you? You have a far-off look of longing in your eyes." McCabe poked Sullivan. "Doesn't he look longing?" The men peered at Thaddeus while still keeping their lines straight.

"Yup, looks longing to me?" Sullivan added.

"Does she smell pretty?"

"She smells far prettier than the both of you idiots." Thaddeus shot them a look. Stephen laughed. He was enjoying his friend being the center of attention. Thaddeus tried to regain control of the conversation. "At least I have a girl. What about you two?"

McCabe was shocked.

"I got me a girl, mighty pretty, too. She gives the best kisses. Tingles a man to his toes." The whole company within earshot laughed. McCabe became red with embarrassment.

"I bet that's not the only thing it tingles, you idiot." A soldier two rows back offered his two cents. "What else does she tingle?"

By this time the whole company was laughing. The sergeant let the banter go on for a short time, before he ordered the company to get serious and keep marching. Snickers and giggles continued intermittently throughout the ranks.

Later that night, Thaddeus and Stephen were ordered to take picket duty. They rested in the early evening and dressed for duty after the sun went down. The night air was cold and crisp. Thaddeus pulled his coat closed around him. He hadn't thought he needed a scarf, but he could have used it tonight. The leaves crunched under his boots. He walked as quietly as he could. Circling the camp became tiresome, constantly on his feet. Thaddeus didn't hate picket duty; he just longed for his bed. Sleep was the only place he could dream about her without interruption.

The scent of cigar smoke caught his attention. Thaddeus listened and strained his eyes to watch for movement. The faint footsteps continued walking toward him. Unnerved that the presence did not identify itself, Thaddeus finally demanded him to identify. Silence. Thaddeus did not hesitate to load his musket and fix his bayonet. He walked back toward the campfire light in hopes someone would see him. Stephen was too far on the other side of the perimeter to help him now. Demanding one more time, he called for the person to identify himself. Raising his musket, he walked toward the sound. Thaddeus decided to use his bayonet, if needed. He did not want to waste the musket ball, but he could injure the trespasser and decide to use the ball later. He hoped Stephen would be there to help shortly. Just inside the wood line, Thaddeus shouted at the figure to halt. No scuffle, no charging. The voice had a deep chuckle.

"Congratulations, soldier. You showed great restraint, and I thank you for not killing me." The voice was from Sergeant Duwey. Thaddeus breathed a sigh of relief. "You showed good restraint and common sense, son. I have been watching you. You would make a good officer."

"Thank you, Sergeant." Thaddeus was willing his heart to slow its beating. He became terrified at his last move. He put himself in grave danger. If this were a band of rebels, he understood he could have been taken prisoner or killed. The whole situation was nerve-wracking.

The sergeant was direct. "Very good, you passed. Now, don't tell anyone else. I will be testing them too. Is that clear, soldier?"

Thaddeus shook his head. "Yes, very clear, sir." With that, Sergeant Duwey left. It took a moment before Thaddeus remembered to resume his picket duties. As he turned the corner of the camp, he saw Stephen waiting for him.

"What took you so long? Did you have to use the woods?" Stephen demanded in a whisper. Thaddeus walked past him, grumbling. "Yeah, something like that."

"Oh." Stephen continued on his picket.

The night got colder as it passed into dawn. The fatigue set in just as Thaddeus and Stephen were relieved of their duties. Exhausted, the boys fell into bed to sleep until breakfast.

As he warmed under the blankets, Thaddeus fell into a deep, restful dream. He saw home for the first time in months. The feeling of happiness overcame him as he walked up the driveway. At the door, he saw Emilie, dressed in a work skirt, blouse, apron, and kerchief in her hair. He could plainly see she had been working in the house. She was beautiful, despite her weary but happy look. He could see her lips move, but no audible words came from her. He struggled to understand her. He took her in his arms and held her, smelling the lavender in her hair. As he pulled her closer, he felt something between them—a firm bump pushed against him. Looking down at her belly, he heard an explosion. The sound startled him into awareness. Heart beating wildly, he didn't know where he was. Looking around the tent, he heard the men assembling outside. It was time to wake up. Stumbling out of his bed, Thaddeus met Stephen.

"Come on, we are going to be late. The artillery is practicing." Stephen pushed Thaddeus back toward the tent. He was standing in his shirt and little else. Thaddeus dressed and hurried toward the artillery field. Today must be Sunday. Ever since General Mc Clellen ordered Sunday as a day of rest, the army did not move unless it was necessary. Today they would spend downtime making repairs and attending services. The company chaplain was a fiery Irishman who spoke of heaven and hell with excited conviction. His sermons were informational and entertaining.

It had been weeks since the last mail call, so when the courier rode in that afternoon, there were many lined up to hear from their loved ones. Camp life needed a break from monotony, and mail was always the perfect distraction.

Stephen was surprised to have two letters: one from his mother and the other he kept a secret. Thaddeus received a letter from his mother, Ian, and Emilie. No packages for either of them came this week. Thaddeus found a shade tree to sit under to read awhile. He sat back and carefully opened the letters.

He knew Ian's letter would be fast. He read about Ian's hardships at the farm. Chores were the least of his worries. Since his last run-in with the law, Ian had been working at the Bayle farm to earn extra money that he now owed the Borough of Gettysburg. Thaddeus read the lamentations of how soldiering would be far easier than his current plight. Thaddeus laughed; he missed his brother but did not miss saving him from his antics.

The second letter was more serious than the first. His mother wrote to him about general topics such as the end of growing season and she was preparing preserves for the winter months. She said she was sorry she did not send a package this time, but apple butter and apple jelly were taking up all her time. Thaddeus thought fondly of her. His mother, as long as he can remember, always worried about others before herself. Was that a typical trait of all women, or was he simply lucky to have a good mother who always made him feel important?

Finally, he opened Emilie's letter. The fear he felt from the dream came back to haunt him. He began to worry about her even before he read the first words.

> Dearest Thaddeus,
>
> Gettysburg is still the same old town you left. I can't say exactly the same, because you are missing. The fall harvest is a good one. Mother and I planned to make preserves and jellies for the winter season, until I got a letter from Seth.
>
> It seems he and his family is in danger at the old plantation. Father, Mother, and I decided it would be best to go see if they are safe. I know we talked about it before, but they are not slaves to us. They are more like family. Father and I are on our way there now.
>
> Since I haven't heard from you, I suspect you are not at Camp Wayne anymore. I hope you are marching far away from danger. It must be dreadfully boring to march and

drill all day long. If it keeps you safe, I want you to be bored to tears. I am sorry if that offends you, but it only means I love you and want you back to me as soon as possible. I pray every day the bullets go anywhere but near you.

Father says we should be near Washington by mid-September. If you are there, I pray whole-heartedly we meet by chance. I would love to feel your arms around me. I feel secure and safe in your arms. I feel all of your love pouring to my heart.

I had a horrible dream you forgot who I was. I know this isn't true, but it feels better that I tell you. I haven't forgotten you. I look at the ring you gave me every day; it reminds me of our promise to love and cherish each other. I won't ever forget you.

We are leaving soon, so I must end by saying, take care of you and know I am as close to you as one can be in my thoughts.

Yours,
E. K. P.

Just as Thaddeus finished the letter, Stephen interrupted his thoughts about her. "Did you get a letter from Em?" Stephen sat down next to his friend.

"Who?" Thaddeus had never heard anyone call her that before.

"Emilie? Did she finally write you?"

"Yeah, did she tell you she was going to Richmond?" Stephen showed Thaddeus his letter. "Better yet, did she tell you she was writing to me?" Thaddeus took the letter from him to look it over.

"Yes, she asked me long before we left for camp. She wanted you to get letters too." He spoke as he looked over what she said. "She asked me again just a few weeks ago. Looks like you had better write her back. She is asking you questions."

"She really asked your permission to write me?" Stephen was surprised. "I didn't think she asked anyone for permission for anything." He thought some more about her. Stephen admired Emilie for her independence. He didn't like how stubborn she was and how she spoke her mind, but he didn't have to worry about that. She was marrying Thaddeus; that was his problem now.

"She didn't want to upset me. Of course, she asked." Thaddeus still didn't understand how Emilie could ruffle Stephen into a tizzy. He knew Stephen liked her, but she could make him angry by the smallest action.

"How do you do it?" The question came out of nowhere. Stephen was serious. He waited for Thaddeus to answer. Stephen's eyes watched him, waiting for some words of wisdom.

"Do what?" Thaddeus smiled. He knew what his friend was trying to ask. Thaddeus looked at him, willing him to ask what was on his mind.

Stephen took a deep breath. "No disrespect, but how do you put up with that woman's…" Stephen could not find a word that described her. She was so diverse, stubborn, independent, aggravating. He tried again. "She is not like any other women. She is everything I wouldn't want in a wife." He was failing at trying to be tactful.

"Well, I am glad you are not marrying her. If you take some time to watch and listen to her, she is stimulating and exciting to be around. I am not talking about her looks. Look at how she thinks. She keeps me alive with her questions. She keeps me excited to want to see life through her eyes. I would be bored with any other woman. Emilie is amazing. You try to box her into what a woman should be. You can't. See her for who she is, and you can't help but fall in love with her." At the end of the speech, Thaddeus was smiling ear to ear. It was as if she came and energized him. Stephen watched the transformation. Before they talked, Thaddeus was tired and quiet. Once he explained her, he brightened up and filled with energy. Stephen was speechless. He could not explain what just happened to his friend.

"That, my friend, is amazing." Stephen got up ready to take his leave. Thaddeus gave him his letter. He noticed Stephen's letter was plain paper. It did not smell of her lavender perfume. The script she wrote to him was done in a careful, formal manner. In this, Thaddeus was certain: Emilie did not love Stephen. The letters were directly opposite, and for that he was proud of her.

"Stephen, do not keep her waiting for your letter. I don't want to hear about it in my letters," Thaddeus teased his friend. "She will never let you hear the end of it."

"I won't." Stephen could not imagine anyone giving permission to write his lady. He felt honored. Stephen headed back to camp to write to his family and Emilie.

The camp was quiet tonight. Most men refrained from cards and gambling in respect for the Lord's day. Early evening, some men went off to the river to bathe. Others washed their laundry. Everyone knew Monday would mean more marching. Washington was close, but not close enough for Thaddeus to catch a glimpse of her in the busy streets. He prayed he would hold her in his arms soon.

FAMILY CONFLICT

Family quarrels are bitter things. They don't go by any rules.

—F. Scott Fitzgerald

❧

LATE OCTOBER 1861

Travel from Washington to Richmond was mostly uneventful. Emilie found herself observing the changes in the trees and her surroundings as she traveled. Richmond was warmer than Fredrick or Washington. There was only rain at night, leaving the days sunny and bright.

"Will we send word to Uncle William announcing our arrival?" Emilie broke the silence of the morning. The two travelers had been busy with their own thoughts most of the morning. Emilie longed to sleep in a real bed. She missed her blankets and pillow, and how the down feather tick surrounded her in comfort. She missed the comforts of home. She hoped Aunt Jeanie would invite them to stay despite the upcoming confrontation.

"I don't think it would be wise to announce our arrival."

Emilie saw the serious furrow in her father's brow. He was worried. Was he changing his mind? Emilie didn't know what to say except offer encouragement.

"We are doing the right thing?" Emilie said, her inspiring words turned into a question.

"Yes, we are. Never go back on your word, unless you're forced to. I promised them freedom. I will see to it they are free." Jacob took a deep breath and continued driving the team forward.

The Prescott Plantation was as beautiful as Emilie remembered it. It stood majestic at the end of the oak-lined drive.

She remembered the trees always being taller than she. She smiled to herself when she remembered how she challenged herself to race down the lane without stopping. She could do it as a child, but now, she was not so sure she could. The house was splendid. Tucked into the trees, the front opened to the sun. The clearing revealed a circle driveway. The center of the circle boasted a beautiful rose garden lined with hedges and a quiet seating area in the center. Emilie remembered how she pretended to hold tea parties there as a small girl. This house gave her good memories.

The footman greeted them at the front porch. Greeting them politely, the man asked if he could announce their arrival.

"No, thank you. I am William's brother. He knows I am coming." Jacob was short with the man. The man bowed his head. "Please park the carriage for now. I don't know how long we are staying."

The footman helped Emilie out of the carriage. She stood on the front porch waiting for her father. "Papa, may I go see Seth?" She wanted to see him right away. Jacob straightened his jacket and adjusted his clothes to announce his arrival.

"Go, then come right back." Jacob waved her away and then walked up to the door. Jacob did not want Emilie to witness the confrontation he was about to have with his brother. The housemaid greeted Jacob. Her pleasant demeanor faded when Jacob inquired about Martha. Martha had always answered the door in the past. Her absence struck discord with him.

Jeanie arrived in the foyer to greet Jacob with a smile. "Jacob? What a surprise!" she leaned in to give him a friendly hug. "What brings you here? Let me call for refreshments." Jeanie leaned over to pick up the bell.

"Thank you, Jeanie. Where is William? I have some important business with him." His stern voice caught her off guard. He looked at her to see if she would tell him what he wanted to know. Jeanie was always faithful to her husband. A strong woman, if there was something she should not tell him, he would be hard-pressed to get it out of her.

"William went into Richmond. He has business there today." Jeanie did not make eye contact with him. "He will be home late tonight or early tomorrow morning."

"What kind of business in Richmond?" he inquired.

"I am not sure. William does not tell me all of his business dealings. Please come in and sit down." She gestured to the parlor. The settee looked more inviting than the carriage seat. She rang the bell to summon the maid. After giving her direction, Jeanie showed him a seat. "Do you need a drink?"

Jacob smiled. "Do I look like I need a drink?" They were both nervous and dancing around each other like cat and mouse. "Relax, Jeanie, I have no issue with you." He sat back and relaxed into the settee. "Where is Martha?"

The question surprised her. She looked terrified. "She no longer lives on the plantation." She nervously wrung her hand in her skirt. "We were not getting along. I was not Julia, and I…she did not adapt to my running the house."

"Where did she go? You didn't send her to the fields, did you?" Jacob knew Martha was a delicate woman. The field work would kill her. She belonged in the kitchen, she was comfortable there, it was her domain.

"The Sprees took her on in their home. Constance needed another slave to manage her house. The last one ran away. The posse caught them and killed them in a struggle to come home. I hear it was gruesome." Jeanie went on telling the story as if she was gossiping with her neighbors—her eyes bright, hands animated, and her voice eager with storytelling excitement.

❦

Emilie hurried toward the cabin. Located through the grove, she pushed through the trees. Expecting to see a few cabins, she was surprised to see rows of newly built structures. Each had fires built in front with large pots of water boiling for laundry. The makeshift clotheslines hung clothes to dry. There were more people here than when she left months earlier.

Looking out to the fields, she saw the rows doubled, tripled, and quadrupled in size. It went on forever. Uncle William expanded both farm and workers. Her heart sank when she realized the plantation was not the same place her family struggled to make profitable years before. It was a large plantation full of slave labor. Her eyes filled with tears. She walked through the small village; she began to realize there were many eyes watching her. She was a stranger here.

"Is you lost, miss?" The woman's voice had a thick accent. She held a large stirring stick. There was a small child hanging on the woman's skirt. The little boy's eyes were big and dark. He was leery of strangers. When Emilie looked at him, he pulled his mother's skirt around to cover his face.

"I am looking for Seth and Big Jim, ma'am." Emilie politely smiled at the woman. "Are they home?"

The woman laughed, her white teeth accenting her beautiful, dark skin. Emilie was attracting a crowd. Everyone pointed at her, mumbling and whispering to themselves.

"Is he home? Lordy girl, you think he's a white man in the big house? That funny, miss." She was a jolly woman; Emilie knew she would like her, if she could get to know her. "He in that field." She pointed in the general direction of the large parcel of land. Emilie's eyes grew big with anticipation. She pointed out to the land.

"Which part?" that was all she said. Emilie could not believe the changes to her former home. This caused more ruckus laughter. Confused but humored by their reaction, Emilie laughed too. "Things have sure changed around here."

The woman stopped. "Is you the former owner's girl?" The woman eyed her with suspicion. Looking Emilie up and down, the woman waited for the answer.

"Um, yes, my name's Emilie." Emilie started getting anxious about finding Seth. She tried to see beyond the crowd that was forming around her.

"Yous the girl he be talking about. Yes, you is as pretty as he says." The women around her began nodding in agreement. They no longer looked at her with fear, but with a friendly regard.

"Thank you," Emilie said. "Where is Seth?" A young child came up beside her, grabbed her hand, and led her away. Emilie found herself guided through rows of new cabins, each looking well inhabited. She went around two outbuildings, and they stopped at the edge of the clearing. The fields were neatly manicured, plowed under because of the season. In the distance, she saw a large group of men working. They were hoeing, plowing, and picking rock. Each man focused on his job.

Emilie turned to the small girl. "Thank you. I'll go find him." As she set out into the field, the girl pulled her skirt. The small voice whispered, "No, there." She pointed.

"What?" Emilie tried to understand what the child was saying. The small girl shrunk with fear. Emilie realized she must have shouted at her. "I'm sorry, please tell me." Emilie's softened her voice to encourage her.

The child pointed to the center of the field. She could barely make out a man with a whip in his hand. "Seth!" she whispered as she stepped into the field. Running was impossible; the uneven ground made her trip on her skirts. This part of the field freshly plowed made her trip and fall. Emilie did not care. She was going to bring Seth and Big Jim back to the house, and no one was going to stop her.

She closed in on the group. One and then another noticed her presence. She nodded to them as she passed by. Finally, stopping, she asked, "Where is Seth and Big Jim?" No one answered her. A man simply pointed to the man with the whip. Exasperated, she marched over to him, pulled on his shirtsleeve, and demanded, "Show me where Big Jim and Seth are."

"A woman in this field? You can't talk to me that way." The man looked down upon her as if she were a fly sitting on the edge of a bowl of cream. He looked cantankerous enough to push her in and watch her drown. He twitched the whip to remind everyone he was in charge here. Emilie didn't know him. He was obviously an overseer. It didn't make sense why Big Jim didn't have the job. He knew this land better than anyone did, spending long, laborious hours tending, plowing, and pruning the plants of this soil.

"They are working, no time for you." He addressed her in such a way she felt less important and small. He flicked the whip close to her shoulder. She felt it through the fabric of her dress. Emilie glared at him.

"I have business with them. Will you please show me where they are." Demanding now, Emilie was determined not to back down. He refused to look at her. She was out of place here, and he wasn't going to give her the time of day. They stared at each other in silence. Emilie finally stomped away. She began calling for them. Her outburst distracted all of the workers. The rhythm of the field was broken as all of the hoes and equipment stopped.

Finally, she saw him. Seth was standing at the end of a row, waving to her. Emilie picked up her skirts and hurried down the row, tiptoeing over large clumps of dirt and skirting around rocks. Across from Seth was Big Jim. Tall and serious, Jim kept Seth close to him in the fields. He didn't want his son to be singled out for any reason. When he saw the young woman jigging through the plowed field, he knew who it was in an instant—Emilie Kathryn. He was grinning with excitement to see his former owner's daughter. Emilie brought joy to his heart with her smile and explosive personality. She could brighten any room with her presence. More importantly, she brightened his heart.

Making her way to level ground, she called out to them. As soon as they waved to her, she was off like a rabbit. She hugged them as close as family.

"I have missed you so much. Big Jim, why aren't you overseeing these fields? You do it better than anyone I know." Emilie looked up to the large man. He was big but as gentle as can be. He held her close, chuckling at her. Oh, how she brightened his world.

She looked up at him with a big smile, relieved to see they were both all right. "Girl, what are you doing in this place? You don't belong here anymore." He set her gently back on the ground.

"You don't either, Big Jim. You did your share and your promise is fulfilled. Come with me to the house. Pa is here." She turned to see Seth. She smiled at him and moved in for a hug. Seth backed up.

"Miss Emilie, I am too dirty for your hug."

He looked embarrassed.

Realizing she was being over exuberant, Emilie stepped back to save him further embarrassment. "Sorry, Seth." She smiled at him. "Well, let's go!" She waited as the men only stared at her. "Let's get Martha and go. Pa wants to see you."

Disappointment washed over their faces. Emilie didn't understand. Big Jim looked uncomfortable. Seth looked away. "Where is Martha?" Neither man said anything; they could not tell her for some reason. They only shook their heads. Emilie had a sinking feeling; like a dark cloud covering over the sun, she felt cold despite the warm fall sun. "Don't scare me—tell me." Emilie tried to choke back the panic.

"She doesn't live with us anymore." Seth's voice was quiet and sad. "She was sold to Mr. and Mrs. Spree."

"She can't be sold! She is free just like you!" Emilie burst into tears. "Pa is here. He will tell you. Come back with me. He will show you. What happened, Big Jim?" Emilie couldn't stop talking, the words spilled out of her pushed by sadness and frustration and anger.

Big Jim was as gentle as he could. "Miss Emilie, I can't leave the field. That overseer likes his whip and will whip us endlessly. Go tell you father we all right. We can't come to him just now."

She stared at him through the tears and confusion, not moving. He gently turned her around and nudged her. "Go now," he whispered.

Emilie turned to look at Seth. Seth only nodded. Emilie walked carefully through the field until she reached its edge. Once on solid ground, she ran as fast as she could back to the house. The crowd she had entertained earlier had gone back to work. Once out of the grove with the house in sight, Emilie collapsed to sit on a rock to catch her breath.

When she arrived on the steps of the house, she tried to dry her eyes and compose herself. She could not present herself to her aunt and uncle looking so disheveled. Opening the door, she found another woman on the other side. This woman doing Martha's job infuriated Emilie even more. The emotions flooded over her again.

"Where is my father?" she demanded. So angry, she could not be polite. This was the one who pushed Martha out of the house. The maid pointed to the parlor. Attempting to announce Emilie, the maid went in front of her to open the door. Furious, Emilie pushed her aside. "I will announce myself. Go!" Her words were thick with disgust.

Emilie grabbed the oak doors and shoved them open. The bang startled both Jeanie and Jacob, who were having a quiet conversation. Jeanie squeaked with surprise. Jacob stood up as if he sat on a pinecone.

"Emilie Kathryn Prescott! What has gotten into you?" Emilie heard his words but did not see him. She focused on the demure Jeanie Prescott, looking very surprised at her niece. Emilie was a sight to see. Tear-streaked face, cheeks red from exertion, she was boiling over with anger. In three strides, Emilie walked up to her aunt and slapped her hard.

"How dare you! They are free, and you have rebound them with your greed for money and lust for power." Emilie sputtered and swung as her father grabbed her around the waist to keep her from attacking her aunt. "You sold Martha to the despicable Sprees. Have you checked on her? She could be dead. They are even more cold-hearted than you and Uncle Will."

Jacob held his daughter close. "Watch your manners, young lady. Thou shall not accuse without proven guilt," he whispered in her ear, both cautioning his daughter and trying to soothe her.

Emilie collapsed in his arms and fainted from lack of oxygen. Her corset restricted her air after running from the field. She was out of breath from anger and exertion. Jacob gently lifted his daughter and set her on the settee next to the open window. Jeanie rushed to get smelling salts and a glass of water.

"She sure has a temper, that one," Jeanie said, handing him the handkerchief of smelling salts. "Where did she come from? She is a mess."

"She went out to the field to see Seth. I am sure she saw everyone out there. It is shocking to her." Jacob gently patted Emilie's hand to help revive her.

"Will she be violent when she wakes up?" Jeanie did not want a repeat surprise from her niece. She backed up and returned to sit on the chair.

"She will be fine." Jacob watched his daughter open her eyes.

Emilie woke disorientated. Her body felt heavy with exhaustion. First, she saw her father's concerned eyes looking at her. She felt the familiar surroundings of the parlor. All of the emotion came flooding in, and she burst into tears of defeat and guilt. "I'm sorry," she whispered. Emilie remembered how angry she was and how she took it out on her aunt. She had never felt the overwhelming feelings of wanting to protect the ones she loved. Yet in this instance, she felt helpless. Saving them was out of her control. Emilie never experienced emotions so strong before.

"I think your aunt needs to hear your apology more than I." Jacob was firm with this daughter. He understood how she felt, but her actions were inexcusable.

Emilie hiccupped, trying to control her emotions. She felt shame for acting so out of control. "Aunt Jeanie. Please accept my apology for hurting you with my words and actions." The words came very hard for Emilie. She knew she was going through the motions because she blamed her aunt for looking the other way while her husband ran a plantation of kept people.

Jeanie looked at her niece. She heard the apology and felt sorry for the child. Emilie was jaded by her family's beliefs. They sounded more and more like Northern sympathizers every time they met. She hoped their business would be finished soon so they could leave her house. Not wanting to stir any more emotion, Jeanie simply said, "Apology accepted. Would you like to clean up before dinner?" Jeanie reached for the bell. "I will call Maggie to show you to your old room."

Emilie sprang up from the couch. "No, thank you. I don't mind going myself. I remember where to find my room."

Jeanie flinched. "As you wish. Someone will be up with water soon."

Jacob intervened. "I will send up some fresh clothes. Once you pull yourself together, we will discuss what just happened."

Emilie bowed her head, humbled. "Yes, Father. Thank you, Aunt Jeanie."

Once Emilie left the room, Jacob turned to Jeanie. "I am sorry. We will be happy to go back to town to stay."

"Don't be silly, Jacob. I think the worst is over. The girl is just taken aback by the changes here. Once she get comfortable again, she will be fine. I'll get water sent up to her." Jeanie excused herself, and Jacob went out to the carriage to tell the stableman to tend the horses and bring in their trunks.

The evening meal was almost complete when Maggie announced William–returned from Richmond. William was in no mood to see his relatives from the North. His wife filled him in on the details of the day, as he went to refresh himself before greeting his family.

Opening the parlor doors, William entered the room, cozy with fine curtains and their best furnishings. Jeanie made him a drink and held it out to him. Seated on the settee were his niece and brother. He noticed Emilie glared at him the moment he entered the room. Jacob stood to greet his brother.

William raised his glass to his brother. "What brings you here so late in the year?"

"I have a few last items of business to attend to, dear brother." Jacob and William were beginning to set up the verbal fencing match. They often danced around each other's words as sport, testing the limits of each other's temperaments. William would rather fence tonight than give in to his brother's pending request.

"I am here to make sure our agreement is being kept." Jacob started the conversation.

"I don't know why you came all this way. Everything is in order here." William smugly countered, taking a large drink from his glass of scotch. He walked over and sat down next to his wife, kissed her on the cheek, and turned to his family.

Emilie, watching the verbal exchange between the brothers, worked hard to refrain herself from bursting out at her uncle. She saw her father was well in control of the situation, but Emilie wanted to get to the heart of the matter quickly before anything else went wrong. This whole trip was not turning out the way she had planned.

"I see Big Jim and his family are still on the plantation. When are they leaving? Surely, you have enough workers to finish preparing the fields for winter." Jacob got to the point.

"Is that what you are here for? Checking to see where those darkies are living? Really, Jacob, they have not told me their plans. Maybe they would rather stay. Living in the North has made you more Union than Confederate." William rolled his eyes.

"If they stay, will you put them on your payroll? I know they cannot stay within Virginia as free blacks." Jacob shook his head.

He should have made sure they were freed before he left. "We are here to take them back with us."

"You have no use for them. I want them here. They are good workers." William emptied his glass and got up to make himself another drink.

"They are not yours to use. I freed them. You were only borrowing them until you got things going here." Jacob made his point by putting his glass on the table with a thud.

William thought it over as he poured himself a drink and walked over to retrieve Jacob's glass to refill it. Returning the full glass to his brother, William sat down.

"Fine. Take them. I have more to take their place. You will have to talk to Spree about the woman. She belongs to them now." He nonchalantly put his arm around his wife, showing his brother they were united. He owned this plantation now, and the message was clear. He didn't care what anyone thought, he was master of this land, and he was running it as he pleased.

"Sounds like you will have to make an exchange, brother. Martha is not to be sold. She is free." Jacob was disgusted. He knew the Sprees beat their slaves. He worried Martha would be another victim. Martha was a strong woman, but could she withstand them?

"You want her? You buy her!" William shot back, knowing the words would sting.

"You had no right," Jacob countered, knowing the words had no effect.

"It is she that has no rights. I own the land and everything on it. They are on my land, and they were sold with the property!" William shouted angrily. "No paper of yours has any say here." William sat at the edge of his seat. "She is worth plenty. Buy her back. Then free her. She means nothing to me."

"What was her price?" Jacob coldly asked. His anger bubbled just under the surface. He was having a hard time keeping his cool.

"I traded her. Constance wanted an experienced housemaid, and I needed two laborers. It was a fair deal." William coolly continued to push Jacob's patience.

"Who are you sending over as trade? That girl who answers the door now?" Jacob recovered from his defensive position. "I am sure there are plenty out there you can train for this house."

"Maggie is a good girl. She stays," William countered. "This is your problem. You work it out with Spree."

"Fine, you don't supply me with another body. I will have to take what is not his, and he will knock on your door for retribution." Jacob set his glass down. "We won't bother you any further. I will talk to Big Jim and Seth in the morning and then leave by noon." Jacob stood up to take his leave. Emilie followed behind him.

William called after Emilie before she left the parlor. "Young lady. If you ever decide to slap my wife again, I will tan your hide with a whip. Is that understood?"

Emilie glared at him with distaste. "If you ever touch me, Uncle, I will see you dead by morning." Emilie could no longer mind her manners; her emotions were many, at the surface, too hard to control. Uncle William had no regard for human life; looking at him made her sick. Without another word, she left the room.

Jeanie turned to her husband. "What are you going to do? Horace is going to want a replacement for Martha." Her words grated on his nerves. He hated Spree, he was an evil man, and William owed him many favors. Maybe someday he could break the ties, but now, they had to stay entwined, indebted to each other.

"Let my brother try to steal from Horace Spree. It will be a large mistake for Jacob." William drained his glass, walked out to the veranda to smoke a cigar. He thought about how his brother once again intruded on his life.

FREE AT LAST

Freedom is what you do with what's been done to you.

—Jean Paul Sartre

NOVEMBER 1861

Jacob woke Emilie early the next morning. Still groggy from lack of sleep the night before. She had been awake most of the night, excited to leave, worried how the day would all resolve itself. Emilie could not wait to have everyone in the wagon on their way back to Gettysburg. Her body finally gave in to sleep just before the sun rose that morning.

"Get dressed; I will take the bags downstairs. When you are finished, we will ride out to Seth and Jim." Her father was serious and curt with his words. He had one thing on his mind, and that was leaving Virginia as soon as possible.

Emilie hurried as fast as she could. Within twenty minutes, she was outside waiting in the carriage seat. The house was eerily quiet; no one was moving around this morning except the kitchen staff. Her father met her with a napkin filled with warm biscuits and bacon. He handed her a hot mug filled half full with coffee, strong and black. Emilie's senses immediately woke to the sensuous smells of good, hot food and coffee.

"Drink more of that. It will spill." His orders were still short and direct.

Emilie carefully tested the coffee. It was good. She flinched as the hot liquid touched her lips. "Ow!" Emilie blew on the coffee, the tin mug now hot to the touch. The ride out to the cabins went more direct than Emilie had gone the day before.

"Good god! What has he done here!" Jacob saw the land transformed into a massive working plantation. The rows of cabins lined the path like a city street. "How did you find them?"

Looking up from her coffee mug, Emilie explained she found the men in the fields. She confessed she did not know which cabin belonged to them. Jacob exclaimed; he found it. He pointed to the cabin with a red door. The window box was vacant of flowers where it once boasted dainty yellow and blue crocuses.

Jacob smiled as he remembered its significance. "I remember making those boxes for Martha. She raved about seeing them and wished for one. Seth and I made it for her birthday. Sad to see it doesn't have flowers in it just now."

Emilie was finally getting a chance to taste the coffee, and she enjoyed its bitter dark flavor. Just as she finished, the carriage bumped over a rut, sending the splashing coffee on the front of her dress. She yelped with surprise. Emilie scurried to take a piece of the napkin to brush away the wetness off her bodice.

"Thank goodness it will blend in." Emilie smiled. Her brown calico print showed no coffee stains, only a wet spot. Jacob stopped the carriage. Emilie waited until he gave her the signal it was clear for her to enter.

Jacob knocked on the cabin door. Jim opened the door, surprised to see his friend. The men shook hands and exchanged words. Emilie waited patiently. Finally, Seth came out to talk to her.

"Is it true, Miss Emilie? Is we leaving with you just now?" Seth was in shock, but excited by the idea. The sun was behind him, accenting his smile. Seth looked refreshed and happy; the plans for his day had changed. "Pa invites you in." Seth held out his hand to help Emilie out of the carriage.

"Seth, we really have to work on your speech, and, yes, we are taking you back to Gettysburg." Emilie was happy to see Seth was all right. Inside the cabin, Jim and Jacob discussed what had transpired.

"I have your papers, Jim. Everyone is free. You just can't stay in Virginia. You know it is illegal to live here once you are free." Jacob looked around the cabin. "We only have a little time. I told William we would be off the property within two hours. We have to pack."

"Thank you, Jacob. What about Martha?" Jim was worried about his wife. "She ain't here. She left for the Sprees early this mornin'." Jacob started gathering things together and setting them on the table. "I have a wagon and horses I own in the barn. I'll send Seth to fetch it."

The men continued to make plans as to how they were going to free Martha. The house packed quickly. Seth and Jim loaded the wagon. Emilie squeezed into the last small space in the wagon. Seth put down a stack of blankets, taking care to make sure the boxes would not shift. When he finished, he helped Emilie into the wagon.

"I hope yous comfortable, Miss Emilie." Seth smiled. He loved taking care of her.

"It will be fine, Seth. Thank you." Emilie sat ready to go again. She watched the men gather in a small circle. Their backs turned to her. She saw Jim reach in his pocket and give something to her father.

Inside the circle, Jacob took the gun from Jim. "This is very dangerous for you, Jim." Jacob knew the ramifications of a black man who carried a gun.

"I have to protect my family," Jim said. "You take it. You may need it to free Martha." His big, brown eyes begged his friend to bring his wife back to him. "I only wish I could do it myself."

"There is plenty of time to protect your family. It is best I take care right now." Jacob felt for the man. He was helpless in a society so biased and suspicious. It was ironic the white man feared those who they kept down. With so many contradictions in this society, Jacob was glad he left it.

"I will bring her back to you as safe as I can. Now take Emilie, head north, and I will meet you within the hour. Do not leave this road." Jacob gave directions like a military officer. "She has your papers in her knapsack."

Jacob waved to his daughter and turned the carriage around. Jim drove the wagon. Together they drove to the Spree's drive; Jacob turned in, as Jim, Seth and Emilie continued north. Emilie waved to her father as they drove away.

A footman greeted Jacob at the front of the Spree home. It was a large plantation house with a wraparound porch. The second floor had a small, turned-out landing near the master bedroom. The two-story brick home was simple but very elegant.

Jacob waited at the large, oak door. When the door opened, he sighed in relief. Martha opened the door dressed in a fine, dark dress and crisp, white apron. Her face lit up when she saw him. "Mr. Jacob. What a great surprise!"

He took her hand, greeting the woman as warmly as he could under the peering eyes of the other servants. Pulling her close, he whispered, "Go get your things. You are leaving with me." Louder, he said, "Is Mr. Spree home, madame?"

Matching his voice, Martha answered, "Yes, may I announce you, Mr. Prescott?" Her head motioned toward the dining room. As they turned around, Horace Spree appeared at the doorway.

"Jacob Prescott! I am surprised to see you." Horace stepped forward to shake his former neighbor's hand. Jacob took his hand cordially.

"I am here to bring Martha back to Pennsylvania with me. She was sold to you, under false pretenses. William will give you retribution for your loss. Martha, are you ready to go?" Jacob was direct and to the point. He was not waiting around for any confrontations.

"No, she was traded to me fair, Jacob. You cannot free what isn't yours or his." Horace was on edge. He disliked the older

Prescott brother worse than he did the younger. They were a strange family, and he was sorry he had to share land with them.

Jacob unfolded Martha's paperwork, showing Horace the paper that announced Martha was a free woman. Horace shook his head in disbelief. "This was signed in 1861. What was she still doing on the Prescott plantation?"

Jacob saw Martha return with her basket. "Go seat yourself in the carriage. I will be with you momentarily." He nodded toward the door. Martha dutifully left. Jacob waited for Horace to finish reading the document. "You can't just take my property without a fight."

Horace's posture changed from defensive and stiff. Jacob took the paper back and stuffed it in his jacket. It was too valuable to leave in the open. "She is not for sale." Jacob tried to remember if the man could read. "The document is signed by Attorney Abbott. It is binding." Jacob turned to leave. He heard a scuffle behind him. Turning back, Jacob saw the barrel of Horace's rifle pointed at him.

"If you think you can steal my property, you are mistaken. Try to leave. I will shoot you." Horace's face turned red with anger. "That paper means nothing to me."

"I am not one of your slaves, Horace. Shooting a man in the back is dishonorable. Do you really want to be remembered like that?" Jacob reached in his pocket, wrapping his hand securely around the pistol. "Take out your anger on the right man, Horace. My brother traded you stolen goods." Jacob kept his voice calm. He knew Horace had a temper. There were many suspect burials of his slaves in the past. They could not have all died from sickness. It was a well-known fact that Jacob chose to ignore, as he was surrounded by a society that did not care.

"I am protecting what should be protected." Jacob watched the old man step forward, gun still pointed at him. His face was set like a stone statue. Jacob watched the man's finger nowhere near the trigger. Horace was trying to intimidate him. Jacob drew his gun and pointed it back toward the man.

"Horace, shooting me will do no good. She means nothing to you. Let her go." Jacob heard someone gasp. Constance Spree witnessed the scene in her foyer: two men, guns pointed at each other. They stood staring each other down like a fox watches his prey. She wasn't sure who was the fox and who was the prey.

Not taking his eyes off Jacob, Horace shouted to his wife, "Constance, go find Ben. Tell him I need him here." He barked the orders to her as he would order his employees. She shrank back into the dining room and disappeared.

"I am leaving, Horace." Jacob turned to reach for the door. Suddenly he heard the gun shot. The bullet whizzed past Jacob's head, embedding itself deep into the oak door. Jacob turned to see the old man, sprawled on the floor, the rifle skittered across the hardwood floor, hitting the doorjamb of the parlor.

Horace lay lifeless on the floor, blood oozing from his head. Jacob suspected he tripped on the foyer rug. He left the man on the floor, knowing his wife would return soon.

It was a long time before Martha spoke. She looked horrified when Jacob returned to the carriage. He put the pistol under the seat, and they drove away. "Mr. Jacob?" Martha's timid voice spoke softly. "Is he dead?"

"No, Martha. He slipped and fell. The rifle went off when it hit the floor. He will have a headache for a few days, but he should be fine." Jacob was relieved to leave Richmond. His anxiety returned after they traveled an hour and half without meeting up with the others.

"You look worried." Martha had been watching him for the last few miles.

"They should be here soon. We could not have been that late." Jacob went over the logical routes and timing repeatedly. Traveling over a small hill, he saw a covered bridge. The scene was beautiful with trees lining the riverbank. The grassy area looked inviting to the weary travelers. Martha tugged on Jacob's sleeve. "There they is." She pointed to a small group waiting by a carriage. Jacob felt instant relief as he recognized them.

"Found them, theys waitn lunch for us." Martha smiled at the sight of her family. She was surprised at how mature Emilie looked. She had grown up in the year the family was gone.

Jacob stopped the carriage, helped Martha down, and rounded up the men to talk about what transpired at the Spree Plantation. The ladies finished setting out lunch. As everyone enjoyed their meal, Jacob told them what they needed to do. "We cannot slow down. Horace is angry, and I am sure he sent men after us. I would feel safer if we made some more time ahead of them." Everyone agreed. They finished eating immediately and packed up quickly. Martha joined her family in the carriage, and Emilie rejoined her father to continue the journey. They did not stop traveling until well after dark.

HOME TO CELEBRATE

Everyone is kneaded of the same dough, but not baked in
the same oven.

—Yiddish proverb

❦

LATE NOVEMBER 1861

"We is not put on this earth as equals. You must stop fussing
so. I's embarrassed wit your fussing, child." Martha's words stung
Emilie's pride. Embarrassment was not what she wanted. Emilie
only wanted others to recognize her friends as people, not slaves.

"I never want to embarrass you. I just want them to see you
like I do." Tears stung Emilie's eyes. "The same as me. We are
equals, Martha. The only difference is our skin color. Yours is
beautiful, full of color and contrast. Mine, pasty and sickly white.
You tell me who is beautiful." Emilie touched Martha's hand.
Despite all of her manual labor, her skin was soft and smooth.

"You're beautiful not on your skin, you have soul child. A soul
of an angel. You are as fierce as a lion. Protective as a bear. Your
smile makes people smile. You will make a great mama someday.
I knows it." Martha loved this girl like her own daughter. She
was as proud as a woman could be. If her daughter had lived,
Martha would have wanted her to be as strong as Emilie. The
weary travelers pushed harder to get back to Gettysburg. The
winter rain and winds were harsh. Lodging was difficult traveling
with a black family. Emilie stopped being offended after the first
week of disappointment. She wore herself out ranting about how
unfair she felt about the whole situation. Martha finally pulled
the frustrated girl aside to chat.

"Miss Emilie, I see you angry at how whites treats us. You
don't have to fuss." She gently talked to the girl whose face was

red with anger. "Folks don't sees us like you family does." Martha sat down next to Emilie, looking kindly into her eyes. "We will be fine. We knows our life is not going to be easy, but we is awfully thankful we have you and your family. You helped us get free now you have to let us live, free." Martha's eyes welled up with tears.

"You will always be family to us." Emilie gave Martha's hand a squeeze. "I will watch my temper, and most of all, I am sorry."

Martha chuckled. "I know you are. Lets get going 'for your mama worried about us. We been gone a long time. Does it warm up here?"

Emilie laughed. "Not until April." The ladies rejoined the men, who were waiting patiently by the fire. The nights were very cold; with no lodging last night, the group huddled together in the wagon. The thin blankets shared between everyone. Only a day's ride from home, they all thought the same thing: Push until we get there.

Emilie sat in the carriage next to her father, pondering her conversation with Martha. She started to create a mental list of what the family would need to live on their own. Blankets, for one thing, that was at the top of her list. Emilie was confident in the knowledge the black community in Gettysburg would receive her family. Emilie was glad they would be close again.

The day dragged on, Emilie began thinking of things she needed to do when she got home. Writing Thaddeus was her top priority. Now that everyone was safe, she began to think of life as it was before she left for Virginia. She missed his letters. She hoped there were several letters waiting for her when she got home.

Late afternoon the next day, the carriage pulled up to the house in Gettysburg. Emilie was excited to be home. Tired of travelling and missing her things, she hurried to the house to see her mother.

Julia saw them coming. She and Emilie almost collided as they rushed toward each other. Emilie hugged her mother. Together they went to help carry their things into the house. Julia brightened when she saw Martha. The ladies hugged and chattered on, catching up on lost time. Greeting Seth and Jim, Julia turned to her husband. Their embrace lasted a long time as they whispered to each other. Emilie smiled, knowing how her mother felt. She would have given anything to hold Thaddeus that way. He seemed to be gone for so long. Emilie felt the ache of longing deep in her heart.

"It is so good to see all of you. I didn't expect you until tomorrow." Julia smiled for the first time in weeks. "I have everything ready for you, Martha, Big Jim, and Seth. We only have one room for you, but it is cozy, and the trundle should be..." She stopped short, eyeing Seth. He had grown so much taller than she remembered.

"Seth, you shot up by a foot or more since I saw you last. I hope you will fit." Julia pulled some belongings from the wagons as they all started for the house.

"Missus Julia, You work your fingers to the bone. We will be fine to stay out here." Jim pointed to the loft in the barn. Julia stopped in her tracks.

"Where?" she asked. When she saw Jim pointing at the barn, Julia laughed. "Oh no, you won't. The nights are very cold now, and I won't have any of you sick all winter. We have plenty of room. Now come."

Once inside the house, Emilie spied the stack of letters on the table. She picked them up and sat down on the chair in front of her. All the letters had the same free-hand scrawl. Thaddeus had faithfully written to her, despite her letters ceasing. She looked at each one. All in date order, she had a lot of reading to do. No time to be with him now, Emilie spent the next few hours settling her Seth's family. Dinner that evening was a happy celebration of togetherness.

Jim and Martha had thought long and hard as to what they wanted to do with their freedom. After dinner, Jim and Jacob reviewed the newspapers to look for land and work. Seth spent time with the men, mapping out the family's future. Martha, Emilie, and Julia cleaned up the dinner dishes and talked about life in Gettysburg. It would take time for the family to get acquainted with both their freedom and their new location.

Once the excitement settled down, Emilie excused herself to go to her room to read and write to Thaddeus. The lamp set the room in a warm, yellow glow. Emilie felt the chill of the winter months seeping through the windows. She started a small fire in the fireplace; setting the small flame to tinder, she nursed the spark into a feeble flame. Feeding it slowly and carefully, it grew hot enough to burn small twigs, then larger branches, and finally, small logs. Its warmth filled her, making her feel secure and happy. Sitting on the floor, tending the flames, she opened her letters to read.

> My darling Emilie,
>
> I must admit I am not happy you have travelled to Virginia. I understand why, but I worry about your safety. I am secure in knowing that you will write to me as often as you can. I miss you, my sweet girl. I miss holding you in my arms and smelling your sweet hair. I am lucky to dream of you often.
>
> We are firmly entrenched here at Camp Pierpont at Langley, outside of Washington, for the winter months. We are "bored to tears," with constant camp duties and working to stay warm. I am thankful for the quilt you made me. It is getting tattered as I use it all the time to stay warm. How I miss the fireplace in the warm parlor with your company.
>
> The mail is coming very regularly. It is exciting to get letters and gifts from home. The holidays will soon be upon us. Do you remember our first Christmas? It was the day I first met you. From that moment on, I knew my life changed forever. If you are not busy preparing for the holidays, I need more socks and a scarf. I lost the scarf

two weeks ago. Know I am healthy; some men are getting sickly as the winter drags on. We are sending some home for burial, but know I am healthy and safe. The socks and scarf will be a great help.

Take care my little one, and know I love you. Dream of me kissing you sweetly. Please write as soon as you are able. I miss you.

Yours always,
Thaddeus

His words always made her feel warm and safe. It felt like a long-distance hug. Emilie stood up from her spot on the floor. She stretched, but her legs protested the sudden movement, picking and tingling as she realized her legs had fallen asleep. She sat a bit longer, making sure she could stand. Exhilarated by his news, Emilie was eager to write to him.

Stirring the fire, Emilie added another log before she sat down to write him the letter he deserved. Emilie filled him in on all of the details of her trip to Virginia and the trip home. She reassured him she would start knitting a new scarf, and she would ask her mother to knit some warm socks. Julia was more proficient at socks, and he would not have to wait months to get them. Emilie finished her four-page letter late in the night. She heard the rest of the family settle in for the night. Emilie banked the fire and finished getting ready for bed. The warm covers wrapped around her felt cozy; she fell into a peaceful sleep for the first time in months. The comforts of home, her things about her, and Thaddeus's words echoing in her head, she slept well into the next day.

❧

The end of the year came quickly. Traveling four weeks left no time to decorate. This year's holiday decorations were at the bare minimum. Emilie was too busy knitting scarves and mittens for everyone. Her present list was long. Jim, Martha, and Seth needed scarves. Thaddeus was waiting on warmer clothes too, and then there was Aaron, Henry, and lastly, Stephen. She didn't want him to feel left out.

Boxes laid out on the table, Emilie made sure each box was packed with plenty of padding so the jars of preserves would not break. She took great care to ask for donations for each box. If they could not be home for Christmas, Emilie wanted to send Christmas to them. Emilie finished care packages for the boys, filling the boxes with scarves, mittens, socks, baked goods, and other small presents. Emilie hoped the mail would arrive before Christmas. She mailed the packages a week before Christmas.

The neighbors came calling during the week between Christmas and New Year's. The celebrations were smaller and more private due to the effects of the war. Inflation began taking its toll on everyday items, such as sugar, tea, and fabrics. Emilie, Martha, and Julia spent time in the kitchen preparing for visitors. There were plates of gingerbread cookies, molasses, and snicker doodles. Warm pots of apple cider and cinnamon simmered on the stove. It looked like Christmas, but everyone still felt the hole of missing family and loved ones this year.

As the year finished, Emilie was grateful. Everyone was happy and healthy. Letters from Aaron and Henry came after months of little word from them. Both brothers seemed to be doing well and staying healthy. Christmas this year filled with prayers of thanksgiving and prayer of safety for all of those missing at home.

WAITING TIME

I love thee to the depth and breadth and height my soul can reach.

—Elizabeth Barrett Browning

❧

FEBRUARY 1862

It was a quiet start to 1862. Emilie welcomed the year with high hopes. The war seemed to be waiting for spring. The men were still in winter camps, waiting to finish their war. The men's war was not with one another; it was against the cold, disease, and boredom. Illness and cold continued to threaten the lives in both great armies.

Emilie relaxed in her favorite chair in the parlor. The Prescott home was vacant of family and friends that moved on. Big Jim and his family found a home, jobs, and a new community to start their new lives free. Emilie enjoyed helping Martha sew curtains and move their things to the new house at the other end of Gettysburg. Big Jim worked six days a week to make the best of the family's newfound freedom.

Tonight the house was quiet after a busy day. Longing to escape into a good book, Emilie picked up a new novel, *The Marble Faun* by Nathanial Hawthorne. The new book was tightly bound. Emilie loved the thick paper and the smell of newly printed book. The thrill of opening a new page never ceased to excite her. Settling deeper in the chair, her long, brown hair fell in curls around her shoulders. Free from the hoop and corset, Emilie allowed her skirts to wrap around her legs, and flannel shawl snug around her shoulders. She felt warm, cozy, and very relaxed. It was times like these that she longed to feel Thaddeus's arms around her. The comfort of being close to him, head on his chest, listening to him breathe—that was the sanctuary she longed for, where the world and all of its trouble melted away. She missed him. She longed to feel his lips on hers, see his clear, blue eyes look through her. She wanted to feel that tingle when he touched her.

Her attention shifted between her story and the ones she missed. She wished she were deep into the plot; it would hold her attention, not letting her mind drift. There had been no word from her brothers in about a month. Emilie didn't worry about them; she figured they would care for each other and come home as soon as it was all over. Letters regularly came from Thaddeus and Stephen. It was entertaining to read about Stephen's antics. Thaddeus always wrote about the seriousness of camp and then changed the subject to courting her. Emilie loved his words. She knew he wrote them with thoughtful dedication. She felt its meaning through these black, inky words. The realization of how much she missed him washed over her. It was no use trying to read. She closed the book, leaned her head back, and closed her eyes to give in to the bliss of sleepy relaxation, her mind drifting dreamily from images of him and memories of them.

Somewhere in her head, she heard, "My god, you are even more beautiful than I remember." His voice was only inches away from her ear. She felt his breath tickle her cheek, his lips soft on her ear. The smell of smoke and wet wool made her realize this was no dream.

Opening her eyes, she saw his clear, blue eyes looking only inches from hers. Emilie squeaked with surprise and threw herself into his arms. Thaddeus was caught off guard and fell back onto the parlor rug; Emilie's legs caught in her skirts, and she fell on top of him. She kissed him first all over and then deeply on his soft, hungry lips. When she stopped, she looked at him, sputtering, "Oh my god, I'm not dreaming! How, when, why?" Overwhelmed by excitement, Emilie could not speak a full sentence. "You didn't tell me you were coming!" She finally found her wits to speak; she smacked him. He cringed and laughed at her. Her slap had no effect on him except to make him smile at her.

Thaddeus smiled. "All of these questions without a proper hello?" he taunted her playfully. He had planned this meeting for some time, and he enjoyed her reaction. She looked happy. He could not stop looking at her. His stay would be short, and he wanted to refresh all the memories of her. He looked into her eyes, enjoying her weight on top of him. Her hair tickled his face as it fell in front of her face. He could smell her fresh, clean hair and enjoyed it very much. Emilie touched him, feeling him in her hands. She kissed him. His mouth felt so good on hers.

"I missed you." Her voice was husky with passion.

He held her tight. "I think we should get off the floor first. If your parents see us." He didn't take his eyes from hers, he wanted to look at her as long as he could. They were locked onto each other, unwilling to look away. She shook her head. The move from the floor to the settee, accomplished without breaking the touch they established from the moment they had linked.

Unwilling to break contact, they held hands while they talked. Emilie filled him in on her adventure to Virginia. She answered all his questions. He told her of the challenges of the winter camps.

"We will be getting ready to move out in the next few weeks after we get back," Thaddeus said. "It will feel good to move. I want to get this war over with before my darling finds another love." He slipped this in to catch her off guard. He waited for her reaction.

"I can't wait till you come home." Confusion crossed her face. "What? Who is finding someone new?" She saw the smile on his face. The big grin on his face told her he was playing with her. Laughing, she shook her head.

"The only one who can steal my heart is you, Mr. Marsh." Emilie pushed him. He didn't move. He sat solidly on the couch. Muscular and defined, she leaned into him, putting her head on his shoulder. He slipped his arm around her and kissed the top of her head.

"How long will it last?" She was nestled into him.

"Forever," he murmured into the top of her head. He enjoyed the hint of lavender and wood smoke smell on her hair. He wished to remember this and every part of her. It gave him strength.

"The war, I mean." She felt the rough wool on her check. Not minding it a bit, she felt secure in his arms; this was the sanctuary she dreamed of only moments before.

"I don't know. I suspect we will be fighting good and hard this year and hopefully come home soon after that." He took her delicate hand in his, raised it to his lips, and kissed it gently.

Their conversation went on until the parlor doors opened. Emilie saw her parents waiting anxiously to talk to Thaddeus. Seeing their daughter smiling, bright with happiness, they entered, bringing in a tray of refreshments.

The family sat and visited well into the evening. At the end of the night, Thaddeus took his leave, hugging his fiancée close. "I will see you tomorrow, until then, sleep well." He spoke softly in her ear. "Always, always remember I love you." With that, he left her standing on the porch. She watched him leave. Seeing him go, sadness washed over her; suddenly she remembered he would see her tomorrow. She felt renewed and happy for the first time in months. She could not wait to start her life with him. She imagined what it might be like to fall asleep and wake up with him every day. They would pick up where they left off; if the war ended—and it would end—she vowed to remember how hard it was to let go of him. When times got rough in their marriage, she hoped this feeling would remind her he was worth fighting for.

> Dear diary,
>
> I cannot believe he is home! I held him in my arms again. I am giddy with excitement. I wish time to slow down so I can keep him as long as possible. Seeing him healthy and well is refreshing to me. I am happy our love

has endured this long separation. I hope this war finishes in the next few months so we can start our lives together. I am amazed our reunion was not awkward, it was as if he never left my side.

I must try to sleep. Tomorrow will be here before I know it. Thaddeus will call on me again tomorrow afternoon.

E.K.P

Morning chores finished, Emilie sat in her room, sorting through more material. She wanted to start her wedding quilt. She had plenty of scraps left over; the quilt would continue giving her hope for their future. Her fabric chest lay open, fabric strewn all over the chest, and her bed looked like a kaleidoscope of color. Emilie had colors and patterns sorted in order of favorite to least favorite. She wanted the quilt to be bright. She hated the drab brown and black fabric. These colors were strictly for work clothes. There was no room in this quilt.

Wrapped up in her thoughts, Emilie turned to see her mother at her door. "Em, I need you in the kitchen." Julia loved watching her daughter create. Emilie always made beautiful projects. She was a meticulous artist, and her work showed it.

Emilie smiled at her mother. "I will be right there. What do you think about these two colors together?" The red and yellow swatches lay across her arm. Her mother shook her head and wrinkled her nose. "That's what I thought. They just don't work." Emilie tossed the fabric on the bed. "I will get back to this later."

"I thought we weren't going to start baking until after dinner?" Emilie was sure her mother told her that plan.

Watching her step on the landing, they started down the stairs, Emilie following her mother. "I thought we could get started to finish early just in case you have visitors today." As they entered the kitchen, Emilie noticed Joe Bayle in the yard, talking to her father.

"Why don't they come inside? It can't be that warm outside?" Emilie went to the door. She waved at the men outside. They were in deep conversation. Emilie saw the stern look on their faces.

Julia took the soup pot out of the cupboard. "I don't know." She busied herself in the pantry. When Emilie went out to the root cellar to gather the potatoes and onions, she walked past the men.

"Hello, Mr. Bayle. How are Mrs. Bayle and the children?" She always referred to the Bayle children as a group. Somehow, she always missed one when she tried to mention them by name.

Joe looked tired, dark circles around both eyes. The creases in his forehead told of worry and stress. "We are not having a good month. The children are sick. The doctor is coming out to see Jane and Robert. They have awful colds."

"I am sorry to hear. Please call on me if I can help in anyway." Emilie left the men to their conversations. On her way back from the cellar, apron full of vegetables, Emilie saw them coming up the drive. Thaddeus and Stephen came to visit. Emilie ran to the house, dropped the vegetables on the table, and scurried upstairs to attend to her looks.

As she passed by her mother and father, she heard, "Where's the fire girl?" The bewildered parents figured out the cause of her distress moments later when there was a knock on the door.

"Emilie, you wouldn't believe how many soldiers are sick this winter. We are boxing them up and shipping them home almost daily." Stephen went on about the conditions of the winter camp. "If this keeps up, good ole Lincoln will have to recruit more volunteers." He took no notice of Emilie's distain, her eyes wide with disbelief and her nose wrinkled with disgust. She could not believe the living conditions were cold and drafty. No wonder the men were sick.

"What do you do for fun?" She was trying to change the unpleasant subject.

Stephen grinned, looking from Thaddeus and then back at Emilie. Emilie noticed something different about Stephen. His newfound independence suited him well. He had a carefree, upbeat note to his presence that she had not seen before. He was exciting to talk with. He laughed more than she had ever known him to do. Emilie didn't miss his sour, sullen pessimistic, dark-cloud attitude. He had almost become carefree despite the darkness of war.

Clearing his throat, he said, "Well, there is plenty to do in camp for entertainment, but I am not sure it is proper to discuss in the company of ladies." Stephen shifted uncomfortably in his seat.

"I think she is talking about cards and writing letters," Thaddeus offered with a warning glare to his companion. "Miss Emilie does not need all the details about soldier antics. It can be very unsettling, my dear." Thaddeus patted Emilie's hand.

"Think of it this way." Thaddeus began explaining how the camp was a melting pot of different cultures and personalities. He summed it up in terms Emilie quickly understood. "Imagine your brother's antics and multiply it by a thousand men. What would you get?" Thaddeus watched her think it over. First, her eyebrow arched thoughtfully; then shock crossed her face. Emilie smiled.

"I don't think I want to know the details," she concluded, laughing. "My brothers were a whole lot of mischief when they were young. Pa made several trips to the woodshed with each of them. I think they learned more in the woodshed than they did in school."

"Do you like reading my letters, Stephen?" Emilie asked.

"Yes, very much. There is gossip around camp as to whom you will choose in the end. My friends are confused as to whom you belong to," Stephen said.

"Why don't you tell them I am your sister?" Emilie interjected.

"It's more fun when they think you are writing me without Thaddeus knowing it." Stephen enjoyed the attention of his friends. "I just let them think about it. You should hear the questions they ask me. It provides hours of entertainment."

Emilie wasn't comfortable being the center of camp banter. It was this kind of talk that ruins a girl's reputation. Emilie wanted no part of that. She eyed Stephen skeptically, considering her next move. If she told him she wanted to be considered his sister, would he abide by her wishes or just laugh? What did it matter anyway? Most of these boys were from other counties miles away.

"I think you are getting 'the look,' Stephen." Thaddeus studied her eyes as they changed shades as her emotions passed over her. Emilie suddenly became serious, her eyes narrowing and her jaw set in an unhappy tenseness. Thaddeus knew she was not pleased with his friend's antics.

"Come on Em, don't fret." Stephen laughed off the seriousness of the situation.

"This is my reputation you are playing with, Stephen," Emilie interjected. "It is not something to joke about."

"I would never allow your reputation to be tarnished." Stephen watched her unchanging expression. He conceded. "All right, if it will make you feel better, you have officially become my sister." He smiled at her, hoping to make amends with her. He didn't want her angry with him. He truly liked her, yes, more than he should ever like his best friend's fiancée.

The afternoon winds and rains raged outside. The last winter storm blew through Gettysburg that day. No one in the Prescott home seemed to mind Mother Nature's last attempts at winter as it blew dark, wet clouds through the town. Everyone was safe and warm inside the parlor, enjoying one another's company.

❧

It was a different story at the Bayle residence. The wind knocked at the pane glass windows while Jane lay in bed, battling a cough that ravaged her body, leaving her struggling to catch her breath with each spell. Low-grade fever, pale complexion—her eyes had very little life in them. She was weak as a newborn kitten but still attempted to smile as her father patiently fed her some chicken broth.

"The doctor will be here this afternoon," he calmly assured his daughter. "I am sure he will find a cure for that cough." He smiled at her, trying to get her to smile back. She looked like a vacant shell. Her eyes were hollow, cheeks sunken; Jane lacked the spunk she once possessed. She was as white as her cotton nightgown. Joe tried to cover up his worry by reading her a story. Jane fell asleep, dreaming about princes and horses.

Harriett tended the boys' dinner needs. She was relieved Robert finally slept for the first time since early morning. His little body was taken by the same cough as his sister. The toddler struggled to breathe while he slept. His body was growing weaker every hour the sickness remained. Harriett struggled to keep Robert fed. He ate little, struggling to swallow. This worried her the most. She anxiously watched the yard for the arrival of Dr. Huber. He was due this afternoon, but by the looks of the wind, she expected him to be delayed. Her fears became bigger as her head told her the children ailed with diphtheria. She began to pray she was wrong. Harriet desperately hoped she was wrong. This disease took so many children; she didn't want any of them to be hers. Her thoughts echoed repeatedly in her head. Tears rolled down her cheeks she was worried and tired to exhaustion. She didn't bother wiping them. Her hands wet with dishwater, she wept as she washed the last few dinner dishes.

Harriet struggled to control her emotions, weeping silently to herself. Joe comforted his wife with a warm, reassuring hand on her shoulder. He rubbed her back and whispered, "Jane is sleeping. Let me help you." Joe had a soft, loving side seen most often by his family. He didn't need to ask his wife if she was worried; he knew she was crying by her silence and the subtle quiver of her shoulders. Her strength was being challenged. He knew she would come through this bravely. Joe wished at this moment that he could hold his wife close, smell her hair and savor her scent. He longed to hold her hands, strong yet delicate, despite their calluses and cracked skin due to dishes and housework. No matter what shape her hands were in, she still handled her family with a firm gentleness. Joe could not imagine another woman in his life. Harriet was everything he hoped for. She worked hard as a mother and a wife. Her dedication was steady and strong. Their relationship grew over the years. As their children grew with them, he knew this was the life God had planned for him.

When the doctor arrived, his sharp knock on the door startled them both. He handed her the towel and went to answer the door. The door was forced open by the wind. Joe struggled to hang on to it. "Dr. Huber, thank you for coming." Joe invited the doctor inside.

"Looks like winter is not over yet," the doctor commented as he set his bag on the table and shed his coat. The wind came up sharp and cold. I am glad to see the clouds don't look like they will bless us with snow."

Once the coat was hung, the adults got right to the subject at hand. Harriett reviewed Jane's and Robert's symptoms—the onset of cough and low-grade fever. Dr. Huber looked concerned. He went to examine Jane first. He asked about her eating and sleep patterns. Dr. Huber watched her breathe. The small body labored with every breath. Looking into her mouth, the doctor's face set into a grim tone.

"From what I can see inside her mouth, she is showing advanced stages." He hated giving news like this. "Keep the rest of the children out of her room, and we need to quarantine the baby and Jane together."

"Is she still swallowing?" Dr. Huber looked at the pair hopefully.

Joe said, "Yes, she ate some broth not thirty minutes ago." He held his wife's hand for reassurance.

"Good, good. Let's check on the baby." Dr. Huber tucked the blankets around Jane's frail body, felt her head again, and left the room. His demeanor changed considerably. This was a potential grave situation, and he was no longer feeling like socializing.

Young Robert fussed as the doctor examined his small body. His body was warm with fever, and his face flushed pink. Robert gave up squirming in protest as the doctor poked and prodded him.

"Harriett, is Robert eating?" Dr. Huber looked up at her, eyes serious beyond all measure. The toddler lay limp in his lap.

Harriett burst into tears. "No, he is not eating well at all. It's like he has forgotten how." They watched Dr. Huber stick his finger into the boy's mouth. Gently, he encouraged him to suck. They watched him protest and struggle to breathe. Finally, the doctor gave them the news.

"The children have diphtheria. Robert is not going to make it. He has lost his ability to swallow due to paralysis of his mouth. Keep him comfortable. It won't be long." The words stuck in the physician's throat. News like this was never easy, no matter how many times it was given. "Jane also has the gray lining in her mouth and throat. I am hoping she is strong enough, but oftentimes, this is what strangles the children. I am sorry." He went on to tell them his instructions for patient comfort and insisted the others do not come in contact with their siblings. Dr. Huber checked each child and adult for symptoms and encouraged them to find a home for the healthy ones for a few days. It will be just a matter of time.

That sentence echoed in Joe's head for hours after Dr. Huber left their home. Tearfully, he and Harriett began preparing to find a home for the others to keep them from getting sick. Joe left to search for a home for Billy, Joe, Van, and Sam. Harriett quietly prepared the boys' things and tried to explain what would happen. Billy stepped up and announced he would take care of the boys while they were away. As the next oldest, Joe did not want to be outdone by his brother and vowed the same.

"Don't worry, Ma, I will make sure everyone listens and eats their supper. We will help with chores and not be a nuisance." He looked to his brothers to agree with him. The boys were wide-eyed with worry.

Harriet beamed with pride. Billy was changing, becoming more responsible and less a carefree child. "Thank you, Billy. I don't know where you are going yet, but we depend on you to help as much as you can." The family would stay strong. It was all they had. Billy nodded in agreement. Van continued to hold on to his blanket for security, and Sam watched Billy for what to do next.

"Ma, will they be better when we get back?" little Joe asked timidly. The child sensed there was something dreadfully amiss in the house.

❧

Family dinner smelled delicious. The table set as usual: Jacob at the left, Julia at the right, and Emilie at the back. Each family member was sharing tidbits about their day, enjoying one another's company. The knock came quite unexpectedly. Emilie could see only the top of a man's hat in the window. Jacob got up from the table to answer the door.

The quiet house changed dramatically with the addition of four young boys. They arrived sullen and sad, but once they settled into Henry's old room, they started smiling and feeling more comfortable with their surroundings. Billy took charge of his younger brothers. Little Joe was next in command, repeating orders issued by his older brother, reminding them of their manners and speaking for Van who was very sad and reserved.

Emilie thought stories would distract the boys from their worries. She remembered this was how they settled in before sleep at night. After warm milk and cookies, the younger boys went to the parlor with her. Billy offered to help with the chores. Sam and little Joe sat in front of Emilie. Van stood in the middle of the room, unmoving.

"Van, do you want to pick a story?" His big eyes stared back at Emilie, no smile and no response. Emilie waited. Holding the book in her hand, she watched him from the settee.

Sam hopped up on the settee and sat next to Emilie. He whispered to her, "He wants to sit on your lap."

"Thanks, Sam." Sam smiled and moved in closer to have the best vantage point to see the pages. Seeing his brother sitting next to Emilie, Van moved in to sit on her lap. Emilie loved having the small boy sit there. She kissed the top of his head as he snuggled closer to her as she read. Thirty minutes later, the stories read and the boys tucked into bed, Emilie came back downstairs to say good night to her parents.

"How are they doing?" Julia asked as she finished putting away the last of the dishes. Julia was glad to welcome the boys. She missed the house being a bustle of activity.

"Everyone is doing fine. Van won't let go of that blanket. Sam watches him like a hawk, and I think the other two enjoy bossing the little ones around." Emilie smiled.

"Billy has sure grown into a young man," Julia commented.

"Yes, he certainly has more responsibility about him. Did Joe say when they were coming back? Will they be visiting?" Emilie asked thoughtfully. She knew the boys were aware that their siblings were sick, but she didn't how much information was being shared.

"No, your pa told Joe the boys could stay as long as needed. Both children are very ill. I think we should prepare ourselves for the worst." Julia wanted to break the news to Emilie as gently as possible. She had not experienced death in her life, and she knew how hard it would be to know that bitter reality the first time around. Emilie was lucky to have a privileged life. She was too young to experience the loss of her grandparents, and unlike most people her age Emilie never experienced the loss of a sibling, young or old. Julia hoped she would be strong enough to learn about this hardship.

"We are helpless then." Emilie felt it was more of a question than a statement. "How do you go on?"

Julia sat down at the table with a mug of warm milk in her hand. She gently took her daughter's hands in hers. "Death comes and goes. It is an inevitable part of life. You must learn now that loss is a blessing. You are blessed to know that person, and you know they are healthy in heaven. These two blessings are given by God. The pain will go away in time. It is how you deal with it. That makes you stronger."

"Stronger? How does a parent become stronger when they lose a child?" Emilie's eyes welled up with tears. The memories of the children flashed through her mind. How would Harriet and Joe go on knowing memories are all they have now of two of their children?

> Dear diary,
> I can't believe how life changes so fast. Yesterday the joy of having Thaddeus home and visiting with old friends brought me so much happiness. Today I learned Jane and Robert Bayle are very ill. The house is bustling with the rest of the children. Billy, Sam, little Joe, and Van are staying with us while Mr. and Mrs. Bayle tend the others.
> Mother thinks the children will die. I know the chances of recovering from diphtheria are very low. I am hoping for the best. People recover. I just hope they are strong enough. I cannot imagine life without Jane or Robert. They have made me smile on more than one occasion. I love Jane's responsible nature. She will make a good mother someday. Little Robert was the first baby I have experienced. I love how he smiles when he sees me. How can reality be so cruel? I will miss them very much. Mother tried to tell me death was a blessing. I cannot imagine it. All I see is sorrow. How can Harriet and Joe go on living without their children? I want to cry just thinking about it. I hope Thaddeus

and I never have to feel this kind of sorrow. I will pray extra prayers and maybe God will see it in his wisdom to spare these beautiful children.

Saddened by the day's events, I hope my dreams will be good ones.

E.K.P

The Bayle children were laid to rest the following Thursday. The aftermath of death left a blanket of sadness and grief on everyone's heart. Emilie and Julia visited the Bayle residence, helping tend the children and sit with Harriett in her grief. Emilie had never felt such emptiness. She longed for happiness, when life was easy and carefree.

GOOD-BYE, HURRY HOME

The reason it hurts so much to separate is because our souls are connected.

—Nicholas Sparks

Emilie and Thaddeus sat close as they travelled into town, her hands comfortably placed in her lap. She wanted to touch him but knew she shouldn't. It was inevitable; he was leaving in two days; she wanted to keep him as close as long as she could. Quietly, he took her hand and placed it on his lap, his hand still holding hers. She looked at him, surprised.

He smiled at her. "I just want you close to me." Emilie returned the smile and squeezed his hand. "I want you to touch me."

"How did you know?" Emilie was always amazed at how he seemed to read her thoughts. It was as if they were communicating with their thoughts instead of words. It reminded her of a fortune-teller at the circus; if he could read her thoughts, Emilie hoped he could also hear her heart.

Today they were going into town for lunch and errands. Emilie was happy to leave everything behind on Table Rock Road. She felt lighter and more carefree to leave behind all of the mourning. First stop was to pick up a few items to make camp life more comfortable. The list was short: Matches, extra socks and new pair of boots, and some hard candies just for fun. Then they were off to eat lunch at Globe Inn.

Sitting across from him, she studied his features; she loved the defined nose, big blue eyes, and the way he smiled at her. There was love in his eyes, and she was happy to see it was her that made him smile.

"Do you ever think about what we will do when you come home?" she asked after the tea was served.

He eyed her appreciatively.

"Every moment of the day when I think about you." His comment comforted her. "It is how we will change that bothers me."

"Change? Who is changing?" Emilie felt a sudden prick of alert fear in her stomach. She suddenly braced herself for bad news.

"Don't fret, little one." He raised an eyebrow at her. He reached across the table to take her hands in his. "War changes everything. I just don't want it to change me. I want you to recognize me when I get home." Emilie had never thought of this before. She saw some men come home injured and ill. Looking at this man across the table, she didn't want to let go of the person she was looking at now.

"I can't imagine you changing for the worse. Why don't you change only for the better?" She smiled at him, hoping to get one in return. He looked so somber.

"Em, if I don't come back..." The words came difficult to him. He had to talk about this; he needed to tell her. Stories of Bull Run came to his mind. The loss of life and limb, she had to be prepared.

"No, no, stop talking like that." She stiffened, resisting his words. He held her hands tighter, not letting her go. "Thaddeus, I will not marry if it can't be to you! I don't care in what condition, just come home." Her eyes pleaded with him. She held on to his hands, squeezing them for reassurance. "I will be waiting for you."

He didn't press the issue further. He didn't want to scare her. She didn't need to have negative thoughts to ponder with no way for him to calm her. Instead, he smiled. "This is why I love you. So positive and bright."

"Those are your words for *impractical* and *unrealistic*." She smiled at him. He looked at her surprised.

"Stop teasing now, I have to tell you. If I am in trouble on the field, I have told Stephen to return your locket to you. This way you will know what happened." She listened until he finished. "I just want you to know this in case anything happens."

Emilie was happy when the food came to the table. She was ready to change the subject. She understood the words needed to be said between them, but it was the possibility of something happening that she was unwilling to think about. All she had thought about up to now was their future after the war; it never occurred to her that he could be taken from them. Emilie chose to return to the happy thoughts.

"Let's just send you back so you can come home, and we can begin our family together." Emilie patted his hands and then reached for her napkin.

"Good idea, I will hurry home to our future." Thaddeus worried about Emilie not wanting to face the possible realities. Would she be strong enough to get through a bad situation? No matter what they discussed, Emilie always wrapped it up with a plan and a smile. They ate their lunch while chatting and playfully flirting with each other. It was a just the day they needed to get ready for another long separation.

Two days later, Stephen and Thaddeus boarded the train to go back to Washington. Emilie kissed him good-bye, willing him to be strong. Holding him close, she gathered her strength to smile instead of cry.

"I will always love you."

His voice was warm and husky in her ear.

"I know," she said, holding on tight. "I love you too. Hurry home to make me your wife." She smiled as he chuckled in her ear.

"I will make you my wife and so much more. I dream of it every night." He cupped her chin in his large hand. Looking deep into her eyes, he said, "Keep writing to me. It gives me strength."

"I will." She hung on tight to his jacket, willing him not to look away. She loved swimming in the blueness of his eyes.

"I have to go." His kiss captured her mouth, claiming her as his own. Tender and demanding, she gave in to him with her whole being. Longing to melt into him and become one, she didn't want to wait.

The train whistle interrupted the kiss. Reluctantly, they let go of each other, and he boarded the train. Once again he left her standing on the train platform. There were no tears, only the familiar void of emptiness surrounding Emilie as she watched the train pull out of the station.

Dear diary,

He is gone again. I feel so empty without him. I am trying to be brave. Trying to be positive, as I believe that is the only thing that will bring him home safe to me. If I lose my battle and give in to negative thoughts, I could lose him forever. It is so hard to carry this burden. I have to smile when I want to cry from the loneliness. I don't know how many other ways I can ask God to end this war. God seems too busy to hear me. I know God must have matters that are more important with men dying and families in need. I will remain positive this will all work out in our favor.

E.K.P.

LETTERS FROM
THE FRONT

Nothing makes the earth seem so spacious as to have friends
at a distance; they make the latitudes and longitudes.

—Henry David Thoreau

The summer of 1862 saw the war gain momentum. The action
stayed clear of Pennsylvania that summer. The guns roared through
Maryland, Tennessee, and the Shenandoah Valley in Virginia.
The victories changed sides—Union and Confederate—evenly
throughout the summer months. The whole matter seemed so
far from Emilie's reality; she began to lose patience with the
whole thing.

Stories regarding the casualties and wounded made Emilie
extremely nervous. With every battle report she read, Emilie
worried about Thaddeus's safety. Letters from Thaddeus and
Stephen came regularly. They were upbeat and positive. Emilie
hoped he wasn't writing about good things and keeping the hardships to himself. She wanted to share those hardships with him.
Thaddeus was a protector. She knew he would keep his worries
to himself. He would make a devoted provider and protector, but
now she just needed to know whether he was doing all right.
Emilie struggled with these doubts every day. When she felt she
could not manage her worry, she took long rides with Starlight.
She visited the places she and Thaddeus frequented before. She
felt close to him there. Emilie wrote daily letters to him from the
time Thaddeus left. She clung to the hope that if she remained
positive, he would have the strength to go on.

Letters from Henry and Aaron came about every two months.
They were very general, saying little about where they were, only
that they were under the command of J. E. B. Stuart's division.
Emilie researched their possible whereabouts through newspa-

pers. The boys seemed so far removed from her and her life as she now knew it. They had been gone a year, with little contact; Emilie felt they had somehow slipped away. The last letter Emilie read from Henry boasted about their victories. He sounded happy about the terror he and his men had reined over a small northern town. Emilie saw some of the old Henry she knew. Mostly, the letters didn't say much except both boys were healthy and missed home. Jacob explained the letters were penned in this fashion as to protect both parties from suspicion of loyalty.

"The enemy?" Emilie questioned.

"I can't see either side as our enemy, Father?"

Who is the enemy? Jacob looked at his daughter's bewildered face. She was beginning to understand the pull the war was trying to impose on them. "The enemy is the one who threatens to take away your freedoms," Jacob quietly stated. They rocked together quietly on the porch swing, Emilie's feet barely touching the wooden porch. She pushed the swing with the tip of her shoe to give it a gentle, swaying motion. Thinking over what her father said, Emilie concluded, "How can one consider family the enemy?" She was shaking her head in disbelief. "What will we do if they come home before the war is done?"

"Aaron and Henry are your brothers first. We will welcome them." Jacob was very clear about his point. "We will hope to see them when this is all over."

Emilie handed her father Henry and Aaron's letters and then turned to the sealed envelope in her lap. This letter was from Thaddeus. She smiled as she opened it. The pages smelled like wood smoke. His handwriting decorated the pages with perfect letters carefully written.

> My dear girl,
>   The fighting is getting intense over the last few days. The rebels don't seem to want to give up and go home. We were lucky to make it out alive. The last few fights have been very close, and we have had many casualties. Stephen

and I are safe for the time being. Know it is your smile and memories of your kisses that keep me fighting to get back to you.

The South is hot and very disagreeable. We have been moving constantly since June. The troops are getting tired. Many have been sick with diseases due to lack of sleep and what feels like continuous marching. I long for the warm, breezy nights sitting on the swing next to you on your father's front porch. I long to hear your laugh and see the sparkle in your eyes when I make you laugh; you bring me joy. We arrived back at Bull Run to skirmish again as they did over a year ago. Looks like we are going to be marching back toward Washington. Hopefully, the rebs will not cross into Northern territory. Our boys are tired and cranky toward them and ready to fight. I just need a reprieve; we are all very tired and need a rest for now. I am hoping we will find some time to relax before they come knocking again.

Tonight as I look into the night sky, I am seeing the same stars as you. You feel so far away, but when I come home, I want us to lay in the yard and look at the stars as I see them tonight. They are beautiful, and I long to share that with you.

Stay strong, my love.

Will be seeing you very soon.

Your future husband,
Thaddeus

A tear slipped down Emilie's cheek. She worried about the toll the war would have on him. She knew he was strong enough to do what was asked of him, but his words felt so vulnerable. Compelled to write him, she wiggled off the swing and headed into the house.

Her father looked from his letter. He marveled at his daughter's devotion. She loved that boy, and he was proud at her persistence to keep supporting him through the trials he faced.

The rest of late spring was ever increasingly trying for her. Thaddeus's letters became more descriptive of his trials and near misses. Emilie was thankful they missed most of the battle at Antietam. It was a horrible, bloody affair. It was clearly a battle of wills with no clear victor. The energies she spent writing letters and sending care packages became a ritual for her. Diligent and strong, she was steadfast and devoted to her future.

This fall, the parlor was decorated with the bright cascade of colors of the wedding quilt Emilie worked all summer to put together. It was time to frame and finish it. The large frame took up a good portion of the parlor. Set on wooden workhorses from Jacob's woodshop, the chairs were set all around. Mrs. Bayle, Mrs. Marsh, and Mrs. Byrne, along with Sallie Meyer and some older students from school, were coming to stitch.

Emilie and Julia set up plates of small sandwiches and cookies. They made tea and cider. It was a very festive get-together. Emilie received her guests, and together they sat around the quilt, discussing the happening around town.

"The storekeepers are very nervous since the raid on Chambersburg," Mrs. Byrne commented. "I am finding it hard to get the materials I need to sew a winter cloak."

"I have seen more patrols around town since Chambersburg. The shopkeepers are hiding some of their inventory in case there is a raid here. Have any of you attended those meetings?" Sallie gave a nonchalant description of what was happening in town.

"I don't understand how the Rebs could get past our forces. The poor folks of Chambersburg and Mechanicville are terrified." Mrs. Marsh shook her head in disbelief. "Can you believe the cost of devastation up there?"

Mrs. Marsh retold the story of how J.E.B. Stuart's cavalry swept through town taking supplies and horses then leaving the town warehouses burning. She expressed how embarrassing it was that the union forces could not catch the raiders. Everyone, engrossed in their work, only shook their heads, each concentrating on the stitches before them.

"Joe and Billy have a plan for the horses, just in case," Harriett added quietly. "No one is going to take our livelihood." As she spoke, Harriett's excitement became more animated to emphasize her point. Sarah gasped. "Wasn't that awful? I hear they took thousands of horses, leaving the farmers with nothing."

Emilie looked up from her stitching. "Stealing horses? Thousands?" Her thoughts immediately went to Starlight, suddenly remembering old man Blocher's warning. His words rang in her head: *I have to say, that horse has some spirit. Keep her close when the troops come knocking. They'll take her for sure.*

"Mrs. Bayle? Do you think Joe and Billy would take Starlight with them?" Emilie tried to hide the swelling panic within her.

Harriett smiled at Emilie. "I am sure something can be worked out." The tension in the room ebbed and flowed as the women discussed the war and its effects on their families. Some stories were heartwarming while others tore at the women's heartstrings. Everyone had stories to tell. The war seemed miles away, but its circle of effect rippled closer to Gettysburg more than anyone had expected.

The end of the year brought life as usual to the town. Once the incident in Chambersburg started to fade from their thoughts, the focus changed to the Christmas holidays. Christmas was a quiet holiday with many empty places at this year's table. The neighbors on Table Rock Road had small, quiet gatherings to remember loved ones, both gone and away.

Emilie and Thaddeus opened presents from each other in separate states in the Union, both thinking about the other and praying the war would end so they could begin their lives together.

BLOSSOMS AND RUMORS ABOUND

Trying to squash a rumor is like trying to unring a bell.

—Shana Alexander

The warm winds of spring brought joy to the citizens of Gettysburg. The farmers eagerly planted the fields in the hope of a healthy, profitable harvest come fall. Schoolchildren ran about, bitten by the spring fever. Emilie found joy this spring. Her friend Sallie was blessed with family homecoming. Her father and brother were safely home from the war, both medically discharged and recovering well. It felt refreshing to see her friend surrounded by family and happiness. She smiled, thinking she too could have been bitten by the spring fever, feeling lighthearted and happy.

Emilie tied up Starlight outside Fahnstock Store. The store was bustling with people, looking for bargains of the day. In the corner of the store, six men gathered, talking loudly about the current politics. The small town was normally quiet and subdued except for its ongoing political hubbub. Gettysburg was a hot spot for defined political parties with loud opinions. The newspapers sharply divided the town, each publisher on the opposite side, each embedded deeply into their own political agendas.

Emilie couldn't help but overhear the loud conversation. It intrigued her to listen to what the men were saying. She edged to look at the trinkets on a shelf, bringing herself closer to the conversation.

"All them copperheads should just come clean and move to the right side of the Mason-Dixon Line if they are gonna support them Rebs. We don't need those dirty, grubby rebs any closer to us than they already are."

"Our own citizens support their cause. I don't know what they hope to gain."

"Wonder where they will be when the Union crushes their fight. What will they do then?" The men grumbled, shaking their heads and agreeing with one another. Emilie rolled her eyes amazed at their ignorance.

"Miss Emilie, so good to see you again." Mary Felty smiled at the young girl. "More writing paper? You must have a special beau. Have you heard from your brothers? How are they doing?"

Emilie was taken off guard by her question. No one had asked about them in months. Emilie avoided talking at length about them for fear she would reveal where they went.

"They are doing well. Both fighting for the cause," Emilie casually answered, unaware her comments caused stirring from the group in the corner. She reached in her pocket to retrieve her payment.

"There's another one, so blatantly spouting their allegiance." The gray-haired man pointed a crooked finger at her. "She should go home, like the rest of them."

Emilie felt all eyes on her. She turned, facing her accuser. "I am home, sir." She glared at him.

"Who is she?" the rest of the men mumbled to one another. The men tried to figure out to whom she belonged. They wondered if she lived here or if she was only visiting.

"That's the Prescott girl," a woman beside them pointed out. "She teaches at the Oakridge School."

"Yes, I am Emilie Prescott." Emilie confirmed their questions.

"Is it true, your brothers are fighting for the rebs?" another man asked her directly. Emilie noticed the group of people began closing in on her with questions and curiosity.

"My brothers are fighting for what they believe in, just like your families." Emilie shot back in defense. She squared her shoulders and watched them curiously.

"What side are you choosing?" The question came from the crowd. "Didn't you move here recently?"

"Are you a Confederate or Union?" The man who posed this question seemed to pop out of the crowd just to be heard. He was tall and devilishly handsome. He caught Emilie off guard with his question. To her, he sounded as if he were accusing her of something. Emilie felt guarded and defensive. The time had finally come. Emilie had to take a stand. How could she choose a side, when she plainly understood this war had more at stake than political views? How could political agendas outweigh the human lives lost? Emilie could not pick a side because she was deeply invested in both.

She looked at the crowd and stated, "I am just a person waiting for this war to be done, so I can go on with my life. Until that happens, I am stuck, just like the rest of you. Good day, Gentlemen."

"You didn't answer the question, miss. Are you a reb?" the man persisted.

"I live in the North. That is enough to answer your question."

She grabbed her package off the counter and turned to leave the store. Closing the door behind her, she was ready to leave the hotbed of controversy. As she rode Starlight out of town, she saw two riders race past her into town. Slowing Starlight to let them pass, she heard them shout to her, "Hurry home, miss. The rebs are coming. General Lee is bringing them to us!" Blankly looking at them, Emilie's heart jumped with excitement. How close would this war come? On her way home, she stopped by the Bayle home.

The Bayle yard bustled with excitement. Emilie came upon the confusion. Horses gathered in a large group outside. Billy raced out of the house, with a knapsack flung over one shoulder and a biscuit sandwich in the other hand. Harriett called after him from the porch. Billy nodded in response and motioned to the barn.

Noticing Emilie approach, Billy motioned to her. He could not speak because he had a mouth full of food. She dismounted, held Starlight's reins, and smiled as she saw him try to tie the knapsack to the horse with one hand.

"Let me help you!" Emilie rushed to his side. Still chewing, he nodded. "That is quite a mouthful. What is going on?" she asked, smiling at his awkward fumbling.

After a big swallow, Billy announced, "Pa says the Rebs are coming. We need to save the horses. It's cavalry, Emilie. You better hide her." Billy nodded toward Starlight.

If Joe is concerned, then this is probably true. Emilie tried to quell the panic that threatened to overtake her. "Where's your pa, Billy?" Emilie was determined to save her horse even if it meant she must leave her in the care of someone else.

"In the barn." Billy grabbed his canteen and walked toward the well.

Inside the barn, Emilie found Joe Bayle, tying ropes and fussing with harnesses and bridles for the horses. He had five lined up on the post. He looked up as soon as he heard her enter the barn. He could not see her in the shadows but assumed it was Billy.

"William, did you finish gathering the food from your mother?"

"It's Emilie, Mr. Bayle." Her voice came from the shadows.

"Miss Emilie, you caught us at a very busy time." He smiled at her before turning his attention back the ropes in his hand.

"I came to talk to you about Starlight. I see you are taking your horses away to hide," she began. "Will you hide her too? I don't want to lose her."

"We are not running from the rebs, young lady. I am protecting my own." He sounded irritated and upset.

"I am sorry, sir. I didn't mean for it to sound like that. I came to ask if you will protect mine with yours." Her voice cracked as she finished her request. Letting go of Starlight would be the hardest thing next to seeing Thaddeus leave on the train.

He saw the tears in her eyes. "Emilie, I can't. I would feel awful if something happened to her." Joe knew the horse meant everything to the young girl. "I can't guarantee her safety."

"I would not hold you responsible, just grateful that you tried." Emilie begged him. "I don't know how to keep her safe."

"Keep her in the barn and pray no one comes for her. That is all you can do. Pray no one sees her." Joe felt guilty for turning the girl down, but his mind was too cluttered with everything that needed to be done. "We must go now." Gathering the ropes he was working, he excused himself and headed out of the barn.

Emilie said her good-byes and rode Starlight home, trying to reason why was she afraid. The Southerners were like family. She grew up there; it was all she knew before she came to Gettysburg. Gettysburg was just as comfortable. It felt no different. Emilie concluded she just needed to protect her and her own family from whomever tried to steal from them. She needed a plan.

Arriving home, Emilie noticed the buckboard in the yard. Seth and Big Jim were in the barn, talking with Jacob. The men were in quiet conversation. Emilie went about her business of feeding and unsaddling Starlight.

Inside the house, she found Martha and Julia, sipping tea at the kitchen table. "Emilie dear, good to see you again. My, you are certainly a handsome young woman." Martha's smile lit up her face when she saw Emilie come into the house.

"Martha, it is always good to see you too." Emilie could not help but return the smile.

"Come sit with us, dear." Julia went to the cupboard to get another teacup. "It looks like you could use some tea."

"Thank you, Mother. It has been a trying day." It felt good to sit down and tell them about it. "I am worried. Everyone is in a tizzy about the rebs. Do you think they will come?"

"I can't see what they would want with Gettysburg," Julia concluded.

"What did they want with Chambersburg?" Martha interjected, her Southern accent still noticeably strong. "The folks up there are scar'it. Our folks are all looking to move farther North. Somes says those rebs will take us back to slavery again."

"Do you have a plan?" Emilie couldn't believe what she was hearing—all the work they did months before, only to have her friends kidnapped and sent back to a plantation.

"Your father and the men are talking about a plan. I am sure when they come up with something, we will know soon enough." Julia took another sip of tea. "Until then, why don't you and the boys stay for dinner, Martha. We have plenty. It will be good to visit with you again."

"We haven't seen you in months." Emilie was excited. "What have you been doing since we saw you last."

Martha chuckled. "Why, you right. It has been some time since we visited. We will stay only if I can cook with yous."

"Be our guest," Emilie chimed in. "I miss your cooking, Martha. You spoil us."

Martha smiled with pride. She missed working for this family.

Later that evening, the families discussed plans for the possibilities if the war came to town. The raid of Chambersburg last October left the families with a resolve to be prepared for anything. Jim and Seth discussed the dangers the black community was facing in Gettysburg. The rumors were very real to them.

Emilie told of her day in town. She explained about the troublemakers in Fahnstock's and her request to Mr. Bayle. "Everyone is looking for trouble. All this talk makes things so uncertain."

"Mister Bayle is a smart man. Them rebs will steal anything they please. They sufferin froms no food. Theys hungry all the time," Seth said proudly.

"Which newspaper are you reading now, Seth?" Jacob was proud of the young man, who was coming into his own. He easily discussed a variety of subjects.

"All of them." Martha laughed. "I at least have enough paper to get my fire started."

"I thought our table had a new covering," Jim teased. "It always has papers on it." Everyone laughed.

"I think it best if you move back here with us," Jacob offered. "We can keep you safe here."

"Jacob, we respectfully decline." Jim was grateful to his friend, but his constant need to protect them felt awkward to the family. "We has a home, and cattle, and gardens, and our own to protect. We can't leave it behind."

"We have to protect our own. Looters looking for anything they can steal," Seth added in.

"We have our life now. It's not right livin wit you again." Martha felt this conversation was well overdue. The Prescott family had always been there for them. The families were like family, but Joe, Martha, and Seth needed to stay independent. They only hoped to make the Prescotts understand without offending them.

The families were quiet for a long time, each pondering the events of the last few weeks. Jacob broke the silence. "I understand what you are saying. I only ask that if you need us in anyway, we are here for you."

"We will call," Jim assured him with a big smile.

"That is what family is all about," Emilie added, happy to know a plan was in place. Everyone parted that night feeling secure about the uncertain future.

Before bed, Emilie gathered her writing desk and sat down to write Thaddeus a joyful letter.

> Dearest Thaddeus,
>
> It has been a very strange day today. There are rumors abound regarding possible attacks on Gettysburg by the Confederates. People are running about town, stores are shipping goods to Harrisburg, and our dear black community is terrified of being kidnapped and sent South again. I

can't imagine how horrible that would feel. Please tell me if any of this is true.

I hope all is well with you and Stephen. The papers are saying the fight is getting worse every day. I pray many times a day for your safety. I heard from Henry and Aaron. They are well and fighting just as hard as you. Why don't you all just shake hands and agree to disagree? Sometimes this doesn't make sense to me. It must be my simple female brain. Overall, I am doing well, just can't wait to feel you safe in my arms again. Stay strong, my love.

I have a plan for Starlight. When Mr. Bayle comes back, I will beg him if I have to. I have to know she will be safe, and I trust him to care for her. I can't bear seeing someone ride away with her. My heart aches just thinking about it. Will we ever stop worrying about the simple things? I can't wait for life to be normal again.

My love is with you always. Take care of you!

Yours,
Emilie

News of the battles came in, giving the citizens of Gettysburg more reason to worry. The small town was determined to protect itself at all cost. Banks and businesses prepared for the worst as Lee and his army crossed the Potomac with great intentions of marching north to Washington.

The news from Thaddeus and Stephen stopped. When Emilie had not received a letter in three weeks, she began a constant vigil of worry. She began having bad dreams. Her confidence began to erode away.

Watching their daughter's personality deteriorate, Julia brought up the subject to Jacob. "It has been weeks since she's gotten a letter from him." Julia sat next to her husband. She handed him a cup of tea and snuggled into the crook of his arm.

"I see she is changing. He may be sick or missing. I was worried this was going to happen. I should have never given them our blessing." Jacob was upset his daughter was missing her bubbly personality.

"What are we going to do if he doesn't come home?" Julia knew this was a real possibility. She tried to avoid thinking about it, but it felt as if the war was like a wolf pacing outside their door.

"We will have to get her back to living as soon as possible." Jacob had already thought this through. "I know the Sullivan boy has been interested in her for months. He keeps asking about her."

Julia set her cup down with a clatter. "Marry her to someone else?"

"You know she won't marry anyone for a long time. The reality is that she is getting old to marry. She will miss out on family and children. If we don't force the issue, Julia, it may never happen. Look how long it took to get her to this point?"

"An arranged marriage? It's not what I want for her." Julia knew her daughter was in love; would it be fair to push her onto another man just so she wouldn't become a spinster?

"It's the best thing we can do for her. She will never experience love if she doesn't get her feet wet. Sometimes, you have to be pushed into the water to learn to swim." Jacob kissed his wife. "She will be fine. You'll see."

Julia shook her head. "I don't think this is a good idea, Jacob. If we force her to marry, she will be unhappy. That is not what I want for our daughter. She doesn't even know the Sullivan boy."

"There have been arranged marriages since the beginning of time. If they didn't work, neither you or I would be here. Our parents and their parents were arranged. They learned to love each other over time. She will be fine."

THE CAVALRY COME TO TOWN

The most persistent sound which reverberates through men's history is the beating of war drums.

—Arthur Koestler

Emilie patiently listened, praying Annie would get this right. The redhead wrinkled her freckled nose, pondering the next letter. She twisted her apron nervously and then looked at Emilie, asking, "What was the word again?"

Emilie smiled in spite of herself. This little girl is growing up fast, and Emilie had the privilege to teach her everything she knows. Emilie felt Annie's struggles were her own as they together learned the ABCs and addition and subtraction figures.

"Your word is *absolute*." Emilie nodded her head at the girl.

Annie took a deep breath and started again. Just as she was about to finish, Carrie came in to the classroom, looking frazzled and very concerned. She clapped her hands together to get their attention.

"I was just informed the rebel cavalry has been seen coming this way. Everyone, go home at once. Do not stop until you get there." Carrie moved out of the way of the children as they filed forward to leave the room.

She turned to Emilie.

"Go! We will resume class when they leave town."

Emilie put some of her things in her bag and grabbed for a set of papers on the desk. "I will grade these in the next few days and bring them back." Stuffing the papers in her bag, she tied the bag and left.

Outside the school, Emilie found a group of girls worrying about which way to go. They fussed at one another, trying to make their point; they looked like tiny chicks in the yard running around not knowing where to go.

"Stop fussing, ladies. I am going that way. Let's go." Following their teacher's lead, they fell into a line and walked with Emilie toward town. The group soon broke rank and chattered all the way into town. Each girl giving her rendition of what may happen next as they became more animated with their tales, the group slowed down.

Emilie grew impatient with their pokiness. When she was about fifty yards ahead, she turned to address the group. "Ladies, the rebs will be on us if you don't hurry." Their eyes grew big with fright; they quickly picked up the pace to town. At the foot of Chambersburg Street, three girls stopped to look to see if they were coming. Sensing she lost a few, Emilie turned around.

Just as she was about to say something, she saw the dust and riders crest the hill. Realizing what they were seeing, the girls squealed with fright and ran. Now it was Emilie's turn to keep up. She maneuvered the girls into the lobby of the Eagle Hotel. The girls turned to watch the spectacle of horses and riders approach town. Some townsfolk watched from their porches; others stopped their daily routines to watch them ride through the streets. The girls began to fuss with anxiety at seeing the cavalry arrive.

Emilie took charge of the situation.

"Ladies, let's wait here and see what happens."

"Will they kidnap us or kill us?" Sarah nervously twisted her apron in her hands.

"I want to go home." All eyes looked at Emilie with fear. They depended on her. She would have to come up with a plan.

"What will they do with us? I hear they kill women and children just for fun."

Emilie was shocked by these words.

These children believed the Southerners were as evil as their imagined monsters under their beds. This was a completely different view than she ever thought.

"What would they want with you?" Emilie sounded defensive. Emilie knew she needed to calm the girls, but she realized she still protected the Southern ways she grew up knowing. She rephrased her statement. "Think about it. I don't think they have use for us. We aren't soldiers. We have nothing they want. Why would they harm us?" She saw all eyes were on her, each girl thinking about what Emilie said. "Let's make a plan to get you home."

The streets of Gettysburg were like a circus. The cavalry came in with a show of guns and wild behavior. Emilie searched each horse and rider for a glimpse of her brothers. The showy shooting of guns and horse handling reminded Emilie of how Henry liked to show off.

While Emilie arranged to see the girls safely home, the infantry of General Gordon's brigade arrived. Passing along the streets with her last girl in tow, Emilie heard the nervous talk of some of the onlookers. Fear of looting and burning was foremost in their minds. Many were discussing whether to try to leave town or stay. Horrible memories of the events in Chambersburg last October came back in everyone's mind.

On the way back up West Middle Street at the corner of Baltimore Street, Emilie saw David Kendlehart, borough council president, moving up the street from his home. He walked fast. The man looked worried but very much determined. Emilie fell in a few steps behind him as they walked toward the diamond at the center of town. Approaching the diamond, Emilie saw a sea of horses, riders, and infantry. They all waited for their next set of orders. Everyone milled around. The last Emilie saw of Mr. Kendlehart was him disappearing into the law office of Attorney William Duncan. Feeling curious about the new visitors, Emilie looked through the crowds, hoping to see Henry or Aaron. The men were dressed in rags. Their uniforms so ill fit, she wondered how some stayed covered. There were holes in their jackets and pants and boots. Emilie wondered how Thaddeus and Stephen were faring. Some men wore no shoes, their bare feet dirty and swollen from walking barefoot. Emilie eyed up the horses in the area. She noticed how beautiful they stood with their riders, dressed in riding boots and jackets with decoration. She admired how well dressed they looked in comparison to their infantry comrades. Looking over the crowd, she felt someone touch her.

"You best run home, missy. We are taking over your town." The toothless solider grinned at her. The man next to him leered at her.

"I am not worried," Emilie calmly stated. "We have nothing here for you. Best you boys leave us alone. You got nothing out of Chambersburg. You will get nothing here." Emilie was surprised she wasn't the least bit intimidated by these men. Standing in their ranks, they posed no threat to her just now.

"Oh, we have plenty to do. First, we will cut your telegraph wires, burn your railroad bridges, and then loot the town as we please." The man acted nonchalant about the laundry list of to dos he posed for her.

"You are no gentlemen." Emilie felt the anger rise within her. "I don't know where you come from, but you, sirs, are no Southern gentlemen." She glared at him.

The men laughed. "What do you think are we doing here? Our general is asking politely for permission from your city. We are waiting for permission."

"It won't matter in a few months," said the man next to him. "We will have the run of the whole country. Then we'll see who comes begging for permission."

All the pieces fell together, Emilie thought to herself. Mr. Kendlehart must be holding an emergency meeting to determine what the city will do with the demands. Emilie shook her head and walked away.

Making her way across the diamond, Emilie started for home. Believing their occupation would be temporary; she wished she had the opportunity to see her brothers. She missed them both. The smell of unbathed men finally got the best of her. She saw no sign of Henry or Aaron. She was growing tired of the day's events. The excitement of the day had worn off. Emilie hoped she would not have any trouble walking the rest of the way home. She was very happy she left Starlight home today. She just wondered how long the horse would have to stay cooped up on the farm now the rebels were in town.

That afternoon, the Confederate troops swept through Gettysburg, gathering all the supplies they needed. Much to the citizen's surprise, most of the goods were paid for with Confederate money. With supplies satisfied, they cut the telegraph wires and burned the rail bridge over Rock Creek. Just as the soldiers promised, they tore up rail track, confiscated horses, gathered free blacks, and took war prisoners. By Sunday, the last of the Confederates left town. Its citizens rejoiced with Sabbathday services with "life goes on" naiveté as the city was cut off from the world and the Confederate campfires burned on South Mountain. The campfires were a silent reminder that things may not be back to normal for Gettysburg.

> Dear diary,
> The war is on our doorstep. The sights I saw this week are startling. The Confederate troops are the most rag-tag poorly dressed group I have ever seen. I cannot imagine these men as anything but badly mannered. I know they must have come from all occupations in the south, but they were no gentlemen. They talked about bringing harm to our city. This is none of the manners or culture I was taught. I am ashamed to think they are from the south. What scares me most is that these men consider me Union. I don't feel like either Union or Confederate. I am precariously balanced in the middle, wishing this would end.

I have not received regular letters from Thaddeus in a long time. I am deeply concerned for his safety. I pray for their safety every moment I think about them. My nightmares are becoming more frequent. I know this is because I worry more than I have hope right now. There were no signs of the armies today. We went to church services. I did not see troops anywhere in town. I hope the Confederates have left town for good. Please God, let this is the end of it.

E.K.P

WAR COMES HOME

War grows out of the desire of the individual to gain advantage at the expenses of his fellow man.

—Napoleon Hill

On Sunday afternoon, the Union cavalry arrived into town only to leave again Monday. Still unable to communicate with the outside world, Gettysburg felt apprehensive and vulnerable. It was an eerie feeling to see the enemy fires only seven miles off in Chambersburg. Everyone knew in their hearts that last Friday was not the last of their interactions with the Confederate Army.

The three miles between home and town buffered Emilie and her family from the growing apprehension in Gettysburg. Reassured by the departure of Confederate troops on Sunday, Emilie went about her day in a business-as-usual manner. School on Monday and Tuesday went on with little sign of trouble from the troops outside her town. She seemed oblivious to the army's movements in and around the town. By Tuesday, it became clear Confederate officers appeared on Seminary Ridge. The news spread quickly through the town.

"I thought they were gone," Emilie said, frustrated for the intrusion on her life.

"They never left," Carrie informed her. "The Union Army is said to be down the road. I am worried about getting caught in the middle of some skirmish."

"What do they want with us?" Emilie shook her head. "Didn't they get enough last week? They took all of our supplies from the stores. What will we live on? I heard the railroad cars can't get in." Emilie's complaints trailed off into silence. She realized she did not like the way she sounded just now.

"It is haunting to know we are cut off from the rest of the world, but I don't think it is us they want," Carrie answered meditatively. "I think they just want each other, and we are in the way." The words haunted Emilie all the way home that day. She desperately wanted to ride again. Starlight seemed so unhappy cooped up in the yard. Emilie knew keeping Starlight home was best for her; she would not risk losing her. As long as there was army near town, Starlight would have to be content at home. With the army's continual interruptions in her daily life, Emilie began to feel as if she were being held against her will. She longed for the carefree days of normal life. This all had to end soon.

Emilie finished her morning chores early. The early-morning sun declared it would be a hot day; the humidity became more intense as the sun rose in the east. The rains overnight added to the oppressing humidity of the day. Emilie wanted to get out from the garden as soon as she could. Her list of chores seemed endless. Emilie longed to finish her sewing project, but work before pleasure was the rule. She ate a quick breakfast; she grabbed the list off the table.

"I will be back as soon as I can," Emilie announced to her mother. "What if they don't have all of this?" She pointed to the list.

"Get what you can. We will do without the rest. I don't like you going to town by yourself," Julia warned her daughter. Emilie stopped and looked at her mother. She had a way of telling her mother she was still going to complete her job. Julia resigned. "Hurry home."

"I will, Mother. I want to get back so I can finish that collar. It will be light longer tonight. I can finish today." Emilie loved finishing projects just as much as she liked starting them. "See you!" those were her last words before Julia heard the screen door slam.

Emilie hurried into town. She walked at a brisk pace. She was unaware that almost directly west of her, the fight had begun. Horses and men bustled in and around town. There were more soldiers than civilians occupying the streets. Something told Emilie this was not a social visit for them. Large groups of men moved as one unit. Officers barked orders to move the troops along to an unknown destination. Just as she reached the center of town, she heard a whistling noise immediately followed by a loud explosion. The sound made her jump. In the confusion, she looked around for the source of the noise.

The officer barking orders never flinched by the explosion overhead. Emilie squeaked at the sound; her heart pounded in her chest. She wanted to run; every part of her being said run. Run where? Looking around for a clue, an officer barked orders to her.

"Go home, missy. You are in danger here." He was dressed in a dusty, tattered, blue uniform. His hair slicked back under his hat gave him an unkempt look. In his hand, he held a sword that he used to direct his company to the fight.

Emilie moved forward to the store. She was stopped again. "No! That's where the fight is. Go the other way!" Men were barking orders all around her. Emilie turned around to head back toward home. She felt like a mouse in a maze. Every turn meant turning away from the fight. By the third redirection, she threw up her hands and said, "Where? Where shall I go?" Another explosion and bursting shell lit up the sky. The noise was deafening.

A soldier pointed toward Baltimore Avenue, the exact opposite of home. "All's quiet...." Another shell explosion drowned out the last of his words. Emilie needed to think. For the first time since she arrived in Gettysburg, she felt scared and helpless. Every road was blocked, the noise of the cannon fire and muskets popping, urging her to run and hide. She ran down Baltimore Avenue, trying to think of another way home. Emilie realized she was very much a creature of habit, she never strayed far from what she knew, be it hobbies or roads in and out of town. Emilie looked around all of the window and doors of the residences were closed. With every new cannon blast, more doors and shutters closed up tight, trying to keep the pending fight out.

Emilie stopped for a moment to sit down on a stoop. The house was locked up tight. Its shutters and front door closed out to the battle in the streets. She wondered if the occupants were out of town or in hiding. If they could see her, would they let her in for safety? Emilie sat there for a bit, willing herself to be calm. Taking deep breaths to slow her rapidly beating heart, she forced herself to think about happy things to calm her jumpy nerves. Not one happy thought entered her mind. Emilie decided to find a place to hide. Wait it out and go home later tonight. As she stood up, she heard yelling and musket fire down the street. A swarm of fighting men ran down the street toward Emilie. Shouting, gunfire, and chaos—it was coming her way. Emilie jumped up franticly, looking around for a place to hide. She did not want to be in the middle of this melee. Emilie pushed herself into the doorway of the house. The doorframe was wide and thick; it was the only shelter she could find, the swarm was coming upon her fast and angry. She prayed the door would open, but it held tight against her body. Pushing herself into the nook of the doorframe, pressing herself against the door, she banged on the door hoping someone would answer. No one heard her.

The noise rumbled like thunder over the mountains. The screaming unnerved her. The agony of the injured and dying echoed in her ears. Wild yelling and curse words mixed with screams of agony, she could only hear the scene coming her way, too afraid to peek around the doorframe. Her heart pounded wildly with anticipation. When she gathered enough courage, she peeked out and saw men running, shouting, and shooting. A stray bullet whizzed past her and hit the doorframe, shattering wood splinters everywhere. Emilie willed herself to stay still while she instinctively covered her face. Her basic instincts screamed at her to flee. Her fingers dug into the wood, keeping her there as she prayed for her safety. The crowd passed, no one noticing the girl pressed into the doorway. In its wake, bodies lay in the street, yelling in agony while others lay still, unmoving.

The street was quiet and still except for the litter of men left behind. Emilie felt drawn to help the ones lying in the street. Just as she let go of her hiding place, she heard a buckboard rattling fast down the street, its driver steering wildly to avoid the men in the way. The man shouted to her, "Get in if you want to save your life." Emilie stared in disbelief, still too frightened to move. "Are you daft, girl? Come on!"

Emilie ran, meeting him in the street. She grabbed the wagon and swung herself into the back. He slowed enough for her to make her way up to the front seat. Emilie settled into the seat next to her rescuer. He turned and smiled at her. Emilie recognized him as the man who confronted her at Fahnstocks a week or so ago. She was intrigued by his good looks then and did not change her mind about him today. Thankful he saved her, she smiled at him.

"Ahh, it's you, rebel. What are you doing here?" His gray eyes shined with amusement. A hint of humor in his smile made him less intimidating as he was last week. "Where are you headed?"

"I am trying to get home, but it seems the army is out that way, and I have no place to go." He saw the look of fear in her eyes. "I guess I will have to find a way to go around."

He chuckled. "No, I think we are well surrounded. You will stay with us." Emilie started to politely protest when he interrupted her. "Look, the fight is northwest of town, and I don't know where it will be tomorrow. You can't get home. You can either stay in the streets or come home and hide at my place until this is over." His choices were not optimal, but she'd rather have walls and a roof over her head than hide in an entryway of a locked residence.

"I don't even know who you are." Emilie felt defeated. She really wanted to return to her home. However, this man was right; she was not going there today.

"My name is Jefferson Adams. I live outside of town with my wife, Sarah, and our children. Once the fight is over, I will see to it you get home safe." He was sincere; Emilie felt safe for the first time since she entered town today.

"So what is your name, or do I call you Rebel?" His question made Emilie laugh. This man had a good sense of humor; he reminded her of how Thaddeus could make her laugh when she least felt any humor in the situation.

"I much prefer Emilie, thank you." The wagon traveled down Baltimore Street out to Tanneytown Road. Union was setting up cannon on Cemetery Ridge. The men stopped the wagon to inquire where Jefferson was going. They told them to hurry as they expected an attack anytime. The wagon slowed with the deep mud in the road. This road well travelled was deeply rutted by wagon and still wet and muddy. The horses pulled the wagon past a large orchard of trees onto a small farmstead. The house was small and modest with a low rock wall around its exterior. This decoration made the homestead inviting. The side yard boasted an unassuming garden, well groomed, and a clothesline to the right. The family had chickens, goats, and sheep. The small barn housed the rest of the livestock for this modest family.

Jefferson stopped the wagon and got out to help Emilie. He reached in the back for his cane. Emilie now knew why he did not participate in the war. He had a terrible twisted leg that required a cane. The limp looked painful. You would never know it, this man made strangers feel at ease with his quick wit and warm smile.

Jefferson introduced his family to Emilie. Sarah was about twenty-five years old. Her face round as her swollen belly, she was slow and deliberate with her movement. Sarah looked as if she was due at any moment. Her face glowed as she smiled a picture of good health. Isabel and Isaiah, ages five and three, welcomed Emilie too; they were excited to see a new visitor at their home. Emilie enjoyed their warm reception. They sat on the edge of their seat, listening to her story of the day's events. Sarah chimed in, "I picked all of the garden vegetables that were ready. The troops are in this area. I am sure they are looking for food."

Isaiah, getting comfortable with his new friend, told an animated story about waiting behind the large oak tree to shoot any rebel that walked by. His small, round face beamed with excitement. "I shoot them, Pa. *Pop, blam!*" His little fingers were making shooting gestures. His face screwed up, trying to close one eye to look as if he was aiming with the other one.

"He shoots the blue coats and horses and big gun and loud ones." Little Izzy eagerly listed the things that passed her by that day. Her hair was frazzled and coming out of its braids from the hard work and play, she did all day.

"Not the blue-coated ones, Isaiah. Shoot the brown- or gray-coated ones." Jefferson smiled at his boy. The evening progressed quietly. The children chattered all evening about the noises of the day. Izzy was still concerned about the day's events and refused to sleep in her room. Sarah and Jefferson sat with her until she fell asleep. The house finally quieted of children's noises; Sarah waddled out of the house to join Emilie on the porch. The ladies sat, each lost in her own thoughts, enjoying the peaceful evening.

The air was still humid, but the night was quiet with no sound of gun or cannon. The road near the home was busy with troops passing by the house. She didn't care to think about where they were going; she only hoped they were leaving town. Emilie sat on the porch swing, thinking about home and wondering if Thaddeus was near. She heard him in her thoughts. She remembered his smile and wished she were in his arms. She missed him more knowing he could be closer than he had been in months. She wanted to know if he was all right. She needed to know he was still alive but too busy to write. She needed reassurance from him. This need grew stronger as the night wore on. Emilie dreamed of him and worried about him the moment she awoke.

The next morning, Jefferson went back into town to see if it was safe to take Emilie home. Emilie stayed behind with Sarah and the children. She wanted to go, but Jefferson encouraged her to stay. He was leery about the possible dangers, and he wanted her to be safe. The afternoon ticked by slowly as marked by the old wind-up clock in the parlor. Off in the distance, they could hear popping of muskets, but everything else seemed quiet and unmoving. Sarah continued with her work: baking bread and making the afternoon and evening meals. Emilie helped as much as she could, keeping one eye on the doors and windows for change. With each *tick tock*, the tension in the house grew more unbearable.

Around 4:00 p.m., the sound of cannon fire penetrated the quiet farmyard. Izzy and Isaiah both ran to the house, slamming the door behind them. Izzy's face was full of terror and her little body shook uncontrollably as she sat with her hands over her ears. Isaiah hid in the broom closet. The slam of the closet door signaled he was in a safe place.

Sarah began in earnest to watch for signs that Jefferson was safe. Once the cannon fire began, it seemed the war had restarted itself, and the women began to pace with worry. Not long after the women began to think he wasn't coming home, Jefferson appeared in the drive. Sarah waved from the door, as she was too scared to leave the safety of the house.

Jefferson, once again, had someone with him. A Union officer followed him to the house. Jefferson introduced the man, and Sarah offered him some food. The officer looked thin and very hungry despite his business-like demeanor.

"The fight is all around you, folks. I suggest you get in your cellars and wait this one out. We are finishing up Culp's Hill and the battle rages at the hills just over there." He looked dejected and frustrated. "I don't know how those rebs are damn good at keeping us on our toes. We pulled in your homeboys and sent them fresh up there." The officer pointed to the Round Top. At the sound of *homeboys*, Emilie's heart skipped a beat. Could Thaddeus really be here, so close to home? Too excited to wait, Emilie exclaimed, "Please, sir, do you mean the First Pennsylvania Reserves?"

He smiled at her. "Those very ones. Some of those boys haven't seen home in a few years. They are a good fighting unit."

Jefferson told the ladies how dangerous it was to be in town. "It is a war zone for sure. You can't travel up Baltimore Street past a certain point. Sharpshooters are camped out in our neighbors' houses, shooting anything that moves. I hurried home only to get questioned by soldiers. Luckily, I used the story that you desperately needed me home, because the babe was on his way." He put his arm around his pregnant wife, holding her close. "I didn't say exactly when the little one was arriving; just he was on his way. They let me pass. Then I met this officer, who escorted me home." Jefferson kissed his wife's forehead; she instantly smiled back, dissipating all the worry and fear from her beautiful face.

Emilie listened to the stories, trying to concentrate over the thoughts of, *If I could only get to see him…I must know if he is safe.* The lack of letters from Thaddeus made her apprehensive imagining the worse. Her vivid imagination only resulted in more worry. She reasoned for her peace of mind; if she could see him again, everything would be all right.

The guns quieted late that night. The skirmish on the Round Top and below lasted well into the evening hours. Emilie waited until she could not hear them for over an hour. She rested and tried to sleep, but thoughts of him consumed her. He was so close; all she needed to do was find him.

TEARS OF LOSS AND HOPE

While I thought that I was learning how to live, I have been learning how to die.

—Leonardo da Vinci

Stepping into the warm, humid night, Emilie quietly latched the door behind her. She walked thinking only of him. She briefly thought about how to stay out of the way of the snipers. If she ran into a soldier, she figured they would help her find him. It would all work out she assured herself. The night was dead quiet now, a much-needed reprieve from the battle earlier that evening. She walked silently down the road when she noticed the lightning bugs dancing in the fields with their gentle, green glow. She remembered the thrill of chasing them through the field catching them and putting them in a jar to watch them flicker and glow. Her first experience with lightning bugs ended tragically when they died quickly. In her innocence, she forgot to put holes in the top of the jar. Never forgetting her mistake, Emilie kept a jar, complete with holes for the next time she wanted to catch lightning bugs.

The walk was long, but she was determined to go; she wasn't sure where, but the need to see him drove her harder. The pitch-black darkness made it difficult for her eyes to adjust to the dark when it happened; stifling a scream, she walked into what felt like a sack of flour. Solid as a brick wall, Emilie could smell the man had not bathed in weeks. The Union soldier stopped her with his gun.

"Who goes there?" The voice that belonged to the stench was demanding and harsh. He shined a lantern on her face. The brightness of the light made it hard to see. Emilie covered her eyes from the offending light. "Speak now or I will shoot you."

Trying to control her panic, Emilie squeaked, "I am a citizen of Gettysburg. Who are you?"

"You are breaking the city's curfew. What's your business here?"

"City's curfew?" Emilie found her voice. "We are not in the city, sir." She spoke with authority and force. "Besides, what I am doing here is none of your business."

"It is exactly my business, especially since I have seized your town." The soldier was growing impatient. *What woman in her right mind would be out in the dark after curfew?*

Emilie stared him down. "I see," she commented coldly. "Not for long. Excuse me, sir." Emilie tried to push past this vile man. His arm shot up, stopping her from passing.

"You have a Southern accent." He crooked an eyebrow. "How can you be a citizen of this town with that talk? I ask you one more time, miss: what's your business here?" He was so close to her, she could smell the tobacco on his foul breath. She was repelled from the stench.

Emilie watched the man leering closer to her, demanding and expecting her to shrink with fear. She read his actions and countered by squaring her shoulders. Emilie was keenly aware of the social differences of men and women. Men expected dominance by action or word. Women never had the chance to dominate anything, except small children to raise and rear them properly. She much preferred the man's world.

From out of the shadows came a voice. "What cha' got here, Charlie?" The man's voice had a country accent.

"I think I's got me a spy, Luke. She won't tell me her business, and she is out past curfew. She says she's a townie, but she got a rebel accent." Emilie felt exposed.

Emilie defiantly announced, "I am not a spy. I am looking for my husband and—"

"Yous not wear'n a ring. Where's your wedding ring?" Charlie shot back. He could see this girl starting to squirm. He just knew he was right. *She is a spy.* Charlie smiled smugly to himself, conjuring up stories of heroism and praise. President Lincoln would praise him personally for capturing a spy.

"I…I am not telling you that," Emilie was indignant. She searched her hand for the engagement ring. Emilie remembered she left it at home. She took off the ring when she baked pies two days ago. Emilie suddenly felt alone. She desperately tried to remember how she outwitted her brothers in the past. Her thoughts bought her courage and time.

Again, the darkness produced yet another voice. "What is going on here!"

The officer came into the light of the street lamp.

"We have a spy, sir. What would you like us to do with her?" The men changed their demeanor as they recognized the officer approaching.

"Take her to the captain. He will get to the bottom of this. Connors, Turner, you take her and be quick about it." The officer turned and disappeared from where he came.

Luke shoved the point of his musket into her ribs and shoved her toward a horse. "You heard the sergeant. You's tak'n a ride to see our captain. He'll know if you's a spy. Move, lassie" They put her on a horse and started to move. Emilie found herself riding farther away from the answers she was seeking and farther still from the security of her home.

Emilie knew she was headed toward Emmitsburg Road; she knew the landscape like she knew the Mozart concerto her mother loved to hear. Her years here were full of accomplishments and pride. When they arrived a few years ago, Emilie was a farm girl from Virginia. Now she was a respected teacher and betrothed to her first love.

The sound of rushing horse hooves startled Emilie, and she turned on the back of the horse. Her sudden movements pushed the soldier off center. The horse startled. "Don't do that you stupid girl. You'll get us both bucked off," Charlie hissed as he tried to calm the horse.

"Courier is coming. Let him pass." Charlie reined the horse over and turned to face the oncoming rush of horses. Surprisingly, the oncoming courier stopped to give Luke and Charlie an urgent message.

The man identified himself and announced that the men were supposed to go to the north side of town to deliver a note and then turn back to do their duty with the girl. They were to go at once. Charlie protested, but the courier demanded they go at once. Luke took the note from the soldier, and they turned their horses toward the north side of town.

Emilie dozed as the horses travelled through the countryside. They moved slower because it was full night. Emilie was aroused as the sun warmed her face. She didn't know where she was. She lost track of their direction. It was early morning, and they had arrived at a large whitewashed and stone barn. Emilie could see the barnyard scene had changed dramatically. The livestock were no longer, the scene littered with men, there was a disturbing wavelike movement, some were walking, but most were not. The horses moved in closer; it became clear this was a horrible scene. Blood, blood, blood—it was everywhere. Limbs both on and off the bodies, these men were suffering with pain, some whispering silent prayers, others calling out to loved ones in their delirium. Everything seemed to move in slow motion.

Dear God, she prayed. *Please do not let Thaddeus be in this mess.* Tears started to well up in her eyes from the horrible smells that accosted her nose. She immediately dismounted from the horse before Charlie and Luke could stop her.

"Hey, missy, you stay right here. You's my prisoner," Charlie was shouting behind her. Emilie ignored him and rushed through the throngs of men. She barely heard Charlie cussing under his breath as she stopped looking down at a man, whose eyes blankly looked up at her. She knelt down and touched his face. He didn't move; his face was dirty, smudged with gunpowder and dust. In his hand, he held a locket. Her heart leapt in fear; the locket looked like the one she gave Thaddeus. Emilie took a kerchief from her pocket and wiped the dirt from his face. She didn't realize she was holding her breath as she let out a huge sigh; the man was not Thaddeus.

A deep, gruff voice from behind her said, "That one is dead. There are others to tend." Emilie looked up to see an older, bearded officer, peering down at her. She could not find her voice; her mouth gaped open.

Out of the confusion, she recognized her name being called. Emilie wheeled around to see Stephen coming toward her. "Emilie, what are you doing here?" Through the smoke, she recognized him. Joy for the first time in weeks spread through her instantly. He was limping.

"Dear Stephen, what has happened to you? Are you hurt? Sit down." She pulled him down on a bale of straw near them. Like a mother looking over her hurt child, she examined his arms, legs, face, head. She was becoming frantic. Stephen grabbed her hands, stopping the assault she was inflicting on his person. "Stop, it is only a flesh wound. I'll be fine in a few weeks. Emilie, I need to tell you about Thaddeus. We were caught up in yesterday's fight."

Emilie stopped him instantly. "Wait, how is he?" She felt a warm glimmer of hope in her heart.

Stephen shook his head and took her hands in his. "We marched forward in the engagement, and I lost him halfway through the battle. I don't know where he is right now, but I know he is not on the dead rolls." Reaching into his jacket, Stephen pulled out a letter tied in a red ribbon. "Thaddeus gave this to me in case we got separated in the fight."

Emilie recognized the ribbon. She always tied her hair up in a red ribbon, when they went riding. She remembered the picnic that day. Thaddeus told her he was leaving, but most importantly, he asked her to marry him. She remembered the love in his eyes and how his smile always melted her heart. Emilie smiled at the memory as a tear escaped and fell from her cheek. She could not accept the idea of him hurt. No, he must be helping others on the field or there is another reason but wounded was not one of them. She took the letter from Stephen and held it close to her heart.

Stephen's voice was tender. He could see her heart breaking.

Suddenly, she took a deep breath. "He is not dead, Stephen. I am going to find him if I have to search every inch of this county." Her chin pointed out in stubborn resolve.

Stephen smiled despite himself. "Now that's the girl I know." They were interrupted by the presence of two men standing over them. Stephen looked up to see two Union soldiers peering down at Emilie as if she were a distasteful street urchin.

"That's our prisoner. We're taken her to the captain." Luke stepped forward to pull Emilie up by her arm. "Come on, tart, time to go. The captain is waitin' to hang you, spy." His voice was mocking with a sick sense of joy to it.

"Call me tart again, and I'll…," Emilie sputtered. She was getting tired of their abuse. These men were wasting her time; she had to find Thaddeus. "I am a citizen of Gettysburg, not a spy." Emilie stood up to face her accuser. Anger and fear for Thaddeus consumed her.

"You don't scare me," Luke hissed, meeting her glare. "Time to go, tart!" He pushed her harshly.

Emilie balled up her fist and hit him square in the jaw. Luke reeled back and fell into the dirt. "I am not going anywhere with you!" she shrieked, her voice cutting through the stillness of the farmyard. She turned to Stephen, whose mouth was open with shock. He knew Emilie had a fire in her, but this was the first time he ever witnessed her outright anger.

Stephen intervened. "This girl is no more a spy than your mother. Leave her be. I know her. She is a citizen of this town, and I have known her for years." Stephen instinctively moved between Charlie and Emilie, not wanting to see this beautiful girl break her hand by delivering a fist to Charlie, for who Stephen surmised was not liked either.

The bearded officer stepped into the circle. "What is going on here? What are you boys doing with this lassie?"

Charlie stepped up and explained. They reported that they were going to take her to the captain for questioning. Stephen interrupted that he vouched for Emilie and her citizenship to Gettysburg. The general sent Luke and Charlie back to their regiment; Emilie was to stay at the hospital until arrangements could be made for her to be escorted home. Day 3 of the battle was already in full swing, and no one would be safe.

Emilie stayed at the field hospital, lending a hand to anyone she could. Bringing water to the wounded or sitting with the dying, Emilie hoped someone was with Thaddeus if he were like these men. Late the next day, Stephen was assigned to escort Emilie back home. Given a horse and carrying a white flag, Emilie and Stephen rode through Gettysburg. It looked like a ghost town. The once-bustling streets were eerily quiet and empty. Church windows broken, rubble in the street—the destruction was immeasurable. Danger was still lurking in the dark shadows of the town. Stephen knew Emilie was apprehensive. He could not stand the silence anymore.

"Emmy, what's happening?" His voice broke the silence.

"I am worried about him. I need to find him. I know he is not dead." Her voice was full of conviction and calm. How could she know so definitely about him, when no one else did?

"Stephen, you better let me off at the front door. I don't want you to witness this reunion." Emilie's voice was vacant and sad. Emilie was sure her parents would be more angry than fearful. She did not want Stephen to witness this family argument. The two arrived at the Prescott residence. Stephen dismounted and assisted Emilie down.

"I will not leave you until I know you are safe," he said with concern. Stephen knew Mr. Prescott was stern with his daughter. He understood there was conflict, and he was going to make sure Emilie was going to be all right.

The Prescotts were very happy to see their daughter. They were worried sick about her safety. Stephen escorted Emilie into the parlor and soon found himself in the center of deep negotiation regarding Emilie's future. It was decided that Emilie had two weeks to bring home Thaddeus. Her father's ultimatum did not comfort Emilie. The words bounced off her. Emilie heard them but did not believe her father was pushing her to move past her love for him as if it were a schoolgirl crush. No, she would never forget him and she decided she may never marry again.

> Dear diary,
>
> I can't help but think he is waiting for me somewhere. I did not realize Gettysburg was so big, finding Thaddeus is like finding a grain of rice in the yard. I have searched for a long time and time is running out. I can't begin to think of not being engaged to him. Pa has begun to hint that I should move on with my life. My life will end if I cannot have Thaddeus. There is no one else who can make me as happy as he does. I will search for him until I find him. Our love will make him strong, I will nurse him back to health. I will be his wife.
>
> More searching tomorrow, I will find him soon.
>
> E.K.P.

The search for Thaddeus was exhausting. It was difficult to cover the county, since the battle of Gettysburg was so devastating; every home, every barn, and every available building was filled with the dying and wounded. Emilie searched day after day from sunrise to sunset. She was covering as much land as she could, but time was not on her side. She was tireless and vigilant through the days following the battle.

Tired and weary, Emilie rode up to the last home in the area. Today, Stephen offered to help her search. They searched in opposite directions, meeting again at a designated place. She searched from farm to farm, as every home in area was turned into makeshift hospitals to house the wounded and dying. This farmhouse yard where chickens once roamed was now littered with dead horses and makeshift tents throughout the yard. Weeds were beginning to grow up in among the flower gardens that lined the fence. The lady of the house no longer had time to tend the gardens; she was literally up to her ears in tending the wounded and dying. No one would have guessed six months ago what horrible things would have come to this small town.

Please, God, if Thaddeus is here, let her tender care be enough to make him strong. Emilie felt as if God was getting tired of hearing that prayer, for she had said it before she entered every home throughout this land. Hearing the creak of the porch under her feet, Emilie took a deep breath and reached for the door knocker.

"Hello, madame, I am Emilie Prescott. I am here to inquire about a missing soldier. Do you have a man by the name of Thaddeus?" Thaddeus was not a common name, so Emilie was sure this woman would know by the name alone.

"Hello, miss." The woman smiled pleasantly. "Come tell me about your soldier, and I will see if I can help you." Her name was Sylvia, and she too had lost everything. An innocent bystander in this small town, she spent endless hours tending death and pain. They came to her, and she opened her doors. Now her small home was bursting at the seams. It was good to see a smiling face. Sylvia listened to the young girl explain her missing fiancé. Her eyes sparkled, and her face lit as she excitedly described him and his personality. Sylvia smiled, remembering herself when she was once young and in love.

Suddenly, Sylvia stopped. "What did you say?"

Emilie met her eyes. "I said he has my locket in his pocket. I gave it to him for protection." Emilie's heart was beating with anticipation.

"What else did he have?" Sylvia was hoping she was not correct. She had seen so much; maybe she was imagining and hoping for this young girl. Unable to contain herself, she pulled on the young girl's sleeve. "Come with me."

Sylvia Curtis saw the terror in the young girl's heart. Her eyes sparkled, shiny with the tears she was trying to hold back. She could not watch this girl's pain any longer. She held out her hand and gently said, "Let me take you to him."

Emilie's heart raced with fear and relief. She willingly allowed the woman to lead her through the hall. In front of the thick oak door, she put a hand on the woman to stop her from entering the room.

"How is he?" she asked, desperate to hear good news.

"It is questionable at best." Sylvia opened the door. The room was dark. The heavy curtains covered the large windows of the study. Emilie rushed in.

He hates darkness. She opened the heavy velvet curtains. The sun brightened the room; Emilie rushed back to Thaddeus. His feet were hanging over the edge of the settee. The rest of his body was laying peacefully, his breathing soft and steady; Emilie peered at his face, tears rushing down hers. She moved in close to see his face, kissed his brow, and whispered, "I am here now."

Thaddeus stirred his face in the sunlight for the first time in days. His body ached from head to toe. Thaddeus could not imagine why the light was so bright and warm. He felt the kiss on his brow. Swimming between dreams and reality, he tried to come to the surface of reality. He dreamed in and out of fever. His body was pained and tired. Suddenly, his brain spoke, *Emilie... Emilie she is here.*

"He is fevered with infection. The surgeon doesn't know what will happen. The next few days should tell us." Sylvia left off the final words of her statement. *If he lasts that long.* The light behind Sylvia was bright and brilliant; it bounced off her day cap with a glow. "Talk to him, Emilie. He needs to wake."

Emilie frantically searched him. *Where, where is he hurt?* Moving the blankets and feeling his limbs, she looked up at Sylvia. "Will he still be whole?"

"He will keep his leg, if he can fight off the infection that has taken him. I am sorry, miss." Sylvia had seen this too many times. Over the last weeks of caring for these men, she buried many and watched as others were prepared for the long trip home in a pine box, labeled, and shipped. Others were carried off to be buried by those still strong enough to dig shallow graves. She too was tired, tired of this war intruding on her life and taking over her home. Sylvia slipped out of the room to leave them together.

She barely heard his voice through her grief.

"Emilie. You came."

"Of course, I came. I didn't believe for one moment you were gone." Emilie's joy was exuberant. She was excited that he was well enough to talk to her; she kissed his forehead and gently laid her head on his chest.

"I want to tell you something." His voice was weak, but he was persistent. He coughed and winced with pain.

Emilie pulled herself closer to him, wanting to hear every word. "Before I left, you said you were not going to marry ever again. I was glad of it, but now..."

She felt everything close in around her. "I have searched this countryside for you. You are not leaving me now! How could you choose this war over our happiness?" Anger turned to tears. She caught his eyes begging for her to look at him.

"I chose to fight so we would have a future. Have the best for our sons. I never chose the war over you. I chose it because of you." Tears stung his eyes, overwhelmed by emotion and the pain that raked through his body. "Don't ever doubt my love for you, Emilie Prescott." He closed his eyes to gather his strength.

Hours passed with no change. Emilie placed cool clothes on his forehead and talked to him. She encouraged him to eat with no success. He refused, saying it was too painful and that he was not hungry. Emilie looked at him studying his features. The war made him older. His forehead wrinkled with pain. His body looked thin; he had lost weight since she last saw him. She could see how the last few months took a tremendous toll on his body. Emilie laid her head on his chest and spoke softly into his chest. "Thaddeus, I am here now. Wake up, darling. I am here to take you home." She fell asleep listening to him breathe, still holding his hand.

Through his delirium, Thaddeus began to speak to her in his dreams. "It's time to go home. I will be there soon." He was silent for a long time. "This is the last fight."

She felt a hand on her shoulder. It was Stephen; he had found her here.

"Stephen, I am so glad you are here." She promised herself she would not break down. Suddenly, she could not wipe her tears fast enough. "We need to move him home so he can recover. Help me."

"He is too weak to move. He needs to stay here until he is stronger," Stephen said quietly. He took her in his arms; she felt so good there. He wished he could hold her longer, but now was not the time.

Stephen stood by Emilie through the afternoon and well into the evening. Thaddeus began to struggle breathing, his fever still raging through his body. He was slipping away, holding on this earth by Emilie's hand in his. Silence blanketed the room, dark and heavy. At last, the silence was broken, when Thaddeus clearly spoke. "Good-bye, Emilie. I will always love you." At his last breath, the locket fell from his relaxed hand. Emilie looked down upon him, watching the last breath leave his body; she wept for her loss. She cried knowing their future ended now. They lost the fight for their future together. Emilie was devastated.

Two days later, Thaddeus was buried in the Evergreen Cemetery in his family plot. It rained on the day he was buried. Dressed in black, Emilie wore the locket she gave to Thaddeus, remembering the promises they made to each other. Emilie felt as if the day was crying with her. God cried for the loss in the fields, and Emilie cried for the loss of her future with the only man she ever loved.

Emilie stayed with the Marsh family as long as she could. Misery loves company, and Emilie felt better mourning with those who knew him best. Late in the day, Jacob and Julia finally persuaded her to go home. They understood when she left the Marsh residence it would forever change her relationship with the Marsh family. She was no longer their future daughter in law Emilie, simply Emilie Prescott neighbor on Table Rock Road. They guided her out to the wagon and drove her home.

The ride home was quiet and sullen. Emilie could not imagine ever smiling again. The pain was so great. She felt alone and abandoned. Julia sat with her, encouraging her to finish her tea with valerian root and chamomile for sleep. When she was completely exhausted and sleeping, Jacob carried his daughter upstairs, and Julia tucked her in bed.

There was little time to mourn; the city was in desperate need of all hands to help with the wounded and dying. Julia left for the church early the next morning as Emilie slept in a much-needed, drug-induced sleep. Jacob stayed behind to watch over his daughter.

It was late afternoon when Jacob heard a commotion outside in the yard. He was finishing the last few cuts on the rocking chair he was going to give Emilie for her wedding. Jacob put down his work to see what was outside. Thinking it could be looters or officers asking for more supplies, Jacob prepared to confront the men.

Outside, Jacob saw Confederate cavalrymen walking around the property. Their uniforms dirty and torn, they were a sight to see. Two were looking in the windows of the house.

"Can I help you, men?" Jacob announced his presence. When the taller man turned, Jacob immediately recognized his son. "Aaron, my God! You're safe!"

"Pa, I have missed you. Where are Ma and Emilie?" The men sized each other up, amazed to be in each other's presence again. "Pa, we need your help."

"Where's Henry?" Jacob looked over, noticing the stretcher for the first time. "Oh, my son!" Jacob rushed to his side. Henry was unconscious. His thigh was bandaged with a makeshift cloth, dirty and soaked with now-dried blood.

"He is weak. He asked to come home to Ma and you. I had to honor his request." Aaron was sullen with despair. "He got shot in the leg, Pa. He'll never walk again."

"Let's let him heal, son. With the Lord's help, he may be fine." The men took Henry into the house and laid him in the parlor. "I will heat some water. There is food in the pantry. What about the other men?"

"They are very hungry. Do you have anything to spare?" Jacob and Aaron fed the small band of men before they set off going back to the regiment. Aaron wrote a letter requesting permission for Henry to stay home until well. He stated the caregivers had access to a surgeon and safety in the home. Aaron reported he would follow in the next few days, slipping back over the lines. Jacob wondered how he knew where they were going, but did not ask. The less he knew, the better.

Henry regained consciousness to drink some broth and consume some bread. His eyes were bright with excitement as he saw his father for the first time in years. They talked quietly about their escapades and fighting through the country. He quieted as the pain started to take over. He dozed in and out of the conversation. Jacob filled Aaron in about how the war was affecting them. He told him of Emilie's loss and how he hoped she would sleep a good, long time because what she had to face when she was awake left her no room to mourn.

"You have left us a mess to clean up," Jacob said to his son. "We are going to be hungry this winter. The armies have taken all we could give." He took another sip of his brandy. It felt good to drink with his son, seeing him as a man instead of a young son. The cavalry had changed them both. They were wiser with time and situation, each growing into men.

The sun began to set, when Jacob noticed the time. "I wish your mother wouldn't delay so late at the church." He got up to check the yard, when he heard the back door open. She was home, tired and worn out from the day's demands.

"Julia?" Jacob rushed to greet her before she walked into the parlor.

"It's me, Jacob. How's Emilie?" He heard her putting down her basket and walking toward the parlor. He tried to stop her before she saw them.

"Julia, Emilie is sleeping and—" He was cut off when he heard her gasp.

"Aaron! My God, where's…my baby!" Julia saw him before the men could stop her; she was at his side, looking at her injured son with tears in her eyes. She hugged Aaron tight, holding him close. She then turned her attention to Henry. He opened his eyes when he heard her enter.

"Hello, Mother." Henry smiled through the pain. "I had to see you again." He looked at his mother as she checked him over. When she saw the wound, she shook her head.

"What have you gotten yourself into, son?" Julia scolded him. He took her hand and kissed her fingers. She stopped to look at him.

"Your boy just got in the way of a Yankee bullet. You should see the other guys. They didn't fair so well." The playful Henry smile returned. His eyes sparkled with happiness to be in his family's presence. "I sure wish that sister of mine would get out of bed. I'd like to say hello." Despite his happiness, she could see he was in pain.

Julia ignored his attempted humor. "You rest. I think we have something for the pain." Julia looked up. "We will have to use brandy. There is a shortage of every pain medication possible. So many suffering in town." Julia explained how the landscape changed, the beautiful countryside littered with war.

"I'm sorry, Ma. We left quite a mess here, and now it looks like we are on the run again. There must have been some misunderstanding in the orders. We got cut off by the Union, we could not help our front line. Too many died because of that." Aaron shook his head, feeling the weight of the mission on his shoulders.

Emilie stirred in her sleep. When she reached the surface of reality, everything came tumbling back into her thoughts. She suddenly felt alone and needed someone. She put on her robe and gathered the wedding quilt around her. The comfort of the quilt made her feel better. Descending the stairs, she heard voices in the parlor. Listening closely, she edged closer to the parlor doors.

That voice. Her brain was searching for answers in the drug-induced fog. *Aaron!* Emilie opened the parlor doors, hoping to see her brother on the other side.

The family looked up when they saw her standing in the doorway. She stood there with her curly, brown locks untamed and loose. Wrapped in her wedding quilt, Emilie felt as vacant as she looked. Aaron was horrified to see she had no life behind her eyes. They usually sparkled with love and excitement. Today, she looked nothing like the girl he remembered. In three steps, Aaron gathered his sister in his arms, comforting her as he did when she skinned her knee when she was two. Emilie wept in his arms.

Once recovered, she found a smile.

"It is so good to see you! I missed you."

From the other settee, she heard, "What about me? I wasn't missed?" Emilie turned to see Henry propped up on the couch. He looked comfortable propped up by pillows and covered with a blanket. Emilie turned to him. "Don't you look comfortable?"

"I wish I was, but this dang bullet is not comfortable, I assure you. Looks like you will still have to do my chores." Henry laughed at her and winced in pain. "Still causing me pain, sis."

Emilie ate a light meal as she listened to the adventures of her brothers, the condition of the town, and her mother's newfound work at the church. The armies had vacated the town, and all that was left were the ones that could not be moved. Julia explained that once word reached the outside, people have flooded into town to look for their loved ones. Within days of the battle, outsiders were once again overrunning Gettysburg.

Emilie listened, amazed at how the world kept moving forward when hers felt as if it stopped in its tracks. She had only one choice to make: keep moving or stop. She wondered how she could live with the loss and emptiness, but she could not stay home to think about it. She was fascinated at the stories of the wounded. She remembered how it felt to help at the field hospital. It was her duty to help. When Julia announced she would be returning to town the next day, Emilie followed with a proclamation of her own.

"I am going with you. Sounds like you need some more able hands." It felt good to sound so strong. "Don't worry, Mother, I have seen plenty at the field hospital. Nothing will surprise me." The idea of helping others get home to their loved ones felt like the right thing to do. Emilie knew if she could send one more home, it would heal her pain.

Shocked, Julia could only agree. "Plan to throw your work clothes away. You won't be able to save them. There is no way we can get all the blood out of them."

This statement did not rattle Emilie as her statement shocked her family. "I have an old dark blue gown upstairs." Her mother looked at her with pain and disapproval. Emilie knew her mother expected her to follow tradition and wear black to mourn Thaddeus. "I will wear dark blue but never black. He may be dead, but he is not yet gone from my heart. I don't wish to mourn him, only remember him with love."

The family looked at one another in quiet respect.

Dear diary,

This is my first entry since he is gone. I still cannot believe I have nothing left. I painfully gave the ring back to Mrs. Marsh because it was a family heirloom. I feel so empty. The tears don't stop, they spring up at a moment's notice. What will I do without him? Will I ever feel joy again?

Tomorrow I will go to town with Mother to help at the church. I feel like if I can heal one person, I may be able to spare someone else the pain I feel right now. It does not make me feel better now, but it may in the future. It is so hard to think of my future without him.

On a happier note, Aaron and Henry arrived home. Henry has a bullet in his thigh. He is in constant pain, but he will stay with us. I pray he will heal. Stephen's injury is questionable as to whether he will heal or not. This war did not spare anyone except Aaron, and he has to go back. I never thought it would come to this. War is a terrible thing, tearing up families and breaking men. I will never understand how men can kill each other to prove a point. Most don't live to see the result of the fight.

I have a big day tomorrow; I pray I am strong enough to do some good.

Good night,
E.K.P.

A NEW KIND OF HEALING

The willingness to share does not make one charitable, it
makes one free.

—Robert Brault

Today, she would begin her work to help the many who still
needed good hands and a giving heart. She happily took the old
calico blue dress from the wardrobe. Emilie smiled to herself with
great pride. Today was the last day for tears. Thaddeus was never
coming home, but she felt empowered to do something good in
his name. Declaring she would not wear mourning clothes was
not just a bold statement, but it was her conviction to finally
stop weeping and start living. Emilie realized that even though
she missed him desperately, his memory would be best served by
helping the dying and the wounded. Understanding her logic,
that one should not wear black in the presence of men on their
deathbed worked; it healed those who came from the battlefields
and surrounding homes. It helped not only her patients, but the
bright colors lifted Emilie's spirits. It felt good to move out of the
darkness of death and mourning.

Emilie realized this was the first day she did not hear the battle.
The guns finally quieted after days of constant noise. The crick-
ets and frogs began to sing again. The birds had not yet returned,
too afraid to venture back to their homes. The streets began to
show signs of life, people slowly emerging from their homes still
burdened with sorrow and confusion. They were overwhelmed
with so much work ahead of them. Emilie realized this was one
of those turning points where you realize nothing will ever be the
same. The weather was humid and oppressive, like a wet, gray
wool blanket; the townspeople struggled to understand the ramifications of two enormous, clashing military bodies. The armies
moved on, and now, all that lay in its wake were the wounded,

dead, and dying. The landscape was littered with broken tools of war. It would take the citizens of Gettysburg months to clean up.

The ride into town only reminded her that her life would never be the same. Emilie and her mother rode in silence. Jacob took the ladies into town, assuring them he would return later that afternoon. The heat and humidity was too intense on this hot July day to walk. The horses still needed protection because of stragglers and strangers in and around town. The citizens of Gettysburg were careful to protect their own. Emilie noticed all that she once knew was dreadfully changed. Debris littered the roadside. Dead horses, broken carriages, and, to her horror, dead soldiers lying in all shapes and configurations. Bodies dropped like ragdolls to the floor, arms and legs splayed in inhuman con-figurations. These images became strangely familiar everywhere they looked; there were new sights more horrible than the last. She tried not to think about the families looking for their loved ones. It reminded her of how desperately she searched for him. The fear of the unknown now changed to feelings of loss. It was a horrible sight, but strangely enough, the mass chaos of her sur-roundings made Emilie feel as if she was walking in a strange land. How could this possibly be her home?

The familiarities of the town buildings were no comfort; as she approached the church stairs, she encountered men remov-ing bodies from the church. There was a strange, low note like the bellows of a church organ. Looking franticly around, Emilie could not place the source of that noise. Emilie's brain tried to understand the sights, sounds, and smells that assaulted her. The whole scene overwhelmed her senses so much, she felt as if she was dreaming. If she were dreaming, she willed herself to wake up. Emilie was jolted from her thoughts by her mother's stern, impatient voice.

"Emilie Kathryn, stop staring. And close your mouth." She felt a tug at her left elbow. The vestibule was bustling with women, rushing here and there. Mrs. Thompson greeted the newcomers with a halfhearted smile and open arms as she accepted the basket of biscuits and leftover stew.

"Thank you for coming back. Fresh set of hands to do the Lord's work, and he only knows how much needs to be done here." Her plump cheeks were finally showing a genuine smile as her kind eyes showed relief. Staring over Mrs. Thompson's shoulder, the sanctuary of the church has completely transformed. The pews moved from their neat, tidy rows. Everything cleared aside, leaving room open for rows and rows of men, both North and South, all lying in heaps of wiggling mass of bodies. The low hum suddenly became very clear as she entered the sanctuary. It was the wounded suffering and bravely enduring their pain. It was a sea of bodies with women and men, the able-bodied ones popping up and down as they saw to the need of those on the floor.

"Time to work, Emilie!" Julia handed her daughter a basket of linens. "Cut these in two-inch strips and roll them. The surgeons will need them for bandages. Go, sit over there." Still dazed, Emilie numbly walked to the coat closet and sat on the floor to cut and roll bandages.

Blocking out the sights and sounds of the church, Emilie was actually humming to herself. This always happened when she found herself content in finishing a job well done. Just as she wrapped the second-to-last bandage, a face peering in at her startled her. It was an older woman with strong, fierce features. Her large, beaky nose was the first thing Emilie saw, and her steel-gray, harsh eyes sent chills down her spine.

"Girl, you are needed out here. What are you doing hiding in here? If you are going to be of any help at all, you must get off your lazy behind and work. The Lord doesn't look kindly upon lazy personages." Her large form blocked the light from the foyer. Emilie realized it was the woman's habit that blocked the light. Emilie was astonished at the woman's tone. She thought godly women were supposed to be nice and kind souls.

"Yes, ma'am." Emilie rose from her comfortable sitting spot and gathered the basket under her arm. "I am just about finished with these bandages. What would you like me to do next?" Emilie attempted to smile, although her heart was pounding. The woman towered over her by a foot, and she looked formidable dressed in black and white.

"First, you can start by not looking so pretty. The men are here for our help in healing, and they, I assure you, are not looking for wives or whores." Her words stung like a slap on her check. "Second, you can stop hiding from all of the hard work and get to tending these men. They are dying by the minute, and every one of them needs water and wash. Is it too hard to ask for that kind of help?"

Emilie's eyes widened at the suggestion. "Wash?"

The blush rose to her cheeks.

"Hands and face, lassie. Not anything private, unless you are accustomed to that sort of thing." The nun was getting impatient with this imp of a girl. She needed good workers, not simpletons afraid of work. Walking her over to the steaming kettle of water, she handed Emilie a bucket and several rags. "Here, I'll show you where to start."

Emilie followed the woman down several rows of men. "Begin here and go that way." She pointed toward the opposite side of the sanctuary. "Do not change the water until it is plenty dirty. We don't have enough to be wasteful."

Emilie stared down at the man lying before her. His eyes closed, he looked as if he was sleeping. Face black from battle, she hoped he was not dead. Clearing her throat, Emilie hoped it would be enough for him to open his eyes. No response, his tattered clothes lay loose around his body. He looked like he should eat. She wondered how long it had been since the man had a good meal. Suddenly, he opened his eyes. Emilie smiled down at him. "Sir, would you mind if I helped you wash your face and hands?" He simply nodded. Gingerly, she wet the rag and put it to his face, wiping away the remnants of battle. His features relaxed some as she continued with his hands. Too scared to say anything, Emilie whispered, "I hope this helps." She rose to her feet and moved down the line. With each soldier, Emilie tried to smile and offer some kindness. Some men were too pained to acknowledge her, but she understood. While she tended the fourth man, she jumped at the sound of that dreadful bark. "Get a move on, girl. You will be here all night with your snail pace."

Irritated at the woman's harshness, Emilie struggled to keep her tongue. She stood up, squared her shoulders, and announced, "My name is Emilie, and I am moving as fast as I can, madame." Her angered, green eyes flashed with defiance. She knew she walked the fine line between respect and disrespect, but no one talked down to her like that. Not wanting to shame her family, she glared at the woman and then went back to her work.

"You know, it is not disrespectful to hold your ground." The voice was almost a whisper. "She talks to everyone like that." His eyes were a peaceful blue gray, with a smooth, husky voice. "I could sure use that water and rag."

Emilie turned to the voice speaking to her. "Here you go." She squeezed the water from the rag, handing it to him. His opened a blistered hand to her. The hands showed dark dirt and soot. She smiled at him. "I'm Emilie. Where are you from?" Emilie immediately felt her spirits lift. She enjoyed meeting people, even in this situation.

"Virginia. Not so far from home now, here in Gettysburg," he said with a wry smile. "Sure wish I could get the rest of the way."

"You are a Southern gentleman!" Memories of her home came over her with emotion and pride. "I used to live in Virginia." Emilie genuinely smiled for the first time in weeks.

He smiled with appreciation. "Your accent sounds familiar."

She nodded, taking the rag from him and rinsing it for another try. "Well, maybe you can go home soon. I am sure you have family waiting impatiently to hear from you."

"I think they forgot about me. I haven't been able to write for some time now. Haven't received a letter in months." The brightness in his eyes clouded was over with sadness.

"Tell me about your family." Emilie was hoping to cheer up this man. "If, of course, you don't think me too forward in asking." A blush rose to her cheeks. Her curiosity was getting the best of her, and that always lead to impertinence.

"Not at all. Name's Bob, from Salem, Virginia. I have a farm and a lovely wife and two children. From my wife's last letter, another one's on the way."

"That is wonderful," Emilie said, feeling a pang of sadness in her heart. "I am sure you will go home soon. You are not hurt bad, are you?" She could not see outright injuries to him.

"My head hurts powerfully bad. I was too near a percussion blast from the enemy's cannon. I was forced to sit out the last day." He started to tear up. "They wouldn't let me march. I let my boys down."

Struggling to understand his pain, Emilie eyes welled up. She wasn't going to let emotion take her, not today. She needed to be strong for these men. *You cannot help others if you are all balled up with emotion*, she scolded herself.

"I'm sorry," she choked. "You were supposed to live today." His eyes were far away, taken by the memories and emotion of the battle. Emilie heard the heavy footsteps enter the sanctuary.

Bob patted her hand. "You better skedaddle, or Sister Claire Marie will be back at you again. Try not to cross her too much. She has a temper." He smiled kindly at her, and she quickly moved down the row.

The first day in the church was exhausting. Emilie and her mother enjoyed the ride home. It felt good to sit down. They had been on their feet all day. Emilie looked down at her dress. Her mother was right, the hemline was soaked with blood. Wherever she walked, it could not be avoided. Her apron was filthy with dirt and smudges. Julia's eyes were heavy with exhaustion. Emilie's knees ached from standing and stooping all day. There were so many men with so many needs. How could anyone hope to heal anyone?

The house lights were on when they came up the drive. It looked warm and inviting. Glad to be home, she was looking forward to a good dinner and a restful-night's sleep. Dinner conversation was limited to generalities. Aaron watched over Henry while Jacob helped Mrs. Bayle with the farm until Joe and Billy returned. There were so many chores to tend too. After he finished at the Bayles', he went to the fields to bury the dead. Jacob told of the dangers of live ammunition in the ground. Jacob had no patience for the visitors and looters who combed the fields in search of treasure.

"I feel for those who are looking for their loved ones. The scavengers make me angry, so greedy and foolish. One man picked up a shell and lost his arm when it exploded. It is not safe out there."

After dinner, Aaron packed his saddlebags with some food-stuff Julia set aside for him. Emilie watched him close the buckle, when he looked at her. "Em, will you walk me to the barn?"

Emilie shook her head and followed him out. She didn't want him to go back now that she knew he was safe. *Life hangs on a thin string*, she thought to herself. When he rode away, would this be the last she would see of him? Despite how heavy these thoughts weighed on her mind, she was glad to get to say good-bye in private. The light in the barn was dimming. The windows revealed growing darkness as the sun continued to set. There was not much time left to this day. Aaron felt safe riding in the night.

Aaron turned to his sister. He admired her for making an effort to move on after her loss. He saw her smile more every day; he was confident she would give in to his request. He asked only what he knew she could give and prayed he could return it to her.

Emilie watched Aaron and Starlight ride away. *Please protect them both. Lord*, she prayed fervently, *I trust you will return them to me whole and unharmed.* Emilie walked into the house, through the kitchen and up to her room. Julia spoke to her as she moved through the room silently.

"Be ready by seven tomorrow morning. We need to stop at the Andersons' before going back to the church." Julia looked up from her knitting. "Em, you did good today. Good work."

"Thank you, Mother. Sweet dreams. Good night, Father." Emilie prepared for bed and cried herself to sleep after writing her sorrows in her diary.

> Dear diary,
>
> How much more can I give to this senseless war? Tonight I watched my brother leave with Starlight. If everyone sacrificed this much, I am positive there would be no more wars. I only let him take her because I know together they have some chance to get through this war together. I'd rather Aaron protect her than some stranger take her from me. I lost my husband, my horse, and my brother. I hated seeing him go. Everything felt normal for one brief moment. Aaron is returning to a war I do not see ending anytime soon.
>
> I never imagined war could tear you apart piece by piece. I see its effects on everyone around me. I was foolish to think I could get through this unscathed by its horror.
>
> I pray for strength and hope it all ends soon.
>
> E.K.P

LIFE EVER CHANGING

When you are no longer able to change a situation, we are challenged to change ourselves.

—Victor Frankl

Late summer in Gettysburg focused on returning the town to habitable. Food was scarce due to the scavenging armies and battle-ruined crops. Visitors poured into town as soon as rail service returned to aid or search out loved ones reported lost here. Demands of the city were still higher than supply. The heat of late summer brought horrible smells of decaying, rotting flesh of human and animal. Pennyroyal and peppermint, used in handkerchiefs, were in high demand to help stave off the stench that permeated the area. Those involved in the long hours of cleanup began to feel the ill-effects of the bad air and stress. These conditions caused illness and sometimes death.

Gettysburg had no time to mourn its once-peaceful existence. They took to working hard in sincerest hopes to find their own peace. Men and women, army and civilian continued the ongoing care of those left behind. By the third week after the battle, the wounded were moved to a new army hospital called Camp Lettermen outside of town. This relieved most of the citizens of their nursing dedications.

Many women followed the men in their care while others let go to return to a new normal life. Everyone knew they could not go back to life before the battle, but they struggled to create a new normal for themselves.

Emilie found joy in working with the soldiers from North and South. She didn't see them as enemies, only people in need of care. She was more than willing to give all she could to see them go home, healthier than when they came. In the instances that she could not help heal, she sat by to write letters for their loved ones and comfort them how ever she could before they passed. The whole experience for her was surreal. She felt her heart become harder against death. She could not decide if she didn't care about death or if it lost its mystery after she had seen it so many times. Death had already taken the only thing she cherished. She felt it was important to comfort the dying as they missed their loved ones. Emilie realized she was blessed to be able to say good-bye to Thaddeus. Many died without such comfort at their side.

This afternoon the last of the men were moved out of the church to Camp Letterman. Emilie swept the floor of the now-empty sanctuary. The ladies left behind to return the church to its former glory did so in an upbeat fervor, not seen in weeks. Everyone felt a little happier knowing there would be church services held there on Sunday. It seemed without these services, their faith waned under the stress and constant reminder of death and sadness.

Emilie felt proud to be part of the healing that happened here, but she was more relieved to see it done. Her sweeping continued as the other women scrubbed the floor. The blood stained the beautiful wood floors.

Lost in her thoughts, she watched the dirt push forward with each stroke of the broom. She heard the sound of heavy boots on the floor. Looking up, she saw Bob waiting at the door of the sanctuary. Emilie smiled at him with a wave.

He closed the distance between them with a few long strides. His eyes were bright with happiness. She could see his pain was gone. He no longer winced and closed his eyes when he talked.

"Miss Emilie, I want to let you know that I am going back today." He was shy, looking down at the floor smiling. "The doctor says I will be fine." He took her hand in his, squeezing it gently.

"Your headaches are gone?" Emilie liked this man. He always had kind words for her, and he was grateful for her help.

They spent a lot of time together while he recovered. She would miss him.

Bob shook his head. "Not entirely, but I am able to go back to regular duties. I want to thank you for your companionship while I was here. You are an angel."

Emilie smiled, shaking her head. "No, just doing my best to help. God did the rest." Bob kissed her hand and gave it back to her.

"Thank you, my lady. I will always be grateful for your kindness." Bob looked into her eyes. The tension between them was palpable. Emilie felt the need to back away, for she knew he wanted to embrace her. She wasn't ready for that; her feelings for him were dangerously intimate.

Instead, she replied, "You're welcome." She knew he had to get back to his life, but she would miss him. It was hard to say good-bye again. "When you see your family, give them my regards."

"My wife and children will be eternally grateful for you." He turned to leave the sanctuary. Emilie waved good-bye. This was one more step to getting back to life as usual.

That afternoon, Stephen arrived at the church. Emilie just finished throwing out wash water when he surprised her. "May I carry that back for you?" Stephen's limp was much more pronounced than weeks earlier. He was getting weaker instead of stronger. With him not returning to the regiment, Emilie found him by her side almost constantly. He saw her every day in some way. It was a comfort to her. Stephen had a way of making Emilie laugh even when she didn't think it was appropriate.

Today she saw he had a satisfied smile on his face. He had some news she was sure, but he seemed to hoard it to himself for the moment. "Thank you. I am tired of carrying these buckets all day."

"That floor will be sparkling by Sunday service," he commented.

"Yes, if blood stains sparkle," Emilie added.

"The blood will forever stain these floors. No one will forget what happened here."

"Does this mean you are ready to go home?" Stephen's hair had not been cut in months. The wind blew it into his eyes. He fought to brush it out of his eyes. "Egads, it stinks in this town. I hope this stench doesn't last forever."

"I am always ready to go home." Emilie couldn't wait to walk out some of the kinks in her knees from scrubbing the floor most of the afternoon.

"Good, I will escort you." He made it sound more like an announcement than a request. Stephen set the bucket down as Emilie gathered her basket. "Will your mother be joining us?"

"Mother isn't here. She had to stay home today. The doctor was coming out to see Henry today." Together they walked down behind the church to the buckboard Stephen had brought into town.

Emilie watched Stephen as they rode back to Table Rock Road. She saw him smiling as he watched the road, seeming so content with himself. He sang to the horses. This was something Emilie never heard from him. She stifled a giggle. He caught her laughing and demanded to know what she was doing.

"Me? You are the one who looks like a cat who just ate the mouse." She peered at him, still laughing. "What is it, Stephen?"

He slowed the wagon and stopped. Stephen turned to her. It was an announcement she never expected to hear. "I just got word. I am not going back."

"What?" Emilie was surprised. How could he be happy not to return to what seemed to fit him so well? Stephen was a changed man since joining the army. He became lighthearted and jovial. He truly liked his work there. She knew he didn't like the fighting and would worry if he did. The job he did as a solider made him a new man, not the cynical sourpuss he was before he left. She didn't want to figure out how it happened; she was only grateful for this new man.

"My knee infection doesn't go away. It feels better, then it's bad again. I won't be able to take the field and do the job of a soldier anymore. Since I am so close to the end of my term, I have been medically discharged." Stephen smiled, hoping Emilie would be happy for him.

The joyful news overwhelmed her. Emilie threw her arms around him, hugging him. "That is great! Not your injury," she quickly corrected herself, "but the news you are home to stay." Emilie turned, thinking the announcement was over.

Stephen took her hand, looked into her eyes, and asked, "May I court you, Emilie?" His eyes were sincere. His hands gentle on hers. "I know it's too soon, but if I wait any longer, someone else will claim you."

Emilie felt as if she were plunged into an ice-cold stream. The announcement took her completely off guard. Memories of her and Thaddeus flooded through her mind; she felt a pang of loss and sadness. Tears filled her eyes. Emilie didn't know what to say.

Stephen pulled her close. "I am sorry. It is too soon for you." He looked into her eyes; she was still so vulnerable. "I was so excited to be home. I am so ready to begin living again, and I want to do it with you." He took her hands into his and kissed them gently. This was just another side of Stephen she hadn't seen before. It excited her to see him so personable and sincere. Thoughts flooded through her head. Could she imagine herself with another man? It was only weeks before she lost the love of her life. Her future dissipated like the midmorning fog.

"What about Thaddeus?" The words were said without her thinking them. It was like someone else spoke them. She felt overcome with emotion. She needed reassurance he would not force her to forget him. She would never forget him. Stephen cringed at the name; he thought it was all over. Maybe it was too soon.

Stephen cupped her chin in his hands. The intimacy felt strange, but she did not pull away. His eyes were always gentle when he looked at her. He watched her, his smile encouraging her to feel again.

"We will never forget him. He was my best friend and your fiancé. We are here, alive and living. We must not stop living. What would he tell you to do?"

Emilie suddenly remembered their last conversation. He implored her to go on living, marry, and have children. Tears streamed down her cheeks. She could hear him telling her good-bye, but he did not tell her to stop living.

"I don't know what to say." Emilie felt fragile. Was she ready for another commitment like this?

Stephen saw all the questions in her eyes. He knew that given time, she would commit again. Thaddeus had warned him to handle her with kid gloves. If pushed in any situation, he said, she will fight you like a wildcat. Given time and patience, she eventually comes around. Emilie is a headstrong woman who knows what she wants. Stephen finished his thought. *If I want her, I have to be patient and wait.*

He kissed her on the forehead. "I know it is a lot to think about. I just want you to know, I care and I want you in my life." Stephen placed her hands back in her lap, smiled at her, and resumed the ride home.

Parking the wagon at the front of the house, Stephen hopped out of the wagon and limped around to help Emilie down. Henry stood on the porch, leaning on homemade crutches. He waved at them.

"Looks like your brother is doing better. Is he walking again?" Stephen was surprised to see Henry up and about. Emilie rarely talked about her brothers. She did not want to draw attention to where they were. Stephen was told after much prodding they enlisted to fight for the Confederacy.

"He is improving slowly. He has a bullet in his thigh. Doctor says he may have a bullet in the leg bone." Emilie filled Stephen in on the details of Henry's injury.

Stephen met Henry on the porch and shook his hand. "Good to see you. I see the war set you out too." The two friends smiled at each other. They walked over and sat down on the chairs.

"It was a nasty bullet from the Yanks. Those boys know how to shoot." Henry laughed. He saw Emilie's eyes get big with shock.

Stephen shook his head. "Well, you rebs are sharpshooters too. I took one too, and now I can't get rid of this infection."

The men chatted about war stories, each not saying anything about strategy or secrets. Both still dedicated to their cause. Emilie waited to see how the conversation would end. Rumors around town were hot with political accusations of Southern sympathizers giving favors to the South. Innocent townspeople were arrested for these accusations. Some townsfolk seemed ready to take out their frustrations on anyone.

Henry finished the conversation with, "So when are you going back, Stephen?"

Stephen replied, "I am medically discharged. I am ready to start living at home again. Looks like I will need to get the farm back on track before we starve this winter."

"I won't be going back either. It looks like we are citizens again. No longer enemies on the field." Henry eyed up his friend, making sure he and Stephen understood each other.

Stephen shook is friend's hand. "We are friends first. It doesn't look like you or I could harm anyone. Your political preference is safe with me, Henry."

"Thank you for your friendship." Henry was sincere.

The threesome continued their conversation well into the afternoon. After Stephen left, Henry looked at his sister. She smiled back at him.

"He likes you!" The glint in Henry's eyes reminded her of the old Henry.

"I know, he wants to court me," Emilie said flatly. "I don't know what to do with that."

Henry eyed her, considering all she had been through and the past that Stephen and Emilie had as friends. His sister looked like she had grown older since her life was touched so brutally by the war. Was it the war or just time passing by?

Henry lit a cigar. After a long draw, he shook his head. "Stephen could be good for you. He's not so bad. Nice as men go. I think you should give him a try." He meditatively sat, enjoying his cigar. Emilie watched him, realizing gone were the carefree days of their youth. There was no more teasing. Henry had become a man drawn into maturity through war and pain. His personality showed through his witty remarks, but he was no longer the boy she disagreed with regularly.

"I don't know how father feels about him." Emilie said. She was convinced he may welcome any man interested in his daughter. If she could fall in love again, she knew she could be happy. It just felt so far away. When would it happen?

> Dear diary,
>
> Stephen asked permission to court me. I like the new Stephen. I can see us working well together. I am not in love with him, but we are good friends. Is it enough? I feel like I am betraying Thaddeus. I know he is gone, but he still lives in my heart.
>
> I know it will take time. If I give Stephen a chance, maybe we can be happy together. I will allow him to court me. Maybe I will fall in love with him. He makes me laugh. He is not as intense as he once was. He seems to understand me more than he ever has in the past. I wonder if Thaddeus talked about me when they were in camp together. Would Thaddeus approve of us?
>
> Stephen is right, we are left on this earth to live. If it wasn't meant to be we would be dead. I choose to live and will hopefully find love again.
>
> Why is the future so hard to see?
>
> E.K.P.

That night Emilie fought with sleep and thoughts of Stephen and Thaddeus weighed heavy on her mind. Emilie wanted to talk to Thaddeus. She wanted his approval. She struggled with her feelings about letting go of him. Moving on to live her life felt like the biggest obstacle yet.

Sleep for her was riddled with questions racing through her mind. Not realizing she fell asleep, she was surprised to see Thaddeus. He walked up to her and pulled her into his arms. Emilie felt uncomfortable there. Thaddeus did not speak to her. She watched him greet Stephen with a handshake. Holding her hand in his, Thaddeus took Stephen's hand, placed Emilie's hand in his. Emilie felt joy. It overwhelmed her. Thaddeus smiled at her and nodded his head toward Stephen. Emilie struggled to ask questions, desperately wanting to speak but she had no voice. She only watched Thaddeus disappear in the mist. Her hand still in Stephen's, Emilie felt peace.

Emilie awoke that morning refreshed. The dream she had the night before calmed her worries and put peace in her heart. Emilie was ready to live again.

TIME HEALS WOUNDS
SEEN AND UNSEEN

Sadness flies on the wings of time.

—Jean de Lafontaine

The armies, North and South, chased each other through the Southern United States, leaving Gettysburg to get back to the small-unknown town it once was. Just as many things changed that year, the people of Gettysburg realized it could not go back to being quaint unknown town in southern Pennsylvania. The three-day battle left an indelible mark on the people and the land. Gettysburg would forever forward remind our country of passion and strength of its people both military and civilians.

The burial of war dead got the officials of Gettysburg thinking about how to memorialize what happened here. Plans for a national cemetery and preservation of the battlefields began weeks after the last of the healed soldiers began leaving town. The town watched as Attorneys Wills and McConaughy argued where the best cemetery would reside. Governor Curtain finally employed Mr. David Buehler and Edward Fahnestock to mediate and settle the dispute.

The Gettysburg National Cemetery was founded that year. On November 19, 1863, it was dedicated to all that fought here in a dedication ceremony. The event brought joy and jubilation to Gettysburg for the first time in four months. The town planned for a large celebration but again underestimated how many out-of-town visitors would attend.

❦

Emilie took one last look in the mirror. The stray piece of hair was finally staying in place. She had fought it all morning. Pinching her cheeks one last time to bring forth a rosy glow, she snatched up her bag and left the room. Moments before, she heard Stephen in the yard. She knew someone would be calling her soon.

Swishing out of the room, she descended the stairs. Emilie saw Henry and her parents waiting for her. Jacob helped Julia with her wrap as Henry laughed with Stephen.

"Hurry or we will miss the parade." Jacob's role never changed. He should have been a railroad conductor, always reminding his family about the time.

Stephen eyed Emilie as she came into the room. Her satin, blue-and-green gown made her eyes sparkle greener than he had ever seen them. She lit up a room with that smile. He was proud to be hers. The courtship was going very well for them, and they were very happy in each other's company.

Riding into town, everyone chatted about the excitement of seeing the dignitaries and President Lincoln. Henry had resolved that his loyalties were still to the South, but he would not express this boldly after seeing how everyone suffered. Rather, he chose to live with his family and their values until the war ended. No, he was not happy with President Lincoln but would smile and be cordial if need be.

Arriving at the cemetery, Henry commented on the sparse look of the site. Hundreds of plots shown by small mounds of raised dirt reminded everyone how many suffered here. Each state represented here; all men who fought and died in the three-day battle were returned to the earth. The ground demanded respect and solemn reverence. Everyone spoke in hushed tones to show their respect. As the family reached the top of the hill, they heard the regimental band in the distance. Turning to its sound, Emilie was overwhelmed at what she saw.

A sea of people gathered on these grounds led by cavalry and the regimental bands. People and dignitaries followed close behind; the new cemetery was overwhelmed with crowds of more than fifteen thousand people who had turned out for this event.

Everyone gathered to listen. Stephen stood close to Emilie, pulling her into him, so she could lean on him as they listened.

Two hours after Edward Everett took the stage, President Lincoln was introduced for his speech.

"What do you think he is going to talk about?" Julia asked her husband.

Henry piped up, "Probably about how he has failed to win, and he now believes the South is right, and we should all join them." He tried to sound funny, but his statement came off sarcastic and sharp. Henry's smile could not cover up his true feelings.

Jacob gave his son a sharp look of disapproval. Emilie smiled at the way he still shrank from his father's glare. They all turned to listen. As their attention turned to the podium, Emilie felt Stephen pull her in closer. She felt secure in his presence, and she enjoyed his touch.

The president gave a short three-minute speech, which brought Emilie to tears. She understood what he was saying, and his words brought back memories of what she and everyone around her went through. As a tear slid off her cheek, she noticed a handkerchief appear in front of her. It still smelled of pennyroyal, but he knew she was thinking about Thaddeus. He offered her the kerchief in silent comfort.

As she wiped the tears from her eyes, Emilie felt Stephen's warm breath on her neck. He whispered so only she could hear. "We will always remember him." The words shook her very soul. Emilie cried silently, her shoulders shaking. Stephen squeezed her tight.

On the way back to the house, Stephen requested a meeting with Jacob before they went into the house. Both men went to the barn to unhitch the team and to have their say.

Emilie and Julia prepared afternoon tea and refreshments. Henry went to lie down; the excursion into town tired him. The men joined the ladies minutes later in the parlor.

Emilie poured out the tea and waited. Both men looked as if they wanted to say something, but neither knew how to say it. Emilie smiled at how they looked, as if they both ate a bird and were waiting to get caught. How sheepish they both looked. Jacob nudged Stephen. Emilie and Julia looked at each other, surprised at the men's behavior.

Stephen finally got up, set his teacup down, and knelt in front of Emilie. Julia took the cup from her daughter's hand and sat back to watch.

Stephen tenderly took her hand in his and said, "Emilie, I have loved you from the day I met you. I felt like the luckiest man at that moment to be the first to know you." He cleared his throat and smiled a sheepish grin. "When Thaddeus got you first, I was heartbroken. Please forgive me; I treated you badly in those months before we left for war." She saw the regret in his eyes. Before her knelt a man who realized his love for a woman he could not have. He went on. "I am a changed man through the circumstances of war. I feel I am a better man for my experience, and now I am ready to become a responsible man of a wife and family. I ask you, Miss Emilie, please do me an honor and become my wife." His eyes watered; he fought back the heartfelt tears as he made this request of her.

Emilie felt a tug at her heart. At this moment, she was thinking about her and Stephen's future. Thaddeus was not present; she felt a part of him leave her heart, making room for her future. Somewhere in her mind, she heard Thaddeus say *Go. I want your happiness.*

Looking into Stephen's eyes, she saw how he loved her. It melted her, opening another space in her heart. He belonged there, and she knew it. "I accept your love, and I would be honored to be your wife."

Stephen took her hand and kissed it. He slipped his hand in his pocket, pulled out a beautiful stone ring, and placed it on her hand. It was a delicate garnet set in gold. "Thank you," he whispered. She winked at him, too emotional to speak.

Julia and Jacob held each other close. They had just witnessed what they had been praying for since the birth of their daughter. Julia wiped a tear from her eyes. Emilie would finally have a chance at love and motherhood.

"Congratulations," Jacob said, standing to shake Stephen's hand, and hugged his daughter. Julia embraced Stephen and hugged Emilie, tears still streaming down her cheeks.

A loud knock on the door interrupted their celebration. Julia jumped in surprise. Jacob opened the door to see the constable and Mrs. Spree standing there.

Before Jacob could greet them, Constance Spree announced, "Arrest him, he stole my slave, and killed my husband." She worked herself into frenzy, pointing a crooked finger at him.

"Good to see you, Constance." Jacob's voice was calm and quiet. "Constable, pleasant evening."

"I wish it were, Jacob. I am afraid you need to come with me so we can sort this out." He looked exhausted. Jacob surmised Mrs. Spree did not just arrive in town.

Jacob cleared his throat. "Is it pressing? My daughter just announced her engagement. I would like this time to celebrate with them."

Mrs. Spree glared at Jacob.

"You have no right celebrating when you are a murderer. You finally married off that little wench. Who's the poor soul taking her off your hands?"

The men looked at her in surprise. Jacob smiled. "If you were a man, Constance, I would shoot you for that." Jacob loathed this dramatic, whinny, and spoiled woman. He didn't know how she got up here, but she was certainly trying to make her point.

"I am sorry, Jacob. No one will sleep until we resolve this. Do you know where the slave is now?" The Constable's voice was flat and business-like.

"Yes, Martha works for your neighbor, Thomas. She is a free slave and has been since she arrived here in 1862. I freed them in 1861 when I left the Prescott Plantation."

The constable shook his head. "Do you have papers?"

"Yes, I will bring them in tomorrow, and as far as killing Horace, he tripped over the rug and hit his head on the table. I never touched him."

"Liar! You killed him. I saw you!" she shrieked at a pitch that would make a dog cringe.

"You were not even in the room. He sent you to get Ben." He glared at her evenly. "Please, constable, with all due respect, I will be happy to be in tomorrow, and I will bring witnesses and her emancipation papers."

"I will see you at 10:00 a.m., and you may bring a lawyer with you." The constable turned to leave. He asked her if she would like a ride back to town or if she was walking. Constance huffed and puffed, calling the constable names for not doing his duty. She raged on and on until he threatened to lock her up for the evening. She snapped her mouth shut, crossed her arms, and sat in the carriage, saying no more.

Returning to the parlor, Jacob smiled to himself. Tonight he was going to spend time with his family. Everyone was happy again; this was a feeling he was not willing to let go.

> Dear diary,
>
> I am so happy. It was a long time in coming, but I finally feel alive and happy again. Stephen asked me to marry him. It felt right, in my heart. I feel like I am letting go of Thaddeus a little every day. I feel good about living. I do not want to be a mournful old woman missing life.
>
> Stephen and I discussed my teaching. He still opposes his wife working, but will concede until the babies start coming. I believe compromise is the best in this situation. Stephen is still very strong willed about some things. I am happy again and feeling more in love every day.
>
> I am getting married!
>
> E.K.P.

OUT OF THE ASHES

Sometimes in tragedy we find our life's purpose—the eyes
shed a tear to find its focus.

—Robert Brault

OCTOBER 1864

Stephen paced across the floor for the—oh, he lost count. She
woke him at 3:00 a.m. with the first pains of her pending motherhood. By 6:00 a.m., he returned with Julia and Jacob in tow.
Martha had joined them later that afternoon. She told Emilie
and Stephen she would not miss the birth of the next generation.
Arriving with a satchel in hand, Martha greeted the men and
then disappeared into the bedroom. Emilie had been in there for
hours with little sound coming from behind the door.

Jacob finally got up from his chair and steered his son-in-law
outside. The air in the room was stale and stuffy. Stephen looked
at him, questioning. "You are going to wear a trough in the parlor
floor, son. Let's get some fresh air."

The men busied themselves looking around the gardens, discussing next year's crops, when Julia came out of the house, smiling from ear to ear. Smiling with pride, she motioned to the men.

"Stephen, come meet your son." Julia cried emotionally. Julia
looked weary but very proud. Stephen noticed she could not stop
smiling. He was shocked to see tears come to her eyes.

Stephen panicked. "Are they all right?"

Nodding her head, Julia struggled to control her tears. She
took him by the shoulders and steered him toward the bedroom.
The family had been moving him around all day because he was
overwhelmed with worry for his wife and child. Stephen felt like

he was walking in a dream all day. Not knowing what to do and overcome with concern.

He went into their room cautiously. The room was dim, the shades partially closed to shut out the harsh sun. Emilie rested peacefully, her hair loose and curly on the pillow. She was beautiful. This is how she looked after they shared their love. He loved seeing her that way. She was peaceful, relaxed, and angelic. He kissed her tenderly on the forehead.

"Hello, new momma."

Her eyes opened, and she smiled at him.

"Did you see him?" she said. "He looks like you."

"No, I just want to look at you, make sure you are all right."

Martha interrupted his survey of her. "Say hello to your son." She handed him the tight bundle of blanket. Stephen felt light-headed. He closed his eyes. Martha grabbed his arm and sat him next to Emilie. Martha placed the baby in Stephen's arms. "I will leave you two alone. You give the child to her if yous feeling faint, you hear me?" Martha waited for Stephen to answer her before she closed the door quietly behind her.

Emilie felt drained. Julia told her she had an easy labor. Emilie wondered what *hard* was like. She watched her husband look in awe at their son. He was lost in wonderment. Stephen counted his fingers, looked at his ears and gently unwrapped the infant to look at him. The baby squawked in protest. He didn't like being inspected by his curious father. He wiggled and squirmed, voicing his opinion. Emilie took him from Stephen.

"He's hungry," she assured him wrapping the baby tight in his blankets.

"Oh." Stephen watched mother and child bond as she put him to her breast. Emilie watched how attentive her husband was to their son. She saw him flinch when she reacted to the baby's hearty latching to her breast. Relaxing into her new feeding routine, Emilie was ready to approach the subject they both avoided for nine months.

"They are going to ask soon. We need to decide." She looked at him. It was a hard decision to name the first child. Stephen said she could name the girl, but he was torn about his son's name.

Emilie looked at him and her new son with wonder. She thanked God for all of the blessings he bestowed upon her. At every moment, she thought God wasn't available, he always blessed her with something new.

She made up her mind. "We will name him Thaddeus Stephen Byrne. It fits him perfectly."

She heard him hesitate; then he reluctantly said, "It's perfect, baby." She felt him kiss her cheek. They sat together for a long time bonding as a family. After the baby was fed, they were ready for eager visitors. Jacob and Julia were ecstatic about becoming grandparents. Martha was just as proud. She offered to stay behind to help with the first few days of their new life. Emilie and Stephen wanted to be alone with their new family. The visitors reluctantly left that night, promising to return tomorrow to look in on them.

Emilie felt exhausted by the day but still wanted to record this event in her diary.

> Dear diary,
> You have been my trusted confidant for many years. Today I become a mother. I feel so much joy now. The sorrow that clouded my life seems lifetimes away. The baby is strong and healthy. He eats heartily and is very active. I am proud to open this chapter in my life. Stephen and I have become very close as husband and wife. I feel confident God blesses our marriage.
> I am happy to find my new normal in life. Life is good and I am as happy as I can be. I think little of Thaddeus now, as I am busy with the baby. We named him Thaddeus to honor him. I am ready to move on and move past the last few years. There is more life to live and a new life to raise. Speaking of, I think he is hungry again.
> Happy and very tired new momma.
>
> E.K.P

The moon was high in the night sky, lighting the room where her husband slept. The baby was sound asleep as Emilie tried to coax another burp from him. Tears flowed down her cheeks. She was happy despite the sudden bouts of sadness that overwhelmed her in the last few weeks. The baby was good as could be. He ate on schedule, slept a lot, and wailed when he needed attention. Tonight, Emilie sat with him, struggling with feelings and what ifs. What if Thaddeus hadn't died, she would be holding his son. How would things be different?

Emilie spent the last few days fighting these thoughts that she believed were gone for good when she married Stephen. Stephen asked her several times what was bothering her. She could not be honest with him, not about this. She did not know why, but her thoughts focused on the what-ifs with Thaddeus. She missed him. She hadn't thought about him for a long time and suddenly he returned to her thoughts and the ache in her heart still as strong as before. Allowing her tears to flow, she felt him near her. She kept these feelings to herself. These feeling usually bring her joy, but tonight she wholeheartedly missed him.

Nursing always made her sleepy. Emilie dozed with the baby tucked securely on her shoulder, both mother and child rocking quietly. She dreamed about him. Thaddeus stood behind her, stroking her hair.

"He is a beautiful baby, Emilie." His voice was excited and full of joy.

"I named him after you," she whispered.

"Good, very good. Now that I know you won't forget us, I can go." He wasn't sad, just matter-of-fact. His hand still on her shoulder, she felt him kiss her cheek.

"Thaddeus, don't go. I love it when you are here with me. I don't want you to go. I need you." Emilie felt a tug at her heart.

"I can't stay. You have a family now. Stephen loves you. He will be good for you. I will always love you, my girl. Make room in your heart for him. My time is done here." She felt his presence fade away. He was gone and she knew he would not come back.

This time she felt her heart let go of him, she felt the tender connection between them break like a ping of a fiddle string. Emilie woke when the baby made a snuffling noise in her ear and sucked noisily on his thumb. Emilie kissed his head, enjoying the smell of his fine downy hair. Kissing him one last time, she tucked him securely in his cradle.

Emilie slipped into bed, next to Stephen. His body was warm and inviting. He rolled over, and she moved closer and put her arm around him. Before she fell asleep, everything made sense. Life is about change, death is about growth, and memories keep the whole experience into perspective. The what-ifs no longer matter because life will not wait.

EPILOGUE

War does not determine who is right— only who is left.

—Bertrand Russell

🍃

JULY 1865

"What are you feeding this boy? He is getting heavier by the week," Henry commented about his nephew's weight. Little Thaddeus seemed to grow faster than a weed. Emilie smiled as she nestled closer to her husband on the swing.

"Are you sure he doesn't need a diaper change? He always gains a few pounds when that happens." Stephen's comment made Henry's eyes grow wide with horror. Emilie laughed and Julia stood up to take the baby from his uncle.

"I will take him inside to change him." Emilie loved coming home. Julia latched onto the baby and cared for him all the while they were there. Emilie enjoyed the respite from the demands of motherhood. They settled back into conversation when Emilie noticed Henry struggle to stand up. His leg injury would be something he would struggle with for the duration. He was recovering very slowly. Henry now progressed to a cane instead of crutches. Through it all, Henry maintained his sense of humor. She noticed him looking down the road.

"Good god, he made it." It was barely audible, but Emilie caught the shock in her brother's voice. She sat up to see a stranger riding up the drive. Emilie immediately recognized Starlight. She was older and walked slower than she remembered.

Emilie left her husband's side to greet her brother and her long lost friend. Emilie grabbed the horse's reins.

"Hello girl. How are you? I see Aaron took good care of you." Still an experienced horsewoman, Emilie examined Starlight. She had a few new scars. One on her hindquarter and another on her front right leg, but overall she was in good condition.

She waited as Aaron greeted the family. She noticed he changed. The loss of the war changed him somehow. Thaddeus's words echoed in Emilie's brain. "*War changes everything. I just don't want it to change me. I want you to recognize me when I get home.*" Aaron looked much older. He was tired and hungry. Emilie knew he rode long and hard to get home. He was out of uniform and looked happy to be home.

"She is a great horse, Emilie," Aaron said over her shoulder. "You raised her well. Starlight became the best horse I ever had during the war."

Emilie hugged her brother. "Thank you for bringing her home. Thank you for coming home." Emilie could not believe he was there. The war ended three months ago. No one heard from Aaron until today, when he rode up the drive.

"You mean that beast didn't try to kill you?" Henry butted in on the sibling reunion.

"No Henry, she did not try to kill me. I didn't whip her with a willow stick either." Aaron smiled at his brother. Realizing what he was talking about, Emilie was shocked.

"Henry! I knew she was trying to throw you for a reason." Emilie referred to their ride up to Gettysburg so many years before. "You are still forbidden to ride her." Emilie shook her finger at him, scolding him like she did as a young girl.

Julia interrupted the sibling squabble. "Em, the baby is dry and hungry again." Thaddeus was squirming in his grandmother's arms, searching for food and wailing in protest. She handed the baby to his mother.

Aaron smiled at his sister's new occupation. She was a momma. He beamed with pride. He hugged his sister much to the protest of his nephew. "I better take him inside," she said, trying to calm the baby.

On the way back to the porch, Aaron said. "Pa, I have bad news about the Prescott Plantation." No one had heard from William or Jeanie since the war broke out. It was almost out of sight, out of mind with everything happening in Gettysburg.

Jacob suddenly felt guilty for not thinking about it sooner. "What is it, son?"

Aaron told them about the raid on the plantation. There was little left of the outbuildings, and the house was pillaged of some good heirlooms. The kitchen was in need of repair from the fire. "I think it can be rebuilt," he said with pride, his face becoming sullen. "Pa, Uncle William and Aunt Jeanie are dead. I don't know how it happened. When I checked on the plantation on the way home, I found a few house servants still watching the place. They didn't tell me much."

Jacob felt a pang of loss for his brother and sister in law. "You know what this means, don't you Aaron?" He looked as his son, not knowing how he would take the news. Aaron shook his head, not comprehending what his father was about to say.

"You are the owner of what is left of the Prescott Plantation," Jacob announced to his eldest son. "I hope the legacy is kinder to you than it was for me."